Badge of Honor

A Medieval Romance

The Sword of Glastonbury Series

Book 10

Lisa Shea

Cover design by Lisa Shea
Book design by Lisa Shea
Visit my website at LisaShea.com

This book is a work of fiction. Names, characters, places, and incidents either are products of the author's imagination or are used fictitiously. Any resemblance to actual persons, living or dead, events, or locales is entirely coincidental.

First Printing: May 2012

- 8 -

Print ISBN-13 978-0-9798377-0-8
Kindle ASIN: B007WMKZUY

I grew up longing for stories
In which women stood up for themselves,
Embraced full honesty,
Faced the consequences,
And lived life with equal measures of
responsibility and pride.

I offer this story to all readers
Who crave this same world.

Badge of Honor

Contents

Preface

Welcome to my Sword of Glastonbury series. I'm thrilled you've joined me in this adventure! These full-length novels share my adoration for all things medieval. I've belonged to the Society for Creative Anachronisms for many years and delved fully into my medieval personae. I've researched the language, clothing, education, and outlook of medieval women. I've practiced swordfighting for years, too. I'm joyful to be able to share the fruits of this research with you!

Each of the novels in this series is fully standalone. While there is a sword passed from heroine to heroine to flow the stories together, each book can be read on its own and involves its own set of characters.

If you've read the series in order you've probably read this preface before :). If you're just joining us, then hello!

Did you know that many words like "wow" that we think of as modern are actually quite old? And that words like "hug" that we consider timeless are actually fairly recent? You can learn more about medieval language, clothing, and other related topics in my appendices in the back. Medieval people loved slang words, traded in goods from the far reaches of the Earth, and had some fairly "modern" views about what women could or could not do.

Especially during these Crusades years, when countless men were off at war, large numbers of public offices were held by women. Many keeps were ruled by women. Women fought with blades to defend their homes and keeps; some even went on the road to fight in the Crusades. Queen Eleanor of Aquitaine was a powerhouse of strength and a model for all women of these years. During this time it was wholly expected that women should be respected in positions of power and were quite capable of actively defending their lands.

It's only later, when peace moved in, the Church solidified power, and courtly love traditions developed, that women were demoted to restrictively passive roles.

It's good to shake off some of the misconceptions created by everyone from Errol Flynn to Game of Thrones and examine what our real-life history has to offer.

Badge of Honor is a clean romance. There is no explicit intimacy. The few swears are period-appropriate such as "God's Teeth" or "God's Blood." There is sword-fighting but no explicit violence. As such, it is suitable for teens and up.

If you ever have any questions or comments for me, I would love to chat! You can find me on Facebook, Twitter, Instagram, Google+, Pinterest, Wattpad, and most other social networks. Just check the 'about the Author' section or do a search for Lisa Shea in your system of choice.

So sit back, relax, and enjoy a virtual vacation in the entrancing world of medieval England!

All proceeds from this series benefit battered women's shelters. Be the change you wish to see in the world.

Chapter 1

England - 1213

Honor is the reward of virtue.
-- Cicero

Catherine drew in a breath of the frigid night air. A thousand shards of ice lanced her throat; she bit off a moan, holding still against the pain. Winter had not yet released its glacial grip on the town. Arctic gusts caused her breath to puff out in frosty clouds of shimmering white. She snugged the thick hood of her cloak closely in around her face, pressing tightly against the alley wall, seeking even the slightest shelter from the cutting wind. The warmth of the inn's fire was tantalizingly close, just around the corner and through a door, but she pushed the image from her mind, steeling her resolve. She would not abandon her watch post, not now, not with so much at stake. It was only a matter of time before the threat appeared, before she balanced on that knife's edge between courage and foolhardiness.

There – she caught the glimpse of movement in the distant shadows. A small group of rough mercenaries loped down the cobblestone alley facing her, one of the men blowing into his cupped hands to keep his fingers limber.

The group's leader came to a light-footed halt at the edge of the deserted square, and the men drew to his side. She watched them with careful appraisal, judging. They were now near where the alleyway opened up into a large cobblestone intersection, ringed on all four sides by multistory stone buildings. The courtyard was brightly lit by the waning gibbous moon. A brilliant exuberance of stars coated the clear January sky like a dense school of sparkling minnows in an ebony pond.

Catherine's eyes focused in on the man in front, and she shivered. Conrad. Of all the men to have been sent … she shook her head. She knew him well, knew his cold heart, his ruthless sharpness, his clinical efficiency in dealing out death. A band of iron pulled tightly around her chest, and she let out a long breath, willing herself to relax. She had faced many challenges in her life, and as desperate as the odds seemed, she would see this through.

In a few days she would have to put this life behind her. If this was to be one of her last actions taken as Shadow, her alter-ego, she would make sure it represented her very best.

It seemed her opponent was taking no chances tonight. Conrad waited without moving, absently brushing the long mane of white-streaked hair out of his eyes with a gloved left hand. His sword hand held at the ready near the hilt. He stayed well in the shadows thrown by the edge of the building, his dark clothes helping him to blend in.

Catherine's eyes creased in confusion as she waited, motionless, looking over the group. Tall and haggard, Conrad had maintained his domination of the bandits for many years despite numerous attempts by rivals to unseat him. Now nearly forty, he usually disdained such trivial tasks as this. Why was he out with his crew on this desolate night, crossing her path?

Bitterness shadowed her heart; she pushed it away with fierce resolution. The man was a scorpion. She would have rather faced almost any other team than his. But he *was* here, and she had to ensure he did not succeed.

She could follow his gaze as Conrad's eyes roamed smoothly over the landscape, focusing carefully on potential danger spots. To his left a wooden sign hung from a pair of iron chains over a decrepit doorway. A black rooster was sloppily painted on the sign's cracked surface. The creaking of the rusty metal, swaying unsteadily in the breeze, was the only noise in this desolate corner of town. There were no signs of candles or movement in any of the windows. The other walls presented only dark windows and alleyways.

His voice was low, oily, but even so it carried to her across the crisp air of the courtyard. "Marc - that seems to be the only inn on the square," Conrad commented to his second-in-command, a wiry blond. Catherine glanced over at the shorter man, her eyes noting Marc's thinning hair and scrawny build. The flicker of a smile crossed her face. *No threat there,* she thought wryly, nodding. It was undoubtedly why Conrad had chosen Marc for his right-hand man.

Conrad was speaking again, and she pulled back her hood to make out the words over the brisk wind. "Let me make this clear, so we do not have a repeat of the Mercador debacle. We will search the inn room by room. When we find them, we will hogtie them, gag them, then haul them – kicking and screaming if need be - to the meeting point." The mercenary glanced up at the building, pausing for a moment. "If they are not there, then we start on other buildings in this area, clockwise, working our way outwards. Our orders were final. We have to find them tonight." His eyes swiveled to skewer Marc's. "No distractions this time," he added sharply.

Catherine had heard enough. In her experience half of any conflict was mental - the chess-game of setting expectations and bluffing power. It was time for her to begin. She pulled her scarf across her lower face, drew her hood down over her eyes, and pressed away from the shelter of the wall.

She slid out of the alleyway across from them, gliding through the open courtyard in silence.

Conrad froze as he sensed the motion. She watched as he scanned up her form with a practiced eye, judging the danger. She knew he was trying to ascertain her threat from her appearance. She had given him little to go by. She wore low, soft black leather boots, dark leggings, and a loose black tunic without adornment. A heavy black cloak was joined at her neck with a matte iron clasp. Her hood was up and pulled low, shielding her face from view, and her scarf completed the mask.

Her cloak swirled in a gust of wind as she smoothly crossed the center of the square, revealing the long scabbard at her left hip. She let them see the glimpse, then furled the cloak around her again, protecting her body from closer scrutiny.

As she approached, the group instinctively lowered their hands to their swords. Marc moved up alongside Conrad, his thin body tense. The rest of the wolves' heads looked to Conrad with curiosity, watching for a sign of how to react.

Conrad's hand, like that of his fellows, rested casually on the hilt of his blade. She drew to a stop, leaving about five feet between her and the men. It was close enough that they could talk quietly, yet far enough that they would have to take a step before a sword blow could reach her. The distance, along with the moon at her back, would help ensure her disguise remained intact.

Conrad flashed a wide, ingratiating smile, nodding in recognition. "Shadow, what a surprise," he welcomed. "What might you be doing in this particular corner of the world?" To hear his voice, the two might have been old friends catching up on news at a country wedding.

Catherine bowed her head in greeting, acknowledging the name of her alter-ego. She kept in the darkness while looking up at Conrad, who was a good five inches taller. "It has been a while," she gave in low reply, maintaining the same style of even tone. "You have admired my bluntness in the past; let us be so here. I am here on a job, as I imagine are you."

Her eyes moved past Conrad to scan the five men who stood behind him. "It is important that our assignments do not ... collide in any manner."

Conrad's grin grew toothy. "Well, now, let us see what we can do. Why not start by telling me what *you* are after."

Catherine's eyes returned back to meet Conrad's, considering for a moment. She let the pause linger, waiting until Conrad's brows narrowed, until she could see the tension pull in at his shoulders. Only then did her low voice rumble from the depths of the hood.

"Fair enough," she agreed, smiling inwardly as the tension released slightly, as she eased their strings like marionettes. In their eyes she had just made a concession. Their trust in her would ratchet up a minute amount. It was a game of inches, of subtle encroachments.

"I am here to protect a certain asset and to ensure that no ... local constabulary interference results. It is therefore critical to me that whatever it is you are up to is done quickly and quietly." She could not help herself, and added lightly, "Unlike, for example, the incident in Kidderminster."

Marc pushed forward, his shrill voice piping up with anger. "Hey, that was *not* our fault!" he shot out, his voice rising. "How were we supposed to know -"

Without looking, Conrad silenced him with a sharp wave of a hand. His eyes remained fixed on Catherine. "We will do what we have to do to get our job done," he replied smoothly, his smile icing slightly. "Now, if you do not mind, we have a task to perform." He nodded to his men and the group of six moved past Catherine toward the darkened inn.

"The priest is not there," offered Catherine with a soft chuckle.

Marc spun at this, his eyes blazing with fury. His hand dove toward his sword's hilt. "How did you know -"

Catherine reacted instinctively, knowing her control of the situation was all she had in her favor. Before he could complete his thought or action, Catherine's blade was glinting in the moonlight, the tip pressed tightly against the thin man's neck.

The group froze, all eyes caught by the tableau. Her sword was clearly of fine quality, but held no engravings, no markings of any kind. Catherine's black leather glove held the hilt in a gentle but firm grip, keeping the point steadily in position.

"You had better acquire a leash for your pet, Conrad," she suggested, her smile hidden by the scarf across her face but quite evident in her tone. "He might find himself injured."

"Marc, back off," ordered Conrad brusquely. Marc hesitated a moment, then pulled away from the sword, stepping back a pace, his face surly. Conrad kept his eyes locked on his opponent's, contemplating. "Now, why would you believe we were after a priest?"

Catherine resheathed the sword in a smooth movement and furled her cloak back tightly against the winter chill. "I know many things about your organization," came her inflectionless reply. "As for the priest, I have been watching this area of town for the past week. I made it my business to know who has been going in and out of these buildings."

Conrad eyed her speculatively. Without turning, he spoke to one of the smaller mercenaries who had been skulking in the back of the group. "Mouse. Go in and check out the inn - but do it *quietly*. If our quarry has truly flown, there is no sense in risking town watch involvement." Conrad's eyes flicked to Catherine for a moment, then he continued. "We will wait here with our ... friend."

Mouse nodded and ran with light-footed grace across the cobblestone square. Glancing around one last time, he eased open the inn's front door and slipped noiselessly inside.

Marc glared at Catherine with venom, absently fingering his sword hilt. "If this Shadow knows so much," he growled with quiet but clear anger to Conrad, "I say we give him a few cuts and convince him to tell us everything. Why trust his word?"

Catherine ran a steady eye down the line of five bandits. In addition to Conrad and Marc, the other three men were clearly seasoned warriors, in good shape despite their rough appearance and shaggy hair. She had no doubt they were well worth the coin paid to them. Each man wore leather armor and carried a scuffed longsword at his side.

To a man they appeared ready to draw on command and to take whatever action was required for the job. Catherine knew that any fight with this group would be a formidable task to win. Conrad alone had more assassinations to his credit than any man she knew of, living or dead.

Conrad glanced at his companions, then back at Catherine. "Interrogate Shadow. It is certainly a thought," he agreed, smiling with cold amusement.

Catherine flicked back a shoulder with a smooth motion and the swirling cloak exposed the sword blade's hilt. In the bright moonlight the men could see the moss-green-dyed leather wrap on the hilt, held in place with bronze wire. In the ensuing silence, one of the bandits murmured to the other, "He is a Bowyer."

Catherine nodded in agreement. It was time to increase the stakes. "I see you have heard of my clan and our sword fighting reputation. Let me assure you that if you try to prevent me in fulfilling my current assignment, I will spill the entrails of at least one of you. I may even slice open two or three of you, ensuring an agonizing death, before I am done." She created eye contact with each mercenary in turn, confirming with each man that he was her chosen first victim. When she spoke again, she pitched her tone to be a melding of ice and steel.

"Which of you will volunteer to be the first to die screaming?"

The silence stretched on for a few moments while the men eyed the potential threat speculatively, sizing up the challenge. Catherine did not move. A tense calm settled across the group. Each person there had been in many fights; there was no compunction about one more. It would only take a word from Conrad to start a fierce, coordinated flurry of swords.

Catherine knew she had little hope of taking on all five well trained mercenaries, but there was no backing down now. With practiced ease she first tensed then relaxed each muscle group, watching for any sign of movement. The command would come from Conrad; these men were too disciplined to move until the signal was given. She would need to subdue Conrad first – if such a thing were even possible.

The mercenaries had changed their stance subtly, settling into combat readiness. The four subordinate men were focused on Catherine, but clearly watched Conrad for a sign.

A movement came from the courtyard; all eyes instinctively turned toward it. Mouse came scurrying out of the inn and ran quickly across the cobblestones to Conrad's side. The smaller man seemed oblivious to the tension in the air and gave his news to his boss in a rapid, soft whisper.

"Shadow told the truth. There is no sign of the priest or his followers," he reported in his barely audible voice. "I checked every room. Now what?"

The mercenaries relaxed slightly at hearing this information. Conrad took his hand off his sword and glanced over at Catherine. "So, any other interesting information to share with us?" he asked, his smile glinting in the moonlight.

Catherine returned Conrad's gaze without saying a word. There was a long silence which Conrad made no move to break. When Catherine finally spoke, she pitched her voice to be low and reluctant, as if she were providing an unplanned concession.

"It is in my best interest to tell you, I suppose, as it will get you out of this area," she offered in a growl. "The priest and his entourage left the inn earlier today in a great hurry. They headed north; in that direction lies the old stone bridge."

Conrad eyed Catherine for a long while, considering. He crossed his arms, fingertips drumming on the heavy muscles of his forearm.

"Here is what I will do," he offered at last. "We will make our way to the bridge and see if we pick up the trail. Yes, I am sure it is in your best interest to have us leave, and I will take that at face value." His eyes sharpened. "However, if we find you have misled us for any reason, we will be back. When we find you - and we will - we will make sure you greatly regret having caused us to waste our time."

Catherine nodded amicably and stepped back. "Good hunting."

With an answering nod, Conrad turned on his heel and strode northwards. The mercenaries moved in closely after him.

Catherine remained motionless and carefully watched their movements until they had dissolved into the obsidian night. Then without a sound she turned and retreated down the alleyway in the opposite direction, regaining her watch position, furling herself back into the shadows.

* * *

In a window high over the square and opposite the Black Cock inn, Jack sat back in the ancient leather chair, its decaying hide crackling beneath him. He ran a hand through his thick hair, contemplating what he had seen.

The second floor room had been too high up to hear the conversation clearly, but an alliance between Conrad's well trained mercenaries and Shadow's sword prowess was definitely not a good thing.

Jack looked over at the elderly priest who lay slumbering peacefully in the corner of the room, surrounded by his three young acolytes. His brow furrowed as he considered his options.

He would be very happy when he had delivered the group safely to Worcester Cathedral.

Chapter 2

Jack cursed at his bad luck, careful not to let Father Berram hear him. The winter rain, freezing cold, was pouring down for the third day straight. The forest road was swamped in mud, grabbing greedily at their boots and allowing coarse roots to poke up in unexpected locations. Their dark brown cloaks were soaked through and draining their body heat with every step.

They could not afford to stop, however - the danger was too great. They had to press on to get to the cathedral.

To their credit, the three weary novices did not speak a word of complaint about their heavy, ice-water-logged clothes or the long hikes briefly interrupted by hurried meals. The young men assisted their elderly priest in turns, their huddled cloaks moving alongside his stooped form in a silent, steady march.

Jack ranged ahead and behind the group, his long, lean form taking the muddy road with ease. In his thirty-two years he had dealt with far worse weather conditions, but it did not make the task enjoyable. His dark hair, hanging wetly to his shoulders, lay matted against his head. Despite the icy cold against his neck, he refused to draw the hood up. Experience had taught him to put off any comfort which might interfere with hearing or seeing an enemy. Beneath his cloak he wore light leather armor and carried a long sword at his side. He hoped he would not have to use his weapon on this trip. If they came across bandits, he would be hard pressed to keep all four of his charges safe at the same time.

He was scouting in front of the group when a sharp cry split through the rain's drumming. His sword was out in a flash and he sprinted back to check on his wards. To his relief, no bandits were in sight. Instead, one of the acolytes – Michael, the tall, thin member of the trio - was sitting on the ground, wincing in pain and holding his ankle. His two friends, Walter and John, crowded around him, examining the injury with sympathy.

Michael blinked away tears. "I think it is broken," he murmured in a tremulous voice, a stalwart look masking the suffering evident in his motions. "I must have tripped over a root." From his sitting position he hesitantly pressed the foot into the ground, then winced. "I cannot put any pressure on it."

His eyes dropped guiltily. "I am sorry; I know I should have been more careful." He rubbed at his ankle as if somehow the blood flow would heal the injury in seconds.

Jack scanned the surrounding forest, holding back another oath. He prayed Michael's cry had not carried to unfriendly ears. "We should get off the road," he directed. "I will see if I can find a solid walking stick for you. You are too big to carry, and we have to keep moving."

He bustled the group into a small clearing and found them the partial shelter of a large oak tree. The men settled down to rest, sighing in gratitude as they crossed from the drenching rain into the quiet peace beneath the large branches. Jack ensured they were secure, then searched carefully through the nearby woods, looking for an appropriately sized staff to cut down for the injured lad.

A few minutes later, Jack found a likely young oak and hewed at it with his knife. He focused on the task, working his way through the hard wood with practiced ease. What a time for Michael to have tripped. The teen was rather gangly, and the ground had been rough, but still ...

Without knowing why, Jack suddenly froze in his motions mid-cut. An overpowering sensation of being watched pressed in on him. He automatically closed his eyes and listened intently.

The forest seemed quiet, but not hushed. There was the muted warbling of birds in the trees, the steady patter of the rain cascading down through the leaves all around him. Still, he quickly sheathed his knife; his hand strayed to his sword.

Opening his eyes again, he turned around in place slowly, trying to pick out distinct sounds amongst the constant wet splush of cold rain impacting soaked mud. The trees glistened around him, light and dark stripes patterning his world.

The feeling of being watched only grew.

At last the words burst from him. "Who is there - show yourself."

A moment went by, then two ... then a form slipped from within a stand of trees. Jack found himself face to face with Shadow. The man's hood was drawn forward as he'd seen a few nights ago. Jack tensed, his breath coming out in slow, frosty clouds. Shadow could easily be the advance scout for the wolves' heads.

Jack flexed his fingers on his blade's hilt, but Shadow made no move to draw a sword. Instead, the cloaked figure stood still, silently watching Jack, apparently considering him.

Was Shadow an ally or a threat?

Jack could not afford the luxury of time. He glanced around again, but saw no other sign of movement. Jack brought his eyes back to meet Shadow's – and stopped, realization hitting him.

Shadow was furious.

Jack now saw the sharp glint of anger in the eyes, the tightness in the form that was more than battle readiness. The heat was also quite evident when Shadow finally spoke in a tightly controlled, low growl.

"Why in God's name have you stopped, Southerner?" Shadow snapped in exasperation. "Conrad's crew is nearly upon you. They will have you in another ten minutes. They have brought a tracking dog with them; hiding cannot be an option."

Ally.

Jack let out a breath, counting his blessings. He almost chuckled at Shadow's use of the epithet *Southerner*, the name hurled at him when he scouted north past Wolverhampton.

Apparently the man hailed from that region. His mind clicked through the available defensive options with lightning speed.

"There are still six of them?" He looked Shadow up and down, considering how Shadow had stood against the bandits in the courtyard, if indeed Shadow had not been working with them. He came to a quick decision. "If you are willing to help, I think we have a chance."

Shadow's head was shaking no even before Jack finished. "There is no way we can keep all four of them completely safe from harm," came the furious objection. "I refuse to take a course of action that risks injury to any of the four." There was a pause, then Shadow continued half to himself, "Circumstances have drawn me in too far as it is."

Jack did not waste further time arguing; in a flash he turned and sprinted back toward the clearing, scanning the area rapidly as he reached it. The four religious men huddled beneath the tree; they looked up, startled, at his fast approach.

The elderly priest's wrinkled face peered turtle-like from within his soaked cloak. "Is everything all right?" he asked tremulously.

The group looked past Jack as Shadow strode into the clearing behind him. Walter's portly face beamed with pleasure, and he called out in surprise.

"Shadow!" With effort, Walter pushed himself up to a standing position, brushing his tousled blond hair out of his eyes. "It is great to see you again!"

John had stood with Walter, but at Walter's outburst he flushed crimson in anger, his face almost matching his copper colored hair. His well-toned body flexed as he turned to send a hard elbow into Walter's side.

Walter gasped at the impact, then flushed in shame and, sealing his mouth tight, looked down to the ground.

Jack was surprised that the novices would know this rogue swordsman, and wondered why they were reluctant to reveal that knowledge. An issue to investigate at a later date. Right now Conrad's team was bearing down on him. He had to defend his charges.

Shadow had dropped down at Michael's side and was deftly examining the ankle. The thin lad's foot was swelling up by the minute; the wound was lumpy, violet, and Michael winced at each gentle touch. Shadow glanced at the two friends' troubled eyes, then back at the injury. The hooded figure cursed softly in the lilting tones of Welsh. "It is broken. He will never get clear of the drawing net with his foot compromised."

Jack dropped to a knee beside Shadow, answering in the same language, keeping his voice low. "I know you do not want to alarm the boys, but we must make a choice. Time is short and my choices are few. I have to stand and fight. *Will you help?*"

* * *

Catherine's eyes flickered to Southerner in surprise. Her switch to Welsh had been instinctive, designed to shield the acolytes from her out loud musings. She hid in the lyrical language often, one of her childhood games she had never quite outgrown. That the Southerner knew Welsh was quite unexpected.

His sturdy arm brushed against hers, and she flinched away. She had been confused when the notorious loner first arrived in town. What odd coincidence had brought the wanderer in to meet the men she had been watching over? When he had prodded the foursome to leave, she had almost dropped her disguise, had almost stepped in to interfere. Instead, as always, she bided her time. In short order it had become clear Southerner had some sense of what he was doing.

Since then he had guided the religious group, surely and carefully, through the mud and rain along their path. She would not have expected that attention from the recluse she had heard tales of, the half-crazed outcast she had avoided deliberately when their paths had almost crossed on lonely roads.

Who was this man?

His arm grazed hers again, shaking her back into reality. Suddenly realizing how close Southerner was, Catherine quickly turned to look toward the ground so that deep shadows fell within her hood again. She saw that his sharp eyes were aware of her motion, but he did not press her further on it. Instead, his eyes went to the muscles of her arm, the sword she wore at her hip, and then over to look for a moment with tenderness at the four religious men clustered around them.

He kept his voice low, and she appreciated his care. Even though it was unlikely that the foursome spoke Welsh, they could still infer meaning from tone, and the last thing she wanted to do was to panic them.

The lilting rhythm flowed soothingly from his lips. "I know I have no right to ask you for assistance, but please, for their sakes ..."

Catherine heard the power behind his message, and it soaked into her very core. It would be so easy to stand by his side, to unite publicly against Conrad's team, to ally herself with Southerner's clear strength and skill. It could be one of Shadow's last acts … the culmination of a four year legacy …

The longing rose so strongly that it became an almost tangible connection between them. She dropped her eyes to the ground, frustration growing and overwhelming her. Finally she ground out, "I cannot. I swore a vow."

Father Berram's tremulous voice came from behind the pair. "What is it that you two are saying? What is happening?"

Catherine took in a deep breath, then let it out slowly, looking down into Michael's pained eyes, holding his gaze for a long moment. There was no time to agonize over this. The wolves' heads would be on them in only a few minutes. Something had to be done.

Standing quickly, she gave a short, descending whistle. Within moments a tall black stallion with a white blaze on its forehead moved quietly into the clearing. Catherine strode over and laid a hand fondly against his mane.

She reverted to English, to ensure the group understood the plan. "I will take Michael myself," she instructed. "If we split up, and you have the ability to move quickly, we have a chance."

Southerner and Michael both cried "No!" in unison, causing her to turn in surprise.

Southerner spoke first, his voice clipped. "How can I know I can trust you? These are my charges. The last I saw, you were holding conversations with the mercenaries. This could all still be a trap."

Catherine scoffed in exasperation. "It is because of my intervention - at great personal risk - that you made it out of town alive," she retorted hotly.

She turned to look down at Michael. "Michael, surely *you* trust me ...?"

Michael's thin, pale face blossomed crimson. "Of course I trust you, Shadow. However, we made a vow - Walter, John, and me. We promised to stick together no matter what. What kind of a vow would that be if I ran off at the first setback?"

The accusation struck Catherine to her core. With everything she was facing, with the brutal choices which lay before her, it was as if Michael had chosen the one statement which caused her soul to echo in understanding. For a long moment she found she could not speak.

Finally she brought herself back to the dangerous present. "You are right," she agreed, her voice somber. "A vow should be held to even when it is most difficult. Perhaps *especially* when it is most difficult."

The man by her side turned to her, the gentle, musical language of Welsh coming to her again, and her tension eased at its sound on his lips. The message, however, was a velvet-wrapped reminder of danger. "This brings us to our main problem, that of Conrad closing in on us."

Catherine nodded in agreement. He was right, of course, and time was growing short. She raced through her few options, glancing at Father Berram's shoulder pack for a long moment. "I would wager the bandits do not really want the religious men. They want what they carry. They will therefore seek to track and apprehend anybody who they feel has that object."

She stood holding the reins of her black horse, staring off into the distance, trying to calculate if her insane plan had any chance of success. If only the pursuers had been Carl and Craig. She would have gladly stood with Southerner to slay those two abominations, her Council's orders be damned. Against Conrad's team, though, the odds of failure were just too high.

Finally, she nodded, closing her eyes for a brief prayer.

"I will make for Worcester," she stated, giving her steed a tender rub on his neck. If ever she depended on his legendary speed, now would be the day. "Once safely there, I will send Peter with a team back to get you."

Southerner made to interrupt, but Catherine pressed on. "Drive west until you reach the lightning-split oak tree by the pond. Peter will be able to find that easily. If you do not see Peter by nightfall, you will know that I was caught." She turned to face Southerner. "By then, though, your trail will be cold and you should be able to make it to Worcester without being spotted."

The man held Catherine's eyes, his deep gaze somber with growing understanding. "You are going to draw the mercenaries off us."

Catherine nodded in return. "It seems the only remaining solution. It gives the best chance of all four staying safe. That is the key concern here."

Southerner paused for a moment, holding Catherine's attention. When he spoke, his voice was low and respectful. "I have heard many stories about you, Shadow, and I had a quite different impression of your character. I am sorry to have misjudged you." He put out his hand.

Catherine joined him in a firm clasp on the forearm. The man was sturdy, strong, and a surprising warmth flooded through her as their arms linked. She blinked in surprise at her reaction, caused so incongruently by this rogue wanderer. She pulled back quickly, staring at him, baffled.

His gaze was tense. "What is it?"

Despite all her training, she answered with the first thought on her mind. "It could be that I have misjudged you as well," she offered in full honesty. "I have been told that you were a hostile, almost crazed loner who should be avoided. There have been several times I have happened on your campfire; each time I made substantial effort to avoid contact." She flushed at the revelation, but found herself adding, "I wish now that I had taken the chance to talk." She turned and quickly climbed onto her horse.

Southerner looked up into her eyes. "Good luck," he offered solemnly.

She nodded in return, then wheeled her horse to ride out of the clearing. She pushed hard through the dark brambles and gullies, waiting until she was distant from the innocents who needed her protection. Finally she pushed her steed to clamber carefully up the slippery slope of a small hill. She stood there for a long moment, drawing in a lungful of air. She pitched her voice to carry far across the trees.

"Cry all you want, damned priest, but it is mine now!" she shouted in triumph, hoping her message reached Conrad's crew and drew them in to her.

"You and your novices will do well to retreat home, for the prize is taken!"

She kicked her steed into a gallop, thundering down the hill, and almost instantly she heard the cries of challenge, the crashing of brush as the mercenaries gave chase.

She had certainly done it now.

She sent a fervent prayer that Southerner would get the foursome to safety, that they would find a sanctuary at the lightning-struck tree, and that she could get the message to Peter before she was slain, or worse.

Chapter 3

Catherine flew at a hard canter, the past few hours merging into a rain-streaked blur. Mouse had been the first to lag, his smaller horse unable to keep up with the thunderous pace set by the group. Catherine had twisted and turned, hurdled brooks, dodged around stone walls. One by one the other riders had faltered, losing a pace here, a length there. Still, like stubborn ticks embedded in a tasty host's side, Conrad and Marc had obstinately remained a mere heartbeat away.

The trio moved almost in unison now, Catherine only a few strides ahead of the two flanking men. Catherine was coming to recognize their voices as if they were life-long neighbors. There, to the left, were Marc's taunts, his running litany of curses, jeers, and insults. His imagination seemed to know no bounds.

But on the right … Catherine allowed a quick sideways glance in that direction. Conrad wasted no energy, no movement in his efforts. He guided his steed with a sure hand, his malevolent eyes focused on the black horse and rider before him. His coiled muscles seemed to ripple in the rain. If Conrad was able to catch up …

Catherine leant even lower over her horse's neck, reseating the slippery reins in weary hands. Her stallion was reputed to be the fastest in the land, but even quick steeds could falter, could turn an ankle on an unseen rock. She had to lose the men and reach safety, both for the sake of the five men she had left behind in the woods as well as her own. If she was caught, her death would be long in coming.

A thought struck her, and she found herself shaking her head at the corkscrew twists that life presented. Here she had hidden away for four long years, respected her Council's wishes, and allowed the world to think she was dead. Only her alter-ego Shadow had been seen outside the city walls. And now, on the cusp of finally being able to re-enter the world openly, she was about to be slain by men who would tumble her broken body in a ditch, never to be found.

An ominously dense hedge loomed before her, pulling Catherine out of her bleak musings. Catherine did not pause for an instant, desperately plunging into its depths. Perhaps this was the chance to finally scrape the wolves' heads off, to slip unseen into the twisted woods beyond. Branches and brambles dragged long welts along her face and arms. The stabs of pain went on for many long minutes as her horse valiantly struggled through its depths.

Finally they cleared the thickets, and Catherine's heart rose. There were no answering echoes …. they had done it …

From both sides, the sound grew. The mantra … the song … the drumming of hoofbeats. There would be no escape.

Catherine leant low, whispering a prayer, focusing on the path. Her black stallion's flanks were heaving, and Catherine knew her steed could not hold out much longer. The day had already been a long one before this flight began. It might be that the mercenaries' horses were fading as well, but that was a thin hope to thread a life on - never mind the lives of the four religious men.

Catherine strained through the pouring rain for a glimpse of Worcester's spires, very aware of the pounding of hoofbeats that were following close behind. If Conrad caught her ... but that could not be allowed to happen. How far could it be? Could they be on the wrong heading?

Suddenly through the grey mists resolved the familiar shapes so long looked for - the tall, sturdy walls of the cathedral's protective outer layer. Catherine thundered toward that defensive shield, urging her horse into a final desperate burst of speed.

Behind, Marc's voice rang out in heated frustration. "God's Teeth! Faster, you mangy beast!" Both men drove in hard, trying to match her move, to catch their quarry before she reached safety.

Uttering a silent prayer, Catherine flattened down completely on the neck of her horse, willing her steed to get to the gate in time. The hoofbeats of the pursuers seemed almost alongside ...

Catherine burst through the open gate in a flurry of hooves and mane, Conrad and Marc peeling off to either side of the entrance. The church's guard would not interfere with matters outside the church walls, but they stood ready and armed at the mouth of the gate, quite able to protect the sanctity of the holy ground.

The two men wheeled about hard, drawing to a heaving stop some distance from the solid stone walls. "This is not the end, Shadow!" screamed Marc, his face flushed with fury. "We will find you, and make you pay!"

Beside him, Conrad gave a long, steady look at the row of soldiers manning the parapets, then without a word he turned his steed with a controlled movement. Together the pair streamed off at a canter toward the west. Their horses' hoofbeats faded from hearing, and soon they were lost in the rain.

The Cathedral guard troop stood ready at the walls and gates, maintaining a keen watch for any return, any movement in the gloom of night.

Catherine finally turned from the gates and lay along her stallion's neck, drawing in long, deep breaths. A tall, slender redheaded man in his early thirties came running down the steps of the cathedral into the courtyard, a young page keeping quick pace with him. The redhead wore a tan tunic and carried a sword at his side; his build indicated he knew well how to use it.

He shouted to one of the guards as he neared. "I saw it from the upstairs window. The mercenaries left? They did not linger nearby?" He drew up to the heaving horse's side.

"Aye, Peter," acknowledged the soldier with a grin. "They had no wish to enter into that sort of a battle. They are long gone."

Peter nodded and stopped alongside the weary steed, taking a hold of its reins and patting its neck with fondness. He looked with concern at the rider. "Shadow, my lad. Thank goodness you are all right. You must have run into the priest, if Conrad's men were on your heels."

Catherine nodded, her heart twisting with fondness and regret as she glanced down at her childhood friend. She longed to talk with Peter, to take comfort in his wise advice – but she knew she could not. The charade had to be maintained for the remaining few days, until her life as she knew it came to a crashing halt.

Sadness swept through her, and she pushed it away with exhausted effort. Keeping her hood forward, she half climbed, half slid down from the horse.

Peter whispered an instruction to his page, and the freckled boy ran off to the side wall, returning quickly with a long stick. He handed it over to Catherine, who took it with a nod of thanks.

Peter spoke more slowly, taking care to enunciate clearly. "Where are the holy men now?"

In response, Catherine drew a simple image of an oak tree in the dirt with the stick. Quick movements then added a lightning bolt in the center of the tree, and drew a pond before it.

Peter nodded even before the image was complete. "I know the place well. I will leave immediately with spare horses for them all. Will you stay a while?"

Peter did not seem surprised when she wearily shook a negative and then with effort climbed back up on the tired mount. "I understand," said Peter, giving the steed another pat. "As always, we thank you for your efforts. Your help has been invaluable." He paused, then looked up into the hooded eyes. "Take care of yourself, Shadow."

Catherine nodded, regret settling into all corners of her being. *Shadow*. The name would soon be lost to her – the name and all it stood for. She had agreed to the path now before her, but it did not make it any less hard.

Resigned, she pulled gently at the reins, turning her horse's head, riding back out through the gates that had so recently provided a solid shield from harm.

Chapter 4

Jack looked up in alarm. From the south came the ever increasing sound of a mounted troop. He quickly gathered up the four men and had them huddle in a damp nook beneath the elderly oak tree. Drawing his sword, he stood vigil on the low, grassy rise, waiting for the forces to come in. If Shadow had failed ... well, he would hold them off for as long as he could.

To Jack's great relief, Peter came into view at the head of a mounted group of soldiers, trailing several riderless horses behind them. Peter drew up alongside Jack and dismounted easily, coming over to clasp Jack warmly on the shoulder.

"Jack, my friend," he greeted, his voice echoing his smile. "I am so glad to find you are all right." He looked behind Jack as the priest and his novices climbed out of their hiding spot. They moved with weary slowness, but smiled with gratitude at the arriving soldiers.

Peter turned back to the dark-haired man. "You had no difficulties after Shadow left you?"

Jack shook his head. "None. Once Shadow drew away Conrad's crew, we saw no one at all as we made our way here. Since then the forest has been completely quiet, if rather wet. My only worry was that he might not make it to you - but I see that he was as good as his word."

Jack paused a minute, then added more quietly, "I had greatly misjudged him. He put himself at serious risk to save us. I am glad that I was able to talk with him before he left us. Is he at the Cathedral now? I would like to speak with him again to express my thanks."

Peter tilted his head to one side, a confused look crossing his face. "Surely you mean he drew you symbols," he commented, clarifying.

Jack was utterly lost. "No, I mean we spoke."

Peter's mouth hung open, then he winked playfully. "What, in English?" he asked in a teasing tone.

Jack nodded, thinking back. "Well yes, we talked in English first, then when he was worried about upsetting the acolytes he switched to Welsh. I am fluent in both, and found him equally facile in both languages."

Peter's mouth dropped open again in amazement. "Maybe we should start from the beginning, Jack. Shadow has *never* spoken - not even once - in the four years I have known him," he explained. "I had decided he was mute, or had taken a vow of silence." He paused for a moment, blushing slightly. "To be honest, I assumed he was mentally challenged as well."

Jack scanned back over how eloquently Shadow had expressed himself. "Surely you are joking?"

Peter shook his head. "Before I came to Worcester, Shadow would provide escort occasionally for monks or nuns who were traveling in our region. I saw him a couple of times a year. He would visit for a few moments when dropping off or joining with a party, but would never agree to stay for longer. I assumed he was a private person, perhaps working off a sin of some sort. He was a great boon for our travelers; I was happy for his help."

Peter scratched his head. "Why in the world would he refuse to speak around me, yet talk so freely with you?"

Jack thought back to the encounter. "I first heard him talking - only faintly - when he had a discussion with Conrad's team near Wolverhampton. At the time I thought he was working with them, but I understand now that he was attempting to send them off our trail."

His mind drifted back through the past day's events. "Then, when Michael twisted his ankle, we were forced to stop to find a walking stick. Shadow did not seem like he *wanted* to talk with me. With the danger pressing in on us, perhaps he had no choice." He thought about the stops and starts in their conversation. "He seemed angry to be drawn into it, but with Conrad drawing near ..."

At mention of the threat, Peter became serious. "There will be enough time for discussion later," he commented quickly. "Let us get everyone mounted and back to the safety of the cathedral."

Jack first helped the priest and lads onto their mounts, then vaulted easily onto a black stallion and pulled alongside Peter. The two men nodded to each other, and the group began moving south toward safety.

The men rode cautiously down the muddy road, the guards maintaining a watchful gaze for any sign of a threat. They moved the horses at a relatively slow pace. The elderly priest was able to keep his steed under control, but they had no wish to risk danger with a fast canter or gallop. Peter and Jack rode side by side at the head of the group, alertly scanning for danger.

Jack glanced to Peter. "Is Lord Epworth back at the cathedral yet?" he asked as they moved through the rain. "No doubt he is eager to lead the debate regarding the Pope's anger with King John. I heard he was returning from Rome sometime this month."

Peter shook his head "It should be another week or so before your foster father returns," he explained. "His boat landed a few days ago and they are coming cross-country."

Jack's mouth turned up in a wry smile. "He loves to be the center of attention, and this political situation has given him quite a stage," he commented. "It may have been bad luck that caused his own holdings to fail, but getting himself temporary stewardship of Worcester Cathedral while a new Bishop is appointed was a stroke of genius."

Peter's eyes brightened. "Yes, he certainly has his talents," he agreed, nodding. "He has nearly converted the extensive complex into his own personal keep and gardens. I imagine he will feel regret when he has to move along to Ireland, to his secondary holdings."

He paused a moment, then continued on another topic. “Tell me again what you learned about Shadow.”

“I am sure I saw the green leather hilt,” Jack stated, recounting the details of the courtyard meeting to Peter. “I also heard mention of the Bowyers. Given Shadow’s willingness to stand up against Conrad’s team, and their apparent respect for him, I am sure he must be one of that clan’s members.”

Peter nodded in understanding. “That makes sense, and would explain his language fluency. The Bowyers are known for their skilled swordsmen and for their talented negotiators. It is said they teach their children three languages simultaneously when they are young, so that they maintain that fluency through adulthood.”

Jack’s mind clicked back through the events of the afternoon. “It would also explain something else,” he added, his eyes brightening with insight. “When Shadow spoke to me, he called me ‘Southerner’. The Bowyers are based up in the northern woods, and in that region I am known by that nickname. He must have seen me or heard of me up there.”

Peter became lost in thought. After a while, he commented, “One of my best friends when I was growing up was a member of the Bowyers.”

Jack looked over in curiosity. “Who was he? Have I met him?”

Peter shook his head. “It was a she, and I imagine not. Her name was Catherine. She traveled a great deal and visited me often, but when I talked about a visit to Worcester, she said that she had never been there. She was quite an exceptional woman; I miss her greatly.”

“What happened to her,” asked Jack gently.

Peter looked into the distance at the memory. “She was killed in a scouting foray. The patrol was attacked by a group of wolves’ heads. That was about four years ago. It still seems like yesterday to me. She was perhaps twenty-two; she was too young to have died.”

Jack nodded slowly to himself. “I think I heard about the event - Catherine was the daughter of the Bowyer’s Lord and Lady? Their sole heir?”

“Yes, that was Catherine,” agreed Peter. “Normally even Bowyer women do not go on patrols, but she was quite the rebel. She had been training as a swordswoman since she was a teen. I know she was not as strong as the men, but she was agile and quick. She was really something to see, with her long, dark hair curled back in braids, sparring rounds in the practice arena. She was not to be taken lightly.”

Jack sensed the sadness in his friend’s eyes and a thought occurred to him. “Were you two ... special to each other?”

Peter looked up and chuckled softly. “Oh, it was not like that,” he corrected with a slight smile. “She was a best friend, but we were quite different from each other. She often joked that I was the ‘sunlight on a grassy meadow’, while she was ‘moonlight in a forest glen’. We appreciated each other greatly, and spent many long hours in discussion - but we were not meant to be a couple.” He rolled his shoulders. “Still, for someone so strong to be cut off in the prime of life, it gives one pause.”

Jack nodded quietly, and the two rode the rest of the distance in contemplative silence.

Chapter 5

Jack blinked awake in the bright warmth of a midday sun. He stretched, noting that the aches and bruises of the previous days had eased slightly with the long, much needed rest. He dressed quickly, making his way down to the main hall. The large room was dotted with tables and benches, half-filled with diners and servants, wafting with mouth-watering aromas.

He smiled as he spotted Peter at a small table by the fireplace, and moved over to sit with him.

Peter waved at a servant, then nodded merrily to his friend. "About time for you to wake. Feeling rested?" Food was delivered promptly, and Jack ripped off a piece of the warm loaf with pleasure, downing a long draw of the cool ale.

"Yes, I am quite refreshed, thank you. How are my charges?" He leant back and looked around the sunlit hall, his eyes scanning the diners.

"They woke perhaps an hour ago and headed promptly into the altar area," commented Peter with a chuckle. "Apparently the four of them feel their safe arrival here had divine assistance, and they have pledged themselves to two days of prayer in thanks."

"It was a rough journey," agreed Jack readily, taking some more of the bread. "I would count my thanks that Shadow found us, however, more than any hand of God in what happened."

"Maybe the two are not that different," replied Peter, raising an eyebrow. "It is quite fortuitous that he found you when he did, after all."

Jack nodded in consideration. "I still am unsure of what triggered the convergence of forces that night," he mused. "Shadow must have been there before I arrived. How did Conrad know where to find his quarry? How did Shadow know to be there to intercept them?" His eyes moved up to Peter's. "And what exactly is in that book? Father Berram was rather elusive when I asked him about it."

Peter chuckled, leaning forward. "As well he might be," he confided in a low voice. "It is not something the church is proud of. It is a private diary that one of the fathers kept in addition to his official church records. It lays out the actual genealogies of the region, of who is related to whom, of bastard children and other relationships."

Jack looked at him in confusion. "Conrad wanted to get his hands on a diary? Does he have something to hide?"

Peter shook his head. "I imagine he was hired by someone whose motive was simple greed. From what I have heard, an unethical person could blackmail a number of wealthy men in the region with the information. He could threaten to reveal connections that their wives and families might not approve of."

"I see," considered Jack, sitting back again. "If people would just tell the truth, they could never be tripped up later by lies."

"Not everyone sees the world the way you do," smiled his friend, toasting him with his mug. "If they did, then I imagine the world would be a far simpler place to live in."

"What does Father Berram intend to do with the book?" asked Jack, considering.

Peter shrugged. "Apparently the material does have some value, in a historical sort of sense. A friend of his out in St. Albans, Father Oswold, is a well-respected historian. It seems Berram wishes to bring the book to him for safe keeping."

"Sounds fine by me," agreed Jack. He downed the rest of his ale. "Are you up for some sparring?"

"Always," agreed Peter with a smile. He stood easily, and Jack led the way out toward the barracks to gather up their gear.

* * *

Saturday's steady stream of incoming guests, drenched by the rains, kept Jack busy from the moment he woke until long after dark. He was grateful when Sunday rolled around; few would travel on the holy day. He was doubly thankful when the heavy rain eased into gentle mists, boding better weather as spring finally began its soft approach.

He smiled with pleasure as he approached the entrance to the main area of the church and came up to Michael, Walter, and John. The lads welcomed him warmly. Jack could see that Father Berram was already seated in the frontmost pew, his wispy hair combed into neat order. Jack moved with the three young men to sit alongside him, and soon Peter had joined them as well. The service moved by with quiet dignity, the unusually large throngs of visitors adding extra meaning to the morning.

Jack offered Father Berram an arm, helping him slowly walk the distance back to the dining hall, settling him in at one of the smaller tables with the three acolytes. In short order the four were supplied with ale, relaxing and enjoying the hubbub.

Feeling content that they were comfortable, Jack's eyes sought out Peter, and together they walked out the back door, moving into the soft afternoon of drifting dew. Jack smiled with pleasure, relishing the quiet. Their feet followed the familiar wending of the gravel path behind the cathedral.

"So, Peter, we finally have a moment. It is impressive how many have come to be heard in this debate. While I appreciate their desire to help, it is also nice to be away from their babble for a while. Tell me, what have you been up to these past weeks?"

He looked about him as they moved. The rains of the past few days had broken into an almost warming sunshine, and he took in a long breath of the fresh air, smiling. He felt rested for the first time in many weeks.

"Did I tell you I was eyeing that young stallion the baker had for sale?" asked Peter with a grin. "I think I can talk him down to a reasonable price, and even get some fresh rolls thrown in as well."

Jack shook his head, smiling at his friend. He and Peter had known each other for almost twenty years now, and the familiar ease of conversation warmed his soul. Their words flowed like a sparkling summer stream, moving from horses to the state of events in London, then on to the political issues being caused by King John's unpopularity.

The afternoon faded on into a chilly evening, and still they wandered the grounds, reluctant to return inside to the throngs of visitors.

They found themselves at the far back end of the cathedral, where a small fish pond was nestled in a curving length of ivy-laced wall. The sun was setting behind the cathedral, shining across their shoulders, sending their shadows walking in front of them. Ahead, a short bridge crossed the back edge of the pond for decorative, rather than practical, reasons. The sun shone full onto the bridge giving it an otherworldly quality.

Jack stopped to appreciate the quiet scene. A woman in a ground-length black cloak was standing on the bridge, her body at an angle to him, looking down at the water with a pensive gaze. Her long black hair cascaded down her back, falling nearly to her waist. Her left hand rested on the railing, her outer dress and inner chemise sleeve both reaching to her wrist.

Jack found himself struck by the woman's countenance. Her eyes were sad and weary, while her lips held a resigned acceptance.

Jack turned to ask Peter who the woman was, then stopped in surprise at the look on Peter's face. Peter had gone white, first in shock, then transforming into a beam of bright joy. In another moment Peter sprang into motion, running in a dash toward the woman, crying out, "Catherine! Catherine! You are alive!"

Catherine looked up at the call, and a warm smile spread across her face. She held out her arms both in a welcome to her friend and in a quiet effort to slow his pace. "Gently, gently," she called out in a melodious voice as he raced enthusiastically toward her.

Jack jogged along behind Peter and saw that, as Peter went to draw Catherine into a large bear hug, she held him back with her arms outstretched. “Please, be easy,” she called out in a more concerned voice. She turned to look at the men full face.

Peter gasped, then brought both hands tenderly up alongside her cheeks. “Who did this to you,” he asked, his voice a steely rasp.

Jack came alongside the pair and saw that her right eye was black and closed. There were smaller cuts and injuries on the rest of her face. Reaching down, Peter drew back the long, draping sleeves which covered her left arm. She moved to resist, but he slid them enough to show that her arms were also mottled with bruises.

Peter looked up sharply, holding Catherine’s gaze. He spoke out again, his voice anguished. “Tell me who did this to you,” he insisted, the anger choking his throat.

Catherine looked up with a fond smile and moved in to tenderly embrace him. Peter hesitated a moment, then carefully wrapped his muscular arms around her, holding her close without putting any pressure on her injured body.

Catherine sighed. “Oh, Peter,” she murmured softly against his chest. “I have missed you so much. I am sorry that I had to lie to you along with everybody else. I had no choice.”

More than a few moments passed with her relaxing in his embrace, him holding her close, resting his cheek on her head. Finally she pulled back and looked up at him, her eyes brimming with tears. “Please believe me. I wanted to tell you I was still alive,” she vowed, brushing the dark red hair from his brow.

“Alive, but barely,” ground out Peter, his gaze focused on her blackened eye.

Catherine’s voice became flat, emotionless. “As for the bruises, the perpetrators have already been brought to justice. That is fully resolved.”

"Oh, Catherine," he sighed, bringing a hand to rest against her bruised face. "What in the world did you get yourself into? How can I help?"

Catherine broke his gaze and looked down, as if uncertain she wanted to continue. A long moment passed, then she spoke more softly, not meeting his eyes. "I wish I did not need to ask, but if you have some of your healing salves available, I would be most grateful if I could use them later in the evening."

Peter looked down at her in concern. "But surely Lord Epworth's -"

Catherine's response was quick and short. "*No!*"

Peter was shocked into silence.

She took a deep breath and continued more calmly, meeting his gaze again. "I do not want to involve him. None can know the full extent of my injuries." Her eyes came up to meet Peter's with serious focus. "I need to have your word that this will remain between us."

Peter nodded uncertainly. "If that is what you wish, then yes, of course."

Catherine gave him a tender hug. "I have always been able to count on you," she half-whispered, before drawing back, turning her eyes finally to acknowledge the second man in the group.

Peter gave himself a shake. "I am sorry, Catherine, let me introduce you. This is my good friend -"

"Let me guess," she commented with a knowing smile. "You must be Southerner."

Jack chuckled softly at hearing his alias twice in such a short period of time. "I am known as Southerner near your homelands," he agreed amiably, bowing slightly. "However, I do have an actual name. I am Jack, foster son to Lord Epworth."

Catherine's face stilled, and she looked between the two men quickly. "Surely you cannot be both men, both Southerner and Jack ..."

Jack regarded her with quiet intelligence. "You have been *told* that these were not the same man," he replied, making it a statement rather than a question.

Catherine slowly nodded, her face a study of concentration. "Yes, and by those who would have known better," she commented quietly to herself.

She glanced up at Peter, and she shook herself; her face lightened again. "That does not matter right now," she smiled to him, fondly taking his arm in her own. "I am starving – let us begin by finding some dinner! Then we can talk to your heart's content."

Peter allowed himself to be led back toward the cathedral, matching his pace to Catherine's slow movements.

Jack unobtrusively remained at her other side, fully aware of the tender limping that marked her progress. His mind half followed the conversation of shared remembrances, but it also wondered at the hinted, deliberate deception someone had made of his character. For what reason?

The possibilities swirled through his mind as they moved into the main dining hall, as they found seats and were brought food by the alert servants.

* * *

Catherine laughed in delight. "Mmm, I am still famished," she called out, reaching over to grab a drumstick from Peter's meal. Her shoulders finally eased their tight tension as she settled into the comfortable presence of her long-time friend. She could see the questions dancing in his eyes, and she knew that, once the room cleared of strangers, they would be voiced. For now, he carefully kept the conversation on casual topics, and she appreciated his caution.

Peter smiled at her fondly, calling for a fresh round of ale, which the page quickly delivered in large, solid pewter tankards.

He gave her a playful nudge. "Speaking of healthy appetites, how is Marcie doing?" His grin grew. "And is Susan still impressing everyone with her archery?"

"Yes, my friends are doing fine," she agreed with a smile, taking a healthy bite out of the meat. "Susan asked after you, you know."

"Oh, did she?" Peter's eyes brightened. "I always did have a thing for blondes."

"She will be glad to hear that," chuckled Catherine. She looked up as the three novices came over to the table.

Walter's round face was flushed with drink. "We are off to our prayers."

Peter turned in his chair, waving a hand toward Catherine. "Gentlemen, I would like to introduce you to an old friend of mine."

Walter grinned with glee. "Oh, we have already met Catherine, earlier today," he offered. "She kindly joined our game of cards to make a foursome. She played quite well, too."

Catherine winked at him. "I could have had you, if I had thought to hold onto that three," she teased. "You are very good at the game."

Walter blushed even deeper scarlet, then gave a low, courtly bow. The three moved off toward the main church area.

Catherine looked around as she finished off her remaining bites of meat. The other household members were rising and slowly ambling toward their rooms. Another pair of visitors made their ways to their chambers, and at last only the three remained alone in the darkening hall. The fire was dying down, the low flames sending tongues of orange scattering amongst the shadows.

Jack leaned back against the table, gazing steadily at the fire. Peter sat sideways on the bench, watching Catherine as she nibbled at the meat and licked her fingers. Neither man spoke as she finished off another two large rolls, washing them down with the ale.

Finally satiated, she sighed with pleasure and eased back against the table, taking care to avoid the many bruises and wounds. After a moment she brought her ale up for a long draw. The silence drifted on in comfortable relaxation, and she stretched her arms out in a long yawn.

She felt Peter's eyes on her, and turned her head sideways, giving him a fond smile. She had missed him these past few years. It was good to be back in his company, if only for the short while her Council had allowed her.

The room grew quiet and still, with only the occasional popping of a log breaking the silence.

Peter held Catherine's look for a long moment. Finally he spoke. "Catherine, we have known each other many years now. We have been through a lot together. I hope that you trust me."

Catherine tilted her head to one side, contemplating Peter. "Of course I do," she replied fondly, putting her hand over his on the table. "I count you among my closest friends."

Peter sat forward. His voice was low and insistent. "If you trust me, please tell me what is going on with your supposed death and this beating you have been given. I can help if you let me know what is happening."

Catherine's eyes flicked quickly to Jack. He had turned slightly to face the other two, and was watching quietly. He held her gaze for a moment.

"I am happy to leave you two alone," he offered without hesitation, "although I promise that I am quite able to keep a secret, and I would also be willing to assist. After all, only Peter and I know about the extent of your injuries."

Catherine held his gaze for a long while, pondering the man before her. She looked over the firm set to Jack's face, his well-muscled body, the leather armor that he wore almost as a second skin.

Most of all, she looked into his grey eyes, saw the intelligence, wisdom, and concern that lay within. Her lips pressed together, and she nodded.

"I cannot divulge the details of my current injuries; there is a confidence issue there which I cannot violate. However, as we are alone, I will tell you what I can of my reported death."

The doors to the room flew open with a loud bang. Jack and Peter immediately stood on either side of Catherine, their stance protective and alert. A short, sturdy man in his late forties thundered into the room, dressed in a heavy, dark blue tunic, long grey traveling cloak, and thick, scuffed leather boots. He wore a broadsword at his side, and his flaming red hair matched the fury in his eyes.

He immediately spotted Catherine and strode over to stand a few feet in front of her. "How dare you!" he stammered in rage. "How dare you feign your death in order to sabotage the Wilmslow negotiations!"

Both Jack and Peter dropped their hands to the hilts of their swords, their eyes locked on the soldier before them. Between the two, Catherine slowly stood, putting a hand on each man's arm at her side to gently restrain them. "Easy," she cautioned them under her breath. She took a step forward to face the newcomer.

"Sir Magnor," she greeted smoothly, her posture regal. "I am glad you have found me so that we can discuss this. It seems that I have caused some confusion about what took place. Take some ale and sit with us; I will make everything quite clear to you."

She stood still, holding her hand out to indicate a seat for him. Magnor huffed for a moment, then gave in to proper formal behavior and came around to sit opposite her at the table. Ale was quickly brought, and Jack and Peter retook their seats at Catherine's side.

Magnor took a drink, then glared at her, his voice only slightly more under control. "That treaty was necessary for our area's safety," he spat out. "You were responsible for conducting those negotiations, before your *death*."

Catherine nodded in agreement. "Yes, I was," she responded, her voice equanimous. "However, a few weeks before the main meeting was to take place, it was discovered that a group of mercenaries had been handed full plans to the hall's layout, including security, guard assignments, and more. The mercenaries had been tasked with my assassination."

Magnor stared in amazement, disbelief changing to fury. "That cannot be true!" he responded with angry shock, leaning over the table to shout at Catherine. “That hall is deep within our territory. No enemy of ours has ever been to it!”

Catherine slowly nodded, her eyes on Magnor.

Magnor sat back, his mind sorting through the options. His voice lost some of its stridency. “Surely you cannot think that one of us was responsible for this heinous plot?”

Catherine’s eyes remained steady, and her voice was light but steely. “Surely you find it more than a coincidence that my father’s assassination was also on your soil, in one of your halls?”

Magnor’s face paled. “That slaying was clearly done by someone else!” he protested. “We have been cleared of all guilt in that situation!”

Catherine said nothing, simply sitting and looking at Magnor, her face impassive. Magnor’s look became serious. “Who were the mercenaries,” he growled in a low voice. “We will make them talk.”

Catherine shook her head. “That angle has already been meticulously examined over the past four years. The task was done extremely thoroughly, from the inside. We are now quite certain that they do not know who hired them. The assignment was given through a complex anonymous system which cannot be breached. That trail has been chased and is bone dry.”

She paused for a moment, her gaze locked on Magnor’s. “The pursuit must take place from the source - with the people who knew the guard schedule and the castle’s layout. We have done what we could from our end. It is now in your hands.”

Catherine took a long drink of her ale, then leant forward. “That is why you were asked to meet me here. I am willing to answer any questions you might have of me - but the packet you received contains all of the factual details.”

Magnor nodded in agreement. “I read the material, but I did not believe the documents. However, looking in your eyes, I see that you speak the truth. You did not abandon us. Someone within our walls has betrayed us.”

He shook himself slightly. “With the details you have provided, we should be able to narrow down the person or persons through the process of elimination. Although,” he added, his voice becoming edged again, “this would have been far easier if you had brought it to us four years ago, when it was fresh.”

It was Catherine’s turn to be short. “It could not be,” she snapped briefly. “You had to be cleared of all complicity first. Also, as you see, I have been occupied with other things.”

Magnor seemed to notice the bruises covering her face for the first time, and he flushed with embarrassment. “Yes, of course, and your own safety naturally would come first.” He paused, and then continued more slowly. “It seems I might have misjudged you,” he admitted. “I promise that we will give this our full attention, and bring the culprits to justice.”

He stood abruptly. Nodding briefly to Jack and Peter, he turned on his heel and strode out of the room.

Catherine watched him leave, then closed her eyes and gave a deep exhale. She rolled her shoulders to release the tension, and took a long drink of ale. She carefully put the mug back down into the ring it had left on the worn oak table.

Wearily, she leant back and looked to each man in turn. “Thank you for being there,” she murmured with a steady gaze of appreciation. “Magnor is not the most stable of men, and I am hardly in any shape to face physical conflict right now.”

She rolled her right shoulder again, and her breath caught at the searing pain which lanced through her body. She held back an oath, closing her eyes for a long moment. “I cannot put it off any longer,” she sighed, looked up at Peter. “You said you had salves with you?”

“Of course,” he agreed readily, and turned to Jack. “I will return in a short while,” he added.

“I will be here,” Jack replied quietly. He looked over at Catherine. “Until tomorrow, then?”

Catherine looked contemplatively at Jack for a moment, then nodded. “Yes, until tomorrow. Good night,” she added softly, then turned and walked out of the room with Peter at her side.

* * *

Jack was staring into the embers of the fire, deep in thought, when he heard footsteps approaching. He looked up to see Peter stride into the room, his body full of taut-strung tension. Jack stood immediately, walking over to his friend in concern.

"What is it," he asked quietly, clasping Peter on the shoulder.

Peter put a hand on the mantle above the fireplace, leaning on it and looking down into the embers. He took a deep, steadying breath. "Catherine was not just beaten," he grated, anger making his voice hoarse and raw. "She was thrashed to within an inch of her life. There is barely a square of skin not crisscrossed with bruises or cuts."

Jack's blood ran cold. "How recently?" he asked after a moment.

"It happened two, maybe three days ago. I am surprised she lasted the evening with us without succumbing to the pain. Whoever patched her up did an adequate job, but she should *not* be up and around. She should be in bed for days yet, if not weeks."

"Yet she still refuses to let anyone know of her injuries?" asked Jack, his mind running over the permutations.

"She adamantly rejects any show of weakness right now," confirmed Peter. "Apparently she has let it be known that she received her black eye falling from her horse. Beyond that, nobody other than you and me know anything further about the extent of her injuries. She insists that the local medical staff, and Lord Epworth himself, never learn of this situation."

"Which means," replied Jack, thinking through the chain of events out loud, "that either the person who did this to her was not in fact brought to justice ... or that he *was* and it was done in a way the law would not approve of."

He retrieved his tankard from the table, walked to the smaller wooden bench near the fire and sat down, taking a long swallow.

Peter clenched his fingers. "I think the culprit must still be out there," he declared with anger. "She is shielding him for some reason - maybe misplaced loyalty. She is not married - maybe it is a boyfriend, or someone she knows." He slammed his fist down on the mantle. "I *will* track him down. When I get my hands on him …"

Jack slowly turned his tankard in his hands, shaking his head. "I do not think that is the case," he commented quietly, focusing on the rotating rim. "She is showing no fear of follow-up violence. A woman with an abusive person actively in her life would not be so complacent here - would not have been so cool when Magnor came storming into the room."

Peter paused for a moment, then turned, nodded in agreement. "She handled that very smoothly," he offered, considering. "She did not seem like a woman nervous about being tracked down and attacked."

Jack thought back to when they had first met on the bridge. "Catherine's eyes when she spoke about the battering were flat," he mused. "It was not something of active interest. She considered the matter in her past."

Peter's mouth twisted into a frown. "Perhaps she had just given up hope of bringing him to justice," he growled.

Jack shook his head. "Catherine is undoubtedly very aware of her duties to her family. Being the sole heir to her lands, if an assassin was out there, or a threat, something would be done about it."

Peter's eyes snapped with anger. "Her family should have kept her safe in the first place!"

"Her clan is renowned for their sword work," rebutted Jack evenly. "I agree with you on this point – surely whoever hurt her has been made to pay for his deeds."

Peter rolled his shoulders, coming to sit beside Jack. "I would agree. What she told us would seem to be the truth – that the perpetrator has been slain."

Jack took in a deep breath. "Not only that, but I think that the person was of some importance."

Peter looked up in surprise. "Why would you say that?"

Jack met his friend's eyes. "If the family needed any justification for the actions they took, they need only show some of Catherine's injuries to any sheriff, and the sheriff would find cause for those actions. They could say he posed an imminent threat to finish the job. Instead, they are choosing to try to hide the entire event. To me, that indicates that it could cause them great trouble if they were known to be the ones involved."

He paused, then added, "It would also explain why Catherine is so tight-lipped about the matter. It is loyalty - but loyalty to her family, not to the abuser."

Peter took a deep breath, then sighed. "I imagine you are right," he agreed slowly. "In any case, I will not violate her trust and mention this to anybody. If it is truly her wish to hide her injuries, I will do the best I can to assist her in that."

Jack nodded. The two men sat in silence for a long while, staring into the fire.

Chapter 6

Catherine glanced down her outfit one last time in the small hand-mirror. She had chosen one of her favorite dresses, a long, rippling gown of moss green, to draw on over her white chemise under-dress. She had carefully braided her hair along her temples, and it cascaded down her back in rich waves.

She peered at the bruises on her face. The eye was still fairly violet, but the remaining visible injuries were thankfully fading into quiet. Her long sleeves and floor length dress hid the many other cuts and mottling from view.

Satisfied, she carefully picked up her necklace – an elegant double spiral on an emerald green background. She reverently laid the heirloom against her chest. Then, drawing in a deep breath, she was ready to face the world.

The dining room was bustling with activity and noise as she entered. Jack and Peter were already eating at the head table, choosing from engraved copper plates of scrambled eggs, cubes of turnips, and piles of well-spiced sausage which set her stomach rumbling. The men looked up, and Peter waved her over with warmth.

She started across the room at a quick pace, drawn in by the luscious aromas, but immediately her bruises and healing cuts ached in protest, and she stiffly reined in her stride.

Jack's brow creased, and he half rose; she made a quick, small shake of the head. The last thing she needed was to be treated publicly as an invalid, to raise suspicion and questions. He pressed his lips together, but retook his seat, his eyes steady on her slow, careful progress across the room. As she approached, he pulled out his chair so that she could more easily get in to sit between the two men.

Peter gave her a nod. “Good morning, Catherine. How are you feeling?” he asked solicitously, his tone of voice light and casual. His eyes reflected a different mood, serious and concerned.

Catherine touched his arm gently. “Your salves are really a wonder,” she replied softly. “Truly, I feel much better. Thank you.”

Jack passed over a steaming trencher of food. “Breakfast for you, m’lady,” he offered. Catherine’s eyes lit up with delight.

“I am *starving*”, she admitted, digging in immediately to the offering. She ate ravenously, devouring everything before her. Jack smiled, watching her for a moment.

“It does look like you are feeling better,” he commented quietly, nodding to Peter. “It appears, my friend, that your herbal talents continue to be worthy of acclaim.”

Catherine sopped up the last of her drippings with a loose roll, then reached for another from the wicker basket. As she did so, a look of sadness swept into her gaze. “Oh, that is a shame,” she commented quietly.

“What is it?” asked Jack in curiosity, looking over at the basket to see if something was wrong with it.

Catherine glanced up at him, her eyes regaining some of their brightness. “I apologize, I did not mean the food,” she replied with a half-smile. She motioned over at the center of the table, where some of the first flowers of spring had been strewn for decoration.

“It is a shame that they killed those blooms just for a breakfast meal. The crocuses could have given us weeks of beauty out in the garden, growing in the spring sunshine. Now they will be wilted in a few hours and discarded into the compost pile.”

There was a movement behind her; Magnor was passing through and turned to smile down at her.

“You look lovely this morning, Catherine,” he praised her heartily. His hand dropped heavily on her injured right shoulder in a strong pat. It was all she could do to hold in a cry, and despite her best efforts, a sharp wince shuddered through her body.

Beside her, Jack's body went rigid, and she could almost feel the self-restraint it took him to remain quiet and motionless. Only his eyes blazed with suppressed anger.

Catherine straightened up with careful movements, her face arranged in a smile as she brought her gaze to meet Magnor's. "Good morning, sir," she greeted him smoothly.

"Morning to you, lass," boomed Magnor, giving her shoulder an extra pat. It took all of Catherine's focus to maintain her gaze, to keep her smile in place.

There was a call from across the room, and Magnor looked up, his eyes tracking to a reedy redheaded man. His smile broadened, and he removed his hand, turning to walk on. "Duty calls. Please, enjoy your meal. I am sure I will be talking with you later on, during the day's discussions."

Catherine's smile slipped a little, and her eyes slid to the side. "We will see if I have time to make it to the meeting," she replied casually, her voice tight. "There is a lot going on ..."

Magnor nodded absently, then walked toward the far end of the room.

Peter turned to Catherine, his face creased with confusion. "You are here representing the Bowyers, and you would miss one second of the intrigue?" he asked, shaking his head. "You love to debate! You and I have argued for hours about matters of little consequence, never mind the political changes which this meeting was set up to evaluate. You would never pass the opportunity up voluntarily!"

Catherine's throat closed up, and she looked down at her meal. She was not ready for this discussion, not now when she was just regaining her much-missed friendship. She gave a push to the eggs before her, but she had suddenly lost her appetite.

Jack nodded slowly, his eyes moving from her tense shoulders to her tight jaw. "She apparently is *not* here for the debate."

She could not help it; she turned her gaze to meet his, to the warmth and understanding she knew would lie there.

The gentleness of his eyes was almost more than she could bear. Her smile slipped, the turmoil of her heart bubbled closer to the surface, and she pressed it down with much-practiced effort.

His brow creased for a long moment; when he spoke again, his voice was low. "If you are here for another purpose, it would seem that purpose is not of your own choosing."

Peter leant over, taking her hand in his own, his lips pressing into a thin line of anger. "Someone forced you into something? Does this have to do with your injuries? If you would only tell me ..."

Catherine cut him off with a sharp look. This was getting out of control. She could not talk about the issue, not here, not like this.

"I was *not* forced," she hissed sharply, glancing around at the others who shared the table. Thank the Lord; none were looking their way. All were enthusiastically engaged in other conversations, completely unaware of the chaos of her thoughts.

A long sigh escaped from her, and she sat back for a moment, closing her eyes in weary resignation. She knew she would have to discuss the situation eventually. She had only hoped it could be put off for longer. She drew her eyes open and looked back to Peter, at the concern in her friend's eyes.

"Rest easy, my dear friend," she reassured him, her voice more even. "What I am doing, I am doing of my own free will. One's actions simply are not always what one would wish them to be. Loyalty, honor, and respect can lead to compromises in one's path through this world."

Iron bands constricted around her heart, mirroring the narrowing of her choices, and it was as if the room pressed in against her, stifling her, holding in her breath. She gave herself a small shake. She had to get away before she said something she regretted. "I am afraid I will leave it at that for now, gentlemen. Please excuse me."

She moved to stand, almost stumbling, sharp pain shooting through her side. Jack's firm arm was there beneath her, subtly helping her to her feet.

She drew in a long breath, fortifying herself, and then she stepped away from him. She moved slowly, carefully toward the back wall door. Then she was stepping through it, making her way toward the quiet garden path which wended its way behind the cathedral.

The sun streamed brightly through the frosty air, adding a glistening sparkle to the world. Catherine moved with deliberate slowness along the path, taking in several long, deep breaths as she reached the herb garden. Her tense mood sloughed away as she inhaled the fresh crispness, as the glow of the sun permeated her. Nature was refreshing the soil, the plants, even the very air. The chives were already sending young spears of green sprouts through the crisp soil, and their gentle fragrance was soothing and refreshing.

Her heart was comforted as she continued more slowly through to the gravel walkway that led toward the pond. It was lined with a glowing jewel-colored progression of crocuses in blue and purple. A sense of serenity infused her, and she dropped to one knee to breathe in their fresh fragrance, a delicate scent that could only be appreciated up close.

Jack came up quietly behind her, standing with her for a moment. "They are beautiful, are they not?" he praised softly, his eyes running down the row of color and ending on her upturned face. "It is a shame the blooms only last a week or two."

Catherine, feeling almost renewed, smiled up at him. "That makes the flowers even more special," she replied. "It means that I can look forward to each unique day, to coming down this walk and sharing their glory with every other person here. It is part of what makes our world so wondrous - that each week offers something new and miraculous to appreciate."

She took one last look at the velvety petals, then pushed up with her right arm to stand. She gave a soft whimper of pain as her arm did not take her weight.

Jack immediately leant over, putting a strong grip beneath her left forearm, gently helping to raise her up. He slid his fingers down to her hand as she made her way to a standing position.

Catherine, nodding her thanks, looked up at him. He did not release her hand, and she did not seek to withdraw it, either. The warm spring sun shone down in a golden shimmer, and she became lost in his tender gaze.

She could not fall for Jack. Not when ...

Her face flushed in a wave of heat. She pulled her hand from his, turning her gaze back down to the delicate flowers.

After a few moments, Jack took a deep breath and spoke softly. "You are here to be wed to my foster father; to become the lawful wife of Lord Epworth," he stated with quiet certainty.

Catherine's face could have been doused in hot water, so strongly did her cheeks flare at his words. She began to shake her head, to postpone the discussion for at least a little while, but his voice came again, sure and even.

"There is no need to deny it," he soothed her. "I have known for some time that he craved a son of his own blood. He has been sorting through potential candidates for months. Your credentials are impeccable; you are just what he has sought. Your sudden arrival here, just as he was about to return, speaks clearly to your purpose."

She wrapped her arms around herself, turning away from him completely. All of her painful, submerged feelings came streaming to the surface. The aches of her shoulder, her ribs, her legs almost faded away beneath the soul-shattering frustration and longing.

She felt his hand, ever so gentle, on her arm, and it only made it worse, made her impotent fury at her situation boil over and fill her, bursting into every corner of her being.

His voice was tense with concern. "Catherine?"

"Please!" she cried out in angst, pulling her arm free, not sure what she was asking him to do, just knowing that she was in pain, so much pain, and she wanted it all to stop. She pulled her arms tightly around her, her eyes stinging with held-back tears.

Jack moved to stand before her, his shoulders so sturdy and strong, his eyes steady, wise, caring. Suddenly she was lost. The words bubbled out of her, escaped her control, flowing as if a dam had caved in, burst beyond all repair.

"My life has been dedicated to protecting the villagers, the people I love," she rasped, her throat tightening with emotion. "I trained daily. I pushed myself through every obstacle, all so I could serve them with my very best skills." Her breath hitched, and the enormity of her situation threatened to overwhelm her. "Now I am ordered to flee to Ireland with Lord Epworth, for my *safety*? To become a *brood mare*?"

The tears started and she pressed her lips tightly together, fighting to regain control. It was bad enough she had spilled out her most intimate frustrations. She would not – could not - allow herself to break down like an unschooled farm girl.

Jack's gaze became protective, and he put a hand gently against her face, to where the purples of her injuries were fading to mottled patches. "To be safe from the aftermath of the attack?"

Catherine barked out a harsh laugh. "If only it were for such a noble sentiment," she growled, turning from his concern, looking down the path, no longer seeing the beautiful flowers, only the hopelessness of her life. The pain of her trap twisted in her heart, coiling there like an angry snake. She put a hand there, willing herself to relax, to rein in her feelings before she lost control of them.

"My council feels that political unrest is inevitable," she ground out, her voice raw. "It is why we are not being represented at this debate. They have given up completely. They are sure that the land will be razed by the conflict, and want me off hidden in Ireland, where I can create a new Bowyer clan."

She ran a hand through her hair in frustration. "Here we had finally finished the due diligence with Magnor, and I could at last re-enter the world. It is just at that moment that my council immediately orders me to marry a coward and abandon the lands I love forever. They want me to turn my back on those I vowed to defend."

She shook her head in anger. "Our clan was founded on honor - on protecting those around us. The new clan will be founded on me running away and breaking faith with everyone I hold dear." Her voice turned cynical. "Now *there* is a trait to pass on."

Jack turned her face gently with his hand to look into his eyes. "Surely they will take your feelings into consideration," he offered reassuringly. "If you have strong concerns, they will listen to you."

Catherine chucked without mirth. "Yes, I was given a choice," she snapped bitterly. "The order is to marry Lord Epworth and join him as he deserts his homeland, all to ensure the continued line of the Bowyer family. I have been granted a few weeks to 'decide', up until Lord Epworth leaves with his feathered entourage for his palace-in-exile. Either that or ..." She looked down with frustration.

Jack's voice was quiet. "Or?"

Catherine took a deep breath. "Or I will be cast out. My council will banish me from my own lands and strip me of all rights. I will be forever separated from my dearest family and friends."

Jack shook his head slowly. "They cannot mean that; surely that is an idle threat. You are the sole heir."

Catherine turned and walked over to a carved stone bench, wearily sitting down. "You know enough about political games to realize that is never true," she reminded him. "You are Lord Epworth's foster son, and yet after all these years he is suddenly seeking to marry in order to have a biological son to supplant you. Not the most noble of actions."

She dug a toe into the dirt. "In Bowyer, my mother has a cousin who is about your age. He has always been furious that I, a mere female, was in line to inherit, and not him. Raymond is well respected by the council. He was one of those who lobbied most strongly for this current situation I am now in."

Her mouth quirked wryly. "Raymond forced me into hiding for four long years. Now he will cause me to be sent as far away as possible. I am fortunate he did not hit upon a scheme to send me off to Rome itself."

Jack sat beside her, nodding in understanding. "If you accept the marriage, you end up far away from him. Any family you raise is not a threat. If you refuse to wed, you have proven your disloyalty to the council and he waltzes in to take your place." He looked across at her, his voice softening. "Either way, you are cut off from what you have been working for your entire life."

Catherine's anger slowly drained out of her, leaving a hollow sense of resignation. She turned wearily to look at Jack. "On the other hand, I am now twenty-six years old. I have spent my life exactly as I have wished. I chose to be a negotiator and was provided with that training. I wished to become the best swordswoman I could and was given that opportunity as well. My mother was at times reluctant, but she gave me my head."

She rolled a rock along with her toe, staring at its progress. "I am now, as my mother repeatedly informs me, at the proper marrying age. Yes, many women marry older still, especially in these hard times, but …"

Jack was shaking his head. "Eleanor, our Queen, did not marry King Henry until she was thirty," he pointed out. "Together they had eight fine children, and one of those is now our King."

Catherine brought her eyes up to gaze at her sword hand, slowly flexing it. "I also shoulder the extra burden of being an untraditional bride," she murmured. "My skills with blade and tracking are not ones that many men would appreciate." She gave a sigh. "My mother warns me that I should be grateful that someone as well stationed as Lord Epworth would overlook my *strangeness* and bless me with this opportunity."

Jack's eyes were suddenly sharp with anger. "Do not ever think that way," he replied harshly. "Every person who is born deserves to reach their greatest potential, whatever that may be. We are, each of us, God's creatures, on Earth to do His will." He drew in a breath, reigning in his emotion with effort. "You deserve to be with a man who appreciates your skills, not one who wants you to hide them away in shame."

Catherine brought her eyes up to his. "Whatever I might feel personally about Lord Epworth, my mother has made it clear that this alliance is very important to the family. Surely loyalty has some part in what I choose to do?"

Jack maintained his gaze, but his eyes shadowed, swirling with conflicting emotions. "Loyalty where it is earned is perhaps the most important quality a person can have. But loyalty for no reason, or for the wrong reasons ... that can be the cause of great evil." He dropped his eyes.

Catherine took in a deep breath, running her hand through her thick hair. "If I lose my honor, then I have little left," she murmured. She gave herself a shake. "I should get back to my room; it is about time for some fresh bandages," she added quietly.

Jack stood immediately, putting out an arm, helping her slowly to her feet.

"I would be happy to escort you …"

She shook her head before he could finish. "I will do fine on my own," she replied, her voice somber. She kept her gaze low, not willing to meet his eyes, to be drawn to stay with him, to talk with him, to share her heart. Instead, she resolutely turned and began the lonely trek back toward the main building.

* * *

Catherine looked up from the dinner table for at least the tenth time, half listening to what Peter was saying at her side, wondering when Jack would ever finish with his duty at the debates. She knew the first day of introductions would be long, even interminable, but surely the man had to eat? She rolled her shoulders, grateful at least that the grinding aches were slowly easing from her bones, the wounds were tentatively drawing together and healing. Peter was indeed a talented herbalist.

She smiled suddenly – there he was. Jack's muscular build, his steady stride brought a quickness to her heart. His grey eyes, the color of a misty morning, scanned the room as he moved, lighting up with pleasure as they met hers. In a moment he was crossing through the other tables and chairs to come up to them.

Peter glanced up as he approached, calling out cheerfully, "There you are; we are almost finished, but certainly, join us." Jack made his way around the head table, and Peter waved for another ale. "Did you hear?" he added, grinning from ear to ear as Jack drew near, "we are going to have some music tonight, and Maya will be singing!"

Jack settled down on Catherine's other side, and nodded with a welcoming smile. "Indeed, we were told about it during the debates."

Catherine looked down sharply at the mention of the debates; a wrenching sensation twisted at her heart. She shook it off with resolution. She stabbed perhaps a little too heartily at the piece of chicken she was finishing off, ripping a section of flesh away, before drawing in a deep breath.

Calm. She had to remain calm.

A soft curse came from her side, and then Jack's voice was gentle, drawing her in.

"Catherine, have you heard Maya sing? She has a most exceptional voice, almost an angelic quality to it. My father invites her here frequently."

Catherine gave a halfhearted attempt at a smile. "I did meet her earlier this afternoon," she agreed. "Tall, blonde hair, blue eyes? She looks like an angel; I suppose it is no surprise that she sounds like one as well. I will be very interested in hearing her voice."

She took in a deep breath, then turned more fully to face Jack. She would not dodge the issue. "You were sweet to change the topic, but I cannot hide from the debates." Her voice dropped low. "I need to learn to accept the path I am on."

Jack looked as if he would counter her statement, but after a long moment he nodded. "If that is your choice," he offered, his voice neutral.

A weary sense of acceptance settled into Catherine's soul. "I agree I will not be attending the debates, as much as I might wish to. However, even if I cannot be present, I am still very interested in hearing what is taking place in the sessions."

Jack's response was instant. "How can I help?"

Hesitance hitched at Catherine's heart. Was it fair to ask this of Jack? Her desire to know about the events prodded her to keep speaking. "I realize it would be an imposition, but would you be willing to give me a summary, at the end of each day, of what was said?"

Jack was nodding even before she had finished. "Of course, it would be my honor," he agreed readily.

A wave of contentment swept over Catherine, and she put her hand on his, giving it a gentle squeeze. "I cannot say how much this means to me," she offered with a smile.

He seemed caught by her gaze, and it was a long moment before he nodded, his face quiet, his eyes not leaving hers.

A servant bustled over with his meal, and Catherine gave herself a shake, returning to her own food. In a moment Jack was going step by step over the introductions, explaining each person's rank and stance on the continuing hostilities between King John and the Pope. Catherine found herself impressed with his memory, with his keen interpretations of the motivations of the various dignitaries. The time flew by, and it seemed only a few moments before the remnants of the meals were being cleared away.

A pair of servants carefully dragged the large harp into the central area of the room while the hall filled with people who were eager to hear Maya sing. The warmth of the bodies, swelled by the roaring fire crackling to one side, brought a welcome counterpoint to the chill winds whistling outside.

The three acolytes stretched out on the dense fur rug before the fire, Michael carefully tucking his ankle in a swaddle of blankets. John, his toned muscles barely flexing with the effort, helped to move him into a comfortable position. Even Father Berram was brought to a well-worn leather chair in a corner and covered with a blanket, his wrinkled face relaxing into contentment.

Jack glanced up, signaling to one of the young pages circling the room. The lad nodded, and in a moment he brought over three mugs of mead to the novices. Jack toasted his friends, and they returned the toast with smiles all around.

There was a flurry of activity at the main doors, and all eyes in the room turned to look.

Maya waltzed into the hall, waving to admirers as she crossed the space. She was wearing a long, cascading ivory dress, replete with gold embroidery on the neck and arms. Catherine chuckled, watching the woman as she flowed across the room. Maya apparently knew of her celestial reputation and did her best to play it up in every way possible.

Catherine shrugged. There was no harm in promoting one's assets, and Maya certainly was beautiful. Her golden hair fell to her waist, and her face was smooth and clear. The crowd quieted when Maya finally took her seat behind the harp and put her hands to the strings.

Jack's voice murmured at her side. "It is a shame Carl and Craig are not here to see this," he offered. "The two men are good friends of mine, and they have a special fondness for female singers."

Catherine's shoulders pulled into tense alertness, and she kept her face turned away in the darkness, willed herself to relax. *Carl and Craig*. Those monsters were in the past now. That they had apparently fooled Jack with their jovial façade was not worth worrying over. Many had been lured in by the fiends' false fronts over the years.

A strumming of strings turned her attention, and Maya's voice floated with ethereal lightness into her thoughts, melting away all other concerns. The crowd sat spellbound as her voice soared and fell, drifting gently through songs of summertime love and daydreams. Peter watched as if he was captivated by her.

Catherine enjoyed the beauty of Maya's voice. It drew her out of her musings, distracted her from her dense web of emotions, her body's jagged aches, if only for this short while.

Maya sang for an hour, then took a short break before singing for another half hour. The crowd applauded their appreciation, and Maya was escorted from her harp by several fans. The hour was getting late, and many of the crowd straggled off for their rooms.

The three young novices came over to sit at Catherine's table. Walter's round cheeks were bright with drink. "She was wonderful, was she not?" he crowed with appreciation.

Peter was still staring dreamily after Maya, and turned at this. "Yes she is," he agreed readily. "If you want to hear a really moving performance, though, you should hear Catherine sing sometime. It is an entirely different experience."

Three young pairs of eyes swiveled to look at Catherine, and the voices all spoke up in chorus. Walter's eyes were bright. "Sing for us!" he cried eagerly.

Michael looked up shyly. "Yes, please do," he added shyly.

Catherine looked around the room. Most of the inhabitants had now left, with only a few remaining to talk or drink ale. The elderly priest was quietly snoring in the corner. If she was going to be pressed to sing, at least tonight seemed like a good evening to do it. "As you wish," she acquiesced agreeably, "although please do not expect anything as lilting as Maya's voice."

John spoke up with rich enthusiasm, "I am sure whatever you sing will be wonderful." The other two nodded in eager encouragement.

Catherine stood and moved over to the far wall, where a small, wooden travel harp hung high on a copper hook. She reached up for it with her right arm, then winced as the wound pulled at her sharply, reminding her of how much healing she still had to do. There was a movement beside her, and Jack was taking down the harp, a quiet smile in his eyes. Warmth swept through her heart, and she nodded her thanks, flustered, turning away instinctively to break the gaze. In a moment she was moving over toward the fire, tugging a small stool into place as she reached the edge of the ember-rich hearth.

It was not long before the others had come to join her, pulling their own seats close. Jack waited until she had settled down onto her stool before carefully placing the small harp into her arms and lowering himself at her side.

The flames were fading into embers now, and a warm darkness had fallen on the room.

Catherine pitched her voice low so that it would carry only to her group of friends. "I am not a court singer, nor trained on harp intricacies," she admitted to them with a wry grin. "I would keep my patrol companions entertained when we were out on the road, playing songs that we could relate to."

Michael's eyes brightened with interest. "You went out on patrol? What areas did you visit?"

Her face fell as she thought back to her friends, to the many long travels they went on together, all gone, all in her past. "I would rather not talk of that," she admitted softly. "Let me share myself through my music instead."

She ran a few passages on the harp, rippling her fingers with ease along the strings.

Jack watched her with quiet interest. "I am surprised the sound is much more earthy and rich than Maya's," he commented to Peter. "I would call Maya's instrument light, almost tinkling. This one seems full and deep."

Peter nodded in agreement. "Part of it is the harp's construction," he explained, "but much of the sound's character comes from the intention of the artist. Catherine, you will find, is very different than Maya."

Catherine ignored the interplay; she made a few small tweaks to the tuning, then nodded in satisfaction. A deep breath, and her fingers were in motion. The song was low yet strong, a melody about the depths of the forest and the darkness of the night. She sang about twilight pools and misty paths.

She lost herself, engrossed in the song, in the memories of her homeland. The verses touched her very soul. She found her breath almost catching …

She wandered mossy pathways
seeking one elusive peace;
A pregnant, furling hush where voices
mercifully cease ...

She looked up, and Jack's eyes were on hers, deep, understanding, immersed in her visions. Her fingers almost faltered on the strings, so powerful was the connection, and she looked away, willing herself to focus on the melody.

When the song faded off into silence, it was almost like coming out of a dream to find herself surrounded by her friends. The group smiled and toasted her quietly, not wishing to disturb the spell.

The ale mugs were refilled, the logs settled into a quiet bed of glowing embers, and she sang. Her longing and sorrow poured out of her as she played. As the minutes passed her emotions eased into an acceptance, a release of the angst that had wrapped her in its tense grip.

A bell rang, and she looked up in surprise. It was prayer time already. The trio of lads glanced at each other guiltily, then rose as one, offering murmurs of farewell before moving out through the main door. Catherine rested her hands on the strings, watching the three go with mixed emotions. She knew that Peter and Jack still had many questions for her. She was bone weary; she was in no shape to tackle the answers tonight.

Before they could speak, she pushed herself slowly to her feet. "I am sorry, but I am feeling quite tired. I think I shall turn in."

"Good night," offered both men in unison, standing to see her off. Catherine felt tempted, looking in their eyes, to stay and unshoulder her many burdens into their tender care – but she knew she could not. Reluctantly, she turned and headed off to bed.

Behind her, she could hear them begin a quiet discussion.

Chapter 7

Catherine smoothed the heather-purple dress down over her chemise, laying the emerald spiral medallion on top with fondness. The combination of colors brought to mind the dappled field of wildflowers which stretched beyond her keep, and a sense of homesickness drew around her for a long moment. She shook the feeling off. She was set on her path, and would see it through as best she could.

She settled the silken white ribbons more firmly into the intricate braid of her hair, noting with satisfaction that her black eye was finally starting to fade. The long sleeves and high neck of her outfit covered the many remaining bruises and scrapes. She smiled at herself in the mirror, and the woman who returned her gaze, while lacking the bright, attention-getting glitter that Maya showcased, did glow with a timeless, honest beauty. She hoped that it would be enough for …

She blushed crimson as she realized that it was not Lord Epworth who came to mind, not the cowardly aging statesman whose face rose before her, but Jack, with his warm eyes, his attentive concern, his intelligent care. It was he that she wanted to be drawn to her, to take her into his arms.

She shook the feeling off with harsh discipline. She was here to be courted by Lord Epworth, and she would focus on that task to the best of her ability.

She put down the mirror with resolution, and in a moment she was moving slowly through the wide hallways, stepping into the noisy hubbub of the dining area, looking across at the head table. The men were there, of course, side by side, and when they looked up in welcome warmth coursed through her heart.

The walk across the large room was far easier for her than it had been the previous morning; her injuries were finally healing in earnest. Jack's eyes did not leave her once as she drew close, and she found herself pinkening under his long perusal. She came around to the seat the men had left between them, taking Jack's offered hand as he helped her into her chair. His fingers were steady, warm, and she felt a reluctance to release them when she was in her place. She deliberately busied herself with reaching for a roll, with drawing the soft dill butter across it.

She scanned her mind for something innocent to talk about, to shake away the longing which was infiltrating her heart, stretching its tendrils into every corner of her being.

"I was watching you and Peter spar from my window this morning," she admitted with a smile, taking a bite of her warm roll. "You two are quite good."

"Thank you," responded Jack, nodding congenially. "That means a lot, coming from you. I imagine you have trained with some of the best in the land."

"Peter seems to favor the high guard," considered Catherine, her eyes glancing over at her friend, "but your style is more … mixed."

Jack chuckled. "You are being gracious," he agreed with a smile. "Peter's father was a crusader and taught him classic sword positions from when he was a young child. I am afraid my own training is much more haphazard. I use what works."

"It appears to work rather well," teased Catherine, taking down a drink of mead. "I counted you achieving seven hits to his five."

Peter gave her a gentle nudge. "Hey, I had six," he argued.

She shook her head. "That last one was weak; it caught his cross-guard," she informed him, the corners of her mouth turning up in a grin.

Peter looked to Jack, and he shrugged, nodding in agreement. "You seemed so pleased by the move, I did not have the heart to tell you," he murmured to his friend.

Peter's eyes sparkled, and he looked back to Catherine. "I think I will have your room moved," he threatened merrily. "Maybe something overlooking the stables."

She swatted him with the back of her hand. "You shall not," she challenged him. "Leave me my simple pleasures in life."

Jack gave her a toast. "You have sharp eyes," he praised. "Not many would have spotted that situation."

She nodded to him, caught by his gaze. "I enjoy swordplay," she admitted quietly. "Watching you in action was a real pleasure."

He smiled in return, and her heart stopped. She was warmed by his gaze, by the closeness of his presence. She flushed, looking away quickly. She was becoming far too fond of Jack - a man who might shortly become her stepson.

Her stomach twisted into a gnarled knot, and she reached for her mead, drinking it down in a long draw. Would he soon come to hate her? In a very real way, her presence would drive as a wedge between him and Lord Epworth.

"How is your foster father doing?" she asked, her throat tight. "Have you talked with him?"

Jack touched her gently on the arm, and she looked up at him. His gaze held understanding and reassurance.

"I do not mind his decision to remarry," he admitted frankly. "Do not trouble yourself about that. I am grateful he took me in when I was a youth. I do not expect anything more."

His face becamc serious. "As long as it is *your* choice, I will support you fully and do all I can to ensure you are happy in our family."

"Thank you," offered Catherine hoarsely, her face heating.

He turned, taking a long drink of his own mead, looking down into the mug. "It would be interesting to have a woman around who could help referee my swordplay," he offered, contemplating.

"I suppose that is not something you find in the average woman your father courts," she replied hesitantly, unsure if this was meant as a compliment.

"Not in any other woman," he countered, his eyes coming up to hold hers, his gaze full, heavy.

A flush filled her body, there was an answering heat in his eyes. The danger in the situation billowed around her with palpable force. Then he had turned again, taking a long moment to track down a servant, to get a fresh round of mead served out. When he looked back, his face was more even, and he offered a half smile.

"I am sure where you come from, there are many women just like you," he commented quietly. "Susan, and Marcie perhaps."

She turned her head away, his casual comment striking her hard. The thoughts of her beloved friends, women she would never see again, added to her sense of loss and longing.

"Please, I cannot talk about them, not right now," she bit out, her throat tight.

Suddenly a hush fell across the room, and all eyes turned toward the main door. A tall, slender man in his late fifties strolled regally into the room. He was dressed in long purple robe held together at the neck with an elaborately jeweled bronze clasp. His hair was trimmed short and was peppered with grey, but his eyes were sharp and alert. The room was filled with quiet salutations of "Lord Epworth" and a wave of bows and curtseys swept across the area.

"Welcome, my friends," called Lord Epworth genially, smiling at his many companions. He shook hands with Father Berram and gave a hearty hug to Sir Magnor. He spent several minutes talking warmly with Maya, who coquettishly fluttered her eyelashes in response. Turning, he spotted Jack, Peter, and Catherine at the head table and headed toward them. Jack stood up and smiled fondly at his foster father.

Lord Epworth pulled his foster son into a solid, hearty embrace. "Jack, it is wonderful to see you," he exclaimed. He held him for a moment, then released him. "We have a lot of catching up to do," he added. "I will look for you later, when I am more settled in."

Jack nodded. "I am at your service," he agreed. "I am happy to see you returned safely from your trip." His gaze gentled, and he lowered his voice. "It could not have been an easy one; you seem quite weary."

Lord Epworth almost seemed as if a mask slipped away for a moment; his face grew older, more tired. "It was a long voyage," he agreed somberly. In another breath the moment had passed, and his presence and enthusiasm had reasserted itself into his posture and movements.

Lord Epworth turned to Peter next, and clasped his arm warmly before drawing him into an expansive hug. "Peter, how have things been around here?"

Peter smiled in welcome to Lord Epworth. "Everything is in order, my Lord. The debate has begun smoothly," he offered. "We are all grateful you have returned to us safely."

Lord Epworth nodded, and next turned to Catherine, who stood between her two friends. She curtsied deeply at his gaze, holding the curtsy and keeping her gaze downcast. Lord Epworth's voice became melodic. "Ah Catherine, my little child, you are even more beautiful than your mother had led me to believe. I am especially pleased to find *you* here in my home."

Catherine took in a deep breath. She had heard that Lord Epworth had arrived earlier this morning, and had done her best to make herself presentable for him. She had made a promise to herself to do the very best she could in fulfilling her family's expectations of her.

Still, being faced with the actual man that she would have to bind herself to for the rest of her life was hard to bear. Hearing him call her a "little child" - she had to fight the instinct to tense and comment on it. She felt Jack and Peter's presence beside her. On one hand, it gave her strength, to know that they were there to support her. On the other hand, it made her realize just what she was giving up in life.

She realized suddenly that Lord Epworth was waiting for a response from her.

She stood from her curtsy, her hands demurely clasped behind her back. She looked up to his chest, to the gaudily jeweled bronze clasp, and then willed herself to meet his gaze.

"My Lord, on behalf of my family in Bowyer and myself, I want to thank you for your kind invitation for me to visit."

Lord Epworth's eyes scanned her from head to toe, his mouth curving with pleasure. "When your mother spoke to me of getting you to safety, I was quick to let her know I could arrange that. My sole thought was for the protection of a friend's only child. Now that I meet you in person after all these years, it seems your presence will be a wonderful addition to my entourage. Greetings, lovely little girl!"

Lord Epworth stepped forward, and Catherine realized that he was planning to give her an enthusiastic embrace in welcome, similar to the bear hug he had given his foster son. She *could not* betray the extent of her injuries. In panic she swept her left hand behind her to find the edge of the table hold on to, to brace herself. Her hand instead swept against Jack's hand.

Lord Epworth began to squeeze and there was no time to seek another option. She clasped her hand against Jack's and felt his matching grip immediately close over hers, holding her tightly. Lord Epworth's arms pressed around her upper back, and he pulled her in hard. Her body screamed out in agony, and the wound in her right shoulder throbbed as if it would split open. She clung desperately to Jack's hand, behind her back, and wrenched her eyes shut.

The agony-laced embrace lasted a lifetime.

At last Lord Epworth pulled away, and Catherine quickly released Jack's hand. She exhaled her breath slowly, hoping that the sound she made came out more like a sigh than a whimper of pain.

Lord Epworth did not notice anything amiss, and stepped back to again look her over with satisfaction. He smiled with pleasure, then turned to talk with Peter. "I need you to catch me up on events; let us head to my study," he instructed, his voice falling into the cadence of an order. The two men walked out of the room together at a quick stride. The crowd settled back down to eat, excited chatter surrounding them.

A group of musicians had come in with Lord Epworth and once he left they began to play light music in the far corner of the room. Catherine's eyes were drawn to them while her thoughts, refusing to focus, flitted like an agitated firefly. There was a drummer with a large, almost frog-like face. The harpist was tall and thin, with blonde hair. The flute player had a shock of red hair and a curved nose. The singer was a small man with tight blonde curls. The sound of music filled the room, but she did not hear a note. She could see the people around her laughing and joking, but she heard not a word. She was bundled in by pain and despair.

Catherine shook her head to clear it, but it was if she was standing in a dense fog, not able to see anything around her, not able to hear a sound. The ache in her shoulder resonated at a mind-numbing throb. Jack was speaking to her, but she could not make out what he was saying. Without a word she turned and walked out of the dining hall, her feet automatically taking the slow, steady path past the herb garden, down the long row of crocuses and over to the bridge at the back of the pond.

She barely took in the beauty around her or the warm spring sun shining down on her. She could only see the path her life was taking. She would be joined for life to a man who treated her like an infant and whose cowardice went against everything she held dear. And yet there seemed no turning back.

The wound on her right shoulder gave an even sharper stab of pain; she automatically raised her left hand to massage it idly while she stared down at the pond.

"Is your shoulder troubling you still," asked Jack with concern. He was standing at her side, his dark hair riffling in the breeze.

Catherine looked up in surprise; she hadn't heard him following her or approach. "Thank you for your support back there," she responded by way as an answer. "I did not mean to squeeze your hand so hard."

Jack chuckled softly. He looked down and flexed his right hand a few times. "I am sure I will survive," he replied with a smile. "I am glad I could help, if only in that small manner." He looked down at her shoulder. "You are sure the wound is not damaged further?"

Catherine rotated the shoulder experimentally a few times, and did not feel the sharp ache again. She shrugged dejectedly. "I imagine it will be fine. Peter wrapped that area up rather thoroughly." She smiled faintly as she looked out at the pond, thinking back. "I have had injuries before, especially during my early years of sword school. I will heal if I take it easy. That was always the challenge for me. I hate to just sit around."

"Peter told me you have been training since you were thirteen," commented Jack with gentle curiosity.

Catherine turned to lean against the railing, to look out at the dark water, a strong resistance kicking in at any thoughts of her past. She should not be sharing her memories, not discussing them …

Jack waited patiently beside her, not pressuring her, his gaze steady, full of understanding.

She took in a deep breath, then let it out. He was to become part of her family, after all. She had a responsibility to make this transition a smooth one, whatever pain it might bring her. He had the right to ask questions about her past and to receive honest answers.

"Most Bowyer youth who have an interest in swords do start training earlier," she commented quietly. "In my case, I did not feel that call until I turned thirteen. The teachers allowed me to join at that late age, and with a great deal of effort I caught up with the other students in a fairly quick time."

"I have no doubt," commented Jack quietly. "There was no issue with you being female?"

"I imagine, with so many sword makers and sword trainers in our area, we have far more women interested in martial activity," she contemplated. "I suppose it would be the same if you grew up in a pottery community, you would want to learn if only because everyone else was doing it. If my mother was upset, it was more that I was avoiding other things I could be learning, rather than that I had specifically chosen to focus on swordfighting."

Jack's moved his gaze to the quiet pond, his voice gentle, almost soothing. "What was it that your mother wanted you to learn about?"

Catherine shrugged, leaning against the railing. "The usual, I imagine. History, dancing, and singing. She agreed with my negotiation trainings. She was pleased that I excelled in those lessons; she felt they were the ideal use of a woman's natural talents." Catherine looked down. "My mother felt, and I see her logic, that a person should dedicate themselves fully to one path in life. She thought that knowing how to beguile an opponent at every turn would bring triumph in the end. To her mind the history, dancing, and singing lessons were all tools in a negotiator's toolbox."

Jack maintained his focus on the ripples on the water's surface. "… but?"

Catherine ran a hand idly along the wood surface of the railing, relishing its weathered texture. "I think it never occurred to my mother that my path was quite different than what she planned for. She envisioned me as an elegant debate participant, drawing in the eye of a polished nobleman to one side, soothing a seasoned warrior at the other. In her mind, having me possess any physical strength would detract from that goal."

Her mouth quirked into a smile. "It was an interesting balance. While my mother did not mind the idea of me being talented with a blade, and took pride in my victories, she *did* worry that I would end up scarring my face or hands. She thought any physical deformity would distract my 'victims' so they did not fully fall into whatever trap I had laid for them."

Jack cocked an eyebrow. "You did not worry about permanent disfigurement? Most women I know -"

Catherine's laugh was short. "I am afraid you will find that I am not like most women," she replied, her voice regretful. "That was always an issue between my mother and me. I could not care less if I wore the latest fashion or hairstyle, while she felt they were absolutely essential to the path she had laid out for me."

Catherine shrugged again, and her face drew tight. "It took her years before she realized that her goals were greatly divergent from my own. It had never occurred to her that what I intended to do with my life was not what her grand scheme had plotted for."

Her hand dropped to nurse her other forearm for a long moment, and her voice lowered. "Yes, I do have a scar or two from my fights with bandits in the area. I always considered them badges of honor for keeping my people safe." Catherine pressed her lips together for a moment. "If my future husband dislikes my scars, that will be an issue for him to come to terms with."

Jack thought a moment, then carefully undid the laces on the elegantly worked leather bracer on his right arm. Catherine realized that the cuff was quite different than the rest of his well-worn outfit. The bracers were far more flashy and almost garish in their design. When Jack had unlaced the leather, he removed it, revealing a nasty gash that ran along the full length of his forearm.

"This is from a fight on the roads north of here," he offered simply, looking down at the scar. "I was escorting a pair of nuns to their abbey and a group of bandits felt they would be an interesting prize." He looked at the wound for a moment, then commented, "When I returned, my father took one look and then had these bracers made especially for me. He asked me to wear them, to hide the wound, because it disturbed him and others to see the injury."

The wound had healed with an ugly red twisting scar, but Catherine did not feel bothered at all. To her, this was the sign of one who had defended the innocent. She put her fingers on the scar and ran them lightly along it, wondering at the stroke that had caused such an injury, at how Jack had fought on despite it. Jack shivered under her touch, almost drawing away. She held him with her tender caress, lost in thought.

Catherine looked down at the scar, thinking of her own wounds, of the choices that lay before her. If nothing else, she could show Jack that not all took such a shallow view of human beauty. She tenderly raised Jack's arm and kissed the end of the scar.

"For Honor," she saluted softly. She could feel Jack breathing deeply and did not trust herself to look up at him. She had already taken a great liberty, giving the responsibilities she had. She should not be encouraging a relationship with the son when she was duty bound to tie herself to the father.

A friendly shout sounded from above them, and the two quickly stepped apart, Jack moving to lace the bracer back on his forearm. Peter came down to join them from the garden path, smiling. "Catherine, there you are. Lord Epworth and I are finished, and he sent me to find you. He would like to have a talk with you; please attend to him."

Catherine bristled at being summoned, but reminded herself again that this was her duty and bit down the annoyance. She forced a smile and nodded. "Of course, Peter. Thank you for bringing the message." She turned to look at Jack. His eyes seemed distant, aloof. "Thank you again," she offered simply.

Jack hesitated for a moment, then turned to look out over the pond. "It was nothing," he replied shortly. Catherine could tell by the set of his shoulders that this was far from the truth, but she did not wish to press the issue. She nodded again at Peter, then turned and walked down the flower-lined path.

Catherine made her way through the stone hallways to Lord Epworth's study. The young guard at the door let her in with a friendly nod. The spacious room was richly furnished with thick tapestries, elegant burgundy curtains, and luxurious brown fur rugs. A large wooden desk stood beneath an intricate stained glass window, and two plush chairs waited by a roaring fire. Lord Epworth was sitting behind the desk when she entered, and came around with a wide smile to greet her.

"Catherine, thank you for coming so promptly," he welcomed her warmly. "Come, sit by the fire. I would love to spend some time with you."

Catherine did as she was told, willing herself to relax. She had worked out many difficult truces - she could get through an hour or two of discussion. The surroundings were certainly pleasant enough.

"That is a gorgeous depiction over your desk," she offered, figuring that praise was always a safe topic. She looked at the leaded glass more closely. A male saint was riding on a boat across choppy seas, sailing toward a distant shore. Overhead, a pair of seagulls soared.

"Is that Saint Brendan?" she asked with pleasure, recognizing the features of the scene.

"Yes, well done," answered Lord Epworth in surprise, sitting back in his chair, looking fondly at his guest. "You are indeed very quick! Saint Brendan is the patron saint of travelers. I always light a candle to him before I embark on one of my journeys. He is my favorite saint."

"He is mine as well," agreed Catherine with a smile. "It is always my wish that travelers reach their destination safely."

"Well, then, we will have a wonderful time of it!" smiled Lord Epworth. "For I love to travel, and you love to keep travelers safe!" He looked her over and nodded. "Your mother was quite right. You are the ideal partner for me. You already have years of training in negotiation. You understand the value of appearance, of deportment, of dress and manner. Your parents trained you in this from when you were young, much as mine did."

He smiled and took a sip of his wine. "My father always talked about how people judge with first impressions, how they react to you before you open your mouth. 'It is not fair, son,' he would say to me, 'but it is the way the world is. You best learn to be wise in this area.' I took his advice to heart. I always seek perfection in my dress and in my surroundings."

"I did learn a lot in my years of treaty work," murmured Catherine cautiously. She did not know if she agreed with his leap from first impressions to a desire for flawlessness, but perhaps he was simply generalizing for her benefit. "So, tell me more about your travels, I would love to hear of them."

As Lord Epworth warmed to the topic, Catherine realized this conversation was going to be a very easy few hours. Lord Epworth launched into a series of long, intricately detailed tales from his latest trip to Rome. He seemed to mention every famous person he had met and every historic site he had visited. Catherine only had to add an appreciative murmur or a well-placed "Oh really" to keep him rolling along.

Eventually lunchtime arrived, and Lord Epworth escorted Catherine to sit with him in the dining hall. Michael, Walter, and John joined them at the main table, and Lord Epworth regaled them all with tales of his trips during the meal. The young novices listened in rapt attention, not having seen much of the world yet and appreciatively gasping over each new tale. Catherine smiled and nodded, taking the time to become lost in her own thoughts.

A movement caught her eye; she glanced up to see Jack enter the hall, followed by Peter. Jack looked over and met her gaze, then looked down again and walked with Peter to the smaller table by the fire. Catherine was washed with a strong desire to get up and join the pair, but with deliberation she remained in her seat and turned back to Lord Epworth. He had not noticed her momentary distraction; he was deep into an epic story and playing off the rapt attention of his young audience.

When the meal was over, Lord Epworth bowed with a smile to Catherine. "I need to go prepare for the debate, a boring chore which I will not tire you with," he apologized. "That begins in an hour. I will see you at dinner. Enjoy your afternoon!" He turned to a nearby page. "George, please tell Stephanie to come by the study. I need her to handle something for me." The page nodded obediently and left. Turning, Lord Epworth strolled down the hall.

Catherine closed her eyes for a moment. Claustrophobia washed over her - she needed to get out of the cathedral for a while, and not just within the walls of the back garden.

She offered her farewells to the acolytes, then went to take her black cloak and dagger from a peg by the entry hall. She strapped her dagger around her waist, hefted her cloak onto her shoulders carefully and strode toward the main gate.

She had just reached the open gates when Jack came up alongside her. He wore a deep brown cloak over his leather armor, and had a longsword strapped against his left leg. His voice was a concerned growl. "You cannot possibly be thinking of going outside the walls alone with the threat of bandits out there?"

Catherine barely checked her step. "I *need* to get some fresh air," she replied with determination. "I will not go far, I just need to get out … away ..."

Jack fell into step beside her. "I will go with you then," he stated firmly.

Catherine strode across the threshold, beneath the looming shadows of the large gates and walls. Her voice was low and bitter. "Conrad and his crew are hundreds of miles away by now, running wild. They are a menace to others now."

"There are other dangers in the woods besides those particular men," continued Jack, his voice still terse.

Catherine did not respond; she simply turned left off the road and into the open meadow beyond. As she left the walls behind, a weight lifted from her shoulders, and she took in a deep, cleansing breath. Yes, she really did need some time away.

There was a cart path leading up into the forest, and she walked along it. Jack stayed alongside her in silence. Catherine was quite comfortable with the quiet, feeling no need to fill it with idle conversation. It began to seem almost natural for the two to be out in the forest, enjoying the beautiful day together.

There was still a fair amount of snow on the ground in the forest; the shadows were keeping cool temperatures. Catherine enjoyed hearing the crunch under her leather boots as they walked. After a while, though, her body began to ache, reminding her that she was far from healed.

She found a fallen log on a rise which gave a lovely view of the cathedral down below. She carefully sat down to rest. Slowly, the peace and serenity of the hilltop location swept through her, and she closed her eyes in appreciation.

* * *

Jack stood at the edge of the clearing, his hand on his hilt, scanning the surrounding countryside, all too aware of just how beautiful Catherine looked as she relaxed in the forest, of how her face glowed with contentment, of how she seemed to almost come to life once nature had surrounded her.

Every sinew in his body urged him to move to sit by her side, to feel her warmth next to him. He resisted with an effort, remaining at the overlook, gazing out at the snowy hills, the grey walls of the cathedral below.

"This was my patrol route," he commented, half to himself, "when I was younger. I have not been up here in a while."

Catherine breathed in the fresh air with a wistful smile. "I loved going on patrols," she reminisced. "We would be out for weeks at a time, walking through the wilderness, keeping an eye on the villagers. Our group was like a small family, sharing stories, relying on each other." She stretched out her legs and sighed. "If I could lead that life forever, I think I would be quite content."

A pang ached in his heart; he knew exactly what Catherine was talking about. He dropped his head in frustration. His loyalty to his foster father meant that he should be convincing Catherine to look ahead, not reminding her of what she was going to lose.

"If you enjoy traveling," he pointed out with a forced smile, "then you will be quite happy going to a new location. Think of all the fascinating landscapes you will visit, the unusual people, animals, and plants you will come across. You could enjoy a world of amazing discovery, and write back to tell your family and friends what you have encountered."

Catherine's eyes lit up. "Yes, that would be quite fascinating," she agreed. "I have to focus on the positive aspects of this task. There will be a wealth of knowledge for me to learn about, and to share." She rubbed her injured shoulder absently. "Still, I will miss many things about my homelands."

"You mean Susan and Marcie," asked Jack quietly. "They were your friends from Bowyer?"

Catherine nodded absently. "I have known them from childhood," she confirmed. "We were inseparable. We did almost everything together. It was very hard to leave them."

"Would they go on patrols with you," pursued Jack with interest. He was glad to have Catherine talking about her past. Until now she had attempted to deflect such conversations, but she seemed to have lowered her guard, out here in the woods.

Catherine laughed merrily to herself, and the sound carried across the clearing. Jack realized that he had never seen her truly happy until now - her entire face lit up with delight. "Oh, no," continued Catherine with a wide smile. "Susan was certainly a good archer, but Marcie was a little on the ...round side. She loved to cook. They would wait for me to come back from patrol, and we would cause mischief around town, but no, they were not the wandering type."

She thought about her friends, and her face tinged with sadness. "We were alike in many ways, but we were also quite different women."

Jack saw his chance to slide in a question he had been puzzling over for days. "Oh, then maybe Shadow was one of your patrol group?" He kept his voice neutral, and glanced over to see what her reaction would be.

To his surprise, Catherine's body tensed, and a look of deep angst came over her. She looked down, scuffing at the snow with her boot. "I do not wish to talk about Shadow," she replied in a low, flat voice.

She stood suddenly and walked to the rise to look down at the cathedral. Her shoulders were hunched, and she crossed her arms across her chest. She continued in a quiet voice, almost to herself, "I will have to forget that name, once I go away with Lord Epworth."

She turned suddenly and strode back down the trail toward Worcester.

Jack's brow creased at the sudden change in her mood, and his thoughts spun through the possibilities. He had expected Catherine to know of Shadow, but their relationship appeared to be more serious than he would have imagined. His face became somber as he stepped forward to catch up with her.

The two remained silent as they returned along the path and through the gates. As they came through the wooden doors into the arched entryway, Lord Epworth came up to meet them. He looked from Catherine's upset face to Jack's thoughtful gaze, and pursed his lips. The silence stretched on for a few moments.

"Jack, it is time for the debate to continue," Lord Epworth reminded him finally, glancing between the two again. "I have been looking for you."

Jack nodded, then bowed briefly to Catherine. She dropped a brief curtsey in response, then turned and walked toward her room. Jack watched her go, his heart heavy. Then he headed with Lord Epworth toward the main hall.

The room was already crowded with participants, and Lord Epworth moved toward the front table, waving Jack to accompany him. The table was already quite full, and Jack shook his head, scanning the room. He spotted the three acolytes in the back of the room, several empty seats nearby. Father Berram sat near them, his hands shaking slightly as he talked with his neighbor.

Jack nodded to his young friends as he took his seat. He was content with his location; he realized in short order that he could more easily watch reactions and hear crowd comments from this position.

The debates started up, but Jack found them slow going. Each speaker had a recommendation to make, but enjoyed the spotlight and took far longer than he needed to in order to lay out his point of view.

Jack turned to talk to Michael during one of the more droning speeches. "How is your ankle doing?" he asked solicitously, keeping his voice low.

Michael seemed grateful for the distraction, and turned eagerly. "Oh, it is quite fine now, thank you," he replied with a smile. His face became contrite. "I am deeply sorry for causing so much trouble during our travel," he added. "It was a blessing that Shadow came along when he did."

The comment reminded Jack of the interchange when Shadow had first entered the clearing and met up with the three novices. He had not had an opportunity since then to talk with the trio alone, and despite the crowd around them now, few seemed to pay any mind to their conversation.

Jack dropped his voice lower, and he looked across the three sets of eyes with serious attention. "You all seemed to know Shadow when we met that rainy afternoon. When had you met him before?"

Walter glanced at the other two with hesitation, then slowly stated, "I suppose, after all we went through together, that we can tell you some of what happened."

John nodded and leant forward, his eyes holding Jack's. He ran his muscular hand through his thick red hair absently as he spoke. "It was about three years ago. We were playing around near a rapids. It was spring, so the stream was raging at a fierce clip. We were horsing around on the rocks and Walter slipped, falling in -"

"I did not slip!" interjected Walter quickly. "You pushed me - I would never have gone in otherwise!"

Michael sighed. "In any case," he continued, shaking his head at the other two, "Walter was in the water and was quickly pulled downstream. We ran along the bank, but he was being drawn to the other side, and the rocks were pretty nasty. We were yelling for him to swim, but he was being pulled under."

Walter crossed his arms over his chest, his voice petulant. “Those rapids were rough! I was trying my best. You know I am not a great swimmer.”

John took up the story. “All of a sudden, there Shadow was, standing on the bank. There was not a moment of hesitation. The cloak came off, Shadow was in the water, and the next thing we knew, Walter was safely on the opposite bank. We had to run down to a bridge to get across, and by the time we got to Walter, Shadow had left.

Jack turned to look at Walter with a piercing gaze. “You saw Shadow without any disguise? You spoke with him?”

Suddenly, Walter clamped his lips shut, and a set look came to his eyes. He shook his head no, then turned to look out at the proceedings.

Confused, Jack turned to Michael. Michael apologized quickly, “I am sorry, Jack.” Michael looked around and dropped his voice lower. “Apparently Walter swore to Shadow never to talk about that. He will not even tell *us* anything. We used to tease him about it, to get him to say something. However, we respect his promise now and defend his decision. I feel shame that we ever used to try to get him to break that vow.”

Jack was frustrated, but he nodded in understanding. “Of course. I am sorry, Walter, I had no idea.”

Walter looked back and gave a smile. “I am just glad to be here, and alive.” He seemed pensive for a moment, looking down. “Now I owe Shadow my life twice.”

Jack had hundreds of questions that he wanted to ask the boys, but he took a deep breath and turned to watch the debates. He would have to find another way to learn what he wanted to know about this Bowyer lone wolf.

Chapter 8

Catherine's injuries were healing, but she was still grateful for Peter's arm as they headed in to dinner. Jack and Lord Epworth had already taken their seats at the head table, and Peter walked Catherine to a seat at Lord Epworth's left, settling her there before he moved to the other side, to sit on Jack's right.

Lord Epworth looked over Catherine's face with critical attention once they sat side by side, and Catherine blushed under the scrutiny.

At last Lord Epworth sighed. "My little one, that bruising on your face is worse than I had imagined." He shook his head. "It is a shame that your council could not send you in a protective carriage, to save you from this dreadful injury."

Catherine flushed to an even brighter shade of crimson. She looked down at her lap, willing herself not to look at Jack, praying he would not speak out.

Lord Epworth took her hands in his own. "Oh, my child," he added contritely, "I do not mean to cast any aspersions on your family. I imagine they thought it best to have you arrive in the manner you did." He paused for a moment, giving her hand a squeeze. "Know that when you join my family you shall always ride safely in a comfortable coach. I shall not allow you to sit on horseback again."

Catherine took in a long, deep breath. He surely did not mean it. He was simply being solicitous, saying what he thought she wanted to hear.

He smiled, patting her on the hand soothingly. "I am sure your face will heal as good as new. Going forward, in my attentive care, nothing further will ever harm the perfection of your looks."

Catherine murmured a quiet thanks, her eyes self-consciously moving to look at her arms. If Lord Epworth thought the bruising on her face was bad … but it was not worth worrying about now. That was a discussion for a later time. Perhaps he would not be as sensitive about scars which were hidden from public view.

Her eyes automatically looked across Lord Epworth's chest to where Jack's bracers were on display in their elaborate glory. Jack had been forced to wear those guards by his foster father; he had been instructed to hide his scars of valor from view. Her face flushed now not in shame, but in anger. That anyone could be denigrated for being wounded while defending the innocent …

Her eyes moved up to Jack's face, and she took in a deep breath. He was gazing at her, his eyes reflecting understanding, support.

Then Lord Epworth was leaning forward again, blocking her view. He smiled congenially. "I will have my physicians send over their finest salves," he instructed firmly. "You will look perfect in no time, I promise."

A pair of servants moved in with trenchers of roast pork and Catherine turned her attention with relief. The aromas from the plates were heavenly, and the group dove into the delicious food with a voracious appetite.

Catherine listened to Lord Epworth's stories for most of the meal, biding her time. Lord Epworth finally leant back in satisfaction, his stomach pushed out with the rich food. Catherine, feeling she had been quite patient, quickly took the opportunity to speak across him to Jack, who had been silent on the other side.

"Jack," she began in a casually friendly voice. "Do tell us what happened during the debates today. I have not yet heard anything about the afternoon."

Jack's eyes flicked to Lord Epworth, then looked back to Catherine. Before he could speak Lord Epworth sat forward again, interrupting their view of each other.

"Now, Catherine, child," he offered soothingly. "The debate consisted of agonizingly boring conversation. Look, Maya is going to sing us a few songs with the musician troupe I came across on my return. Let us relax and enjoy their performance." He patted Catherine's hand, then turned his chair to draw closer to her.

Catherine put on a smile, willing herself to be patient and tolerant. She took a long drink of mead and turned her attention to the evening's entertainment. Maya again looked like an angel come to earth with her porcelain skin and ocean-blue eyes. Her layers of white dress seemed lighter than air.

The dark haired, frog-faced drummer did a wonderful job of syncopating with Maya's summertime songs, and Catherine mused how the oddest pairings sometimes create the sweetest sounds. She noted with amusement that the flute player, with his shock of red hair, bore a striking resemblance to Peter, if only the musician's nose had been a little straighter. The male singer, in his small frame, seemed to have the energy of someone twice his size, and soon had the entire room singing along in enthusiastic harmony.

Catherine looked from the motley crew of musicians over to the aging man at her side. He was well respected by his fellows, after all, and had a gentle demeanor. Maybe she could find some way to make this pairing work. There were far worse men in the world to be matched with. She spent the next two hours in deep thought.

When the performances were over, most of the gathering meandered off to their rooms. Catherine stood when Lord Epworth did and did not resist when he guided her toward the exit. Father Berram, roused from his corner spot, used a cane to slowly come over to meet with the two.

"Ah, Lord Epworth," greeted the elderly man querulously. "If you have a few minutes, I needed to talk with you about some points brought up at the debate. Perhaps if we could speak in private?"

"Of course," responded Lord Epworth smoothly. He gave an absent bow of farewell to Catherine, then dismissed her with a turn and continued on with Father Berram toward his office. Catherine sighed softly in relief. She stood still for a few moments, to give Lord Epworth time to fully leave the room, then she returned to sit by the fire.

She looked up with a smile when Peter and Jack came to sit on either side of her, bringing her a tankard of mead. Jack gave her a half-smile. "I assume you do still want to hear about the debates."

"Yes," said Catherine with a grateful nod, glad that Lord Epworth's behavior had not put Jack off. Jack settled back and went carefully over the details of the afternoon. Catherine and Peter listened raptly, and an hour passed quickly.

Peter nudged her softly in the ribs. "Now, perhaps a song or two?"

Jack retrieved her travel harp from its hook, and Catherine smiled her thanks. She played songs of her childhood, songs of her homeland. Her face became wistful and sad, but she played them so that she would not forget.

* * *

Catherine woke early the next morning, the faint dawn sunlight whispering into her small but comfortable room. She rolled out of bed, threw the thick curtains wide and looked down on the central courtyard. Peter, Jack, and the soldiers of the cathedral were in full motion, working their way through a series of sword routines. The movements reminded her fondly of home, of what she had left behind.

She sat on the low bench by her window, watching the men as she had each morning since her arrival. They were so different, those two. Peter's movements were the crisp, precise actions of a classically trained man. Jack, on the other hand, tended toward more aggressive, full blows, his moves reflecting innovation and fluid response. She wondered what his training had been.

The sun rose higher into the robin-egg-blue sky, and she drew herself away from the window. It was time to get dressed. She first removed her floor length white chemise, examining each part of her body with step by step attention. Her wounds were healing well, the mottled purple fading into gentle pink. Her brow furrowed as she moved her right arm. Her shoulder injury was still the worst of it. She rotated her arm over her head, and her upper arm groaned in resistance. She lowered her arm again and pressed the seam of the scar gently, pursing her lips. She needed to remember to take it easy, to allow the area to heal properly.

Satisfied, she pulled on a fresh white chemise, then a pale yellow dress followed on top. Carefully, reverently, she slipped on the green pendant, running her finger along its spiral design. The sunlight caused the glass to sparkle with an inner glow.

It looked so warm outside, so refreshing. She decided to take a short walk through the crocuses before breakfast and relish the fresh air.

She was delighted to find Michael in the gardens, his thin frame moving steadily on his crutches. He apparently had taken a break from his two constant companions. She spoke up in welcome as she approached. "Are you enjoying the crocuses as well? Are they not gorgeous?"

"Yes, indeed," agreed the young man, his blond hair glowing in the spring sun. "Look at how they occasionally escape their beds, too," he added with mirth, pointing to a lone crocus that had sprouted in the middle of the chive patch.

Catherine lowered her voice conspiratorially. "I have always had this thought that squirrels did that," she admitted with a grin. "Certainly the crocuses are not walking on their own. A squirrel must dig up a bulb, think it is a nut, and bury it elsewhere."

Michael chimed in immediately. "I bet that is exactly it. However, would it really be a squirrel? Maybe it is a mole of some sort, blind as a bat!"

Catherine smiled and hooked her arm into Michael's. "Is not this much better than roaming around the musty cathedral? While I do appreciate the stained glass and carvings, here is a beauty remade fresh each day by nature."

Michael swept his eyes up to the formidable walls of the cathedral looming behind them. "I hear that the vaults below have incredibly intricate wood carvings, gathered from all over England, combining pagan symbols with Christian ones," he replied in consideration. "They were an obsession of the previous Bishop. My parents are historians and spoke of them often. Those works of art might be interesting to see."

Catherine's smile faded. "I have been trying to avoid the vaults," she admitted, her voice haunted. "Lord Epworth is custodian of a great treasure here. From all I hear, those artifacts are indeed worthy of the reputation they have garnered."

Her voice became harsh. "Lord Epworth is about to abandon everything entrusted to his care. The chances of those carvings surviving the month are slim to none. The conservative church members who are moving in will burn those in a heartbeat." She shook her head in anger. "He is abandoning his charge, fleeing without a glance back, solely concerned with his own safety."

Michael gave her a reassuring pat on the hand. "That is a ways off yet," he reminded her gently. "Do not worry about that happening until it becomes set in stone."

Catherine forced herself to smile. "Well, what about you? What are you going to be up to?" she asked with interest.

Michael beamed. "Father Berram is continuing from here down to St. Albans," he told her with enthusiasm. "We will of course be going with him! One of his oldest friends, Father Oswold, is living there. The town is the location of the first martyr in all of England. I have always wanted to go there. The amount of history at St. Albans is just amazing."

Catherine let Michael ramble on about his trip and the research he would do. She was quite happy for him, that he would get to visit locations he had read about for so many years.

As Michael spun his dreams, Catherine looked around and was puzzled to see Jack at the far end of the garden. He did not make an attempt to come over and join the two; indeed, he seemed if anything to be lost in thought. She drew her eyes away from him and struggled to focus on Michael's stories.

After they had walked for a while, the breakfast hour chimed. Michael escorted Catherine in to the dining hall area. They were greeted in the entryway by Lord Epworth and Maya. Maya nodded demurely and left as Lord Epworth smiled down at Catherine. "My child, you look lovely," he complimented, offering her his arm. "You are one of our tiny garden flowers come to life."

Jack came up behind the group and nodded greetings to his father. "She is inordinately fond of crocuses, or so I hear," he commented with a small smile. "I do not believe we have any yellow ones in our gardens, however." He moved past the group to take a seat with Peter, who was already relaxing by the fire.

"Why, then, we will just have to fix that," joked Lord Epworth with a grin.

He led Catherine and Michael up to the main table where they settled in for their morning's offerings. Catherine steeled herself and somehow lasted through the hour of breakfast, followed by another two hours of conversation in Lord Epworth's study. She understood that Lord Epworth was attempting to the best of his ability to be engaging. She simply felt no answering emotion - little interest in his never-ending stories of famous people, and a building irritation at his off-handed dismissal of her views and ideas.

By the time their discussion in the study ended, it was all that she could do to walk at a slow pace when fetching her dagger and cloak to stride out toward the main courtyard.

Catherine was not surprised when Jack fell into step beside her as she crossed beneath the archway of the main gate. The two did not speak as they walked along the cart path, easing from the sunlight clearing of the cathedral's immediate surroundings to the lush, quiet woodland to the south. They strolled along the quiet stream for a while, then ascended the rise up to the overlook. As they walked, Catherine rolled her head along her neck, easing the tensions that had built there.

Jack glanced over with a keen eye. "Are your injuries bothering you?" he asked with concern.

Catherine shook her head no. "It is not my wounds that are giving me trouble," she replied wearily, then bit her tongue and focused on the mossy path ahead. It was not her place to complain about Jack's foster father to him.

Jack did not respond, and Catherine had a sense that he had understood the reference. She knew she should change the topic; move onto less dangerous ground.

Apparently Jack had the same thought. "I have a question for you," he offered, his voice tinged with curiosity. "You indicated when we first met that you had been deliberately misled about me. You had been told that Southerner and Jack were two separate men. Well, then, tell me more about Southerner."

Catherine chuckled, thinking about how to respond. "It is not very flattering," she gently teased. "You are sure you want to know?"

Jack smiled in return. "I am sure I can take the blow to my ego," he responded readily.

Catherine moved across the clearing to the fallen tree, settling herself down onto it with a long, relaxed sigh. It really was quite beautiful in this area. She ran her hands along the trunk's rough bark, enjoying the weathered texture. The sun was warm, in a spring like fashion, and a gentle breeze caused the branches to shimmer all around them. A peace settled over her.

"Come, sit with me then," she offered, smiling up at Jack.

He hesitated for a long moment, scanning the area with a contemplative look, then he nodded, moving to take a seat at her side.

She leant back, soaking in the sunshine. "You want to know about Southerner," she agreed thoughtfully. "Well then, I remind you that you were warned." She looked out over the snowy landscape, thinking back to what she'd been told during the many council sessions. Her voice fell into the measured diction of recital. "Southerner apparently had a tragic family history. His parents were slain in a bandit raid on his village. He was left all alone when only fourteen. This loss affected him immensely. He became a fearsome swordsman, but his mind was unbalanced. He trusted no one. He wished to remain completely alone."

She kept her eyes on the horizon, thinking back. "On our patrols, we were warned to steer a clear circle around him. It was not that we were afraid of him killing us all, necessarily. We had been told that if we enraged Southerner by violating his privacy, he could easily take it out on an innocent villager further along the path. We were informed that this had happened several times in the past. We respected his desire to be alone and had no wish to trigger a murderous rage."

Catherine thought for a moment, adding, "I suppose I thought of Southerner as an injured wolf, lost without his pack. It was not that he was evil ... but his pain made him unpredictable."

She looked over at Jack to see how he had taken this tale. To her surprise, his eyes were shadowed and troubled. He looked up and held her gaze, and she realized he had been wounded by her words.

"Jack...?" she asked with concern, suddenly ashamed of having been so forthright and glib.

Jack gave himself a little shake, and his laugh sounded forced. "It seems they chose to mix in truth with fantasy, as is the case with most rumors," he commented, his voice tight. "It is indeed true that my parents were slain by wolves' heads, and that I was left alone. I have worked hard to gain skill with a sword partially as a result of that attack."

His voice became serious and firm, "However, I swear to you that I have never hurt an innocent person, and certainly would not do so simply because my privacy was violated. You have to believe me."

Catherine put her hand gently over his, softly squeezing his fingers with her own. "Jack, I already know that they lied to me about you being two people, not one. I have no doubt that the deception did not stop there." She gave a small smile. "Besides, I would hope that I am a good enough judge of character to know you are not a man to hurt innocents, based on our conversations over the past week."

Jack put his free hand over hers, holding her gaze. "Thank you," he replied quietly. "That means a lot to me."

He took a long, deep breath, and then let it out again. "Well, go on. What was the tale they spun for Jack, then, if Southerner was a half-crazed hermit?"

Catherine blushed deeply and looked down, drawing her hand away to clasp both together in her lap. "Maybe it is better if I do not tell you this one," she admitted in concern. "I am afraid you will find this story to be even worse."

Jack raised an eyebrow. "Oh, come now," he replied with a wry smile. "They have already made my family tragedy into a twisted story. There can hardly be anything worse than that." He added, half under his breath, "If you do not tell me, my mind will invent a hundred stories far more dastardly than what you were told ..."

Catherine put up her hands in surrender. "Very well, you win," she gave in. She took a deep breath, looked over into Jack's complex, grey eyes, and found that she could not hold his gaze and tell this tale. Again she chose to look out over the rolling hills, with the dark grey of the cathedral resting in the center of the landscape.

She lightened her voice in the sing-song style of a fairy tale told to wide-eyed infants. "Jack is of course the foster son of Lord Epworth, of the Cathedral at Worcester, far, far away." Jack chuckled at the effect and sat back to listen. "Apparently Jack loves to play the soldier. From outward appearances is very much the man of action. He wears high-quality leather armor and carries a finely balanced sword at his side."

Her voice became rich with drama. "However, Jack is a lackluster dreamer. He invents people he has befriended, places he has explored, and battles he has been victorious in. In real life, Jack has abandoned his friends several times when he was needed. He has left his post because he was bored. He prefers elaborate deceptions to actual hard work."

Catherine felt rather than saw Jack's sharp perusal of her, and she took a deep breath to continue. It was best to just get it all out in the open, and then discuss it once it was said. "Apparently this play-actor Jack also built up the image of an ideal woman in his head, which he told to everyone who would listen. She was about five foot seven, to properly align with his height of just over six feet. He was very much about appearances. She was slender yet toned, with long dark hair cascading to her waist. She could speak English, Welsh, and French, useful for travels in all parts of the nearby lands. She needed to be of proper lineage, because station and caste were very important to Jack."

She chuckled wryly and looked down at her hands, blushing. "In short, my council warned me that Jack would become immediately infatuated with *me*, and that he would attach himself to me like a starving leech. They warned me that should I even make the slightest contact - saying hello, allowing our glances to meet - that Jack would insinuate his way into my daily life. He would be impossible to get rid of and I would be miserable for the rest of my life as a result."

Jack stood immediately, his face pale. "My lady, if you think -"

Catherine was on her feet in an instant, turning to face him. "No, no" she insisted gently. "I do not at *all* think you are this man they described. If you have spent time with me, it is because I wished it. I do not feel that you have been untoward in any way."

Jack appeared hesitant, looking into Catherine's eyes while lost in thought. He spoke softly to himself, "Yet once again, it seems that they mixed in ..." He shook himself and asked, "So what do you make of these council statements?"

Catherine ran a hand through her dark hair and slowly shook her head. "Obviously they were taking a great risk in lying to me. They were not making up tales about a dead historical figure. They were building deceptions about an actual, living person who I might run into. In fact, they were building these lies about the relative of the man they expected me to marry. That would be a huge gamble."

She bit her lip, sensing a dangerous territory ahead, but she pressed on. "It means that the danger posed by the truth was worth that risk. They were hoping that I would be wed to Lord Epworth before I discovered the reality."

Jack nodded in agreement, his voice tightening. "It was not just that they wanted you to think ill of me," he added quietly. "They deliberately created stories for each character that would fit perfectly with what you saw at a glance. In both cases, the story painted a situation so dire that you would not even want to initiate contact with me. Even a casual friendship would not happen."

Catherine took a step closer to Jack, looking up into his eyes. The keen look in his made her involuntarily offer a wry smile. It was suddenly crystal clear to her what the council had feared happening.

The fact that her family had gone to such drastic lengths to keep them apart made Catherine's heart beat even more quickly. She had already felt drawn to Jack, with his loyal defense of the acolytes and his wisdom and intelligence here at the cathedral. To know that her council felt he was such a perfect match to her own desires ...

Catherine's voice was hoarse when she spoke. "It is too late to close the box," she admitted, marshaling her emotions. "I cannot erase you from my mind. Still, I will go forward with my appointed task. I must reconcile myself with my directed fate. I must try ..."

Her throat closed up. She wanted to turn her head away, but could not bring herself to do so.

She saw the pain in Jack's eyes, but he nodded slowly. "Yes, of course," he agreed, his voice husky. "It is ... your duty." He cleared his throat and looked out over the glistening landscape.

Catherine's heart ached; his nearness was a physical sensation drawing her in. She could not bring herself to move or to speak further. What was there to say?

It was Jack who finally broke the silence. "We should head in," he suggested quietly, his voice remote.

Catherine nodded, and the pair walked slowly back down to the cathedral.

Catherine focused her efforts on spending time either with Lord Epworth or in solitary pursuits for the rest of the day. Jack did not meet her eyes at dinner, and it was easy enough to allow Lord Epworth to control the conversation. Maya delighted the room with her romantic ballads for several hours, and Catherine let herself get lost in the music.

When Maya had finished, the listeners dispersed. Lord Epworth stood at her side, and she obediently rose, putting her hand on his proffered arm. He escorted her quietly to her room, nodding in farewell as she pushed open the door and walked inside.

Catherine was not sleepy. She sat on the bench by the window, staring out at the night sky. She wanted desperately to know how the debate had gone today; she missed the quiet hours she usually spent talking with Jack and Peter. She knew she had no choice. She needed to cut back on time spent with Jack. It was all too clear to her that she was falling for Jack, and that was a relationship she did not have the luxury of encouraging.

Her mind whirled for hours; it was late before she was able to climb into bed and fall into a troubled sleep.

Chapter 9

When Catherine awoke the following morning she was surprised to see the sun high in the sky, the courtyard beyond her window quiet and empty.

She scolded herself wearily as she climbed out of bed. There were few enough days of admiring the crocus blooms as it was, without missing a morning of them! She went through her injury check, pleased that the cuts and bruises were mending well with the help of Peter's salves. She pulled on a fresh white chemise, then slipped the moss-green dress on top of it. She put her head through the chain of her pendant, then took a few moments to quickly braid back her hair before descending the stairs to the main dining hall.

Lord Epworth and Jack were already at the head table when she entered the room. She walked over to join them, nodding with a smile for her host. Lord Epworth beamed at her, but Jack's gaze was troubled. A wave of guilt washed over her. It was her duty to ease gently into this family, not to rip it apart.

The breakfast was delicious as usual, with buns and raspberry jam being a highlight of the meal. Catherine found herself eating three of them, much to Lord Epworth's vocal amusement.

When the meal was over, Lord Epworth stood, and Catherine and Jack moved to their feet along with him. Lord Epworth spoke fondly to Catherine. "I have some legal situations to work out regarding my pending relocation," he apologized with a smile. "It is boring tedium that I will not subject you to. As an apology, however, I have brought a present for you."

Catherine demurred. “You really do not need to do that, my lord. I have no need of presents ...”

She caught out of the corner of her eye the two large baskets that a young page was bringing over to the table. In them were heaped piles of crocuses, the blue and purple petals already fading and browning.

Catherine’s face froze in shock. A quick calculation told her that they must have cut down every crocus in the garden to fill the baskets. They had killed every bloom, every flower, every last harbinger of spring.

Lord Epworth was still talking. “I thought you could sprinkle them in a bath or decorate your room with them,” he went on magnanimously. “I will have George here bring them up to your room for you to decide.”

He put a hand under her chin. “Oh look, your eyes are welling,” he cooed tenderly. “I knew you would love my present. Have a wonderful day, my dearest little one.”

Before Catherine could think to speak or protest, he wrapped her in a tight bear hug, squeezing her until her right arm nearly exploded with the pain. Finally he released her, gave her a gentle pat on the cheek, and strolled haughtily toward his study.

Catherine was surrounded by a thick curtain of throbbing fire. She turned and strode out of the room, across the cobblestone courtyard, and beneath the shadows of the front gates. Her shoulder was a blaze of red hot agony, and her vision was blurred by tears.

She made it to the small stream in the woods that the cart path paralleled before she dropped to one knee, sobbing silently. The searing pain of her shoulder, mingled with the complete lack of understanding in her future husband, spiraled her down into a whirlpool of despair.

A number of minutes passed before she regained control of herself, slowing her breathing back to normal. She made a cup with her hands and splashed the stream’s water on her face, washing away the tears.

* * *

Jack drew to a stop as he came into the clearing, taking in her shaking shoulders, the weary way in which she brought the water up to her face. A knife twisted in his heart at what she was going through, and in a moment he was moving to her side, dropping to one knee.

There was so much he wanted to say, but he knew that he could not. At last he rasped, "I am so sorry," the words woefully inadequate for the emotion which thundered in his chest. He put down the bundle of cloaks and weapons that he carried in his arms. "It was too late by the time I found out what he had done."

He started to ask how she was, but one glance at her eyes caught the words in his throat. "No, obviously you are not fine," he added quietly. "Is it the overall situation, or did he inflame one of your wounds?"

Catherine gave her face another splash of water and slowly brushed back her hair with her wet hands. She sat back on her heels, not looking up at him. "My shoulder is giving me trouble," she admitted with a grimace. "I think it needs to be looked at."

Jack looked at each of her shoulders, then focused more closely on the right one. "This one, here?" he asked with concern. "I see a growing red stain; the blood is coming through. We need to get this cleaned up before you go back in if you are going to keep your injuries secret."

Catherine paused, indecision clear on her face. Jack met her gaze. "I already know that you were seriously injured. Peter made that plain. Either you let me help you here, or you somehow try to get to Peter to work on it without anybody else noticing your state."

Catherine was silent for a long minute but at last she nodded. "All right," she agreed slowly. "However, remember your promise. Not a word to anyone of what you see."

"I swear it," vowed Jack with serious resolve. He wondered again why she was so insistent on secrecy. He wished she would trust him, would share her sorrows with him to shoulder.

He nodded his head toward a flat, grey stone. "Please sit on this rock by the stream. That way I will be able to clean the wound if it needs it."

Catherine draped the skirt of her dress around her and sat on the long, smooth slab of stone. She pulled all of her hair over her left shoulder so that it would be out of the way. Jack sat immediately behind her and first unlaced the back of the green overdress. He undid enough of the laces so that both shoulders fell down to her elbows, revealing the full white chemise beneath. Catherine let her right hand hang loose so that he could work on that shoulder, pressing her left hand to her chest, holding the fabric of both dress layers there.

"Go ahead," she stated quietly.

Jack hesitated a moment, then carefully unlaced the more slender ties of the delicate white chemise. His face paled when he saw what was beneath the lacing. Peter had not been exaggerating when he described Catherine's injuries. Her back was a mass of welts, cuts, and bruises - the purple and blue colors fading, but giving clear indication of what she had gone through.

He slid the sleeve down her arm and found a white cloth bandage wrapped around her upper arm that had slid loose. A long gash sidled down her bicep - the sides of the wound neat and clean. Blood was oozing from where the gash had been pulled apart by Lord Epworth's strong hug.

Jack looked at the wound for a moment, then moved to Catherine's right where he could work on the arm and talk with her.

"Catherine, this is a sword wound," he commented simply.

Catherine chuckled wryly, meeting his gaze steadily. "Yes, Jack," she replied evenly. "I was in fact there when the wound was made."

"How -"

Catherine made to hold up her left hand, then realized she was holding her dress closed with it. "No questions, remember?" she reminded Jack. "What I need for you to do is to mend the wound, not to discuss its origins."

Jack hesitated a moment, then gently untied the white bandage cloth. It had matted blood on it as well as traces of the salve Peter had used. He rinsed it out thoroughly in the stream, then used it to attend to the wound area. When the injury was clean and dry, he wrapped the cloth back around Catherine's arm, his movements as gentle as possible.

"How about your left shoulder," he asked, finishing up the right arm's bandaging. "Should I look at that as well?"

Catherine's response was quick and short. "*No!*"

She blushed and looked down, taking in a deep breath. "I think you have done enough for one day," she added in a more gentle tone. "My left shoulder is fine."

Jack tucked in the bandage's free end and examined the results. "It is still going to slide if it is touched," he mused, half to himself.

He reached down to his brown cloak and with a quick movement tore off a thin strip from the bottom. He looped that through the white bandage, then looped it over and under her shoulder. "There, that should give you a little more support," he offered, giving a test tug on the bandage. "How does that feel?"

"Ouch!" cried out Catherine suddenly, then she burst out laughing, the peals ringing out down the valley. Jack stared at her, his brow creased in confusion.

"What is it," he asked, looking at the bandage in concern. "I did not touch you after that tug ...?"

Catherine's eyes were glowing with mirth as she turned to him. She held out her right hand, which had a spot of blood forming on the index finger's base. "I was playing with this vine and I have poked myself," she chuckled. "I think I need a doctor."

Jack looked at the tiny spot of blood, back at the sword wound he had just bandaged up, and a smile eased on his face.

"Here, I have plenty of bandages for all of your ills," he offered with a sweeping bow. He ripped a short, small strip of brown cloth and fashioned a mini-bandage for her finger. "For you, my lady."

Catherine's laughter settled down, and she presented her hand to Jack. He held her hand with his left, then slid the brown ring onto her finger with his right. Suddenly tenderness swept over him, and he involuntarily glanced up at her. Her eyes were shining, and she held very still in his grasp. He finished settling the ring onto her finger, and then lowered his lips to her hand, brushing her skin with a gentle kiss.

Catherine was trembling in his grasp, and when he looked up at her, her eyes were shining. Then she let out a long, shaky breath and looked away, flustered.

"Thank you," she murmured softly. "I feel much better now."

After a moment Jack found his voice. "I had better get your dress laced back up," he commented hoarsely. He sat behind her and slowly, tenderly, laced up the white chemise, laying it gently against her damaged skin. Next he re-laced the green dress. He left his hands against her neck for a moment when he was done, closing his eyes as he did so. He could smell her scent, a mix of her natural sweat and rose coming from her body and hair. It was almost intoxicating. He leant away from her slightly and gently swept her hair into place, laying it down along her back.

"They should not notice the spot on your shoulder if you have your hair over that area," he suggested, his voice low. "You should be fine now."

Catherine clasped her hands on her lap and began unconsciously to play with the brown ring. "Yes," she echoed quietly, hesitantly. "I am sure things will be fine now."

She stood and brushed the dirt off of her dress. "I suppose I should go back and ..." She sighed, looking in the direction of the cathedral. "I need to do something with those crocuses," she added in resignation.

Jack picked up the cloaks and weapons and walked alongside her as the two returned to the cathedral. When they reached the main stairs, he handed her the black cloak and dagger. His hands met hers beneath the bundle, and he held them for a moment, feeling their warmth and strength, before she slid free of his grasp.

Her eyes lowered, she turned quickly with her items and headed up to her room, leaving him to stare up after her.

* * *

Jack found himself daydreaming during the debates, and strove to focus on what they were saying so that he could relay the information to Catherine later on. He found his step quickening as he headed toward the dining hall. Lord Epworth was already there, with Maya on one side of him. Jack pressed his lips together, nodding to her in quiet greeting as he took his customary seat on Lord Epworth's other side.

"Is Catherine eating elsewhere tonight?" he asked in a low voice, striving to keep his tone neutral.

Lord Epworth gave a sigh. "I am afraid the poor girl was feeling worn out, and only wanted a small snack in her room before turning in."

Disappointment filled Jack's soul, but he instantly steeled his emotions and nodded noncommittally at the news.

Lord Epworth's eyes sharpened, his look full on his foster son. "You would not know at all why she would be that tired, would you?" he asked pointedly.

Jack held himself steady; he could not betray the trust Catherine had placed in him. "Not at all, sir," he responded with a casualness he did not feel. "I am sure she is simply enjoying your present."

That thought seemed to brighten Lord Epworth's mood, and he nodded, turning to talk with Maya. When the meal was over, the group of musicians played a series of lively songs. Halfway through the first one, Lord Epworth whispered something into

Maya's ear. The two rose to their feet, then walked out toward his study arm in arm. Jack watched them go, his gaze following them in quiet speculation. He stayed in his chair long after the musicians had finished, as the room cleared out and drifted into silence.

The fire mellowed down into glowing embers and the room immersed in shadows. Jack shook himself, picked up his tankard and walked over to the fire to sit on the nearby bench. As he approached he was surprised to find Michael curled up in the corner chair, furtively reading a codex with a finely tooled cover. Michael looked up guiltily as Jack came nearer.

Jack gave the lad a gentle smile. "Is not that one of Lord Epworth's personal tomes?" he chided.

Michael flushed and nodded, hiding the codex beneath a fold in his tunic. "Do not tell him, please? I promise to return it as soon as I am done. I cannot help myself; I love to read. I will devour anything I can get my hands on. My parents were scholars and I am afraid it rubbed off on me."

Jack waved away his concerns. "I am not sure why Lord Epworth is so stingy with his library," he conceded. "It would be better if the stories were enjoyed by many, rather than collecting dust as wall ornaments." His eyes brightened. "Just make sure he does not spot you when you return it, or you will learn what a Worcester Whipping is all about."

Michael nodded nervously and scurried out of the room. Jack sighed and leaned back, taking a long pull on his ale. He sat by the fire alone, staring into the dying embers.

Chapter 10

Catherine woke early the following morning, took her seat by the window, and stretched wearily in the soft dawn haze. She watched with quiet attention as the men parried and thrust in the courtyard below. The sun rose slowly behind them, sending light and shadow in dappled patterns across the stonework.

Peter was sure, steady, classical in his motions, but she found her eyes drawn as if by a powerful magnet to follow Jack's movements. She remembered how he had been willing to fight off Conrad's entire team to keep the lads safe. She could see that same passion in his movements below, the same directed focus. He was a man she would be proud to have by her side …

There was a movement to the right, and John walked along the edge of the sparring area, his eyes watching the men with interest. The lad was well built, and Catherine was surprised he did not join in the activities. Out of the three acolytes, he seemed the one most suited to learn sword work, if only for self-defense. However, for whatever reason, he merely watched for a while, then faded back into the main hall.

She felt that way herself, trapped on the sidelines. She was an observer only, a gulf forming between what she had wanted out of life and what was now an option.

She sat still, even after the men had finished and headed inside, staring at the mosaic of stones. She could not bring herself to take her habitual pre-breakfast walk through the gardens, to look at the many headless stalks that now would fill her favorite pathway. It would only emphasize her growing feeling of despair.

She pressed her lips together, turning away from the window. A part of her scolded: she was an adult; she should not be reacting so harshly to such a minor incident. After all, they were only flowers. Lord Epworth had meant well.

She took in a deep breath, then sighed deeply, looking down. She knew the truth deep in her heart. It was not just the flowers, It was the lack of understanding behind the action. It was the fact that Lord Epworth had no idea that cutting down the entire garden of flowers would bother her in the least.

She pursed her lips, standing. What was done was done. She had already sent the wilted flowers down to the compost bin. She could only try to communicate with him more clearly going forward, to help him understand her more fully.

Catherine decided to find a quiet look for today's outfit. She put on a soft tan dress over her chemise, and braided her hair back with brown ribbons. She suddenly glanced at the brown ring she still wore, realizing that her color choices were perhaps not as arbitrary as she had thought.

She considered leaving the token behind, but could not bring herself to remove it. It made her feel better, somehow, to have Jack's ring on her finger. It made her feel as if she had some small say in her life's path. She had avoided dinner last night, but she could not hide out in her room forever. It was time to go down and face another day.

She was the first of her party to the dining room, and she watched attentively as Lord Epworth and Jack entered together. Jack seemed attentive to his foster father, and Lord Epworth for his part was respectful to Jack. Still, she noticed that Lord Epworth took cares to keep himself between her and Jack, even when the two men walked around the table to join her. Jack gave her a nod in greeting, but was shut out from any attempt of eye contact after that.

Catherine nodded at appropriate intervals during Lord Epworth's small talk as they ate breakfast, but her mind was on the coming hours, wondering what the day had in store for her.

Lord Epworth turned to Catherine as the meal was cleared from the table, sitting back with a smile. "I do not have any duties this morning," he explained with a warm grin, "so I thought I would offer you a special treat. How would you like to come down and see the vaults? There are a few quirky carvings down there that might amuse you."

Catherine could sense Jack's sharp eyes on her, and she remembered that he had been in the garden when she had the conversation with Michael about the pagan artworks. She forced herself to smile brightly.

"Of course, I would love to spend time with you," she replied, holding the smile in place. She stood and put her hand on Lord Epworth's arm, forestalling any attempt at a hug. She willed herself not to look back at Jack.

"We will see you later, Jack," commented Lord Epworth smoothly, dismissing his foster son. He immediately guided Catherine toward the door that led into the depths of the building.

* * *

Catherine strode up the long, dark stairs, pushing the heavy wooden door wide, willing herself to hold in her strong emotions until she was clear of all watchers. The hall was deep in gloom, and a heavy rumble of thunder shook the walls, but she did not slow one step as she marched toward the hooks. She yanked her dagger off of one, grabbed her cloak from the other, and in a moment she was through the main doors and crossing the cobblestone courtyard. She flung the hood over her head as she strode beneath the arched entry gates and out toward the woods.

She was just within the first layer of trees when the sound of racing feet came from behind her, and the skies opened up with pelting torrents of rain. A lightning flash sizzled overhead, immediately followed by a ground-shaking clap.

Jack's voice was sharp with frustration. "God's teeth, Catherine, you could have waited ..."

Catherine continued her stride without a hitch in her step. Jack moved alongside her, pulling his own cloak closed. He glanced over at her for a moment, studied her face, and let his comments fade into silence.

They moved side by side through the thick woods. The trees provided shelter from the storm which raged overhead. There was the steady patter of falling rain landing high above; occasionally she felt the thud of a drop or two that worked their way through the thick canopy.

Eventually Catherine slowed, her inner steam easing slightly, but she could still feel the tenseness in her shoulders, feel the sharpness in her angular stride.

When they reached the top of the hill, she sat on the far end of the log where it nestled up against an elderly oak tree. Jack slowly lowered himself to sit at her side. The thick branches of the oak offered good protection against the rain which fell heavily across the landscape. The rain washed away the remaining snows, leaving the forest glistening and fresh.

Catherine could not draw rein on the racing thoughts which pounded and stampeded within her head. The carvings had been beyond beautiful. The thought of them being destroyed mingled with her fears for the villagers she was leaving behind, with the crash of another clap seemingly inches away, and finally the words burst from her in an explosion she was helpless to stop.

"Those carvings are priceless," she cried in half agony. "They are intricate, they are full of meaning, they are true treasures that should be protected and cared for. He is just going to abandon them! He knows well the dangers that await those things left behind. They will be burned, smashed, and destroyed. He is just going to leave them!"

Another flash of lightning, and her breath caught at the hopelessness of it all. "How can he just abandon all of this?" she railed, her voice shaking with angst. "How can he leave, when he knows so much depends on him ..."

She felt wetness on her cheeks, and she no longer knew if it was from the heavy rain around them or from tears streaming down.

Jack took in a long breath, and she could feel the tightness in his arm where it lay beside hers, the tension in his face. She wished with all her heart that he were free, that she were free, that life's path had not led to this web of agony.

He moved toward her slightly, then stopped, looking down. He paused for a long moment, then murmured to her in a hoarse voice.

"There is always hope, Catherine," he half whispered. "Look what I have found. It is the first snowdrop of the year, right here where we have had our talks. It is our sign of spring ..."

Catherine felt as if a lightning bolt had seared through her heart; her defenses were completely overrun. The torrents of pain and hurt within her exploded into geysers, and she burst into uncontrollable, heart-wrenching sobs.

Jack reached out his arms and pulled her tenderly to him. She collapsed against his broad chest, unable to think or move, only to cry. He held her gently, pressing his lips softly against her forehead.

Many long minutes passed, and Catherine felt as if time suspended. There was only her pain, his sheltering arms, and the curtains of pelting water which shut out the rest of the world.

Catherine slowly became aware of the dripping of the rain from the leaves, the rustle as the branches moved in the light breeze. She felt the warmth radiating from Jack's chest, and it took every ounce of strength for her to draw up, to move slightly away from that protective embrace.

She took a long look at the small snowdrop at their feet, then she moved her hands up to her neck and carefully removed a leather loop that was hidden beneath the white chemise. She took it off over her head and handed it to Jack. Jack examined the carved pendant which hung at the end of the twined strand. It was a white granite snowdrop blossom, a fine work created by a skilled craftsman. She knew the stone flower was still warm from her body heat, and she blushed as he cradled it in his palm.

"That was given to me by Susan and Marcie," explained Catherine quietly, her voice hoarse from the crying. "It has been our tradition, from when we could barely walk. We always tried to find the first snowdrop. It began in January of each year, and we scoured the forests, the roads, anywhere we could, to see who would track down the very first one. You could not cut it, of course. You had to locate it and then bring the other two to proclaim your victory. They would then grant you your prize."

Catherine's eyes welled with fresh tears, and she absently brushed them away. "When I left, there were not any snowdrops yet. I do not even know if snowdrops exist in Ireland. Susan and Marcie gave me this pendant to remember them by." Her voice dropped down to a soft whisper. "As if I could forget ..."

Jack took her hand tenderly in his own. "I am so sorry; I had no idea."

Catherine took a deep breath and looked up into his eyes. "Of course you did not, and I am being silly about it. It is just a flower. It is a silly childhood tradition. I am letting myself get worked up over nothing at all. Nothing that matters." She looked down at the small flower and willed herself to accept her path in life.

Jack's voice came to her as if from a great distance. "What was the prize that was won?"

Catherine smiled fondly at the memory. "It is your heart's desire," she responded simply.

She sat for a long moment, staring at the flower, then gave herself a shake.

"It could be anything," she elaborated, her tone calming. "One year when Marcie found the snowdrop, she insisted she wanted to win that fall's pastry bake-off. We helped her test recipes all summer long, and when fall came, she got her wish. When Susan was the winner once, she decided she wanted a new bow of yew wood. It took us months, but we found her the perfect branch to make it from."

Her mouth quirked into a sad smile. "Our rule was that no wish was impossible or silly. We trusted each other. Whatever it was that the winner decided on, it was the duty of the others to help make that dream into a reality."

Jack's voice was hoarse. "What of my dream?"

Catherine looked up at him, and the world dissolved around them into a misty fog. Nothing else existed in the rain except her and him. His hair was now glistening from the rain; his eyes were tenderly focused on hers. She was lost in his gaze. He moved down toward her, and suddenly they were kissing, their arms wrapped around each other in a gentle embrace.

She closed her eyes and lost herself to the kiss, to the moment. His embrace was an encompassing cocoon of safety and tenderness. His lips were firm, tender, and filled her with a longing she had never known. The kiss seemed to go on forever ...

She pulled back, breaking apart from him with an effort, drawing in shuddering breaths. She longed to lean in again, to lose herself to him, but she could not. It was unfair to lead him on when she knew her course in life.

Catherine's eyes teared again at the warring emotions in her breast. Her voice ached with pain and regret. "Jack, I am so sorry ..."

Jack took a deep breath, sitting back slightly with rigid effort. He looked down to his hand, and with a long exhale he lifted the pendant, offering it back to Catherine wordlessly.

She folded his fingers over the stone carving, and pressed it gently to his chest.

"Please keep it. It is yours now."

Jack shook his head. He reached forward with his other hand and gently stroked the side of her face; she closed her eyes and leant against his hand, sighing.

"The pendant is not what I desire, Catherine," he murmured, his voice ragged.

Catherine opened her eyes and gazed into his. She could see clearly the agony he was going through. She finally looked away with an effort and stood up.

"It ... it is all I can give you," she responded at last, her voice low. She pulled the hood of her cloak up around her face and headed back down the hill.

Jack stood quickly and strode down after her, coming around in front of her when they reached the stream. His eyes caught hers.

"Catherine, I must know the answer to a question," he insisted, his eyes dark with turmoil.

Catherine hesitated, then responded cautiously, "What question would you ask?"

Jack's eyes held hers with serious intent. "If you were to choose not to marry Lord Epworth, to take another path … would there be an obstacle to my courting you? Would you fear Lord Epworth's wrath? Your council's disapproval? Would my birth be an issue?" His voice caught, then grew firm as he forced himself to continue. "Would Shadow -"

Catherine could take no more. She turned her face sharply away, the torment slicing through her. She had abandoned so much which was necessary to her very existence ... and now the most ideal man she could dream of was pleading for her hand.

There was a loud shout. Looking down the path, her heart raced. Three men were approaching quickly, their black cloaks swirling behind them. Her mind snapped instantly back to the here and now, and she cursed that she only had the small dagger at her hip. She quickly stepped apart from Jack, giving them both room to act in case the men were hostile.

Jack reacted instantly to her movement, putting his hand to his sword, his eyes alertly turning to gaze in the direction she faced.

Catherine sighed with relief as the newcomers closed. It was only Lord Epworth with two of his guards. Their cloaks were wet with rain. Her shoulders stiffened suddenly - Lord Epworth's face burned scarlet with anger, and his eyes looked between the two with quick agitation.

Lord Epworth went directly to stand before Jack. "What in the world are you thinking, having Catherine walking on a day like today?" he shouted in fury. "You should have more sense than that!"

He turned to Catherine and his voice softened. "I am so sorry, little one," he apologized. "Your delicate ears should not have to hear this. The soldiers will escort you safely back to the cathedral at once. I will see you later, at dinner."

Catherine found herself being bundled off by the soldiers before she could respond.

* * *

Jack watched the trio move from the clearing, every instinct urging him to remain by her side. It was only firm force of will which kept him in place, had him remain as she faded into the murky woods. Soon even her footsteps could no longer be heard.

There was a clearing of a throat, and Jack was brought back sharply to the present. Lord Epworth was staring at him, his gaze less than friendly.

"Catherine is at my home for a single, express purpose," the man reminded him with a firm voice that was laced with icy coldness. "As my foster son, I expect you to fully support me in my wishes here. I have raised and sheltered you these past twenty years. I have never asked for anything in return."

Lord Epworth paused a moment, then continued with a harsh edge creeping in to his words. "As both your foster father - and as a man about to marry – I insist you tell me the truth. Have you compromised her?"

Jack's face flashed with steel, and he threw his head high, looking steadily at his foster father. "No, sir." he replied tersely.

Lord Epworth eyed Jack for a long moment, then nodded in grim acceptance. "That woman should be grateful I am even considering her," he bit out. "Twenty-six years old? I doubt she is pure at that age, especially given the lifestyle she has maintained over the years." He fingered his broach absently. "Her mother swore to me Catherine has been quarantined these past five months. Any child she bears will be my rightful heir."

Jack stiffened at the word 'quarantined'. Was Catherine some sort of a prize cow to be thus discussed and treated? She was a woman, a woman of intelligence, of wisdom, of strength …

Lord Epworth stared at Jack with a frown. "You are interfering with my progress," he stated coldly. "Whatever immature resistance she is mounting, she will give up soon enough. She needs to accept her life as a docile female of hearth and home. Her main duty will be that of bearing children. These outings are not a habit I will permit when she is my wife. From this point forward, Catherine is not to leave the cathedral."

He stared at Jack for a long moment, his eyes considering. "Also, Jack," he added, his voice now crisp, "you are not to talk with her at all. For any reason. Do you understand?"

Jack nodded shortly. He did not trust himself to speak. Lord Epworth held the gaze for several seconds, then turned on his heel, striding with resolution back toward the cathedral.

Jack stood without moving, the stream tumbling by his feet, the torrents pouring down from the heavens, the waters and spray washing over him in a never-ending deluge.

Chapter 11

Catherine sat by the window, watching as the torrential rain hammered down on the courtyard, the men below working through their sword practice as if it was any other day. Her mouth quirked into a smile. She remembered well the many days on patrol in the mud and grime, the nights when she huddled by a campfire, soaked through to the bone. At least here the men could come inside when they were done, put on dry clothes, and get warm food into them.

She put on her tan tunic again, pressing her hand absently against her chest, to the spot where until recently a small granite pendant had hung. She was oddly content. She did care for Jack. He now carried a token of her affection, and she wore his on her finger. When she married Lord Epworth, Jack would remain a constant presence in her life. She would care for him, would love him from a distance. It would be enough.

She smiled, making her way down to the main dining hall. Lord Epworth was sitting at the head of the table, and she took her place beside him, allowing him to bend his head to kiss her hand in greeting. The servants moved around them, bringing in eggs and sausage.

Jack's seat at Lord Epworth's other side remained empty, and Catherine's heart quickened. It was one thing to be held apart from him – but could she not even see him, to know he was nearby?

Lord Epworth talked in a constant patter, discussing one of his trips to the countryside, naming the people he had met along the way. She nodded, encouraging him, her mind in a whirl.

When Lord Epworth finally stood and headed in to the conclave, she barely saw him go. She scanned the room for Peter, but did not see him either. The rain pounded down outside the windows, sending a constant patter of sound into her thoughts.

She moved absently toward the main door. Jack had always appeared when she went out on her walks, and there was so much they had left unsaid. It would be good to clear the air with him, to explain why her life had to take the path it was set on. She gathered up her cloak and dagger from the hooks, pushing open the heavy door, looking out into the sheets of grey.

A guard on the steps turned to gaze at her with dour calm. "I am sorry, M'Lady," he offered in a low voice. "You are to stay inside the cathedral walls from now on."

Catherine stiffened in unbelieving fury, her eyes swiveling to the main gates in the wall, to the stretch of meadow and forest beyond. She was a prisoner? She was being held captive within this stone structure? The walls closed in, the press of people around her stifled her, and fought to remain calm.

"Of course," she agreed to the guard, turning and resetting her items on their hooks. She made her way to the main hall again, settling herself into the leather chair in the corner, curling herself up in it, staring out as the sheets of rain which blocked out all view of the gardens beyond. She was trapped. In a short while they would relocate to Ireland, and maybe the building there would be even smaller, the breadth of her domain closing in on her. She could not take it. It would overwhelm her spirit …

She closed her eyes, resteeling her focus. She could do it, and she would. It was being required of her, and she had been trained for this type of task. She would find a way to survive, to last in this deprivation. She had thrived on long assignments in pouring rain and deep snow. Surely she could handle this task, held 'hostage' by a roaring fire with delicious food and flowing drink?

Footsteps sounded near her and she looked up with bright attention. Her heart fell slightly; it was Michael who walked over to her, book in hand. She smiled fondly at the lad, motioning to the bench next to her.

"How are you doing?" she asked, turning to look him over. "Your ankle seems well mended."

He nodded, sitting and leaning back. "Yes, thanks to Peter's fine care I am as good as new." He held up the scroll in his hand. "Look what I have found – it is a copy of The Iliad, by Homer."

Catherine's eyes lit up with delight. "How perfect for a rainy day," she mused, tucking her feet beneath her. "Would you read it aloud?"

"I would be delighted," agreed Michael, settling in. He waved a hand at a passing servant, and in a moment they had a pair of tankards of mead. Michael propped open the curled parchment on his lap. The words rolled out in Michael's quiet voice, and Catherine allowed herself to get lost in the story. Time unfurled as a never-ending stream, moving, unwinding …

She glanced up in surprise as the room filled with people. The grey clouds outside had darkened, and she realized that it was already dinnertime. She smiled fondly to Michael, truly grateful for his time and distraction for the long afternoon. She made her way over to the head table, taking her seat, her eyes scanning the room with hopeful attention.

Lord Epworth walked in with Maya on his arm. The two came over to the table, Lord Epworth sitting down between the two women. Catherine found her gaze sharpening slightly. That was Jack's seat the woman was taking.

Lord Epworth noticed the direction of her gaze and chuckled, patting her hand. "Do not worry about Jack," he commented quietly, his eyes distant. "He, Peter, and some of the men are out on a training exercise. They should not be back for several days."

"Out in this rain?" asked Catherine in surprise, looking past Lord Epworth to the heavy sheets of water which still pounded down from the sky.

Lord Epworth pursed his lips. “Yes, well, the men will not melt. Maybe it will do some good,” he commented roughly. He waved for mead, and in a moment food and drink was being distributed to the table.

Catherine descended into a grey melancholy. She had only spent time with Jack for a week, and already he seemed so much a part of her, a constant presence at her side. She focused on eating her food, on drinking her mead. Lord Epworth spent half of his time talking with Maya on his other side, and Catherine relished the quiet periods, her time to reflect.

The musicians came on, the flutist with his shock of red hair showing off his talents with a series of solo pieces. Maya clapped with delight, and even moved down to accompany him on two occasions. By the time the evening had ended, and Lord Epworth moved to escort her to her room, Catherine had lost the will to resist. She closed the door behind her, pulling off her dress, climbing straight into bed.

Chapter 12

Sunday morning dawned as dismally as the previous, with rolling grey clouds and a deluge of steady rain. Catherine sat for a long time by the window, looking down at the empty courtyard, wondering how Jack, Peter, and the other men were faring. Were they under shelter, or trekking through the mud and gloom? She knew the feeling well, the heavy clamminess of leather armor dense with water, the eye strain of trying to make out shapes in the grey mist. She sent her thoughts out to the men before turning to dress.

She put on her purple outfit, the best she had brought, and brushed her hair out well before moving to go downstairs. Lord Epworth was waiting for her with the others, and together they moved into the main cathedral. Catherine found herself smiling as they took their seats. It was a magnificent building, the flickering candles and stained glass windows adding an ethereal beauty to the scene. The Latin mass boomed out in echoes around the room. It was calming, soothing. She reminded herself what she was here for, what her purpose was. She could help maintain the tradition, help bond these ancient families together, help to preserve some part of the past.

When the mass was over, she moved with docility at Lord Epworth's side as he talked with various delegates, greeted newcomers, and caught up with old friends. Soon they were at lunch, then sitting on a velvet couch in Lord Epworth's study, talking with a pair of men from London. At each stage Catherine remained quiet, patient, letting the men talk, letting the words roll over her.

By the time dinner rolled along, Catherine had become transfixed in a dream-like state. She realized Lord Epworth was smiling down at her, and she automatically returned his smile. He picked up his glass of mead, leaning over to clink it against hers.

"Today was wonderful, simply wonderful," he extolled, his eyes shining. "I could not have asked for a more perfect partner. You were beautiful, demure, and completely appropriate. I think this shall work out very nicely." He took a long sip, then carved in to his roast pork.

Catherine nodded at the compliment, but the words rolled around within her like a rock underfoot during a long walk. They itched at her, prodding her. Was this to be her life? Long days of saying nothing, of smiling and nodding at her husband's side while living in some sort of a haze? Is this what she had trained and studied for?

The tall, thin harpist set up his travel instrument, and within moments Maya had come down to join him, setting up her own harp at his side. The two played duets for several hours, delighting the room with their talents. Lord Epworth put his hand on top of Catherine's, and she let it sit there, trying out feelings for this man at her side. He would not beat her, he would not misuse her. Surely that would be enough? Could she grow to love him, to respect him?

He gave her hand a gentle squeeze, and Catherine felt no frisson of pleasure, no response at all. She thought back to her times with Jack. The slightest touch from him, the briefest look would send her heart fluttering, would send waves of joy throughout her body. With Lord Epworth it was as if a cold clamminess settled over her, dampening her emotions, shutting her down.

The musicians ended their set, and Lord Epworth stood at her side, drawing her up. He escorted her to her room, standing patiently as she pushed open her door. She nodded her farewell, closing the door behind her, moving to lay face down on the bed, utterly lost.

* * *

Catherine's life settled into a dull routine. Mornings were spent listening to Lord Epworth discuss one of his trips in exquisite detail. Afternoons would pass reading with Michael, or perhaps playing cards with Walter and John. An evening meal, and then time listening to the musicians for an hour or two. Each night Lord Epworth escorted her to her door, ensuring she was safely within before going about his business.

Catherine could easily see this cycle perpetuating for the rest of her life. There would be no escape, no change, no rescue. She found her will fading, found herself submerging in the pattern.

Finally, Friday dawned with shafts of sunlight streaming through gaps in the grey clouds. Catherine sat at the window for a long while, staring at the empty courtyard, energy rekindling as the sun moved across the stones. Some fresh air would do her good. She would venture on the back garden path to see what remained of the flowers.

She dressed in her tan outfit, smoothing it down over her chemise. She idly spun the brown ring which she had not yet removed from her finger. She glanced out the window again, her mood lightening. Surely Lord Epworth could not intend to keep her locked inside forever. Once spring came in earnest, he would undoubtedly let her go for her walks in the forest, if even with a guard escort.

She moved quickly down the stairs and out into the back garden. The world was misty and wet, a breeze dancing across her face with a gentle touch. The herbs smelled fresh and rich after the long rain they'd gotten. She breathed in deeply, filling herself with their fragrance. To her relief the crocus stems looked simply like thick grasses along the path. Daffodils were coming up alongside to give trumpet shows of yellow and white.

Catherine smiled in earnest, looking around her with pleasure. Nature had renewed itself. She needed to learn to trust in that.

Her heart lightened as she walked slowly down the path, drinking in the beauty of the gardens. Her feet took her around the pond to the bridge behind it. Even the water sparkled with fresh life, and the sun became more effective in melting away the fogs and mists. She looked out across the scene with pleasure.

Her heart caught suddenly in her throat. A man was striding toward her down the long path, his rangy build and dark hair immediately recognizable to her. It was Jack. His movement was quick, sharp, and his face as he approached was darkly serious.

Catherine gripped the bridge's railing with both hands, steadying herself. She had hoped that the week without him would have cured her of her affections, but her reaction told her that if anything the absence had made her miss him even more. He looked so strong and sure, his dark hair framing his face, curling slightly as it reached his shoulders ...

Jack came up and stopped short before her. He spoke without any preamble. "I have just gotten word," he bit out tersely. "Shadow has brutally assassinated two men that I respected deeply - Carl and Craig. They were traveling craftsmen who moved from city to city offering assistance. Good men, good fighters."

His face was set in a serious look. "You must tell me what you know of Shadow, and where I can find him. This heinous act needs to be avenged."

Catherine blinked in shock, her mind whirling through her options. Jack's mind was even more quick, and he took a step toward her. "You were not surprised," he snapped coldly. "You *knew* of these murders?"

Catherine had a firm rule against lying and saw no benefit in changing that now. "Yes," she stated simply, her voice flat. "I knew that Carl and Craig were dead."

Jack's gaze roiled in fury. "You knew, but did not tell anyone here? Surely you knew of their association with our cathedral," he pressed, the anger in his voice held under a very tight rein.

"I did," answered Catherine shortly.

Jack's face flushed at her response. His voice was a sharp demand. "Tell me where Shadow is."

Catherine's back went up; she turned to square her shoulders against Jack's, holding her ground.

"You abandon me for a week, then return to shout orders at me? I most certainly will *not* tell you *anything* about Shadow," she retorted hotly. Fury swept over her and knew she had to leave quickly before she said something she regretted.

She turned on her heel to stride past Jack back to the cathedral.

* * *

Jack could barely hold onto the chaos of emotions which whirled within him. There she was, right in front of him, and so far out of reach. And now she was deliberately holding back information about the death of men he cared for almost as much as her?

Then she was turning her back on him, leaving him, and something snapped within him. He slammed his hand down on her left shoulder, desperate to hold her in place, to keep her there by his side. The week without her had been sheer torment …

A blur of silver streaked into his vision, and all other thoughts stopped.

Catherine had spun faster than he had thought possible. There was the cold bite of metal against his neck, the sharp edge of her dagger pressed along his jugular, and his world narrowed into a pin-point focus. He froze to instant stillness.

Catherine face had distilled to ice, and she gazed into his eyes almost without recognition. He wondered if he imagined the tremor of panic deep within her core. The pressure at his throat did not waver.

He did not breathe, did not move, acutely aware of the razor edge, of the sturdy hand which held it in place, that one small movement ...

"Good God, Jack, what the hell is going on?" came a loud, shocked voice. Peter came running up to stand beside the two, looking from one to the other. "Catherine?"

Catherine's eyes did not move from Jack's gaze, nor did her knife leave his neck. Her eyes were shadowed and her voice came as a flat rasp. "If you ever grab me like that again ..." she bit out, giving a slight turn to her blade. "Do you understand me?"

Jack nodded slightly, and he carefully released his hold on her left shoulder. Catherine took a step back and deftly slid the knife back into its scabbard. Without turning to look at Peter, she strode deliberately past the two men back to the cathedral.

Peter watched her go, then rounded angrily on his friend. "What in the world were you doing?" he challenged in angry confusion.

Jack took a deep breath and rested his hands on the railing of the bridge. "I just found out that Carl and Craig were slain by Shadow. Apparently Catherine knew about this and was shielding Shadow. She was protecting Shadow from me, and from justice.

Peter sorted through this information. "When did the killings take place," he asked, pondering something.

Jack counted backwards. He suddenly went pale. "About two weeks ago," he replied, the blood draining from his face. "Perhaps a day after we first came to Worcester."

Peter nodded. "Which makes it a few days before Catherine arrived here, her body covered with injuries." he agreed, continuing the thought.

Jack shook his head. "Surely there can be no way that those two men are responsible for Catherine's wounds," he argued with heat. "They were men I knew, men I trusted."

Peter looked down into the pond, considering. "If it *had* been them, and if we assume that Shadow and Catherine have some sort of bond between them, then it would explain why Shadow would have taken such drastic action."

Anger surged through Jack's body. He did not know if it was because Catherine had defended Shadow against him or at the thought that the two were lovers. "I refuse to accept that Carl and Craig are involved at all in Catherine's injuries," he repeated firmly. "There must be another explanation."

Peter looked over. "The only way to know is to ask," he responded. "Maybe if we ask her together, calmly, she will be willing to at least confirm or deny any part she played in this situation."

Jack nodded in agreement. "You are right," he ground out in frustration, struggling to push down the jealous heat which flooded through him. "If she was in fact an innocent victim in all of this, then she deserves sympathy, not anger." He thought back to the sword cut she had on her right arm. Surely some sort of fight had been involved to cause that kind of wound.

The two men stood on the bridge for a half hour, discussing the situation and what approach would work best. Finally they headed in to the cathedral to find Catherine.

As the two men approached the main doors, the wooden entryway was flung wide and Lord Epworth stormed out, looking around. He spotted Jack and walked straight over to him.

His voice was low and cold. "What did you say to her?" he demanded with steely anger.

Jack dropped his eyes. He did not want to involve Lord Epworth in this, but apparently the situation was escalating quickly. "My Lord, I am sorry to inform you that Carl and Craig were killed recently. I asked Catherine to provide information on the main suspect, a man from her town named Shadow."

Lord Epworth's eyes flicked with surprise. "That is all?" he insisted, his voice shaded with confusion.

Jack glanced at Peter, then back at Lord Epworth again. "What has happened," he asked, concern rising in him.

Lord Epworth spread his arms wide. "She has gone. She grabbed her belongings and took off on her horse. My guards insisted she remain, but did not feel comfortable restraining her by force when she refused. Nobody knows where she has gone to, or why."

Jack's response was immediate. "I will go after her and bring her back," he promised with firm resolve.

Lord Epworth's reaction was equally quick. "You will *not*," he thundered in anger. "You have already caused far too much harm to my relationship with Catherine, whether you meant it or not. Father Berram will be leaving in a few days for St. Albans, along with his novices. I want you to swear to me that you will accompany them as far as they wish to go. This will be your last duty to me as a son, for I will be leaving for Ireland soon."

At Jack's look of hesitation, Lord Epworth's face became stern. "Swear it," he repeated.

Jack dropped to one knee before his foster father. "I swear it, on my honor," he vowed. Lord Epworth turned away and strode off before Jack regained his feet.

Watching his father leave, Jack's heart dropped. Everything was now lost. He had accosted Catherine in fury, and she had run straight back into Shadow's arms. It was completely his own fault.

He walked past Peter without speaking and strode to the gates. He remained standing there, staring out, until his shoulders slumped and he admitted to himself that she was not going to return.

Chapter 13

Jack's week drifted by as if he were a ghost moving amongst a world long since gone to him. His body went through the motions - eating crisp strips of bacon at breakfast, assisting Father Berram at the afternoon debates, sitting dutifully beside his foster father during the long, bleak evenings. His ears took in the melodies of Maya's angelic voice, the rhythmic accompaniment of the frog-faced drummer. All sounds, all sensations barely registered in his mind.

Each morning he geared up and took on the guards in sparring exercises. Each afternoon he rode out with Peter on patrol of the cathedral's lands. He recognized each fluttering movement of a branch, caught each cry of a distant stag, but none touched him.

Friday came around again. Jack stood on the fishpond bridge for a long while, gazing down at the still waters dappled by the morning sun. Catherine's presence surrounded him, haunted him, filled him with an aching loss. She had stood on this very span of curved wood. Her fingers had laid on this very railing.

He remembered keenly how her eyes had blazed in her defense of Shadow. He could see with crystal clarity her fury when he demanded she sacrifice her loyalty.

He had grabbed her, to force her to give in to his wishes.

He had driven her straight into Shadow's arms.

* * *

Jack barely heard the closing discussions of the debate. As he had expected, the participants resolved to press King John to reconcile his differences with the Pope. Jack had little hope of the exhortations making any real change, but it seemed to give the men in the room a sense of progress. He wondered if Catherine's skills could have brought about a more meaningful result, and pushed the thought away wearily. There was no way to know.

The participants, joyous in their sense of success, bustled out toward the main hall. Jack followed the boisterous group with leaden feet.

A grand feast waited for them in the main hall. The tables were groaning with colorful pheasants, ripe peaches, elegant swans, and a number of rare delicacies brought in from all corners of the known world. Jack took a long sip of his mead, watching idly as Lord Epworth chattered away at Maya. The world continued to revolve and move forward just as if nothing had changed.

John's young voice was rich with laughing energy. "Jack! Are you in there?"

Jack shook himself aware, and looked across the table at the acolyte. "I apologize," he offered with a half-smile. "My thoughts were elsewhere."

"Apparently so!" agreed John, taking another bite of his pheasant leg. "I was saying that Father Berram is finally ready to embark on his expedition, now that this tedious talking is all done with. He thinks tomorrow night, or Sunday at the latest, and we will be off! Is that not exciting?"

"Yes, that is good news," agreed Jack quietly, his heart dropping. Once he left, then even if Catherine did return, he would never see her. She would meet up with Lord Epworth, the two of them would embark for Ireland, and she would be gone … gone …

Peter gave him a gentle pat on the arm, startling him from his musings.

"Would you like some company on the road?" asked his friend with quiet earnestness.

"Surely you have work here?" replied Jack, looking up at Peter with curiosity.

Peter shook his head. "Lord Epworth is almost complete with all of his preparations. I was never intending to accompany him to Ireland, and the incoming clergy already have their own soldiers and men with them. I would welcome the chance to go out for a few weeks."

"If you truly are willing, I would be pleased to have you on the ride," agreed Jack, a soft easing coming to his soul. "It would help to pass the time, and I could use a second sword hand."

"Consider it done, then," smiled Peter, clinking Jack's mug with his own.

"I almost wish we *would* run into trouble on the road," murmured Jack, downing his mead in a long draw. "The poor soldiers are asking me to ease up on my attacks during morning practice. I have a fury of energy within me, and nowhere to vent it."

Peter chuckled wryly, nodding to his friend. "I am afraid you will have little luck on that count," he commented quietly. "I have been paying close attention to the reports on that front. Conrad and his crew have been spotted by numerous contacts in the far north. Whatever they are up to, they seem to have turned their attention away from Berram and his book."

Jack sighed, looking down. "I suppose that is just as well," he agreed quietly.

* * *

Jack and Peter spent Saturday afternoon sitting at the main table with various maps of the countryside, discussing the routes they could take to St. Albans, considering how quickly to ride.

Peter's eyes scanned over the topography. "Are they in any rush?" He tapped his lip in thought. "Father Berram certainly managed his horse when you first came here, but I am not sure we should force him to do that for a prolonged period of time."

Jack nodded in agreement. "I think a wagon would be a better choice," he commented. "Father Berram could ride, and the boys could either ride with him or walk as the mood struck them. You and I would bring our horses so that we could hold off any mounted attack, as unlikely as that would be."

"What do you think, about a month?" asked Peter.

"Yes," confirmed Jack, his eyes going over the landscape. "The boys are looking on this as a grand adventure and are no rush to see it end. Berram, as well, seems to be quite patient and would rather get there comfortably than in a frantic rush. I think that will do quite nicely."

"I will get the kitchen to pack us some supplies," mused Peter, "and we can restock along the way as needed."

Jack nodded to him, and the two headed their separate directions. Jack worked his way through the stables, talking with the wagon master, ensuring all was ready for the trip. When he was done, he felt his feet leading him to the main gate, as they had done every day since Catherine had left. He stood there for a long while, staring down the road, his eyes seeking for any sign of movement down its dusty length.

There was nothing. She was gone; she was not going to return.

* * *

Sunday morning's mass streamed by in a smooth movement of noise and motion; Jack did not hear a word of the sermon. His mind was focused on the day of travel ahead of them. In short order Jack stood with Peter in the main courtyard, the midday sun streaming down across the steady activity that filled the area. He held his horse's reins with casual ease, looking out with growing desolation at the road beyond the main gate.

Behind him, the courtyard echoed with friendly banter as Walter, John, and Michael helped the elderly Father Berram clamber up into the sturdy wooden wagon. It was already well stocked with boxes of dried meat, baskets of apples and peaches, thick wool blankets, and other sundry items.

Jack became lost down the long road, off in the distant horizon. The preparations behind him seemed insubstantial and disconnected. So much was changing, and soon he would be gone from here, perhaps forever.

"You are sure the mercenaries are near Scotland?" he asked Peter for what must have been the tenth time in the past few days. "I have no desire to risk these men's lives again."

Peter patted him comfortingly on the shoulder. "We have numerous independent reports," he stated with certainty. "Whatever they are up to, they are far from here. We should easily make it to St. Albans without issue. The less guards we take, the less we attract attention."

Jack nodded absently. It was true that bandit activity in the area had gone into a lull in the past weeks. It was as if the troublesome elements in the area had gone into hibernation, and were waiting … for what? Why were things suddenly so peaceful?

His eyes flickered - it seemed that there was a small movement in the distance. He shaded his eyes against the afternoon sun, and soon the shape of a rider, coming at a fast gallop, distinguished itself from the background. As the person approached, Jack could make out the black cloak, but nothing else. The steed was also jet black. A flash of sunlight revealed a white blazon on its head.

Jack's eyes sharpened; his muscles rippled with tension. His hand dropped to his hilt, his fingers wrapping around the leather.

His voice was a low growl. "Shadow."

Peter put his hand on Jack's arm. "Wait," he cautioned, watching the figure. The rider came closer, dropping down to a slower canter. A toss of the head threw the hood back.

Catherine.

His breath caught. He would at least be able to see her before he left. She had come back.

His eyes stayed on her as she approached. She did not slow as she came past him through the main gates, instead pulling to a hard stop near the far steps. Her entrance caused a stir; the collected crowd stopped packing the wagon and horses and turned to watch her progress with a loud murmur.

Catherine dismounted easily and unstrapped one of the small packs tied to the horse's saddle. She carefully removed an oilskin wrapped object, then turned and scanned the courtyard area.

Spotting Lord Epworth, who was watching her with a look of surprised pleasure, she strode straight to him and curtsied deeply. "M'Lord, please let us talk for a moment," she requested, her voice neutral. She drew him to a quiet corner of the courtyard.

The servants and soldiers went back to their packing task, but whispered amongst themselves and glanced surreptitiously over at the pair while they worked.

Jack fought a powerful desire to walk over and find out what was being said. He forced himself to stand by the gate with Peter, watching as Catherine sat on a bench with her package, talking at length to Lord Epworth. Lord Epworth paced back and forth, turning occasionally to make statements or ask questions. Catherine unwrapped the package, and Jack could see the flash of blue come from the codex she withdrew from the oilskin. Next to him, Peter sucked in his breath.

"It is the Codex of the Bowyers," he explained, giving a low whistle. Jack glanced over at him, a question in his eyes. Peter continued, "It is an illuminated manuscript, with gold leaf letters, telling the full history of the Bowyers. There are even blank pages at the end of it, so that it can be added to. It is rumored to be a work of art." He nodded over at the couple. "The cover is decorated with sapphires."

Catherine was holding the book up toward Lord Epworth. Lord Epworth strode back and forth before her, his voice still low but his movements betraying his anger. Catherine did not move. She sat perfectly still, her gaze focused on Lord Epworth.

An idea coalesced in Jack's thoughts, and he froze in place, transfixed by the scene. She had found a way to get free.

There was a change in the dynamic; Lord Epworth swore beneath his breath, reached out and took the codex from Catherine with a sharp movement. His response was sharp enough to be heard clearly across the courtyard.

"I will talk to Jack and Peter," he snapped.

Then he had turned on his heel and was striding straight toward Jack. The elder man's eyes flashed with anger and frustration.

Jack's chest constricted as if stones had been laid on his ribs. He willed himself to maintain a neutral expression. He would not do anything to upset his father further, to disturb what Catherine had set into motion.

Lord Epworth pulled to a stop before the pair, his eyes sweeping between the two men with open suspicion. "You still swear you did not precipitate her behavior in any way," he demanded, his voice clipped with hostility.

Peter and Jack both shook their heads, and Jack took a step forward. "I swear we did not, sir," he vowed, his voice firm. "We only asked Catherine about the murders and about Shadow's role in them."

Lord Epworth held his gaze for a moment, then nodded, his face sagging.

"She is not going with me to Ireland," he stated in a terse voice. "Instead, she is going near St. Albans, to talk with Lord Xavier. He could be instrumental in -"

He broke off sharply, and his jaw clenched. "I find her actions wholly inappropriate and will not discuss them further." He took a long, deep breath. "I would appreciate it if she could go most of the way with your party. I owe at least that much to her family. She says she is ready to leave now."

Jack nodded, maintaining an even tone. "If that is your wish, then of course we will comply," he agreed smoothly.

Lord Epworth glanced between the two men, and his tone gentled slightly. "I will be departing next week," he continued. "I will miss you both greatly. We have spent a lot of time together in these past years. I have watched you both grow. If you ever have a chance to come to Ireland - either to visit or to stay for longer ... please do."

He stepped forward to embrace each man in turn. Then, with a final look, he walked back to the main stairs to stand with the courtiers there.

Jack looked for a moment at the man who had raised him from a teenager. Lord Epworth had been his mentor, and had treated him well.

As he watched, Maya sidled over next to Lord Epworth and coyly put her hand on his arm, fluttering her eyes up at him. Lord Epworth patted her hand absently, the move one of intimate familiarity.

Jack shook his head and turned to Peter. "Time to leave," he prodded. He took a hold of his horse's reins and waved at the other party members to move through the gate.

The three novices took the lead, running down the road, their exuberance evident in every movement. The elderly priest came next in the wagon, smiling from the driver's seat, steering the horse with an experienced pull. He appeared quite happy at getting on the road to see his old friend.

Jack glanced back to check on Catherine. She was standing in the center of the courtyard, holding the reins of her dark steed. She looked back once at Lord Epworth, giving him a farewell nod. Then she turned and resolutely walked toward the gate.

Jack watched her as if she was moving in slow motion, her eyes focused forward. As she passed him in the gateway, she looked to the side for a moment, her eyes meeting his gaze. Her eyes were shuttered, unreadable. Then she was past him, moving down the road.

Jack glanced at Peter, and without a word the two fell in at the back of the group, side by side.

* * *

The group walked for an hour in the springtime sun, the three young men laughing and running back and forth up the road, enjoying the adventure. Jack found himself thinking about the life he had left behind and his prospects for the future. He would of course be welcome back at the cathedral when he returned, but Lord Epworth would be gone. He would have to deal with the new Bishop, would have to build a fresh relationship. He did not know if that path appealed to him.

Jack watched with attentive curiosity as Catherine walked in front of him, leading the black horse. He desperately wanted to talk with her, to apologize for his behavior in the previous week. He had not wanted to rush her; he had hoped she would initiate the contact, but he wanted to talk with her before the group stopped for their first break. He did not want to leave their first conversation to take place where there were active listeners.

Jack dismounted and handed the reins of his horse to Peter, then resolutely walked forward to catch up with Catherine. She moved with her head down, keeping aside her black horse. She had not wavered or changed her step since they had left the Cathedral.

When he drew alongside her, Jack took a deep breath. He had been rehearsing what to say for many days now, and it was the time to speak the words.

He looked over into her eyes, and all thoughts of speech fled. Although she was not making a sound, tears were streaming down her cheeks.

Jack acted on instinct; he spun against her and wrapped her into a gentle embrace. Catherine resisted at first, her body stiff and angular. Then she gave a soft shudder, let out a long sigh, and folded against him in surrender. Her breath came in long, slow heaves.

Peter stopped a short distance behind when he saw what was happening. The four religious men meandered ahead, looking forward to the future. To Jack it was as if he and Catherine were in a world of their own; he was her pillar, her foundation. There was a tenuous tremble in her stance, a delicate hesitance in the way she allowed him to hold her close. Aching sympathy for the woman in his arms filled him, and he gently drew a hand down her hair, soothing her as he might a child.

A few minutes went by, then without a word Catherine gave herself a gentle shake, pulled herself slowly away and started walking forwards again, keeping her eyes low.

Jack called after her softly, his voice hoarse.

"Catherine ..."

Catherine held up her hand, motioning him to be quiet, not looking back. "Not today," she replied quietly, her voice shaky. "Not yet."

Jack stood still while she walked away from him. Peter caught up to him, waiting for him to remount. Together the two men followed behind the group, lost in thought.

* * *

Catherine said little when they stopped for an afternoon break, and she was equally silent when dinnertime rolled around. She ate the bread and cheese brought to her where she sat a little apart from the others. Her eyes were focused on the road in front of her, and her gaze was distant.

Jack respected her request and did not press her further, but his eyes stayed on her, concerned. While she may have found a solution to her situation that resolved her own moral dilemma, she had still violated the demands presented to her by her council. As a result, she was now exiled from her family. She was without home, without support.

Jack sighed and tossed another stick into the campfire, watching as the sparks flared in the deepening dusk. He certainly knew how it felt to be without a real home. He wondered what the coming weeks would have in store for them all.

Peter came over and sat beside him. "I will take first watch if you want," he suggested amiably. "It should be pretty quiet, with us being on main roads."

Peter had spoken quietly, but Catherine answered immediately from across the fire. "I will take second, then," she offered, her voice without inflection. “I know that I do not have to,” she added quickly, as Peter began to protest. “I am going to take a turn, whether you ask me to or not. We might as well make it official; we all need our rest.”

“I know you scouted often for the Bowyers,” replied Peter smoothly, “I do not doubt your ability to keep watch. Do you have a weapon?”

Without looking over, Catherine nodded toward her horse, which was grazing to one side with the other steeds. “Yes,” she stated without further comment.

Peter looked at Jack, who nodded. “I am third, then,” he agreed. The two men looked at each other for a moment, and Jack knew it was clear to his friend that they would ensure their own shifts overlapped with Catherine’s. They had worked together for many years and trusted each other implicitly. This trip was their charge, and they would not leave it in another’s hands.

The rest of the party was already curled up in cloaks. Catherine lay her heavy, black cloak down to one side and curled herself up in it, facing away from the fire. Jack found a location on the other side of the fire, and settled in to get his sleep.

Rest did not come quickly. All he could see was Catherine’s hunched up form, curled against the crisp nighttime breeze, her dark hair flowing down to the mossy patch she lay on. She seemed so alone, so sad.

He wished there was something he could do to help. For now, that door was closed.

Chapter 14

Catherine eased awake, the gentle warbling of birds drawing her into a morning drenched with delicate sunlight and whispers of fog. A hesitant sense of hope kindled in her breast. Her world was in turmoil, but for the first time in years her future held promise. She had deftly managed an intricate set of negotiations, had achieved possession of the book, and had convinced Lord Epworth to accept it.

She could remain in England. She was free of her obligation to flee with the elderly churchman and abandon those who depended on her.

The repercussions swept in on her, and a dense fog of pain swirled around her, enveloping her. These precious gifts had come at a heavy price. She could never return home, never see her loved ones again.

She reminded herself firmly that, had she stayed on her previous course, she would have been equally separate from those she loved. At least now it was on her own terms.

Drawing in a long, deep breath, she sat up, taking a fresh look at the beauty around her. She would not have to leave these hills and forests she adored. For the next few weeks she would be able to relax with Michael, John, and Walter, enjoying their company. And then, after that, the world stretched before her. There were many who relied on her assistance, who depended on her for their safety and security.

She put off any thoughts of Jack and Peter for now. That still remained unresolved. She would keep her eyes on the larger picture. She would be able to serve those she cared for, in the way she knew best.

Walter's voice rang out warmly across the clearing. "Breakfast is served!" She smiled and rose, noticing that Jack and Peter were thankfully out on patrol, leaving her free to relax for the morning meal. She moved to join the three acolytes and Father Berram as they poured out ale and served sausages. The boys' excitement about the upcoming trip bordered on bliss, and she found their enthusiasm was infectious. Her heart warmed with joy. When they bent their heads in gratitude after the meal was through, she joined them with pleasure. She had much to be grateful for. She was moving in a direction of her own choosing. Her beloved horse was with her. The air was fragrant with the springtime promise of flowers and sun.

The group packed and set into motion. She had known it was coming, but even so her stomach flittered with butterflies once the boys had run ahead, and Jack's sturdy presence gently approached her. She had not been able to cope with a discussion yesterday - not then, not when her world had just been rearranged like a pretzel. Now that she'd finally gotten a good night's sleep, and time to rest and think, she could be ready for his questions.

"Catherine," began Jack cautiously, giving her a chance to put off the conversation. She nodded for him to continue, and he did so, his speech coming quickly. She could tell that he'd been running over this discussion in his mind for some time.

"I want to apologize for my outburst at the cathedral. I was caught up in powerful emotions, and I took them out on you. Please forgive me."

Catherine took in a deep breath, remembering the fury of that afternoon, the near loss of control. "I am sure we both said some things we did not mean," she replied after a moment. "We have a new start here; let us take advantage of it."

"You brought the Bowyer codex down for Lord Epworth's safe keeping," continued Jack, his voice easing. "A way to preserve the Bowyer legacy, as your council had requested?"

Catherine nodded hesitantly in agreement, her shoulders uncoiling slightly. Perhaps he would leave the argument in the past, would truly let them begin afresh. "It was the only compromise I could hope for," she explained. "In the end I knew I simply could not run away to Ireland myself. There is still too much to hold me here." Her face became somber. "I had to stay with or without the council's permission."

Jack's eyes shone with admiration. "I am sure they will come to respect your choice, and see that it was for the best." He paused for a moment, then looked at the road stretching before them. "Peter mentioned that the codex was stored in London, but that is quite a distance from Worcester. Had it been moved somewhere closer?"

A hint of a smile tugged at Catherine's face. Many men before Jack had been amazed by her horse's speed and stamina. "No, it was still in London," she agreed smoothly.

"But that is a good four day ride from Worcester," protested Jack, his face bright with disbelief. "You were only gone seven days; there is no way you could have gotten there and back again."

Catherine patted her steed's neck fondly. "Oh, I had some help," she offered, giving her beloved stallion a gentle rub.

Jack looked up at the horse, his eyes tracking to the white blaze on his forehead. Catherine remembered suddenly how Jack had seemed defensive as she had approached the cathedral. She was hit by the knowledge that he had seen the horse when she had met him as Shadow, deep in the rainy woods. A chill swept through her, and she realized that she had stepped into a trap of her own making.

Jack's voice went cool. "That is Shadow's horse," he stated with certainty.

There was a long silence. Catherine's smile faded, her hope dimmed, as the feared-for danger blazed into a threatening reality.

"Yes," she replied finally, her voice hollow.

A harsh note of anger flared into Jack's voice. "You *did* run straight to Shadow. And after I told you of his heinous crimes?"

Catherine's fury roiled up from the depths, and her hands clenched. He had *no right* …

Peter pressed his way between the two, his eyes moving sharply left and right, creating space with his body. A long moment passed as they walked down the road three abreast, a tense silence hanging in the air.

Peter's voice was placating but firm. "Catherine, I need to ask you something."

Catherine's throat tightened. "You can ask, but I may choose not to answer," she bit out. She could sense what was coming. Her world closed in around her.

Peter nodded in acceptance. "I realize you hold the trust of many people. Your clan is often called in to delicate situations which require vows of secrecy. I do not ask you to violate any such mandate."

Catherine stared down the road, tension delving into her shoulders, turning them to stone. "Yet you are undoubtedly digging into a double homicide," she snapped.

Jack's voice was sharp. "Carl and Craig were *honorable* men – it is my *duty* to avenge them, and why you continue to --"

Peter held up a hand to quiet him. They walked a few paces in silence again, and then he turned back to the woman at his side.

"Catherine," he offered quietly, "When I saw your wounds, I was ready to kill whoever had done it to you. I would not have hesitated."

Hope drained out of Catherine's soul. She had naively thought that the issue would fade away, would become a distant memory. She had dreamt that she and Jack could create a new start together, could find joy ...

Tears trickled down her cheek, and she shook her head sharply, keeping her gaze down so the men would not see her turmoil. She willed herself to keep walking forward, first one foot, then the next.

She had chosen her path. She would live with the consequences. She took in a long, deep, shuddering breath, and let it out again. All that remained was to give an answer that protected the innocent ones. She knew her words could destroy all chances for a relationship with Jack, but there seemed to be no other choice.

She kept her head lowered as she spoke. "Carl and Craig were indeed hunted down and slain by Shadow," she confirmed in a quiet, flat tone.

Jack gave a low oath, but Peter put a hand on his arm, turning again to Catherine.

"Because ...?"

Catherine's throat closed up. She would not lie, not dishonor the women and girls whose lives were cruelly stolen. She could also not reveal the full truth; it would only taint the futures of the innocent victims who remained alive.

That only left her with one choice; one fraught with danger, one which put her on a collision course with Jack's blade. She had gone over the alternatives for long weeks now, had explored option after option should this situation arise. There had been none.

Her alter-ego, Shadow, would have to take the blame without providing any ethical reason for the two killings. She would have to live – forever – with the knowledge that Jack seethed with hatred for what she had done.

Even knowing she had no other choice, Catherine's throat closed up. The world faded to grey, all color draining from the sky.

Jack's growl burst into the silence. "Did Shadow murder Carl and Craig because they attacked you, or not?"

Catherine flushed. It would be so easy to twist the story, to tell the men what they wanted to hear. But she could not do that. The truth was too important to her to disgrace it with a lie.

"No," she ground out, exhaustion settling over her. "Shadow was tracking them long before I was injured."

Searing pain rippled through her shoulder, embedding into her heart. She knew that, with that statement, Jack could easily decide to seek after Shadow for vengeance. For her own protection she would have to get clear of his presence as soon as she could, to keep herself safe from his sword and fury.

A chill swept over her. It was as if the sun dimmed, as if a cloud passed, as if she had lost her chance at joy ...

The pain swelled, cascaded, and she waved the men away, wanting to be alone … alone …

Peter and Jack glanced at each other, then paused so that she could walk ahead of them. She continued forward slowly, her head down.

* * *

Jack clenched his fists as waves of anger pummeled his heart. Shadow had relentlessly pursued and slaughtered two men who had shown him nothing but kindness from when he was a boy. Not only that, but the man had also embroiled Catherine in the madness, maintaining some sort of a hold over her.

Were they lovers? The thought filled him with a sharp stab of pain. Was that why she had found a solution to her marriage with Lord Epworth? Because she could now be with Shadow?

He remembered back to when they had stood together on the cliff overlooking the cathedral, when he had asked her about Shadow. She had been upset, had said she would need to put Shadow behind her. Had she found the idea too difficult to bear?

He flinched, but looked open-eyed over the past few weeks. Had she been toying with him this entire time, a casual distraction while she planned her escape?

She had run to Shadow after their fight on the bridge. She had said, just now, that she could not leave these lands, that too much still held her to remain.

Had she already pledged herself to stay by Shadow's side?

Hurt and fury boiled within him, and he shook it off, bringing it under tense control with an effort. He mounted his horse, forcing his eyes to look far ahead, down the curves of the road. With careful focus he began planning in detail how he could pick up Shadow's trail, pursue the murderer, and bring him to justice.

He nodded in grim determination. He would start as soon as the priest and his novices were safely dropped off at St. Albans.

* * *

Catherine's resignation grew, expanded, settled into every pore of her being. She had lost Jack. She would have to build a barrier to keep him out, to maintain him as only a distant companion on the road, nothing more. Once they parted ways near St. Albans, she would never be able to see him again. The danger was far too great.

Sharp longing stabbed at her heart, and she muffled it with an effort. She could not afford those feelings any longer. She had known what she risked when she accepted the role of Shadow, and now it was time for her to shoulder that responsibility. Innocent lives depended on her silence.

A deadening calm blanketed her, and she wrapped it around herself, drawing it in tightly. It was the only solution.

Michael, Walter, and John came wandering from the path to climb into the back of the wagon, looking backwards at Catherine. Their faces were furrowed with frustration.

Catherine drew in a deep breath. The young lads were on their grand adventure – she would not let her own sorrows drag them down. She made an effort to smile to lift their spirits.

"Now, my young friends, what has got you so gloomy," she asked with forced cheer, trying to bring back their former enthusiasm. "Worn out from walking already?"

John spoke up, glancing back at Jack and Peter. "We are all over eighteen," he huffed with a hint of petulance. "We are in fine shape. There are three of us. Yet we need nursemaids for a quite common trip to St. Albans on public roads. Surely we can take care of Father Berram and ourselves."

Catherine's eyes brightened. "Of course you can," she agreed readily. "In fact, as I am a lady of fine birth now without a home, I find myself in need of bodyguards. I feel you three would be perfect!"

Walter scoffed, his pudgy face downcast. "Do not humor us," he growled morosely. "Surely those two would do far better for you. What kind of bodyguards could we possibly be?"

Catherine put on a hurt air that her judgment would be so readily dismissed. "You know that I have trained with some of the best swordsmen in the land," she responded archly. "I am a fine judge of character, and I see that strength within all three of you."

She looked to John. "You are an active lad. Tell me, John, why might you feel you are *not* as well suited as say, Jack would be to protect me?"

John looked behind her at the two men, and she turned briefly to follow his gaze. Jack's eyes were flat, and her anger flared. Apparently the man was openly scoffing at the idea. A blaze of anger filled her veins. No person's value should be dismissed so callously. His clear disbelief made her even more determined to see this impetuous act through.

"Well, John?"

John's face grew serious, and he knelt in the wagon, facing her. "Jack is spectacular with a sword. He is tall; he is much stronger than I am. He has been in combat situations many times. He could probably kill a bandit attacker with his eyes closed."

Catherine shrugged, unimpressed. "Fine, let us say that is true. So say a bandit attacker comes and raids our camp. Who will that attacker go for first?"

Three pairs of eyes swiveled toward Jack. "Exactly," agreed Catherine with a thin smile. "So there Jack is, involved in saving his own skin. Who will be around to protect me?"

Michael shook his head. "Bandits will never see us as a threat," he protested. "They will think we are just monks who do not know how to fight." Once he had said the words, his eyes gleamed as he realized the advantage.

Catherine nodded encouragingly. "You will be overlooked, and that will be your strength," she confirmed. "When we stop for lunch, I will show you how."

The three regained their energy and soon they were wheedling Father Berram to stop for an early lunch. At last he caved in with a wry chuckle, and the group drew aside into a clearing.

Once everyone had eaten, Catherine went over to Walter and whispered something in his ear. Then she gave Michael, Walter, and John small sticks, and took one herself. She had Michael stand in the center of the clearing, then took a position in front of him.

"Michael, you are the bandit," she explained. "We will pretend these sticks are our daggers."

Michael nodded with understanding. He posed menacingly, wielding his stick above his head as if he were a cobra.

Catherine smiled in appreciation. "Well done. You are so fearsome, in fact, that apparently you have scared Walter and John silly. So you two, get on his left and right, perhaps five feet away from him. Cower on the ground, put your hands over your head, and milk it for all it is worth."

Walter and John immediately took their positions, cringing and crying in fear.

"All right, Michael the Bandit, come and threaten me," she encouraged.

Michael took a strong step forward, and Catherine quivered in mock fear, wildly waving her arms. "Do not kill me!" she cried out with great emotion. "I do not want to die! I am too young! Please spare me!"

Michael moved in again, glaring at Catherine with theatrical anger. He had only taken one more step before Walter slammed his stick into the back of Michael's knee, sending him to the ground. Walter was over him in a moment, holding the stick to his chest.

Michael looked up, baffled. "Where did *you* come from?" he asked in confusion.

Catherine reached down a hand to help Michael up. "You did not even see him, did you?" she asked with a smile. Michael shook his head no in disbelief. "You discounted them as soon as they curled up," she explained. "You thought of them like rocks or tree stumps - as non-threats. You focused on me because I was active and moving. Your peripheral vision did not extend to where they were after only a step or two. All Walter had to do is take out your knee, and suddenly Michael the Bandit loses all of his advantages - his height, his mobility, his strength. Once he is down on the ground, you can either take action against him or simply run away."

John frowned. "He still has a sword," he pointed out, "and he will know how to use it."

Catherine nodded. "The aim is to finish it quickly," she replied. "This is not something that the bandit is going to learn and grow from. It is a one shot resolution. When you hit him in the back of the knee, he is going to experience a sudden, blinding pain, and he is going to go down hard. His main focus is going to be on hitting the ground softly and figuring out what happened. If you get to him while he is still trying to get his bearings, you have the advantage." She waved over to Walter. "Here, you be the bandit now. Try to see if you sense where the danger is."

Catherine ran them through the drill many times. She had them try different configurations, helping them learn what worked and what did not work. The three were quite surprised that even when they knew an attack would be coming, they usually could not sense from which direction it had been launched until it was too late.

"See," explained Catherine, helping Walter up from a particularly vicious attack by John, "the bandit will be fearing an attack, too. He will be cautious. However, even if he is extremely paranoid, he cannot watch in all directions at once. He will discount your cowering forms as being beneath notice. You will not give him the chance to learn from that mistake.

This means the trick should work for you over and over again on each new enemy you run into."

The group headed out for the afternoon section of its journey, the novices once again in high spirits. Catherine tied her steed to the back of the wagon, walking instead at its front, watching the trio of youths practice mock swordplay with their sticks at the front of the group.

There was a motion to her side, and Peter came up to join her. "That was very nicely done," he commented with quiet appreciation. "I truly think they have more chance against an attack than they might have had before."

"Everyone deserves the chance to feel important and able to defend themselves," replied Catherine, her voice low. "Perhaps especially those who are thought of by others as being not up to the challenge."

The hours flew by in blue skies and drifting clouds, and it seemed all too soon before they were pulling aside for dinner. She busied herself helping Walter with the cooking of the stew. The lad was a master with the herbs, tossing in a dash of sage, a pinch of rosemary, creating a savory smell which set the whole group's stomachs rumbling.

"You have a real talent here," she advised him with a smile, taking a taste of his creation. "I hope your order appreciates your skills.

"Oh, they have great plans for me," he agreed with a grin, stirring in another pinch of salt. "Perhaps someday I will become head cook at Canterbury itself!"

Father Berram tottered by, drawn by the rich fragrance. His wizened eyes scanned over Walter, and he pursed his lips for a moment. "Do not draw your pleasures from distant shores, my lad," he advised somberly. "Every day you have is a gift. Savor the food before you. Enjoy the world around you. Do not lose track of what you have now, in your craving for future glory."

Catherine took in another mouthful of the dinner, its warmth filling her. "The priest is quite right," she agreed wholeheartedly. "I believe what you have created here is just as delicious as anything we enjoyed at the cathedral, and our dining hall is the best nature has to offer. You are a master cook right now, serving the best of friends."

Walter blushed under the compliment, and as they passed around the bowls and bread, the kudos were echoed by all present. Catherine basked in the richness of the company, and in counterpoint it emphasized the loss created by her estrangement from Jack. When the others remained up to talk, she claimed fatigue, moving to her bed area as soon as the sun dipped in crimson streaks below the horizon.

When Peter awoke her for her shift, she sat by the fire without a word, knowing he patrolled the outer ring during the first half of her shift, watching as he woke Jack, the men trading places during the second half. She never saw Jack in his patrol, did not speak a word to him when her time was through, when she curled up in her corner and strove, desperately, to find some sleep.

It was no use. The scene from the afternoon replayed in her head, caught on a continual loop. It showed her speaking the words which divided them, the shuttering of his eyes, and the shutdown of his heart.

* * *

Dawn's glow warmed her eyelids, the fluttering of birds rising to meet the new day tickled her ears, but it was a long time before she willed herself to open her eyes, before she pushed herself off the rough ground to gather her belongings. She tied her steed again to the back of the wagon, moved to the front with the lads, and willed herself to be cheerful and strong for their sake.

The moving cart with its load of supplies and elderly priest became a firewall for her, a safe buffer between her fragile heart and the man who loomed so strongly on the other side. She could feel his presence, could sense his eyes on her. She craved the warmth of his fingers, the strength of his arms. It was all gone. Her path in life had created a chasm that none could bridge.

She ran a hand distractedly through her thick hair. What if she simply told him the truth, that she *was* Shadow, that he should trust in her reasons for having slain the pair of criminals?

She laughed harshly, kicking at an errant rock in the road, sending it skittering across the path. He would never believe her. He had decided that she was in league with Shadow, and would simply accuse her of lying to cover for him.

After all, there was no way to prove her claim. Even if she brought up things said and done during the flight from Conrad's men, Jack believed she had gone off to meet Shadow during her trip to retrieve the codex. He would simply say Shadow had discussed his activities with her during that time.

Her mind searched through her choices as they stopped for lunch, during their quiet dinner, through the long hours of her nighttime watch period as the clouds sent billowing shadows across the moon. There seemed no other escape. Jack simply would not believe her story. She had to get away from him, for her own safety, and for the security of those whom she had sworn to protect.

* * *

Jack watched as the sun slowly crept above the horizon, sending tendrils of orange and scarlet streaming across the sky, as the canopy above tinged from black to indigo to royal blue. This was one of his favorite parts of the day, the fresh beginning, the new start which offered hope.

He looked over the array of sleeping charges in his midst. The past few days had brought them into rural areas, only a scattering of villages interrupting their gentle voyage. There were now fewer locals for any potential troublemakers to blend in with, but also less support to call for if an issue should arise. He remained always on alert, always listening for danger, aware of his surroundings.

The group stirred to life, and soon they were eating Walter's delicious offerings, gathering their gear, and setting into motion. Catherine tied her black stallion up behind the wagon before moving out in front with Walter, Michael, and John, as she had done the past few days. A sturdy knot coiled around his heart, a coldness settled on his shoulders as he mounted and slowly rode at the back of the group alongside Peter. His friend had attempted to talk the first day or two, but had now settled into a somber quiet, which was quite to Jack's liking. It gave him the time to plan out his search patterns to track down and slay Shadow. It had to be done methodically, with careful precision. He could not allow the assassin who had butchered his two best friends to escape from justice.

He considered, for the hundredth time, that Shadow had stood against Conrad and his crew, had risked his life to save the very men now in his care. He shook his head, putting that out of his mind. Past good deeds did not annul a heinous crime. Shadow would be made to pay for those innocent deaths.

A pair of swallows soared and raced across the open sky, but Jack barely saw their undulating flight. The light was fading from his world. Catherine alone seemed to grow more beautiful each day. Each glance reminded him that she was meant for another man, that she had toyed with his heart, had pledged herself to Shadow.

The man would pay.

Another day drained by, and then two, and the quiet villages faded into the past, the landscapes before them open, almost without farmhouse or tavern. His patrol habits drew into play, and for lunch he had them stop on a rise looking over a stream, a chance to catch fresh trout to replenish their food supplies. After lunch, the three boys ambled down to fish while Father Berram retreated to the wagon for a sun-drenched nap,

Jack and Peter were just finishing brushing down the horses when Jack heard a low call. Catherine was sitting at the edge of the rise, looking out toward the stream with a fixed expression.

Her voice was low, urgent. "Bring the bows."

Peter raced to the horses' gear to grab the weapons, while Jack strode over to join her, dropping to one knee alongside her.

"There, behind the copse of trees," she whispered, pointing. Jack followed her outstretched finger and for a moment saw nothing. Then there was a movement, and he spotted an unsavory character lurking amongst the birch, a glimpse of shine indicating a drawn sword. "There appears to be only one," she added.

Jack looked over to the stream as Peter slid beside the pair, handing a strung bow to Jack and preparing the second for himself. The three acolytes were splashing in the water, hooting with delight. They came out of the water after a few minutes and shook themselves dry, then dressed, still horsing around.

The bandit emerged from the woods and stalked toward them.

Jack and Peter both raised their bows in unison. Peter's voice was a low mutter. "Not until he makes a move," he urged. "He could perhaps be a lost gypsy or some such."

Jack snorted in disbelief but did not argue. The three pairs of eyes watched as the bandit made his way down to the bank, his sword ready and drawn.

The three below spotted the bandit and waved in friendly greeting. Catherine could not hear what he barked at the three novices, but their reaction was immediate. John and Walter flung themselves to two sides of the bandit, cringing in fear, rolled up into balls as tight as a millipede. Dismissing them, the bandit turned to face Michael, who was jumping around in a panic, crying out in heartfelt pleas for his safety.

Catherine's breath caught. "Wait ..."

Both men were following the bandit's movements with pinpoint precision, but they held back on launching the arrows.

It all happened in an instant. Walter launched himself at the bandit's knee, sending the bandit face-forward into the sand. John landed on top of the attacker, and it was over. The beach was quiet again.

Jack quickly unnocked the arrow and handed his equipment to Peter. "Get them back on the horse," he whispered, then took Catherine's arm and moved back to the main campfire area. The priest was still snoring in long drones.

"So then Marcie won the cooking contest?" he asked in a louder voice, grabbing randomly for a conversation topic.

Catherine chimed right in, realizing what Jack was doing, nodding her approval. "Yes, she made an incredible apple tart," she responded, her voice warm. "It was the most amazing thing you had ever seen. She laid out the dough to be shaped like leaves all along the edge of the pastry. She used a mixture of apples from different locations to get just the right flavor balance. She was like a woman obsessed, but all of her hard work paid off. She still keeps the ribbon in her room."

The three boys came charging into the clearing, falling over each other to tell Jack what had happened. John's voice echoed across the meadow. "It was a bandit!"

Walter spread his arms wide. "He was *huge*!" he added enthusiastically.

Catherine and Jack turned to face the trio. Catherine quickly scanned the three lads for injuries. "You are all right?"

Michael's voice was rich with delight. "Yes, we are fine," he assured her. "We did it just as you told us to, and it worked! It really worked!"

Peter came to join them from where he was standing by the horses, and in a moment all six of them descended the long slope to take a closer look at the dead body.

Walter, John, and Michael played out the scenario for them several times, providing moment by moment recreations of the event. Jack patted down the corpse, finding nothing of value but the sword in his hand. He undid the man's belt, sliding the sword back into its scabbard, eyeing it thoughtfully.

"Who shall we present this trophy to, then?" he asked the trio.

John and Walter immediately looked to Michael. Walter did not hesitate. "Michael should have it," he announced. "He took on the most dangerous part, to distract the bandit. He deserves to carry the sword."

Michael blushed, then accepted the offered weapon with a wide smile. He strapped on the belt with quiet attention, standing proudly, as if he had been presented with the finest war trophy that could be achieved.

The rest of the afternoon was filled with recounts, reenactments, and descriptive monologues on the day's event. Jack could almost echo the dialogue back at the appropriate part, but he held his tongue, letting the boys revel in their victory. It was long past dusk before the adrenaline had worn off and they tumbled into a deep sleep.

A silence settled across the camp, only broken by Father Berram's low snores. Jack sat back against a roughly barked log, letting out a long breath of satisfaction. He looked in turn to Catherine and Peter who sat on either side of him. The three smiled to each other and settled in to watch the fire.

Chapter 15

Catherine found that, despite her concerns, the days and nights rolled on in an orderly progression. The daytime sword practices became more spirited, with the three lads now secure in their own ability to face danger. At night, she reconciled herself to her path. She protected the innocent. She was not exiled to Ireland, not trapped with a cowardly man who apparently had every intention to keep his mistresses at his side as well.

Life was never perfect. This was a compromise she could be at peace with.

The journey continued to unfurl, step by step, hour by hour. She felt both appreciation that the time would go by smoothly, as well as a hollow, lonely core form in her soul. She knew how difficult the choice had been for her to create the wall, to keep Jack away. It hurt her to see how easily he remained on his own side of that barricade. Had he forgotten her so easily in the brief days she had been gone?

It seemed no time at all that they were about halfway done with their journey, and the lads' spirits had never been higher. They had faced their fears and survived them. They were on an adventure to see new lands. Father Berram looked forward to seeing his old friend Father Oswold and sharing stories with him.

Catherine was less ebullient. Where the four religious men were looking forward, she found herself looking back, second guessing her decisions. Her own future seemed uncertain, hazy.

When she glanced into the eyes of Jack and Peter she saw that they had become drawn into a quiet melancholy. It occurred to her that Lord Epworth's leaving had left both of them adrift as well. She wondered what plans they had, once the trip to St. Albans was through. Would they return to Worcester, to work with the new Bishop?

Jack, in particular, seemed to become lost in thought at every opportunity. She often caught him with a distant gaze as they moved along the quiet road, as he sat musing by the campfire in the evening. He became preoccupied once again during lunch while the boys enthusiastically discussed what new and interesting things they might see in St. Albans.

Catherine chuckled at the list, which seemed to grow with every new dawn. Based on the boys' tellings and retellings, she could count off many of the priority attractions now without thinking. There was the coffin of the martyr, the Roman ruins, the fabled clock-tower.

Walter gave her a nudge of glee, seeing how immersed Jack had become in his far-off ponderings. "I will bring him back," he promised with a grin. He turned to the older man. "All right, there, Jack, time to rejoin the living," he insisted, giving Jack a shove on the arm. "It is your turn. What do you think *you* will do first once we arrive in St. Albans?"

Jack started in surprise, then stretched and put down his mug. "I will probably start in Harpenden first," replied Jack absently, his mind clearly still distant.

Walter blinked in confusion at the nonsensical reply, but Catherine sat up from her lazy enjoyment of the afternoon with a quick movement. She turned to look at Jack, her eyes sharp. It seemed as if a cloud had drifted across the sun, leaving a bitter wind to cut at her, drive away all warmth.

"You are going to immediately track down Shadow," she stated coldly, surprised that she had not realized this before. She exhaled in a long, steady breath. Her hope for a peaceful parting suddenly vanished, as a morning mist evaporates in the bright, harsh sunlight of day. Her voice became bitter, but she forced herself to hold her position; to not turn away to hide her pain.

"You are not even going to wait one day. You are going to hunt him down, relentlessly, like a wolfhound sent after prey."

* * *

Jack froze, realizing he could not un-say what had been said. He held Catherine's gaze with an effort, seeing her disappointment clearly. There was no use trying to sugar-coat or hide this. He had avoided the topic for many days, but now it was here to be faced.

"Aye," he replied simply, wishing that life had led them on a different course. "The moment the boys and Father Berram are set, I will begin my hunt."

A cascade of emotions crossed Catherine's face – frustration, anger, and then finally, a deep seated calm. She drew in a steady breath and climbed deliberately to her feet. She turned on her heel and strode down the slope to the clump of aspens where the horses were tied.

"Wait - where are you going?" asked Jack, standing to look after her, his voice blended with both concern and anger. He had not meant for Catherine to find out like this, so casually. He knew his plans would disturb her, and had hoped to broach them with some context. It twisted at his soul, that she could be so protective of the man who had cruelly slain his friends.

Catherine reached the horses, tossing the answer back over her shoulder as she untied her horse's reins. "I need to be alone for a while," she responded in a flat voice. "I will return soon enough."

She mounted and cantered down the road, quickly vanishing from sight.

Jack slowly sat down again, shaking his head with frustration. There was nothing to be done about it. She would not reveal more details, and he would not push her. She had a tie to Shadow that he might never know the full depth of.

By killing Shadow, he would lose Catherine forever - but he was honor bound to do so.

The boys quieted, some of their lightheartedness shaken by the scene.

Time passed, and Jack became lost in thought, wondering just what the future would hold for him. What would happen after he found and dealt with Shadow? It seemed fated that the act would create an uncrossable chasm between him and Catherine, and all options appeared grey and lifeless. Would he join his foster father after all? Find work somewhere? No path seemed to appeal to him.

When hoofbeat sounded, he did not bother to look up. Whatever Catherine had thought about while she had gone, it was unlikely she would share her musings with him. She seemed to have chosen protecting Shadow over trusting him. He looked at the grim possibility that what he did in the next few weeks could easily cause Catherine to never speak with him again.

A single word from Peter brought him out of his reverie. "Jack ..."

There was no thought necessary - Jack knew that tone and reacted instantly. Immediately he was putting his hand to his hilt, scanning the area, rising smoothly to a standing position.

The horse had stopped several yards in front of the group. It was the same black bodied, white blazed stallion that Catherine had been leading for the past weeks. On him, however, sat a figure in a long black cloak, wearing a black tunic and pants. A black scarf covered the lower half of the figure's face, leaving only the eyes visible.

Jack drummed his fingers down the sword hilt, settling his grip in tightly, and it seemed like the world slowed down around him.

Jack's voice came out as a deep, sibilant hiss, the sound matching his blade as it was drawn from its scabbard. "Shadow."

Shadow dismounted easily, the cloak sliding aside to reveal a green-wrapped hilt worn on a belt scabbard. "Jack," came the low reply, a deep, resigned growl in the voice.

* * *

Catherine's every nerve ending tingled with alertness. She exposed herself to great risk by coming to face Jack openly. The man believed Shadow was a well-trained, cold-blooded assassin. He would have no compunction in killing her.

She had gone over the options in her mind every hour since Jack had made his discovery of Shadow's guilt. In the end, if Jack was going to pursue her, and he could easily catch her unawares. Confronting him directly seemed the only way that provided any chance for a future. She could think of no other way to bring a resolution to this situation that would be positive.

If she simply told Jack of her dual identity, he would never believe her. If she did *not* tell him, he could spring into her life when she was unprepared, and one or both of them could die. There was still hope that the two could talk this through.

She fervently hoped that by approaching him with Peter present, in a situation where Jack felt relatively at ease, that he would be open and perhaps even obligated to discussion rather than combat.

Jack's whole body shimmered with tension, and he held his sword off to one side. He eyed her with steady appraisal for a few long moments, a hint of confusion crossing his brow as she did not approach.

Finally, he asked abruptly, "I want to hear it from your own mouth. Did you kill Craig and Carl?"

She nodded. "Yes," she admitted simply, keeping her voice low.

Jack expelled his breath in a rush. "Why?" he pressed, his voice tight.

Catherine had expected this as well, but still felt the familiar tightening of the throat when her actions were questioned. Her voice held a hint of steel when she responded.

"I would have hoped that the incident with Conrad's men would show you that I act with honor. Peter here can vouch for my character." Pride pricked at her and made her add, "I do not lightly divulge the reason behind actions which may have involved innocents. I cannot compromise others. Either you will trust that my actions were just, or you will not."

Jack shook his head. His voice was ragged. "While I agree you acted courageously when these four were in danger, one brave action does not make up for the callous murder of two respectable men," he insisted. "Now you are making Catherine cover for your behavior as well? Is *that* the deed of a man of honor?"

Catherine's eyes widened. For all of her musings, it had never occurred to her that Jack was jealous of Shadow! She should have realized that there were many components to the antagonism Jack felt.

She smiled without mirth. "I refuse to provide details of the deaths. You apparently refuse to accept my actions as just. I have come here to work this out. How do you propose we resolve this situation?"

Jack's eyes sharpened. "By the powers vested in me by my father, Lord Epworth, I will do justice on you, and sentence you to death. That sentence shall be carried out immediately."

Walter gasped in shock, and Catherine gave a short barking laugh. "By authority of your *father*?" she scoffed, her voice sharp with derision. "I do not accept that Lord Epworth has *any* say over my actions. I also do not accept that you – or anyone else - has the right to mete justice out in his name. Surely he has already abandoned all power on these shores, and fled his duties?" Her hand fell to her sword, and she tossed her head in defiance.

Jack's mouth tightened with fury. His voice became a steely threat. "How dare you declare your actions outside the law?"

Catherine's retort was quick and low. "My actions *are* the law," she stated with heat. "It is the interference of Lord Epworth - that -" Her throat closed up as she realized how close she had come to marrying him. "That *coward's* actions are what I object to. I will not be judged by *that man*."

Jack coiled even tighter, and she prepared for the inevitable attack. Adrenaline surged through her; she was playing with fire, but she found could not help herself. Her emotions were overwhelming her; she struggled to rein them under control.

She had to stop the fight. That was her priority.

She pitched her voice to hold a sharp lack of respect. “So, this is how you honor your vows,” she taunted him, “You know that I have slain two renowned swordsmen, yet you intend to abandon your care of the religious men in order to satisfy a personal vendetta. Tell me, are you so certain that you will get through this fight without even a scratch?”

That comment made Jack pause, and his eyes flickered momentary to the men who stood in a nervous circle watching the encounter. He looked back to Catherine again, giving the blade in his hand a quick rotation to loosen the wrist muscles.

Peter spoke into the thick silence. “I propose a duel to touch only,” he offered in a quiet, almost placating voice. “The first of you to achieve three touches will be declared the victor.”

His eyes sought out Jack’s, and he spoke to his old friend first. “Jack, if you win, then Shadow will swear to return to the cathedral. He will place himself into the custody of whoever is in charge - be it your father or the new Bishop, and accept the judgment of the court there on his actions.”

Jack and Catherine both looked sharply at Peter, Catherine’s eyes flashing furious anger. Jack looked back at his opponent and he seemed startled by the strong feelings shining there. Slowly he nodded.

“Would you swear to do that?” he asked gruffly, a visible calm settling down over him.

Catherine took a deep breath, trying to gain a handle on the anger she felt. Turning herself over to the cathedral minions was the last thing she would possibly want to do. She could think of no worse humiliation. Her council would be beyond furious. Still ... there seemed to be no other solution that would suit all involved. She certainly did not want a duel to the death be the only way around this. Her mind raced to find another solution - but it had tried this task for weeks without coming up with any answers.

"Yes," she finally ground out, her voice reflecting the frustration she felt. "I swear on my honor and life that, should you best me, I will go immediately to the cathedral and turn myself in."

Jack studied Catherine for a few moments, then nodded. "I believe you," he responded simply. He turned back to Peter. "If I win?"

Catherine had numerous ideas for what her victory should entail, but before she could put them into words, Peter spoke up again. "Jack, you would swear to consider this matter settled. You would not pursue Shadow in any way going forward, nor pressure any other person about him."

Catherine found this to be a meager pittance, but apparently Jack felt otherwise. His eyes smoldered as he battled with conflicting emotions. Finally he nodded grimly. "So be it," he agreed, his voice tight. "I so swear." He looked back up at Peter. "I will have you as my second and referee," he added, contemplating the situation. "Who will Shadow have?"

Catherine chuckled softly at the unusual dilemma. "I also choose Peter," she echoed smoothly. "I have no issue at all in trusting him to judge fairly between us two."

Jack's face showed his surprise, but he nodded. "Then we are resolved," he stated in a calm voice. "First person to three touches; no touch shall be injurious in any manner. Failure to hold to these rules is a breach of honor."

Catherine drew her sword with slow precision, saluted in agreement, then spun it out and down, holding it in a low, backward pointing stance. The hint of a smile flitted on her lips.

"Whenever you are ready."

The three acolytes and priest all backed up a few paces, and Peter took a location between the two combatants. He waited until both were settled and had their eyes on him. He gazed with interest between the two figures before him, almost sizing them up.

He held his hand up, then dropped it with a sudden movement.

"Begin!"

Without a sound, Jack launched into a strong attack, apparently intending to finish the fight quickly. Catherine had been watching him daily for the past few weeks and was quite prepared for this, sidestepping easily and turning to counter. She had no such desire for a quick resolution. If anything, she hoped to get in a word or two while they sparred. It might be their only chance, ever, to discuss the situation for which they fought.

Jack moved in again, his swings strong, and she deflected three more blows in quick succession, only doing the bare minimum to keep her body free of the blade. No need to reveal her strengths just yet.

His pace kept up - strike, counterstrike, feint. Catherine found herself unable to maintain the fight pace and get in a word. The thought that her one chance to talk with Jack as Shadow would get by her filled her with frustration. She decided to take a gamble and change the momentum of the melee. On Jack's next run, Catherine leapt completely out of the way, then spun around in a flash, pounding him hard in the back of his thigh with the flat of her blade.

Peter's voice echoed across the clearing. "A hit!"

Jack came hard around with surprise, and looked at Catherine with a new level of respect. Catherine swung her blade up to her forehead in a salute, then brought it down and right with a sharp movement.

"Now then, Jack," she encouraged, her voice cordial and light. "Let us try this again, shall we?"

Jack came in more cautiously, watching her movements, slowly circling her. This was more Catherine's speed, and she fell into the relaxed pace of her many years of practice.

"I am curious," she inquired, moving her feet to match Jack's in the circling. "You will avenge these two men to the death if necessary. I respect that sense of duty - but I find it misplaced."

Jack made a feint, and she parried smoothly, crossing blades with him a few times. When there was another break, she spoke up again. “What have those two done to deserve such loyalty?” she asked with honest curiosity.

Jack did not slow his pace of circling, but his shoulders relaxed a little as he considered the question.

“They were admirable individuals. For example, there was the flood two springs ago in Gloucester,” he noted. “They graciously helped the flood victims. They donated supplies and their own labor to assist the town in rebuilding.”

Without pausing, Jack launched smoothly into a swing diagonally across her chest. Catherine, shocked by Jack’s words, barely parried the blow to her left, and was completely unable to counter as Jack’s sword turned mid-air, came back, and landed with a loud smack against her left hip. She doubled over in pain, and Jack immediately took a step backwards, withdrawing.

Jack shook his head slightly in confusion as Catherine rubbed at the impact location. She realized that he hadn’t expected the blow to hit; he had assumed she’d block that one, and perhaps three or four after that, before he reached his true attack.

Peter’s voice sounded unsure. “A hit …?” He looked at Catherine in bafflement. “That makes it one apiece.”

Catherine took a deep breath, straightening, then wincing at the throbbing pain coming from her hip. She looked up to meet Jack’s gaze, her eyes smoldering.

“I accept the hit; I should have been prepared for any trick,” she growled, her voice grating in anger. “However, if you deliberately lied in order to gain an advantage ...”

Jack’s stance was wary. “I did not,” he replied, his voice clear with conviction. “I have no reason to doubt that the events happened as I explained.”

Catherine nodded and then began circling again. “I was there, in Gloucester, the night the flooding began,” she explained bitterly. “I carried children to safety; I built dams to try to stem the rising water. I spent weeks afterwards helping the villagers dig themselves out of the sea of mud and rebuild their homes.”

She paused, her throat growing tight at the memory. "That is when Craig and Carl *deigned* to grace us with their presence. They showed up with building materials, that is true. However, they charged outrageous prices for them, on terms that no villager could meet. They threatened to foreclose on several properties after only a month."

She chuckled wryly as she remembered the events. "When I paid the debts out of my own funds, the pair threatened to kill me. Maybe I should have agreed to a duel then, and spared everyone the subsequent traumas."

Catherine was swept by the frustration of that time; of the anger of the villagers who were trapped in debt. She swung into action, going through a series of eight-point swordsman exercises. Jack easily matched each one, and the movement became more a dance of blades than an attack.

Catherine filled with fury that Jack had been misled, was using his talents and energies for a pair who was so undeserving. Still, through her anger and disappointment, as the swords flashed in the sunlight, she was surprised to realize that she was truly enjoying herself. It had been a long time since she'd engaged in this style of swordplay, and she had almost forgotten just how pleasurable it could be.

Apparently Jack felt the same way. The tension in his shoulders eased; his face relaxed. He settled into the rhythm of the exercise, not seeking to break it. He matched her moves and went through the paces without seeking to take advantage.

She could sense the interest in the five pairs of eyes attentively watching them. The warmth of the afternoon sun shone down in glittering gold. A wildflower-infused breeze swept by them, sending grass waving in long fields stretching out to the distant seas.

She almost forgot the serious stake for which they were sparring.

Jack's voice shook her from her rhythm. "The wolves at Beeston," he prompted as he created a figure-eight movement against her. "There was a pack of wolves menacing the farmers in the town." He turned through another series of moves. "The two went in and took on the pack single handedly, for no gain at all."

Something inside her snapped, and she drove her sword hard down toward his right shoulder, knowing he would block her, but needing to feel the sharp impact. She did not allow her sword to skitter down his, but held her place, pressing against him for a long moment.

"Those wolves were no threat," she insisted through gritted teeth as she ground her sword into his. "That was a mother with cubs, part of a quiet pack who had lived in those parts for decades. Those two miscreants were out to impress a tavern wench and brought in ..." Her voice choked off, and it took her a moment to recover.

"It was a *cub* pelt they brought in, stretched and distorted, after they tortured him for hours."

Her eyes held his with deep seriousness. "If these tales are the best you can do ..." she threatened in a low rumble.

Jack held her sword at bay easily; despite her best efforts, her strength was clearly no match for his. Still, she could see the confusion swirling in his grey eyes. Her heart danced with a kindling of hope. Maybe he was, at long last, beginning to harbor doubts about his friends.

Jack pushed Catherine off with a move of his sword, and the two began their circling again. His moves were less aggressive, his eyes pondering, and Catherine drew in a long, deep breath, praying with all her might that he was starting to believe. Her wild, crazy plan may just have worked.

His brow furrowed, and she let him take his time without pressing or distracting him. She would go as long as necessary for him to trust in her, in what she was saying. After all, she had proven herself to him already several times over. She had drawn away Conrad's men when Michael had twisted his ankle. He apparently knew how she had saved Walter's life in the rapids. He undoubtedly also knew how she had helped Peter many times with escort missions.

Surely he could come to accept that her reasons for Carl and Craig's deaths were honorable ones.

Jack's feet slowed, then came to a stop. His eyes were full on her. "There is still one claim the two men can make," he insisted, holding his sword in a guard position rather than an aggressive one. "The girls who were harmed at Kirkstall; Carl and Craig were there while it was happening. I know this is true from other people who worked there. The men stayed there to keep those girls safe. I had first told them about that Abbey four years ago, when ..."

Catherine's world came crashing around her, as if the landscapes and sky had been made of glass, and a barbarian giant with an iron rod had smashed them, demolished them, filling the air with shimmering shards of death.

Every muscle in her body tensed in preparation for a full bore assault. Her blade had seemed a light toy for a sparring match; she spun it so its wickedly sharp edge glittered in the bright sunshine.

She barely recognized her own voice when it cut through the wall of fury which seethed from every pore of her skin.

"*You* were the one who told those two about the Abbey?" Catherine raged in disbelief, unable to fathom how the man before her could have unknowingly set in motion so much evil. "That was *your* fault?"

Jack did not have time to answer, for she vaulted into an attack which used every last iota of her speed and accuracy. Jack only had a microsecond to react before each blow, and he parried furiously to keep the quick stinging blade away from his body.

She saw the moment of awareness, the second when his eyes widened with understanding of her aim. Her blows were not being aimed to contact his flesh. They were deliberately being driven to land hard on his sword.

Catherine did not want to gain a hit. She was looking to slam home the anger and fury Jack had unleashed with repeated bone-jarring contact, blade on blade.

Between blows, Catherine's voice came deep and hoarse, held at a pitch meant for Jack's ears alone. "*You* sent them into that field of lambs?" she raged from between clenched teeth. "You, who knew their reputation for chasing women of any age? You who should have known better? Do you know how many girls they hurt? Do you know how many girls they *killed?*"

Catherine's voice rose in intensity with each attack. "Those were my *friends* ... Those were ..."

Jack's face whitened with sick horror; at last he finally realized the truth of what had happened. Catherine was beyond caring. She was drowning in pain, and anger, and frustration, and all she knew was she had to feel the metal impact, hear the thunderous clash.

Jack took a step back, but she would not let him end the fight. Not like this. She lunged toward him, engaging again. Another step back, and another lunge forward.

On his third retreat, Jack gave his sword a twist, sweeping it before him with a long, arcing move to clear space between them. At the end of its movement, Jack's sword whistled by her right shoulder.

Catherine swung up her sword into a high, angled pose to block. Instantly an unimaginable pain nearly drove her to her knees. She leapt backwards, cutting off the assault, her mind unbelieving. Before her, Jack stood still, his breath coming in ragged heaves, but she no longer cared. She threw her sword down to stand upright in the dirt between them. She drew in long, staggering breaths as she brought her left hand up to press against her right shoulder with strong pressure.

She could barely think past the absolute agony streaming from the wound. Jack had violated the terms of the duel. He had deliberately cut her, wounding her sword arm, because he felt it was his only chance of victory. She could not believe he would go to such lengths to win.

She pressed her left hand down hard on the injury, the warmth of the blood coming up through her fingers. She would not last long with this gash in her tricep. She had to finish it now, to win the fight and get away from him. He was a man without honor. Anger hit her in crashing waves, threatening to overwhelm her completely, and she shook as she fought to retain control. How could she ever have trusted him, cared for him?

She stepped forward and forced herself to pick up the sword with a firm grasp despite the agonizing pain moving further out into her body. She could not show any weakness now. Her world whirled for a moment, and she fought with every ounce of her power to maintain her focus for just a while longer.

Her voice was tight with fury as she issued the command. "Raise your sword."

To her surprise, Jack did not move. He seemed to be listening to another voice. Jack hesitated a moment, his breath slowing, then to Catherine's utter surprise he bent over and slowly, carefully, laid his sword down on the ground. He waited a moment, his fingers touching the hilt, then he straightened up, meeting her gaze steadily.

Catherine gasped; disgust and indignation cascaded over her in torrential waves. He was going to refuse to fight her? Was he truly such a coward? She was losing strength quickly; she knew she would not last long. Her voice rasped out, louder and more urgent. "Pick up your sword!"

Into the silence, Peter's voice rang out sharp and clear. She realized he'd been talking this entire time, that somehow her intense pain had been blocking out his words.

"Catherine Maria Bowyer!" he shouted in exasperation, and Catherine could not help her reaction. A childhood spent in the company of strong willed parents mandated that her head turn, her eyes react when her name was called in this manner.

She heard the gasps around her and swore softly in fury. All hope of resolution was now lost. She did not know how Peter had figured out her secret, but he had ruined everything. Her fury and anger transferred from Jack to Peter in a heartbeat.

"How dare you interfere?" she growled, still holding her sword at the ready.

Peter spoke slowly, enunciating carefully as if talking to a child. Even so, it was only on his second pass that the words started to join together to make sense, to seem more than a random collection of sounds. "Your shoulder stitches have snapped. Jack did *not* touch you," he explained gently.

It was as if she had been a bucket full of water, and someone pulled a large plug out the bottom to release the flow. All of her anger, frustration, energy, and focus went whooshing out of her in one long, fast moving rush. She was suddenly hollow, empty.

The ground came racing up to slam into her, and she flung out her hands to keep it at bay. The impact with her right arm was bone jarring, and she cried out in absolute agony, rolling down on her side as her arm collapsed beneath her.

Jack and Peter were at her side in an instant, turning her over and working to remove her cloak and tunic. She did not have the strength to resist; it did not matter. Everything had been lost. Jack's hands were at her back, quickly undoing the lacing and sliding the white chemise off her shoulder to reveal the shoulder wound. It had been pulled open and was bleeding heavily.

Jack groaned. "God's Teeth, Catherine."

Peter hurried to his horse for his medical kit. Jack reached to the other shoulder, pulling aside the fabric to check for injuries there.

Catherine flinched instinctively but had no strength to stop him. It did not matter now, anyway. She felt Jack stop dead when he slid the cloth past her shoulder, revealing a small but clear burn in the shape of an eight sided star with one spoke missing. He hesitantly put his fingers on the mark, and when he spoke again, his voice was soft and incredibly tender.

"Did Carl and Craig do this as well?"

"Yes," replied Catherine, that one word costing her more than a lifetime of spilt blood. "That was a long time ago, when I was a teenager. A kidnapping attempt, barely foiled."

Jack was silent for a long moment. He appeared to be in shock, lost in memories. "Branded like my parents," he finally murmured to himself. He slid the fabric up to cover the scar, but left his hand there, holding her shoulder. "That is a badge of honor," he added softly, his voice thick with emotion. "You should be proud of the battles you have survived."

Peter jostled his way back by her side and knelt to work on her bleeding arm. He prepared the area by first wiping away the blood with a cloth.

He looked up at Jack as he worked, his gaze rich with concern. "She is going to need some drink and something to bite on; this is not going to be pleasant."

Jack glanced around, and Walter was by his side, offering a flagon of mead. Jack took it and put it to Catherine's lips. Avoiding his eyes, she chugged down the warm liquid, knowing well what was in store for her. Then, without hesitating, Jack loosened the laces of his bracer that he wore on his right wrist.

"No," Catherine bit out against the pain, seeing what he was about to do. "That is a present from your father. I will not let you disfigure that."

Jack laid a hand gently against her cheek, and for a moment her pain seemed to fade away. He looked down at Catherine with a mixture of admiration and amusement. "I think it is time we both are able to accept our bodies and our scars. I will volunteer to be the first. I will no longer hide behind this bracer; this leather is far better suited to keep you from pain."

He finished unlacing and offered the soft leather to Catherine. She hesitated for a moment, then took it between her teeth. Jack gripped both of her hands in his own and then turned to nod to Peter. "Go ahead," he prompted. "Let us get this over with."

The pain was searing, even worse than it had been before. Catherine closed her eyes tightly against it, biting down on the soft leather and squeezing Jack's hands. The pain seemed to go on forever, coming in waves that threatened to overwhelm her. Jack's steady voice gave an anchor for her to cling to. After what seemed to be hours, Peter was done and wrapped the bandages against the wound. Catherine finally opened her eyes to find Jack watching her, and she smiled faintly into his concern.

Jack extricated his right hand from her grasp and gently brushed the hair away from her face. “Surely there was an easier way to do this,” he commented, half in jest.

“You know there was not,” she responded quietly, caught in his stare. “I was willing to risk everything to see this through.”

Jack lowered his head to bury his face against her shoulder, holding her gently for a few full minutes. After a while he lifted her easily, carrying her over to a spot by the fire in a mossy bank. “I think we will be calling it a day,” he suggested as he laid her down. “There is no need to get going until tomorrow. You have been told to give that shoulder a rest many times now. Maybe this time you will actually listen.”

Catherine did not have the will to argue; her energy was completely drained. It was hard to even keep her eyes open. The moment Jack laid her on the ground, she rolled onto her left side and fell into a deep sleep.

Chapter 16

Catherine woke suddenly in moonlit darkness, startled out of a dream. She found her hand still entwined with Jack's, his sleeping face only a short distance from her own. He looked so peaceful in rest, his brow no longer furrowed with worry. She reached forward with her free hand to gently trace the side of his face.

He awoke with a start, his own hand coming down on top of hers automatically in a trapping motion. He relaxed when he saw her face, realized who had roused him.

Catherine flushed. "I am sorry," she offered softly. "You need to get your rest."

Jack hushed her with a smile. "There is time enough later to rest," he reassured her in a low voice, his eyes held on hers. "I do not wish to lose a minute with you."

Catherine searched his eyes, melting as she realized that they held not anger or distance, but caring and love. She gripped his hand with her own, overwhelmed that after everything he could still care for her so much. A single tear escaped from her eye and slowly trailed its way down her cheek.

Jack let out a soft oath as if his resolve had finally been pushed to the breaking point. He leant forward and pressed his lips to her, giving her a gentle kiss.

Catherine closed her eyes, bringing her injured right arm carefully on top of him, pressing his body close to hers. His hard muscles stretched against the full length of her form, reassuringly strong and stable. She lost herself in the kiss, surrendering herself to him.

Her breath coming in deep, ragged gulps when at last they parted. She could see by his eyes that he was awash in the same powerful emotion.

Jack chuckled softly to himself, his eyes ablaze with passion. "To think I was jealous of Shadow," he murmured huskily, tracing her face with his fingers. "When I thought that you had run off to him ..."

Catherine took another look at his face, the torment in his eyes, and drew him down into a passionate kiss, yielding everything to him.

When they finally separated, she lay back, gazing into his eyes for a long time. Eventually exhaustion overtook her and she fell into a deep sleep.

* * *

When Catherine awoke the next morning, the camp was already up and active. Jack was at the fire, helping to serve the elderly priest. Catherine kept her eyes closed for a while, sorting through her thoughts.

While Jack had shown his care for her, she had no doubt that he also had many questions about what she had done as Shadow, and the fate of his friends. She would need to find a way to address his concerns while also shielding the identity of the others involved. She was sure that it would not take long for the topic to come up in conversation; she simply had to make sure she took care in how she directed the discussion.

She unfolded herself from her cloak; immediately all eyes turned to her. Jack and Peter quickly came over to help her move to the side of the fire.

Catherine took care to keep her injured arm immobile. "I am fine, I am not an invalid," she protested. She glanced up at Peter. "If you recall, I had far worse injuries only a few weeks ago. If it is only my arm that is bothering me now, I am ahead in the game."

Peter shook his head, his eyes twinkling. He scooped out a bowl of stew and handed it to her. "Yes, and I spent quite a bit of time patching you up that time. A lot of good it did me, with you completely ignoring my instructions to let the arm heal."

Catherine huffed, although her lips curved up into a smile. "I did! I went *weeks* without much physical activity. How long do you think I could last? It was sheer torture ..."

Michael, John, and Walter were watching her with wide eyes, sipping mulled wine from short pewter cups.

John was the first to speak up. "So you *did* receive those wounds while fighting Carl and Craig?" His voice held awe. "How could they have touched you, when you fought so well against Jack?"

Catherine winced; while she had expected the topic to come up soon, surely she could have gone more than five minutes without being drawn into this!

Peter quickly spoke up, turning to fix John with a steady look. "I do not think that is an appropriate -"

Catherine made herself smile and waved Peter off. "No, that is fine," she soothed placatingly. "They want to hear and will be on pins and needles until I divulge some details. Let us just get this out in the open."

She kept her eyes fixed on the trio, but she was acutely aware of Jack sitting to one side of her. She knew that of all the people here, it was to him that her message would be going.

She leant back against the rock near her, took a bite of stew, and thought for a moment. Maybe if she handled this well she could buy herself some time on the more difficult discussion with him.

"There were three main reasons that I was injured so heavily when I fought those two men," she stated, looking at each of the three teens in turn. "As we continue our journey, when you name for me those reasons, I will explain how they affected the fight. That will give you something to think about, and keep me from having to talk non-stop for the next two days. So, what would the first reason be?"

John leapt at the idea immediately. "They were stronger than you!" he cried out, apparently thrilled that he could finally use his personal excuse in a discussion. Michael and Walter rolled their eyes, but looked to Catherine to see what she would say.

Catherine nodded slowly in agreement. "Yes, that is true," she conceded, taking bites of her breakfast as she spoke. "They were taller; they had a longer reach. They had more strength and more physical mass. I was quicker than they were, but if they anticipated my blow and got their sword in the way of it, there was no way I could 'power through' them. They could block just as if I had swung at a stone wall."

She nibbled on her muffin. "Conversely, if they swung at me, my only hope was to deflect the blow. I could not simply stop it. If I tried, they would plow through my block and land against me. Perhaps not with the edge of the sword, but with its pounding force which could be just as harmful."

Michael's voice was thoughtful. "That was not an issue with Jack," he mused.

Catherine nodded again. "You are correct, because we were deliberately fighting to touch only. Neither of us could use strength without risking harming the other. We could only use gentle touches. Therefore my quickness had an advantage over his strength. He could block me, but if I was quick, I could get in anyway. I could block him, because he was not using his full strength against me."

Her mind went back over the fight of the previous day. "Remember near the end of the fight, when I directly aimed swings at his sword?" The three young men nodded in unison. "Those blows were coming down with my full force. Every ounce of my strength was behind those blows - but I knew there was no danger of Jack actually being hurt. He felt the impact, certainly, but the blows would never have gotten through his blocks, despite me using the full power in my body. There would simply be no way for me to muscle through a solid block of Jack's. He is too strong."

Walter's voice was petulant. "So what was all of the story you gave us about us having an advantage?"

Catherine smiled. "Remember, the whole point of my talks with you was that you were to appear defenseless and weak.

You were to elicit a certain feeling in your opponent's mind, so that he reacted to you in that manner. However, when I faced Jack, what did I do?"

Walter brightened. "He thought you were a skilled warrior!" he shouted, understanding spreading over his face.

"Exactly," replied Catherine. "I wanted the confrontation to happen. He would not respect me if he felt I was weak; his honor would not allow it. So I presented myself as strong and capable; a threat. He therefore treated me as such."

Walter's eyes clouded with confusion. "Why did you want to face Jack?" he asked, looking over to where Jack sat behind Catherine.

Catherine didn't answer; she looked down to her stew to finish off the last bites. Jack glanced at her, then quietly spoke up. "Because I wanted to fight Shadow," he responded, his voice thoughtful. "It was something that needed to be resolved, so she presented herself to resolve it."

Catherine couldn't help herself; she turned and looked back at Jack, catching his gaze. The question died on her lips. She could not bring herself to ask it, in case the answer was not what she was hoping for.

Jack looked into her eyes for a moment, then nodded, a knowing smile touching the corners of his lips. "Aye," he murmured softly, his voice pitched for her alone. "It is resolved."

* * *

Catherine rode in the wagon for the morning, stretching out against a comfortable mound of heavy blankets. The sun drifted in golden streaks through the gentle spring breezes. The boys kept up a happy chatter with her, discussing block techniques and arm-length issues. Peter and Jack stayed close behind, adding in commentary and enjoying the travel.

Catherine glanced up at Jack, a warm smile passing between the two. She was more relaxed than she had in many months.

Even her shoulder seemed to throb less painfully as they moved at a slow pace along the well-maintained road.

Lunch and dinner passed with leisurely conversation, and soon Catherine found herself on night watch with Jack by her side. She had worried that he would press her about Shadow, but instead he sat in a comfortable silence, simply being there with her.

After a while had passed, Jack looked over at Catherine. A tightness settled across her shoulders, but he gave her a reassuring smile. He took her hand in his own, turned it over and tenderly pressed his lips to the inside of her wrist, holding the kiss for a long while. Catherine's tension melted away like remnants of snow on a sun drenched meadow.

Finally Jack looked up and put his other hand in the neck of his tunic, withdrawing the pendant that hung there. It was the granite snowdrop. Catherine traced its shape, then looked up into his eyes. He nodded slowly.

"Catherine, I trust that your reasons were ethical and sound. I do not need to hear anything more. I understand if, for whatever reason, you must remain silent. I believe completely in you, and in your honor."

A wave of relief washed through Catherine's soul, cleansing out the remaining shadows, leaving a radiant glow coursing through her.

Her eyes returned to the elegantly carved snowdrop, to all that it signified. She remembered with vivid clarity the day she had given it to him, Her mind followed to how she had been forced to push him away, and how he had asked …

Her eyes moved up to hold his, shining with emotion. "You asked me a question, that day in the woods," she murmured huskily. "One I was not given an opportunity to answer. I will give you that answer now. It was solely my pledge to my council to focus on my betrothal with Lord Epworth which kept me apart from you. If it had not been for that task, I would have encouraged your courtship with all my heart."

She held up her hand, showing him the brown ring which she still wore on her finger.

Jack's eyes went to the ring, and then he was drawing her into a tender embrace, kissing her, wrapping her in his warmth. She gave herself fully to the kiss, becoming lost in him, holding nothing back.

It was a long while before she separated from him, her breath coming in deep draws, her body almost glowing.

A great weight lifted from her shoulders. She leant against him, resting her head on his broad chest. Jack put his arm around her, and the two sat for many long hours, watching the shadows of clouds drift across the ebony sky.

* * *

The three boys were eager and alert when Catherine made her way to breakfast the next morning. Walter barely let her get settled before his voice burst from him.

"All right, we know they were stronger than you were. That was point one. I think that the second point is that they took you on as a team, just like when Michael, John, and I take on enemies as a team. It can be impossible for you to keep track of both of them at once. Is that right?"

Catherine nodded, smiling with pleasure. "Very good, Walter!" she praised him. "You are exactly right. It is not just that you are fighting two opponents. If you had two opponents that did not work well together, that could be in your benefit. However, if you face a team of enemies who are very good at what they do, the problems multiply."

She thought back to the fight, to the way the men had moved. "They were like a pair of wolves," she recalled, her voice lost in the memory. "It was uncanny; they had fought together for so long that it was instinctive to them. They did not have to give any sign at all to each other. One would move, and the other would counter-move. It was spell-binding. I was fascinated by it, even while they pummeled me."

She shook her head to dispel the memory. "In any case, there are three of you," she pointed out to the eager listeners, "which means you have it even easier when you face an enemy. With two, the second person has to be right behind you to be out of sight. With three of you, it is nearly impossible to keep track of what you all are doing. I will show you some more tricks today that should help you really take advantage of that."

The day went by quickly with Catherine, Jack, and Peter taking turns working with the lads as they walked, giving advice and suggestions. The conversations carried on through dinner and it was a while before the three lads settled down into their bedding for the night.

Catherine smiled as their voices continued in a low murmur from the mounds of blankets, then moved to sit beside Jack on a weathered log by the fire. The night sky was brilliant with stars, and her eyes automatically tracked to find Cancer, its quiet shape almost lost in the multitudes.

Her mind was sent back to those nights of torment, thirteen years ago, when she stared in desperation at the shelled constellation, wishing she had her own protective armor to defend herself from her captors.

Her hand moved to her left shoulder, to the brand, and she reminded herself that at long last justice had been done. Her years of training and searching and preparation had, finally, brought some peace to her soul.

She realized that Jack was gazing at her with steady eyes, and she resisted the urge to look away. He had seen her mark, and he had recognized it. Perhaps he was one of the only people in the world who could understand what she had gone through.

Her voice was low but steady when she spoke. "Jack, tell me about your parents."

Jack smiled faintly, nodding, his eyes moving briefly to her shoulder before beginning. "We moved to our village when I was five or six; I only have wisps of memories of where we lived before then. My father was a leather worker, while my mother was talented with herbal medicine. I had, perhaps, a typical childhood. I spent time with the sheriff, learning swordplay and building my skills."

He paused for a moment. “As it so happens, that was where I was on the day of the attack.”

He looked down at his hands. “I came home late that evening, much later than usual. It was already long past dark. Our house was fully ablaze. I pushed my way through the flaming debris and found them both inside, dead. They had been tortured, then killed. The house had been set afire around their corpses, perhaps to cover the attackers’ tracks.”

He paused for a long moment, and Catherine could see the pain shadow his eyes. “A madness took over my brain at seeing my parents laying mutilated and slain. I was only in my teens at the time, but I felt sure if I had been home that I could have protected them from harm. I dove into the woods, determined to track down those responsible.”

He grew quiet, lost in his memories. Catherine waited patiently, allowing him to reveal his story in his own time.

“I became lost in the forest, roaming for hours. By the time dawn came I knew the attackers were far away; I focused on finding my own way back to the village, to tell others what I had seen. It was then that I came across a campfire with two men tending it. They were craftsmen, and they welcomed me in with surprised pleasure.”

Catherine nodded slowly. “Carl and Craig,” she stated, her voice cool.

Jack looked up, meeting her eyes. “Yes.” He took in a deep breath. “I was exhausted and starving. They brought me a blanket and fed me a warm breakfast. They listened with sympathy to my story. I thought I was extremely lucky to have come across their camp. They offered to escort me back to the village, and I readily agreed.

“We passed through a larger town along the way, and the men had me hide in their wagon for my own safety while they went in to get news. When they came out, they told me that the assassins had been through here, and were letting it be known that they were now hunting me down. The two men advised me to go into hiding - to make a new start somewhere where I would not be known, where I would be safe."

Jack looked out into the distance, lost in the memories. "They promised to take up my cause as their own, to track down the men responsible. I could not believe in my good fortune, to have found such loyal men. They took me to Worcester, setting me up there as a page of the household. Then they left, out to track down my parents' killers."

Catherine saw how this would play out. "Eventually they told you that they found them," she guessed.

Jack nodded wearily. "Oh yes, I got updates every few weeks as to their progress, and then came the fateful day. Carl and Craig came back to me triumphant. They had found the mercenaries involved in the attack and had killed them. I still remember how much I looked up to those two men. They were my heroes. I owed them everything - my current station, the revenge for my parents. I would have done anything for them."

Catherine looked down. "I am sorry, Jack."

Jack shook his head, then turned to look Catherine in the eyes. His own were shadowed in pain. "With all you have told me, it now seems likely they were the ones responsible for my parents' deaths. The facts all seem to fit." His lips drew into a tense line. "The question is, why? Why kill my parents? Why lie to me, why hide me away? Were they protecting me, or using me as leverage for something?"

Catherine twined her fingers into his. "Together, I am sure we can figure this out. There must be an answer."

Jack maintained his eye contact and took a deep breath. "Catherine, there is something else."

Catherine had known this was coming, and she resisted the temptation to look away. It was better to face this head on. "My scar."

Jack nodded slowly. "When I found my parents dead, I told you that they had been tortured. My father was a leather worker. They had branded them with his tools, maybe in an attempt to get them to talk. I knew those tools well; I saw them every day of my life." His eyes flickered to her shoulder. "One in particular was an eight sided star. When I was a child I used it for sword practice, and one day I broke off one of the star's points. It became a symbol my father loved; it gave him a sense that we should treasure our full selves, including our imperfections."

His grey eyes were steady, drawing her in. "Whoever placed that mark on you would seem to be the same men who tortured and killed my parents eighteen years ago. They must have taken the tools with them when they left."

Catherine's throat closed up. She had never talked about the incident, not even to her mother. But Jack deserved to know, to confirm his suspicions about his parents' murders.

"It was thirteen years ago that I was captured, when I was thirteen years old," she whispered hoarsely. "It was Carl and Craig who took me hostage when I was riding alone. They … they branded me …" Tears streamed from her eyes, and her voice failed her. She could not do it. Despite the many years which separated her from those long, dark nights, the pain was still too powerful, too visceral.

Jack's strong arms wrapped around her, drawing her against his chest, and she felt the safety, the protectiveness of his body around hers.

His voice came softly in her ear. "I am here for you, whenever you want to talk about it," he promised. "If you want to leave it in the past, then that is fine as well. All that matters is that we are together now."

Catherine curled up close against him, shutting her eyes against the night.

* * *

Catherine sat for a long while by herself the next morning, turning her spiral medallion around in her hands, lost in thought. The day was overcast, and her mood was quiet as well. She was not up for much conversation, and was curious what the three boys would have waiting for her to discuss at breakfast.

She finally stood and went over to join the group, taking her stew from the pot with a quiet nod to the wizened priest. The boys seemed to share in her somber mood; if anything, they seemed a bit sullen. Apparently the third point had not come quite as easily to them. She felt sorry for having affected their usual optimism like this.

"Come now, I know the weather is sour," she prompted, forcing a grin. "Let us see what we can work out on your current puzzle. Surely you have some guesses," she encouraged them gently.

Michael spoke up this time, his studious voice tenuous in the damp morning air. "The others do not agree with me," he stated slowly, "However, I saw the bruising on your back when Peter was stitching you up."

He drummed his fingers on his leg. "I have seen men who have been in fights. If they win, they might have a few minor cuts. If they lose, they could have earned some serious welts. But you went beyond that - you were crisscrossed with bruises on bruises." He paused, then continued more slowly. "I think they beat you on purpose, not as a side result of the fight."

Jack glanced sharply at Peter, who nodded in agreement. Jack then turned to look with concern at Catherine.

She sat, lost in thought for a long while, staring into the campfire. Michael waited in patient silence, as the logs crackled and settled. After a while, she shook herself and looked up.

"Yes, that is true," she finally agreed. "I was not going to count that in with the third point, but I suppose after all that is a part of it. If they had been content merely to kill me, then most likely I would now be dead. Instead, they wanted to send a message. My broken body was going to be that message. They took a long time to do their work, and that gave me the opportunity to find a weakness I could use."

She paused, her mind caught up in the memories. She knew that Jack and Peter were listening intently, and took her time in wording her response. "I had finally, after all the years, caught the pair at an illegal activity that could be proven beyond all shadow of a doubt. I told them they would be brought in for justice." Her mouth quirked in a wry smile. "They thought it ludicrous that anyone could pass judgment on what they wished to do. They wanted to make sure that others thought twice before coming after them."

She took a deep breath, then pressed on. "They used every dirty trick I had heard of, and many more that they had invented themselves. They each wielded a sword and flail, so that they could do as much damage as possible without killing me immediately. They ... they seemed to enjoy it. It was all I could do to keep the blows from falling. Many times I could not do that."

Her voice trailed away, but she forced herself to continue. "In the end, it was their own arrogance that undid them. They felt that no person could stand up to these attacks. They became more cavalier, not protecting themselves during the blows. I saw that, and knew I only had one choice. When Craig went for my shoulder, I let the blow connect. He was not expecting that to happen, and it made him lose his balance for a moment. That was when I was able to send my own sword in to kill him."

Catherine paused a moment at the memory, then went on. "Carl went into a madness when he saw Craig fall. I do not think it ever occurred to him that they could die. His rage made him sloppy, and I was able to get in a blow to him after a few passes. He went down, and the fight was over."

Michael's eyes were wide. "Then what happened?"

Catherine looked up, her eyes holding calm acceptance. "I dropped like a stone," she admitted without reservation. "As far as I was concerned, I was going to die, too. My wounds were serious. However, I knew that I had achieved my goals, the girl was safe, the lecherous pair were finally dead. Beyond that, I did not really care."

"Why you?" pressed Michael. "Why did *you* have to take action? Why not just report them to the authorities?"

Catherine paused for a long while, realizing that she had said more than she meant to. The clearing was silent.

Jack's face was a mask of self-control. It was clear that he wanted to know more, and that he was holding his tongue with great effort.

Finally Catherine nodded to herself. She turned to look over to Peter. "Could you bring me my sword, please? I imagine you put it back on my horse's saddle."

Peter nodded and went to fetch the blade, bringing it back to her in a few minutes. She drew it out of its sheath, looking with fondness down its length. Then she rested it on the ground and unwrapped the copper wire and green leather binding on the hilt.

When she had removed them, she handed the blade to Michael. "There is an emblem that was tucked within the binding. What does that say?" she asked quietly.

Michael worked out the letters engraved on the metal oval, now visible. "It says ... VERITAS," he read slowly. "That means 'truth' in Latin."

Jack's eyes flashed to Catherine's, meeting them. "Veritas - the sword of truth," he expanded to the young men. "That was the name given to the sword that the reeve of the Bowyers would wield. We thought that position was halted a hundred years ago, when the church took over those protective responsibilities."

Catherine laughed without mirth. "As if we would abandon our people because the church claimed they would do a better job," she rebutted smoothly. "No, the position has remained in action, and we still hold tournaments every five years to choose a new reeve. The last tournament was held four years ago." The corners of her mouth turned up in a smile. "It is a swordfight to first touch," she added lightly.

"A fight which you won," replied Jack, a smile growing across his own face.

Catherine nodded. "Raymond, my cousin, was furious. He claimed that it was not fair, that in a real fight he could have easily bested me. Who knows, that could be true. However, these tournaments have been run the same way for hundreds of years. They cannot be changed because one man feels his chances were weakened by those rules."

She sighed, continuing. "Undaunted, then Raymond brought up another problem. I had been declared dead while we investigated the assassination attempt. How could I perform my duties when I could not be seen by outsiders?"

"As a result, you invented Shadow," Jack responded, awareness brightening his eyes. "With that cover, you could travel the lands and help keep order, all without it being known that Catherine was still alive. That is why you were there to rescue Walter, and why you helped out at the cathedral."

His brow furrowed. "If that is the case, why did you say you could not get involved when Michael twisted his ankle? Surely that would be exactly what the reeve would be doing."

Catherine's gaze shadowed. "The council looked with hostility on the church which had stripped its power," she ground out, dropping her eyes. "They held grudges quite admirably. I was instructed to stay far away from any church-related activities, although I made an exception in Peter's case. I wanted to be able to see him when I could, even if it was in disguise. Which reminds me," she added, turning to face Peter. "How did you know who I was, at the end of our duel?"

Peter smiled gently. "Your speech was the first giveaway. I was hard pressed to think that you spoke so similarly just because you came from the same region. Finally, though, it was your shoulder injury. Jack had clearly not touched you, and it seemed an outrageous coincidence that you and Shadow both had a serious injury on the exact same part of your body. Once I realized that, everything else fell into place."

Catherine nodded, then turned solemn again. "I do not mind you all knowing my identity. However, if the church found out we were still active, there would be heavy repercussions on the Bowyer family. I would appreciate it if this stayed within our group."

The men all quickly agreed to this. Catherine lapsed into silence, and seeing that the conversation was over, the rest packed up for the day's journey.

To Catherine's surprise, Father Berram came over to sit with her for a few minutes as the camp was being taken down.

"My dear," he stated in a querulous voice, "I am so glad that you are all right." He patted her hand tenderly with his own.

Catherine smiled gently down at the stooped figure, seemingly so frail that the gentlest of breezes would blow him over. He had been quiet throughout much of the journey, and she had begun to think of him as unaware of what was going on around him.

"Thank you, Father," she responded with a smile. "Soon we will have you to your friend's house, and this traveling will be done with."

"I look forward to that," agreed Father Berram with a nod. "Father Oswold is dear to me." He looked over toward the wagon, and Catherine helped him to stand, then boosted him into his traditional spot in a nest of hay. Michael climbed up to take the reins, and in a moment they were underway.

Chapter 17

The next few days drifted by in languorous relaxation for Catherine. The mornings were spent strolling through the warm spring sunshine, helping the acolytes learn and improve their skills. During the afternoons, Peter took on the training while she and Jack walked hand in hand, sharing the simple pleasures of being together. In the velvet of night, when the rest of the world slept, they shared the watch, unveiling their turbulent pasts to each other's tender care.

Jack had not pressed Catherine about her childhood abduction, nor about the reason she had faced Carl and Craig. His understanding warmed her immensely. There were some things she was simply not ready to broach yet.

It seemed all too soon when they began to near Oxford, the junction where Catherine had to break off to take her own path northwards toward Bedford and Lord Xavier. The parting lay heavy on her mind as she sat alongside Jack in the moonlight, the gentle rustle of leaves stirring all around them.

Catherine raised her hand in the air before her. She ran her thumb along the brown ring, her eyes moving to meet Jack's somber gaze.

"I promise I will come back to you when our tasks are over," she vowed softly. "There is still so much I would like to tell you, so much I would like to learn about you. After I finish this mission at hand, I should be able to speak more freely. However, it is critical that I first meet with Lord Xavier. I believe even more strongly now that he holds the key to much of what has gone on. Now that I am no longer pretending to be dead, I can finally press him for the truth."

Jack nodded in acceptance. He ran his hand tenderly through her hair before drawing her into a strong embrace.

Catherine sighed with pleasure, willing herself to remember every moment of the evening. If only she had met him years ago ... but maybe it would not have been the same then. She might not have been ready to give up her independence.

Jack's voice rumbled out against her. "I still wish that I could accompany you on your path, or that you could put the trip off and come with us instead," he murmured.

She shook her head against him. "You cannot make this trip with me," she replied. "I must do this alone, for several reasons. You need to finish your journey with the boys and Father Berram. I will be back to you soon enough, and the roads here have been quite peaceful."

When Peter took over the watch, Jack came with Catherine to lay down by her side. Jack's eyes were steady on her, and eventually Catherine drifted off into a deep sleep under his watchful gaze.

Morning dawned with a gentle drizzle. After breakfast, Catherine gave each party member a gentle hug, and wished them all good travels. When she came to Jack, she simply pressed her hand against his chest, feeling where the carved flower lay nestled there. He put his own over hers, pressing it against him, his thumb moving gently against the brown ring she wore. He held her gaze for a long time.

She gave a nod. "I will find you soon," she promised softly.

"I will be waiting," he responded with a smile. "Stay safe."

She mounted and nudged her steed to a walk. When she had reached the horizon, she turned and stopped for a brief look back, her hand held high in farewell. Then she moved forward again and the party disappeared beyond the hill.

* * *

Jack watched her vanish from sight, his heart heavy. Turning, he prodded the group into motion, taking the road on toward St. Albans.

Father Berram perked up into greater alertness as they neared the hometown of his childhood friend. The three lads focused with fresh enthusiasm on the fascinating adventures they would find in the town.

The land became more forested and they began to pass a greater selection of travelers. A pair of elderly nuns strolled past them, enjoying a leisurely walk home. A red-haired farmer and four bright-eyed girls passed them in a cart, delighting in a trip to visit relatives. Four merchants in gaudy outfits on horseback, their leader a small man with tight blond curls, overtook them, offering a selection of knot-work jewelry before continuing on their path.

Jack drew solace from the relaxed cheer of their fellow travelers. The roads were safe, and the weather was warm and fresh. Catherine would have a good time of her trip.

With five days left in their journey, they drew into the ring of towns surrounding Oxford. While they were generally avoiding inns and public locations, their path would take them right through the Christ's Church environs, and they agreed to stay there the next evening.

The thought made Jack nervous. He was comfortable protecting the group in the wild, where he could stand watch and listen for horses. In the middle of a bustling town, with people on all sides, it would be nearly impossible to ward off a determined assassin, if indeed any lurked about. But was there really any danger? It seemed that the past troubles had evaporated, leaving them with a quiet calm. Still …

Jack ended up spending the night contemplating ways to keep the religious men safe, and devising methods he might coordinate with Peter to handle sleeping arrangements. When Peter came on watch, Jack talked with him at length about the issues, ending up with no sleep at all. He laughed it off with Peter as the two shook the others awake.

"I did this often as a young man," Jack admitted with a smile. "Maybe it is good for the system, to do it every few years. We can get a good night's rest this coming evening."

Still, as the day wore on and they moved into more populated areas, the strain of watching each new face wearied him. Eventually they found a quiet hill between villages to have their evening meal. Dinner conversation was lively between Peter and the three boys, but Jack found himself hard pressed to get caught up in it.

Dusk drifted into an ebony night, and soon a large, full moon slowly rose in the sky. He acknowledged to himself that he had been quiet since Catherine had left, and was tingeing his observations with that melancholy, but even so the moon looked pale and shadowy through the mists. A chill drifted through his soul.

He waited for the boys to settle down to sleep, then headed out on a long walk while Peter took the first watch. The damp moss underfoot gave a musty smell which soothed him, but a tenseness remained across his shoulders. As he neared the camp again, Peter came out to meet him.

"What is bothering you, Jack," asked Peter, his voice low with concern. "You have seemed on edge all day. You should be asleep now, catching up on lost rest. This is my watch."

Jack rubbed at his neck absently. "I know I will need my sleep, to be alert when my turn comes. I just cannot seem to do it." He cracked a half smile, sighing. "Perhaps I am coming down with something."

Peter patted his friend on the shoulder. "I think we know where your 'illness' lies," he grinned. "If anyone is truly sick, I am," he added. "My throat is killing me!"

Jack rolled his shoulders to release some of the stress that had settled there. "It is more than just missing her," he insisted. "It is a strong sense that something is wrong. Something with Catherine."

Peter looked fondly at his friend. "We have talked about the logistics a hundred times," he soothed gently. "Catherine will be fine. She is somewhere safe, and she is on an important diplomatic mission. She would not be any safer if she was here in the woods with us. She will catch up with us in no time."

Jack shook his head. It was as if something were buzzing at him, gnawing at his memory. "I imagine you are right," he acknowledged without much enthusiasm. "It is just -"

A strangled cry split the night, coming from the direction of their camp. Both men burst into a run, sprinting the short distance to the small clearing.

The campfire had been kicked out of its stone ring, the sprawled logs sending flickering light wildly across the scene. The elderly priest was standing behind it, white with horror, shaking like a leaf.

John and Michael knelt on either side of Walter, holding him up in a sitting position, trying desperately to staunch the heavy stream of blood pouring from a gaping wound in his stomach.

Chapter 18

Peter immediately ran to Walter's side, dropping to one knee to examine the wound. Jack quickly scanned the area, but seeing no enemies, he moved to the priest, taking his arms gently but firmly in both hands.

He strove to keep his voice calm, to focus Father Berram's attentions. "Who was it? Who attacked?"

The elderly priest shook his head in confusion, his grey wisps of hair wildly askew. "We did not see anybody," he insisted, fear causing a tremor in his voice. "None of us did. We woke up when Walter cried out, but there was nobody here. It does not make any sense!"

Peter called over to Jack, his voice low but urgent. "He is hurt badly. I cannot handle this myself. We have to get him to Oxford immediately."

Jack did not question his friend. Within five minutes they had the camp packed into the wagon and were moving at a fast pace toward the cathedral. They had planned on arriving there the following afternoon, taking their time. Jack hoped desperately that they could cover the distance in only an hour or two if they pushed the horses as fast as they could go. Every extra moment reduced Walter's chance of survival.

The travel spun by in a blur of speed and worry. The moment that the cathedral was in sight, Jack galloped on ahead to get the gates open in advance of the cart. To his annoyance, the guards on watch questioned him at length about the group, ignoring his pleas for haste. The Captain of the Guard himself came up to the wall to shout down queries, which Jack tersely responded to. The wagon had almost reached the gates before the guards reluctantly pulled them open. Then each man was thoroughly patted down; all weapons were removed before they could move to the central courtyard.

Walter had not regained consciousness and his pulse was faint. Leaving Peter to get the others settled, Jack picked Walter up in his arms. The wound seemed even worse in the bright torchlight of the hallways, the blood and bile staining his clothes. A young, freckled page appeared, leading Jack through the maze of buildings and hallways to the infirmary area. A pair of doctors waited, apparently alerted by the guards, and went to work immediately. Jack took a deep breath and fell back onto a wooden bench that lined one wall, exhaustion nearly overwhelming him.

He turned to the young page. "Can you tell my companion, Peter, where I am?" The boy nodded and ran off. The two doctors worked in near silence, mopping at the wound and attempting to clear it out. Jack knew better than to trouble them with questions while they worked, and watched with his lips moving in silent prayer.

In about fifteen minutes Peter came in to sit beside him. He was rubbing his throat, his face serious. "The others are settled in a room, and the Captain has put a guard at their door. I did not question him; he seemed rather testy. In fact, the whole cathedral seems to be on alert. There are a number of guarded rooms, and none of the soldiers I passed were in a mood to talk. What is going on?" He gave a few hacking coughs.

Jack shook his head and looked over again at Walter lying motionless on the table. "I do not know," he murmured quietly. "I just do not know."

One of the doctors let out a long sigh, and Jack looked up. The doctor was holding a finger against Walter's neck, and shook his head at the other doctor. The two men looked over at Jack and Peter.

"I am very sorry," consoled the elder doctor, his voice somber. "He lost too much blood. I am afraid he has passed on."

The doctor took a cloth from a nearby table and laid it over Walter's body.

Jack stood and walked over to Walter, laying a hand on the sheet for a moment. This had happened on his watch. He had been responsible for the group, and he had let himself get distracted. This was his fault. Shame and anger burned hotly on his face.

Peter's hacking at his side grew worse, and Jack felt irrationally upset with Peter for disturbing the death bed. One of the doctors gave Peter a large mug of mulled wine and a brown scarf dipped in herbs to wrap around his throat. Peter tied it and almost immediately his cough lessened. Jack bowed his head and gave a silent prayer for Walter.

After a few minutes Jack let Peter lead him away, up the stairs to the room the two were to share.

A wooden platter of bread and pints of ale waited for them in their room; Jack realized he was starving and exhausted all at once. It was a few hours after midnight. The full moon was now obscured by thick clouds, and the candle on the table barely held off the pitch darkness.

The pair ate the bread as they talked, trying to make sense of the evening's events.

Jack shook his head. "Why would they have killed Walter, and then vanished?" he asked for the tenth time. "Why Walter, and not the others? Was anything stolen?"

"No, nothing," rasped Peter, looking down into his ale. "We went over everything we could think of during that ride. There was nothing missing. The others do not remember anything at all out of the ordinary - not a noise, not a movement. It is as if a ghost slipped in, singled out Walter for some reason, and then fled again."

He took a long swallow, grimacing as the liquid moved down his throat. "John and Michael could not think of any enemy at all in Walter's life. No unpaid debts, no badly used girlfriends. Walter was a friend to everyone he met. There was nothing, nothing."

Peter looked up at Jack, an idea flashing into his mind. "You were feeling nervous right before they called out. Maybe you had heard something? Sensed something?"

Jack shook his head, taking another swallow of ale. "That was not it," he avowed, although uncertainty crept into his thoughts. He had been *sure* it involved Catherine. Maybe he had just assumed it was about her, and had missed a vital sign of an attack? Could he have been that distracted? He had not slept for over twenty four hours - maybe his irresponsibility had caused him to overlook something critical ...

A loud knock came at their door, startling both men into standing.

The door opened without further preamble, and the Captain of the Guard briskly strode in. He was middle-aged and robust, with short cropped hair and a full, grizzled brown beard. His body was girded in solid, well used leather armor from neck to ankle. The captain looked between the two men in a manner which was apologetic but no nonsense. "I am very sorry for your loss; I have just heard about your friend," he stated with sincere concern. "You must understand that I was doing my duty ..."

Peter waved his apology away. "We understand completely," he responded hoarsely. "Walter was grievously injured; I did not give him much hope of surviving from the moment I saw the wound. Your infirmary offered but a stray dream. While I am in grief that he did not survive, I do not lay the blame at your feet. That blame lies with the man who put the dagger into his stomach."

"So you are Peter, Captain of the Guard at the Worcester Cathedral?" asked the Captain, moving directly on to the next topic.

"Yes, that is correct," answered Peter, glancing at Jack in curiosity.

"The Bishop asks for you to attend to him directly," continued the Captain, his voice slipping automatically back into the short bark of command. "It involves the Lady Bowyer. Apparently she refuses to talk with anyone but you, and is threatening to leave immediately. I realize it is very late, but as you might imagine the situation is quite a volatile one."

"The Lady asked for me?" responded Peter in confusion. "Why is she here? Why would she want to talk with me?" He shook his head to clear his thoughts. "Yes, of course, I will come right away." He walked to the open door.

Jack fell into step besides Peter. "I intend on accompanying Peter," he commented to the Captain in a low but resolute voice. He would definitely like to hear from Catherine's mother why her daughter had been forced into the marriage, and why the council had lied to Catherine about his own background.

The Captain nodded. "That is fine with me," he responded evenly. "My orders are merely to bring Peter; you are welcome to come as well. If you would follow me, I will take you to where she and the Bishop are waiting."

He took the lead and guided the group down a fieldstone hallway. Torches flickering in wall holders threw spots of light and shadow along their path. The Captain walked steadily, visibly reining in his stride to wait for his exhausted guests to catch up to him. "Again, I apologize for the late hour," he offered as they ascended a narrow flight of stairs.

Peter gave a cough to clear his throat. "How long has Lady Bowyer been here?"

"She was escorted in a short while after dusk," responded the Captain distractedly, taking a left down a hallway. "One of our patrols came across the fighting. There were perhaps seven dead, from which side we cannot yet tell. The Lady was facing down five bandits. The attackers fled as our patrol approached, and the Lady made to go after them. Our patrol had to physically restrain her and bring her back to this Cathedral for her own safety."

He took the next right. "The patrol had quite the time getting her into the building despite her efforts to get free. Even now she is insisting on going out immediately and tracking down those bandits."

Jack felt the ghost of a smile pass his lips. Apparently the mother was much like the daughter. "Surely you cannot hold her against her will, if that is what she wants. Why not send a patrol out with her, to track the vagrants down?"

The Captain snorted in disbelief. "Tonight? Send her out with one patrol? Our carrier pigeon house has not had one moment of rest since dusk."

He held up a hand and began ticking off the messages.

"The entire town of Bowyer has been burnt to the ground. It appears that every man, woman, and child has been slain. Every Bowyer that we know of who was out of the enclosure has been killed by assassins. The visiting sword master in St. Albans, the female diplomat up north, the two herbologists in St. Giles, the elderly nun visiting here in our own Cathedral. Every one. Undoubtedly that is why your group is here, seeking medical help for your friend."

He shook his head, moving quickly down the hallway. "Lady Bowyer is the only noble Bowyer left alive. Her entire immediate family has specifically been accounted for and is dead, perhaps with only Raymond's body still missing. You cannot expect us to willingly let her leave these walls?"

Jack's vision closed down around him. He put a hand out to the wall to steady himself.

Catherine was dead.

He had known something was wrong; he had sensed death in the air. He had not been there to protect her ... he had failed her as well ...

Peter was at his side in an instant, his hand resting gently on his shoulder. "I am so sorry, Jack," he consoled softly, his own voice ragged.

The Captain stopped, realizing the effect his words had had on the two. "I thought you knew?"

Jack could barely get the words out. "Is *Catherine* dead? Are you sure?"

"I am afraid I do not know specific names," apologized the soldier. "I only know what I have been told, that all have been accounted for. Our Bishop was very clear on that point."

Jack's world dropped out from beneath him. "When did it begin?"

"The attacks started right at sunset. We have been receiving reports in every way you could imagine." The man looked between the two newcomers. "I had assumed your party fell victim to one of these attacks."

Jack shook his head, willing the tears away. His mind raced through the possibilities. "It might be that Walter was somehow related," he suggested uncertainly. "If so, he never spoke of it." He glanced over at Peter, who looked as baffled as he was.

"He did not tell me of any such relationship, either. Maybe he was keeping it hidden for some reason."

Jack took a deep breath and forced himself to start walking again. It seemed infinitely wrong that the world continued on as before, and yet Catherine was no longer a part of it. "Let us go talk with Lady Bowyer," he recommended somberly, his voice rough. "Maybe she can shed more light on this."

The two soon reached the end of the hallway, where the Bishop stood in a thick, dark burgundy robe. He was dressed for sleep, and his hair was tousled. The door before him had an outer grate of metal as well as an inner door of thick wood.

The Bishop gave a nod. "This is our most secure room," he explained to the two men by way of greeting. "It is used when we welcome a visiting abbess or other woman of great importance. I felt it appropriate in the current situation."

Jack and Peter both bowed to the elderly man. Peter saw that Jack was lost in thought and gave the response. "Thank you for offering us shelter on this evening," he stated hoarsely. "We will be glad to assist in any way we can. You said I might be of help in this matter?"

The Bishop's eyes went to the closed door. "She refuses to speak with any of us," he explained, his voice tinged with confusion. "Maybe it is the shock of the events. I cannot be sure. The only person she has mentioned at all is you. She said at one point, 'If you had Peter of Worcester Cathedral around, now *he* would be worth my time to talk to.' I do not know why, but when the Captain said that you had just arrived, I thought you might understand."

Peter shook his head. "I have only met her a few times, long ago," he recalled, his voice reflecting his confusion. "However, I will gladly talk with her, and do what good I can in convincing her to stay here in safety."

The Captain opened the metal grate, and then knocked on the inner wooden door. After a few moments, when there was no answer, he motioned for Peter and Jack to head in.

Jack and Peter stepped through the doorway, pausing a moment to let their eyes adjust to the deep gloom. The large room was wreathed in darkness, with only two guttering torches throwing a flickering light from opposite sides. A canopied bed occupied one wall to the right. Shelves on the left held scrolls and pottery. A large bearskin rug stretched out in the center of the stone floor. The far wall held two large windows, both open to the night air. By the left window they could barely make out the back of a figure in a long, dark cloak, the hood pulled up. She stood motionless, looking out past the dark town to the forest beyond. As the door closed behind the pair, she spoke to them without turning.

"I told you to leave me alone," she growled wearily. "I am Lady Bowyer; I am not subject to your commands. You have no right to keep me here."

Peter stepped forward, his voice hesitant. "My Lady, I was told that you had asked for me."

Jack saw the shake of the head, but the figure did not turn. "I do not ask anything of you. I do not need anything from you. There is nothing that I want that you could possibly give me. It is all gone. My entire family is dead. Everyone is gone ..."

Peter waited a moment, then spoke into the silence that she left. "I am deeply sorry for your immense loss, My Lady. Maybe I can be of help. You asked to talk with me. I am Peter of Worcester Cathedral. The Bishop told me ..."

The woman did turn at that, a slow, feline motion that somehow seemed full of malice. Jack saw the glint of long steel at her side and realized that she was fully armed. She had not relinquished her weaponry at the entry gate.

Slowly she strode toward the two men. Her eyes, so much like Catherine's, flashed with anger from the shadows of her hood. Jack felt a dagger of agony strike him as he once again was reminded of the still incomprehensible loss.

She stopped a few feet from them, sizing them up, her hand resting on the hilt of her blade.

Her voice, when it came again, was a deep, sharp hiss. "You dare to come to me, to plumb my depths, after everything that has happened. Your audacity -"

Her voice bit off in fury.

Peter's voice was raspy but earnest. "I am here as a friend, My Lady," he vowed. Jack was sharply aware of the nearness of that steel and the thin edge in the woman's fury. He suddenly wished he had kept his own sword, to block any attack the distraught woman might throw.

Peter's voice continued, placating. "Please know that you can trust me, that you can trust both of us. Tell us about what happened. Maybe we can help."

At this, the woman's gaze slid from Peter over to where Jack stood a few paces back. Her eyes seared into his; her voice came ragged and low. "You, Jack. I would not have thought ... you stand beside Peter in this?"

With her words, Jack again felt the loss of Catherine as sharply as if a knife had been plunged into his own stomach. He was overcome with guilt; he should have been there, should have protected Catherine with his own life.

He lowered himself onto one knee, bowing his head, his face etched with pain. "My Lady, I was ... close ... to your daughter. I should have been there for her when -"

His voice failed him.

It seemed that the figure froze for a moment. Jack suddenly remembered just how strongly Catherine's mother had fought against Catherine ever meeting him. Surely she would not hold that against him now, with everything that had happened.

Then, to his surprise, a cynical smile emerged from the depths of the hood. Jack blinked in shock. The woman nodded slowly to herself. "So that is how it stands," she commented quietly. She stood a little straighter and her voice became more steady. "Well, then, gentlemen. A talk. Let us lay everything out on the table."

She paused a moment, looking up at the two men with consideration. "However, I insist we have this conversation with you on the other side of that metal grate."

Confused, Jack and Peter moved to oblige her request. They opened the thick wooden door, returning to stand with the Captain and Bishop. They closed the metal grate which stood before the doorway. At her instruction, they locked the door and handed the key to her through one of the openings.

She glanced down at it. "This is the only key?" she prodded in a rumble.

The Captain nodded in agreement. "We only keep one key to this door, for security reasons," he responded. "I swear on my honor."

Lady Bowyer put the key on a table by the bed, then returned to stand by the door, secure in the shadowy darkness of the locked room. "Well, then, here we are. Peter, it seems that we have both been confused. You see, I thought you were dead. In fact, I thought that I had slain you." She chuckled wryly to herself. "I nearly took your head off, and yet here you are walking and talking." Her eyes slid to the scarf at his neck, then back to meet his gaze again. "Your medical talents have truly impressed me this time."

Peter looked at Jack, then back at Lady Bowyer. "I do not understand, my Lady," he responded slowly. "We have not seen each other in many years. We certainly have never fought."

The cloaked woman shook her head. "We will get to my proof in a moment. Before we do, show some honor. In this House of God, in front of witnesses, confess to your actions freely. I admit quite openly that my blade connected with your neck, with the intent to kill you. Will you not also admit that you took arms against members of the Bowyer family? That you attempted to kill at least one such person this very night - Catherine?"

Jack felt like he had been punched in the stomach, and looked over at his friend in surprise at this accusation. Peter went white with shock, but when he replied, his voice was clear and steady. "No. I swear to you, I have not laid one finger on Catherine or any of your clan."

The figure's laugh was harsh. "You forget that I was there. Despite your efforts, I have survived your ambush." Her eyes flickered to the Bishop before returning to hold Peter's firmly. "I do not know if you are working with the Bishop or not, but I do know he will not allow you to harm me on holy ground. So, in this room, I am safe for now." She paused for a moment, then said decisively, "I will negotiate terms for my safe passage out in the morning, when the castle is awake and I can request an impartial set of witnesses from the town."

Jack's world was spinning out of control. Where were these accusations spawning from? He spoke up quickly. "Lady Bowyer, I swear to you that Peter was with me all night."

She whirled to face him, and the pain burning in her eyes made his breath catch. When she spoke, her voice was low and grating. "That you could even -"

She turned away with an effort. "Fine. Let us reveal the final truth, if you two insist on maintaining this charade." She paused, eyeing the metal grate, as if gauging its strength. Then, with deliberation, she pushed off the cloak's hood, letting it fall back.

It was Catherine, her head thrown back in sharp defiance.

Jack's heart leapt in a rush of joy and relief. "Catherine!" he cried out, running to the grate. To his surprise, she took a step backwards into the darkness, staying out of reach.

His voice caught. "Catherine," he repeated, "I would never hurt you!"

Her voice shot back immediately, strong and sharp. "Yet I saw Peter there, in the ambush, driving his knife in an attempt to hamstring me. Yet I had to take my own blade to his neck to get myself free. Yet you claim that you have been with Peter all night." Her eyes went from one shocked face to the other, and then back to the Bishop who stood behind, speechless. She drew herself up. "I will require five town witnesses, gentlemen, ere I step foot through this grate in the morning. See that they are present."

With a quick move, she deliberately shut the heavy wooden door in their faces. The bar slid home with a solid thud.

Jack shook the locked gate in frustration. His voice echoed with anguish and joy. "Catherine!"

There was no sound at all from within. After ten minutes of pounding and pleading from both Jack and Peter, the situation remained unchanged. The Bishop and Captain watched the pair with a mixture of suspicion and confusion. The men's efforts were only halted when a page came running up to the group. "My Lord, the patrols have brought in the dead bodies from the ambush earlier. They request that you immediately come down for a briefing."

The Bishop turned to the Captain. "Stay here at the door. Let me know if she makes any noise or opens the door. Do not in any way attempt to harm or detain her. Something odd is going on here." The captain nodded his assent.

His eyes swiveled to stare at Jack and Peter. "You two are with me," he ordered. "You will not be left alone near Lady Bowyer, not with this current state of affairs. She is safe enough in her room for now."

Jack glanced back at the doorway in anguish, but she had not made a sound since closing the door on them. Perhaps he could best serve her by finding out the truth of what was going on.

Jack and Peter fell in alongside the Bishop as he strode down the hallway. Jack spoke with fierce determination. "I swear to you, Bishop, that we had no hand at all in any of these deeds. I do not know if Catherine is in shock or has been misled by someone."

The Bishop did not stop in his quick pace. "We will determine the truth soon enough, Jack. And when we do, we will have a reckoning," he promised.

The trio reached the outer courtyard in a few minutes. A ring of torches surrounded the open wagons that the patrols had brought in. There were several corpses in each one, clothed in purple and yellow livery. Peter looked at the uniforms with shock. "Those colors are of my family," he rasped in surprise, fingering the cloth. "However, the outfits are not quite right; they seem to be cheap imitations. I do not recognize any of these men either. They are not from my household."

Jack's eyes flashed. "Imposters," he stated with flat anger. "Not only that, come look at this one."

Peter and the Bishop walked over to join him. The man in the cart had been cut at the neck; his head was barely attached to the shoulders. Peter's eyes moved from the wound to the face, and he started back in shock.

"That shock of red hair … he could be my twin," he whispered hoarsely.

He reached over to touch the nose, and a piece of putty came off beneath his fingers. "This man was trying to disguise himself as me?" he asked in confusion. "Why?"

Jack was scanning the other bodies. "Look - this one has a face like a frog, and here is a tall, thin man with blond hair. This other one is small, with tight, blond curls. Where have we seen these men before?"

Peter's eyes sharpened in recognition. "The minstrels at the cathedral at Worcester," he replied in surprise. "These were the men who sang with Maya."

"They also passed us on the road here," remembered Jack. "Dressed as merchants. They have been tracking Catherine, and perhaps studying us as well. This had been planned out. Maybe they thought it was the only way to get close enough to her."

Jack turned and strode toward the stairs. "If she sees the bodies, she will know the truth of what happened," he vowed resolutely as he took the steps two at a time.

Peter was alongside him in a moment. "Maybe if we let her rest until morning, she will be more willing to talk about it then."

Jack shook his head. "She will not sleep, and if we leave her alone too long -"

He ran the rest of the way to her room, slowing when they reached the Captain. "Has she said anything yet?"

The Captain's eyes were somber. "Not a peep. However, I am not even sure we could hear through that door, if she made any noise. It is very thick."

Jack walked over and hammered on the door for a few minutes, calling in between thuds with the news. There was no response, not the slightest indication that his message had been heard.

The silence worried him immensely. He turned and raced down the hall. "I am going around to the window," he explained to Peter, who loped alongside him. "She has got to hear what we have to tell her."

The two ran down the halls and worked their way around the main castle building to the back side, where it overlooked the fields. The room was on the second floor, and Jack hoped that she had kept the shutters open so that she could hear his message.

When the pair rounded the last corner, his heart sank. A long ribbon of fabric descended from the window. He had no doubt that Catherine had made her escape while they were down examining the wagons.

Exhausted but determined, he jogged to the stables and tracked down a stable boy. The sleepy lad was helpful but confused. Yes, a woman had come asking for her horse, and he had done all he could to help her get on her way. Had this been the wrong thing to do?

Jack slumped against a wall in despair. It was pitch dark, and she did not want to be found. There was no way he could track her, although every instinct in his brain screamed for him to head out and try. His body was near collapse from exhaustion. He knew he still had the remaining three charges to get safely to St. Albans, and it appeared they were in serious danger. His world was crumbling down around him.

Peter let him rest for a few minutes, then guided him gently back toward their room.

"Let us get some sleep," he suggested quietly. "She will be safe enough, hidden away in the forest. I have no doubt that when we are on our way that she will come and find us in her own time. She wants to know what happened as much as we do. She is not one to shoot us in the back or kill us in our sleep. When she comes, we will talk."

Jack felt completely helpless, but nodded in acquiescence and followed his friend. Despite his worry, the moment his body touched the mat he collapsed into an exhausted sleep.

Chapter 19

Jack found himself being shaken awake by Peter. It seemed he had barely fallen asleep, but he could see the sun high and strong through the window. Peter put a wooden platter of bread and cheese down on the table next to him, along with a mug of ale. "I thought you could use some lunch," offered Peter quietly, taking a seat in a nearby chair. "I held off waking you as long as I could."

Jack shook his head to clear the mists, and rolled over to a sitting position. He took some cheese and bread, layering them before popping them into his mouth. After two or three he began to feel human again.

"How are the others doing?" he asked between mouthfuls.

"As well as could be expected," replied Peter somberly. "They are completely confused as to what happened. They cannot think of any ties Walter had to the Bowyer family. They blame themselves for not having heard the attackers."

Peter paused for a moment. "Apparently Walter's parents are both dead, and the Cathedral is offering to have him buried here. The other lads think it is a good idea, that Walter would have been content. We were waiting on you to begin the service."

Jack finished the small meal and stood. "Of course, just give me a moment." He walked to the dresser and splashed some water on his face, then ran a comb through his hair. He turned and nodded to Pete. "Let us go."

The service was short, but Jack was touched by the care the Bishop put into talking about Walter's life and deeds. The group watched somberly as Walter was lowered into a plot in the cemetery, well-tended and surrounded by flowers. Jack knew his friend would be well looked after here; it was small comfort with the guilt which lay over him like a heavy blanket.

The Bishop urged the group to stay, but more than ever they sensed the need to push on to St. Alban's. Father Berram wanted to get to his destination safely, but Peter and Jack had a different reason for wanting to move on. They both knew that their only hope of talking to Catherine soon lay in being in the open, where she felt safe to approach them. They moved out into the late afternoon sun, with the rainclouds finally easing into patchy wisps.

As they left the immediate environs of the cathedral the landscape slowly changed from built-up town, to sparse villages, to quiet rural roads. At first Jack watched every tree, every hill for a sign of Catherine. As the miles rolled by he relaxed his vigilance. He had no doubt that she was out there, somewhere ... but she would choose the time and place of their meeting. He would need to practice patience and wait for her.

They rode longer than they normally would have, enjoying the quiet of the open road and hoping to give Catherine an opportunity to present herself. They finally stopped only when the last streamers of violet had faded into dusky ebony. They ate their dinner in silence, keenly aware of the missing spots at the campfire. The group turned in early, and Jack sat out for his watch.

Every snapping branch, every gust of wind made his heart leap in hope, but despite his fervent wishes Catherine did not show herself. He thought of walking a short ways into the woods, in case she was nervous about confronting the whole group, but he could not bring himself to do it. The sleeping forms of his friends lay deep in exhausted slumber before him, and he would not let them leave his sight. Not tonight.

Finally the moon had crested its center point; he gently shook Peter awake, turning the watch over to him. It was a while before sleep overtook him.

The next day found them in even quieter woods. The sun was in full force now, and numerous wildflowers were springing up along the roadside. Jack knew he should take some pleasure in these signs of spring, but his concerns about Catherine and fresh grief over Walter's death filled his thoughts, layering a dense fog of darkness over the yellows and turquoises. The cart wheels rolled onward, the group moved along slowly but steadily, and soon it was evening again. They found a clearing by a small pond and ate their meal in silence.

The three religious men turned in early, the recent grief still weighing heavily on their minds. Peter turned to Jack, giving him a gentle nod. "Go ahead and rinse the horses' tack down at the pond," he encouraged quietly. "I will keep an eye on them until you return." Jack hesitated for a long moment, then nodded. The gear needed the rinsing, and he would only be gone for a short while. He gathered up the items and walked down to the quiet shore.

He knelt in the moonlight, swishing the bit and bridle through the water, the events of the night running over and over in his head. How long had Peter been away from the lads on that fateful night? Two minutes? Maybe three? How could any assassin have slipped in so quickly, and then escaped without even a trace to show his passing?

A loud *snap* echoed around him, freezing him in place.

* * *

Catherine watched impassively as Jack stood slowly, turning in place to meet her gaze. She kept her hand on the hilt of her blade, stepping back off the thin branch she had deliberately pressed in two. He was perhaps ten feet away, and she could see the exhaustion lining his face. She had no doubt that her own body held the same signs of weariness and sorrow.

Jack gazed at her for a long moment, then dropped his hands to his belt, undoing the latch and separating the halves. He tossed the whole thing, scabbard, blade, and all, a distance behind him. He stood, waiting, arms out to his side, completely unarmed.

Catherine let the silence stretch out for one minute, then two. She knew that she was unwilling to begin their talk because it could easily be the last time she saw the man she had grown to care for greatly. Once this started, it could lead directly to the brutal ending.

She had gone over the options incessantly since that night at the cathedral. The men would stop at nothing to finish what they had set into motion. Undoubtedly Jack and Peter had concocted a story to explain everything, to attempt to win her trust again.

How could she believe whatever they said, with all that had happened? How could she afford to trust anyone, if she were truly the last Bowyer now alive?

She drew in a long breath, then let it out again in a smooth stream. She would provide them with this one last chance. If there were but the slightest possibility that they remained true to her, it was worth risking. The two men could be her last hope.

"I am listening," she finally offered, fighting to keep the weariness at bay. It was not only her body that was exhausted, but her soul. The grief of the last few days was catching up with her. She looked at Jack, at the familiar lines of his face, at the gentleness of his eyes, and wondered how she could steel herself against believing in the lies he was about to tell her.

Jack carefully lowered himself to one knee, keeping his arms at his sides, his eyes full on hers. His voice was soft, low, and echoed with a sincerity which tore her heart in two.

"Catherine, I swear to you, neither Peter nor I had anything to do with the horrific acts of these past nights," he vowed. "The men you were ambushed by a few nights ago - the ones who were dressed in Peter's family colors - they were imposters."

Catherine made no effort to hide her disbelief. "*This* is the story you have thought up? Imposters? Surely you and Peter could have done better than that in the two days you have had." She took a step forward along the sandy shore of the pond, giving a frustrated kick at the soft surface. Her voice went hard. "I was there, Jack. I saw them - and him - with my own eyes."

Jack nodded quietly, his eyes steadily on hers. "The men that you saw, the ones in his livery. Did you recognize them?"

Catherine shrugged. "Certainly, they were familiar. I must have seen them when visiting his family home at some point."

Jack's head gave a gentle shake. "Perhaps you have seen them somewhere else, somewhere recently," he countered, his focus growing serious. "Perhaps at the Worcester Cathedral?"

Catherine stopped in her tracks, her gaze lost far in the distance as she searched back through her memories. "Maybe ... the man with the blond hair ..."

She turned suddenly to face him. "The musicians. They were the musicians who played for us. The frog faced drummer, the small singer with the blond curls."

It could just be true.

With harsh discipline she shook her head. This was exactly what she knew would happen. They would invent some wild story which had just enough plausibility in it to seem possible. She would cling to it, in her desperation, and she would be lost.

Fury shot through her that they would play her like this. "That proves nothing," she snapped. "Peter could easily have brought those assassins in to Worcester to prepare them for their task at hand. If anything, this proves even more strongly that they were in league with you and him." She paced angrily down the side of the pond, tension building between her shoulders.

Jack's voice remained low. "Think of the musicians you saw at the Cathedral. Then think of the men you saw at the ambush. Were any missing?"

Catherine had had about enough of this. She spun to snarl at him. "How do you know so much about the ambush, then? Were you there?"

Jack shook his head and his eyes dropped, heavy with guilt. "Not only was I not at your side, defending you, but I was not even guarding the three boys. While I was away from camp, talking with Peter, Walter was being murdered. That is what I was doing at the time of your ambush - I was failing you both." His face twisted in pain as he relived the torments of that night.

Catherine froze with shock, and she half started toward him before reining herself in with an effort.

Walter was dead.

"God, not Walter," she whispered. "The lad was innocent in all of this, a sweet, gentle -"

She turned away, looking out across the pond. When she spoke again, it was with a hoarse sadness. "I never dreamt that anybody would have known his connection to the Bowyers."

Jack looked up in surprise. "So he *was* related to your clan? We racked our brains to figure out why he would have been slain. The lads swore that he was not in any way associated with your family."

Catherine felt the ghost of a smile come to her lips, but it did not reach her eyes. "Only a few knew of Walter's lineage. I suppose it does not matter now, if it is told. He was the bastard child of my cousin Raymond; a youthful indiscretion with a local dairy maid."

Walter's laughing face came up before her, and she pushed away the tears. "The maid died in childbirth, and the child - Walter - was sent off to be fostered with a miller's family who already had several children. It was thought that Walter would live his life out there in quiet anonymity, posing no threat to my cousin's ambitions. Only a few of us knew."

The thought reverberated in her mind. Indeed, barely any had known of that situation, of Walter's true parentage. "If the attackers knew about Walter, then they must have been working with someone high up in the council. Even a well-connected enemy would have had trouble knowing about Walter's past."

The thought of an assassin slaying Walter firmed her resolve. The lad had been left in Peter and Jack's care – and somehow he had been killed. Was this further proof that the two men were involved in the heinous actions of that long, dark night?

Her eyes moved to hold Jack's again, and a darkness entered her soul.

"The fact that Walter was slain in your own camp hardly exonerates you," she pointed out, pushing the point with ruthless attention. "Maybe you yourself plunged the blade into his -"

Jack reacted viscerally, leaping to his feet, his face hot with anger. "Never. I would never have allowed Walter to be harmed in any way, and the thought of hurting him myself -"

His voice failed him.

Catherine let out a deep breath, reading the truth of this in Jack's face. She nodded, but her heart still twisted with doubt. "Maybe what you say is true, that Walter was marked for death without your knowledge. That does not rule out your involvement in the other attacks."

Jack deliberately knelt down again on one knee, rolling his shoulders to release some of the stress that had settled there. He looked up at her again, his eyes pleading with her to listen. "Think of the men at the ambush," he insisted again. "Were all of the musicians there?"

Catherine thought back to the evening of the ambush. The group had met up with her seemingly by chance, and she had been thrilled to meet with members of Peter's extended family. She had recognized them as familiar, and they had entertained her with several stories of Peter when he was younger.

She ticked off each band member in her head. The drummer - stocky, dark hair, bloated face. An incessant talker who seemed to like the sound of his own voice. The harpist - thin, tall, with hands that were always in motion. The singer, seemingly the leader of the group, rather small, with blond curls and predatory eyes.

She looked up suddenly. "The flute player was missing. The red-head. The one who -"

Her voice faded away at the realization.

Jack nodded slowly, his eyes holding hers. "The one who looked like Peter."

He had looked like Peter.

Catherine remembered now, how she had commented on that very fact at the cathedral. They had seemed almost like twins. And that flute player had been absent when she met up with the group so conveniently on her trail north.

Jack's gentle voice eased into her thoughts. "The reason I know about the men from the ambush is that their corpses were brought in by cart to the Christ Church, just after we had our talk with you in your room. That is why I stopped hammering on your door. We saw the way they were dressed, and we recognized them as the musicians from my foster home. The flute player had been expertly made up to look like Peter. The resemblance was quite uncanny."

He cocked his head to one side. "Although I still find it hard to believe that you could have been fooled thoroughly. Peter is like a brother to you - surely his voice -"

Catherine chuckled dryly and looked away, faint hope glimmering in her soul. "He kept in the shadows, saying that he was ill and did not want me to catch his sickness," she replied wryly. "He spoke only in raspy sentences. He said that his throat was on fire; that he could barely talk."

Jack gave a short laugh. "You seem to have put an end to that problem - the corpse we saw had his head only barely attached to his body. Your work, I imagine?"

Catherine almost found herself trusting him when she brought her gaze back to meet his. "I was wondering how Peter had survived that wound. I saw it with my own eyes; I saw my sword take the man down. Surely nobody could have survived that blow. But when Peter appeared, with the scarf around his neck ..."

Jack waited for a long moment. "There is an easy way to prove this to you, for once and for all," he offered slowly. "A much quicker solution than returning to the cathedral and having them dig up the bodies from whatever dirty grave they tumbled them into." He paused, and then continued. "Come hold your sword to my throat, and take me hostage. Then allow me to call Peter in here, to show you his untouched neck."

Catherine stood stock still, considering Jack's offer. It was one thing to face both men when she was the only one armed, in the safety of holy ground. It was quite another to take on both of them out here in the forest. If they were lying to her, then this surely would be the trap they would set.

And yet ... she looked into Jack's eyes, into those depths she had come to know and trust these past few months. She could not go on alone for long. Without someone to guard her back, it would only be a matter of time before one night's sleep became her last.

It was her only choice.

Still, it took all her effort to bring herself to speak. "Remember the sharpness of my blade," she warned him, before drawing her sword. "Any move will be your last."

She felt as skittish as a young doe as she slowly walked to stand behind Jack's kneeling form. He did not so much as move a muscle at her approach, although she could see the lines of tension in his jaw. She was alert for any sign of motion, any sense that he was turning to grab at her sword arm, but he remained perfectly still as she lowered her arm and carefully pressed the edge of the blade against his neck.

It seemed that her senses were heightened, that she felt every slight movement he made as he breathed. The familiar aromas of leather, of musk, of the oil he used to care for his blade all rose in a comforting sensation, and she found herself leaning against him slightly, almost against her will.

Beneath her, it seemed that Jack was caught by the same spell. She could feel him almost tremble, resisting the urge to move.

"Bring down Peter," she ordered gruffly.

Jack's voice called out rough but calm. "Peter, come down to the pool for a moment."

They stood in this tableau for a few moments, then the sound of crunching underbrush came to them from the direction of the campfire. It moved closer, and in short order Peter stepped out into the moonlight from the woods.

His eyes flashed in alarm when he saw Catherine standing behind Jack, the sword held close under his chin. He looked between Jack and Catherine without speaking, and dropped his hand to his belt. In a moment he had released his scabbard and sword. He took two steps forward, clearing them.

Jack spoke to Peter in a slow, clear voice. “Peter - show Catherine your neck.”

Peter nodded in understanding. He pulled his leather tunic off over his head, tossing it aside. He then unlaced the white under-tunic to the center of his chest. He pulled both halves clear of his neck area, and took several more steps away from his sword. Lacing his fingers behind his head, he stood there, waiting for Catherine to approach at her own pace.

Catherine knew this was the moment of decision. She could not ask for Peter to come closer without putting herself at risk. She could not leave Jack without being at risk. She could hardly stay here forever, nor could she leave these two - the two men who might be the only help she could trust to stand by her side.

Taking a deep breath, she made her choice. She stood back from Jack, removing the sword from his neck with one smooth motion. In a few steps she was clear of him, and also some distance from Peter. Neither man moved. She looked slowly between the two men, her gaze searching.

“I swore to myself not to believe any story you presented - that it would undoubtedly be full of deceit,” she ground out. “Yet ...” She found herself slowly approaching Peter, hoping against hope that this wild story could actually be true. Her eyes focused on his neck.

She realized that she saw no mark at all on his skin - not the slightest wound to indicate that this was the man that had cut her. Neither Peter nor Jack moved a muscle while she approached her old friend. Both held perfectly still, perhaps even holding their breath.

Catherine was within an arm’s length of Peter now. This was the moment of truth. If their intent had been to draw her in, one more step would put her beyond help. They would easily overpower her and she would be ended.

She looked up into Peter’s eyes, seeing the friendship and caring that had been there for so many years. She looked again at his neck. It was smooth and untouched. She took that next step, and brought her hand to touch, tenderly, his throat. “Oh, Peter,” she groaned, her voice breaking.

She dropped her sword and threw her arms around Peter in a hug, feeling the motions as he slowly, carefully brought his own arms down to hold her in a gentle embrace. The grief and horror of the past few nights flooded over her - all of her childhood friends slain, her family gone, the ambush in the night. She fought the tears, but despite her best efforts, they flowed down her cheeks, and she was tired beyond all reckoning.

She felt rather than heard Jack come over to stand beside them. She forced herself to regain control, and after a few moments she took a step back, wiping her eyes.

She looked between the two men. "God's teeth, to have you back again," she got out between breaths. "Not having you two to turn to made everything else beyond unbearable."

Jack held her eyes with his own. "Catherine, you have my word on this. Never doubt our loyalty. We are here. We have always been here. We always shall be."

Catherine took a deep breath and gazed at her friends. In some ways they were so different - Jack's dark hair, Pete's lighter features. Jack's quiet somberness, Pete's quick openness. However, in the ways that really mattered, they were quite alike. Both were loyal, both were steadfast. She had always seen that in their actions, and she could see that now in their eyes.

A wave of exhaustion hit her and she staggered.

Jack was at her arm in an instant, supporting her. "We can talk more after you eat," he assured her. "Let us return to the camp and -"

A loud scream split the night, coming just west of the main camp area. In a flash, all three had retrieved their swords and were sprinting at top speed toward the sound.

Chapter 20

To their surprise, only John was in the camp area, looking around with wild, sleep-filled eyes. A second cry sounded again, from further to the west. All four ran in that direction, pushing roughly through brush and new saplings. In only a few moments they came to a small clearing. The elderly priest was kneeling in its center, cradling the bleeding form of Michael in his arms. The cooking knife was sticking out of Michael's chest, and the stream of blood from the wound had pooled beneath them.

Peter and Jack immediately went to Michael's side, gently moving the priest away from the body. They tore away the clothing around the wound, and Peter made a dam with his hand to hold back the blood as they quickly evaluated the situation. Jack examined the wound, looking to see how deep it was and what had been struck internally. Catherine circled slowly around the edge of the clearing, looking carefully at the damp ground. John and the priest stood huddled together, wide-eyed at their prone friend's plight.

Peter packed cloth around the wound, doing his best to be gentle even though there was no movement at all from the prone body. The blood flow slowed; Michael's face paled and stilled.

Peter laid a finger at his throat to feel for a pulse. After a few moments, he dropped his head in sadness. He placed his hand on the knife's hilt for a moment, then, with a smooth draw, he removed the knife from Michael's chest, laying it by his side. He laid a hand gently on Michael's head, saying a quiet prayer.

John burst out crying, turning to bury his face in the old priest's chest. "Not Michael, too!" he gulped between tears, his voice ragged. "Not both of them!"

The old priest gently comforted the boy, his wrinkled face contorted with sadness. He tucked the book he was holding into his belt pouch, the better to wrap his arms tenderly around John.

Jack looked up at Catherine, fury and grief mingling in his expression. "Was Michael a Bowyer too? How could this have happened again?"

Catherine shook her head. "No, he was not part of our clan. I know Michael's family; they were scholars from Amesbury. I have no idea why someone would have gone after Michael. This makes no sense."

Peter gently gathered Michael's body up in his arms, and stood. "None of this makes any sense, Catherine," he reminded her quietly. "All I know is that we should push on to St. Albans immediately. We must get the priest and John to their destination, and to safety. Apparently someone is trying to kill them before they can do that." He strode toward the main clearing, with John and the priest following close behind.

Catherine paused, then looked over to Jack. She spoke softly, so that the others would not hear. "I have my horse with me, about a half mile away. I will catch up with you soon."

"No!" Jack's response came quickly and with ragged emotion. "I will not have you alone in this forest. There is a group bent on killing you, perhaps killing all of us."

He saw her face flush, and pressed on. "I know you value independence. Believe me, if anybody understands that, I do. However, remember why you refused to go with Lord Epworth. You wanted to protect your friends, to stand by them. Let your friends stand by you now. If you want to avenge your family, to care for those who remain, you need to start by protecting yourself and accepting assistance."

Catherine's eyes flashed in frustration, but she took a deep, steadying breath. "We do not have much time, but you are right. I do need to learn to trust you ... to not solely rely only on myself." She tossed her head as she held his gaze. "Fine, then.

Take a look around the clearing. There are not any footsteps except our own. Not one. The killer is a member of our group, or Michael committed suicide."

Jack's eyes narrowed. "Are you sure?"

Catherine waved a hand, encompassing the clearing. "Be my guest, but the light is fading as we speak."

Jack went to work immediately, moving quickly but surely along the perimeter of the clearing. Catherine knew what he would find. During the weeks they had been traveling, it had only taken a short period of time before each of their shoe prints had become as familiar as their faces. There was Peter's sturdy leather soles, with the dent by the front toe. In that spot was the elderly priest's tread, with the rippled heel. When Jack returned back to where Catherine stood, he was nodding in slow agreement. "I do not see anything else. I cannot believe it - but it looks like you were right."

Catherine glanced up at the sky, where the sunset was sending streaks across the sky. "There is still the chance that someone threw the knife from further out. That was what I wanted to do - to check to make sure there was not another solution."

Jack scanned the forest. "We will split the work. I will search the northern half, and you take the southern. We should have enough time to get that done before darkness falls."

Catherine nodded and carefully circled the area, staying within sight of him. If there were indeed an assassin still lurking in the woods, she wanted to make sure they faced him together.

It took them until the light was just about to fade completely, but they were certain of their findings by the time they regrouped in the clearing. There were no signs of anyone else being present in the area.

Without a comment, they walked back to the main camp area. The others had gathered up the supplies and loaded up the wagon. Catherine retrieved her horse from the gulley she had tied him up in, and together the party pressed on toward their destination.

Even in the dark, they rode as quickly as the cart would go, the wheels making a surprisingly loud rumble on the rutted dirt road. Catherine and Jack rode at the front of the party, straining their ears to listen for any sound that could signal the hoofbeats of assailants. The moon lit the road well, throwing shapes on the side of the road into sharp relief. It helped them to push along at a fast pace, covering the miles quickly.

It was almost dawn when the group approached the main cathedral of St. Albans. The town was beginning to stir, and a few farmers nodded greetings as the travelers passed by. When they moved through the Cathedral's main gate, Catherine immediately dismounted and spoke in a hurried whisper to the gatekeeper. He nodded and ran inside with her to fetch help. Jack and Peter remained by the cart with the other men, finally relaxing their guard.

In only a few moments the brothers of the house arrived along with house guard. The elderly priest and John were both led off to separate rooms, while a page waited for Jack and Peter to wearily dismount. Michael's body was reverentially conducted to the chapel.

The page looked up with quiet respect. "If you please, we have rooms set up for you."

Jack glanced back at the wagon. "The horses will be taken care of?"

The page nodded. "We have everything in hand, sir. This way."

* * *

Catherine sighed in relief when she, Jack, and Peter were shown into her room and the door closed sturdily behind them. In many ways it was much like the room she'd been given at the Christ Church - two large windows looking out over a quiet countryside, a large, canopied bed, a table to one side with three wooden chairs around it. A warm fire radiated gentle heat from one wall of the room.

She sat wearily in one of the chairs, waving for the men to take the other two. From a flagon on the table she poured out three large measures of mead.

"Drink up," she offered somberly, taking a long sip of her own.

The men were apparently as weary as they looked; they sat without question and eagerly took long pulls on their drinks. Catherine felt the exhaustion hit her again - as well as the anger and confusion. She put her metal cup down a bit too strongly on the table, and the impact rang out loudly in her ears. Jack and Peter's eyes flashed to meet hers.

Catherine found it hard to say the words. She took another swallow before she held Peter's eyes and growled, "There was nobody else in that clearing. Nobody."

Peter's face registered the shock that she and Jack had been absorbing these past few hours. Jack leant forward, his face serious. Peter looked between his two friends. "You are sure? You are absolutely sure there was no other person?"

Catherine looked up at him. "The moonlight was very strong, and the soil was damp from all of the rain. Every step that we took showed up clearly in the surrounding grounds. Jack and I traced the entire circle thoroughly. I looked for broken branches, for bent leaves, for anything. I checked for trees that could be climbed. I found nothing. The only footsteps that went into that clearing were those of our own group members."

She sat back and let her eyes fall shut. "I do not know what to think," she admitted wearily. "I just do not know what other solution there could be. Maybe Michael became overwhelmed with guilt or shock and committed suicide. He was a sensitive lad. Perhaps the priest simply found his body there after that happened."

She opened her eyes again, looking to Peter. "You stayed near the wagon. What did Father Berram say about it, during your ride here?"

"He said he found him as he lay, with the knife in his chest, already unconscious," responded Peter in a quiet voice. "That there was nothing he could do, and he called for help."

At the image, Catherine's eyes welled with tears, and she brushed them away. "If I had not recently sworn to myself to trust you two, I suppose I could say that one of you had done it." She glanced up at their worn faces, and smiled wryly. "But no. I have had enough of that pain. I believe that you both are true, and that you have no hand in this."

Peter's face furrowed with concentration. "Any alternative before us is hard to fathom."

Jack swirled his cup slowly on the table. "If Michael *did not* commit suicide, what other options would we have? Either Father Berram or John would have had to have done it. John could have killed him, then snuck back into bed, leaving Father Berram to discover the body."

Peter wrinkled his brow in disbelief. "The boys were as close as brothers," he pointed out. "But the other alternative is that Father Berram made the killing blow. I do not know if the elderly man is even capable of such an action. He can barely climb into the wagon each morning."

Catherine nodded wearily. "No solution seems even remotely possible," she agreed. "Just in case it was not suicide, I asked for the two to be given separate rooms, and for a guard to remain on each man. At least for tonight nobody else can get to them. We will have to sort this out somehow in the morning."

Exhaustion pulled at her, and her eyes closed again of their own accord.

Peter slowly stood, his joints clearly aching with the strain. "I will let you get your rest," he offered to Catherine with sympathy. He glanced at Jack. "Maybe you could give her some assistance," he suggested, his voice gentle. Then he turned and left, closing the door quietly behind him.

Jack got to his feet, then moved over to help Catherine shakily climb to her own. She half fell against him, and he put his arms out to catch her. The strength of his body was against hers, and suddenly she was clinging to him, her arms entwined around his in a powerful embrace. He kissed her hair, her forehead, her cheeks, her lips.

His murmurs came to her ears in a low rush. “You are alive … you are safe … oh Catherine … Catherine …”

He swooped her up into his arms and carried her over to the canopied bed, laying her down on the soft sheets. She slid her hand down to catch his wrist, holding his hand against her. Looking up, she caught his eyes with her own.

“Please stay,” she whispered, her voice wistful. “I do not want to be alone.”

Jack groaned, kissing her hand tenderly. When she slid over to make room, he pulled the blankets up over her, then lay down alongside her, on top of the covers.

“I would be by your side for every moment, if I could,” he promised in a soft breath, his hand gently tracing the curves of her face.. “Every second.”

Catherine twined her fingers into his, laying her head back onto the pillow. “Stay,” she sighed again.

In another moment she was sound asleep.

* * *

Catherine woke with a start when the door creaked slowly open. She was wide awake in a moment, turning to reach for her sword. She stopped short when she saw Jack lounging in the bed next to her, a comforting smile adding a slight glow to his somber face.

He spoke over his shoulder to the person at the door. “It is all right, Peter, she is awake now. You can bring in lunch.”

Peter’s face poked around the door, and he nodded in welcome to his two friends. “I was starting to wonder if I should just wait until dinnertime,” he offered gently, coming into the room with a large wooden tray. It held an assortment of cheeses, a fragrant loaf of bread, and slices of dried apple.

Catherine pushed herself up into a seated position, and Peter laid the meal across her lap with a courtly bow. He brought a pair of mugs over from the table and set them down on the tray as well. He pulled over a chair to sit next to them, grabbing a slice of apple from the tray and munching on it.

Catherine found that she was ravenous, and ate the food with great relish. Jack sat back against the pillows, his face easing. "It is good to have something to be happy about," he commented quietly to Peter, watching her eat. "What have you found out so far from the morning sessions?"

Catherine paused between drinks to look over at Peter, a question in her eyes.

His eyes shadowed. "They are looking into the murders," he explained. "Is this all related to King John's issues, or separate? It seems a bit unbelievable that so many people have been slain and there is no organization proclaiming credit. Why burn an entire town if your reputation will not grow from your actions? Even mercenaries want their deeds to be known so that they can charge higher prices on their next jobs. Before we get to a 'why', surely we should have known by now the answer to 'who'."

Jack snagged a piece of bread and took a bite, lost in thought. "Any more thoughts on why Michael was killed? Any ideas at all from John or Father Berram?"

Peter shook his head, his face puzzled. "Both hold to their stories and repeated questioning from various people has not shown any change. The only thing we can figure at this point is that the lad committed suicide. Maybe the tragedy of his friend's death was too much for him to bear."

Catherine had consumed most of the food that Peter had brought and was starting to feel more like herself again. She ran her fingers through her long, tangled hair to draw out the knots.

"I have been going over in my mind everything the Bowyers had been working on recently." Her throat caught, but pushed on through it. She needed all of her facilities sharp to help avenge her family. "It seems clear that the attackers had help from the inside for many reasons. The enemy got through our outer wall. Legends are that the wall has never been breached - I imagine that someone from inside let them in. Also, the assassins knew of Walter's lineage, something that was very much a secret."

Jack's brow furrowed. "They could not account for Raymond's body, last I heard. They were still tallying up the bodies ... there was a lot of damage to sort through." He looked over to Peter. "Have you heard anything new?"

Peter nodded. "Raymond's corpse is still missing," he agreed quietly. "There is more news from town. One of the mercenaries was caught. He does not know who hired him, or for what reason. However, he does know that two people were allowed to leave the enclosure before the attack began. He assumed they were spies of some sort."

Catherine exhaled slowly, drumming her fingers on the tray. "It seems unbelievable. I am hard pressed to imagine that any member of my community could participate in such a heinous action. Even Raymond's ambitions did not seem to run so high."

She tapped her lip for a long moment. "Raymond had lands of his own, located between Bowyer and those of Sir Magnor. He had amassed quite a fortune over the years. Maybe he has been kidnapped and is being held for ransom."

She shook her head. "I cannot see the sense of Raymond being involved in this attack. He had won. I was exiled. Even if Raymond had some part in these events, why would he kill the inhabitants of Bowyer? Those were his own lands at that point. Those were his own people."

Emptiness filled her. She looked down at her hands, and the brown ring which still remained there. She drew her focus onto it. She had not quite lost everything. She still had Jack. She clung to that thought with every ounce of her focus.

Jack reached out to hold her hand, and her breath caught. Suddenly it seemed that the shocks of the past few days had created a hyper-awareness in her of a desire to live, to love, to be held by Jack, to lose herself in his embrace. Warmth flushed down her spine, and a ragged breath eased out of her.

Jack raised her hand to his lips, pressing them tenderly against the back of her hand. "I am here for you, always," he promised, his voice as firm as steel.

Peter quietly took the tray and left the room without a word, closing the door softly behind him. Ever so gently, Jack pulled Catherine with his hand until she lay against him, their faces only a few inches apart. Her breath caught as she brushed the hair from his eyes. He was so strong, so skilled - and yet he handled her with such great care, as if she were a fragile doll.

She ran a hand along his cheek. "I will not break, you know," she promised huskily.

Jack needed no further encouragement. With a groan, he pulled her down hard to him, kissing her with fierce longing and desire. She answered his passion with a fire of her own, rolling him over so that he pressed down against the length of her body. He traced kisses down her throat, her chest, undoing the lacing as he went. A small flame leapt out from each place that he touched her.

She lost track of when she slipped the outfit over her head, when she helped him draw his own off. She was lost in the touch of his fingers, the feel of his flesh on hers, the movements of his body against hers.

The streaming sunshine had drifted into gentle evening shadows before she lay, exhausted, on top of him, the sweat of their bodies mingling. She kissed contentedly along his neck, feeling his hand gently caress her waist. Their breath had settled into a more even pattern, and she was happier than she had been in years.

Jack's gaze was steady on hers. "I will never again let you out of my sight," he vowed. "I will never again risk allowing anyone to harm you."

Catherine's grin grew. She nestled herself tightly against his body, causing him to wrap his arm around her waist in a reflexive motion. She gave him a gentle kiss on the mouth before commenting, "I suppose now would be an inappropriate time to remind you that I never made it to see Lord Xavier."

Jack's eyes glanced up at hers, first as if this was a jest, then narrowing when he realized she was serious. "You must be joking," he protested, his voice deep and solemn. "After everything that has been happening, you cannot expose yourself to that risk."

Catherine propped herself up on one elbow so that she could easily meet his eyes. She lay a hand against his face, again marveling at the gentleness and strength that co-mingled there.

"I will not go alone – I will take a group of soldiers for protection. However, it is because of everything that has happened that I *must* go. This is no coincidence, that all of this is occurring now - now when your foster father has left, when Father Berram has decided to bring the Book on its journey to St. Albans. There is a reason behind all of this."

She held his gaze with tenderness. "Someone has gone through an incredible amount of time, effort, and money to cause all of these events to set into motion. We must find out why, and Lord Xavier must be persuaded to tell me. He holds a key to this, because of his involvements in the Wilmslow Negotiations."

Jack did not hesitate. "Then I shall go with you."

Catherine looked down his well-muscled form, down the strong arms, the rippled stomach. The temptation to have him by her side, to be safe in his protection, called to her with a power she could barely resist.

It was several moments before she shook her head. "If I arrive with you, then Lord Xavier will feel the church is involved. Even if you swear you are acting on my behalf and not for your foster father, the thought will linger in his mind. He would never tell me what I need to know." Resolution built within her. "I must do this without you. My task will be delicate and challenging enough as it is."

Jack's face drew in tense worry. "I realize that I cannot watch over you every moment, but surely this can wait? Walter and Michael are barely in the ground. This is not the time to be taking chances."

She felt the rightness of her path as a certainty. “Time is absolutely of the essence,” she gently retorted. “I must go soon.”

He let out a deep breath, nestling his face down into her thick hair. “Surely there must be another way,” he pleaded, his voice rough with frustration.

Catherine gazed fondly down at him. “I felt this exact same way when I left you on the road, so many days ago. At the time, you were in far more danger than I was, escorting the group with their valuable cargo. Every hour that I was away, I envisioned you under attack, fighting for your life. I had to control an impulse to run back to you, to stand by your side. It was the not knowing that wore away at me.”

Jack leant up to kiss her tenderly for several seconds. He drew away again to look at her with concern. “We care for each other because we make a stand for what is right. That is part of the attraction. And yet, that makes it so much harder to be apart from you.”

His words echoed in her very core, into the inner reaches of her soul, and suddenly it was as if she were glowing with a warm, radiant light, one which filled her very being. She knew with complete certainty how she felt.

Her voice was pitched soft and low, but as she spoke she felt as if her words etched the air in crystal relief.

“I love you.”

Jack held her gaze for a long moment, and then he let out a shuddering breath. When he spoke, his voice was hoarse. “It has been a long time since I have heard those words,” he murmured, raising a hand to gently stroke her cheek.

Catherine’s mouth quirked into a tender smile. “Then I shall have to say them often, to make up for lost time,” she offered gently. “I love you, I love you, I -”

Jack rolled over with a groan, covering her with his body, kissing her, drawing her body to his. It was a long while before she could speak coherently again.

As she lay sprawled on his chest, her breathing settling down to normal again, he whispered against her cheek. "You have bewitched me body and soul, my beloved."

His eyes shone as he turned to gaze at her.

"I love you, and will thank God every day that your path led you to me."

* * *

Catherine and Jack spent that night and the next day entwined in each other, with only rare interruptions from Peter who had learned to knock before bringing in food and drink. Catherine found the hours to be the happiest she had known, and a part of her wished this time would never end.

In the quiet moments, though, when she nestled in the crook of his arm, she remembered the loss of her family, her friends, everyone she had held dear. She knew she could never rest until she discovered who had destroyed her family and found justice for them.

Soon the preparations were settled for her trip, and she sensed the approaching departure as a billowing black storm. When they finished dinner, she drew Jack out of the keep, out through the main gates. The sun slipped lower through the azure sky as they followed a quiet path through the woods surrounding St. Albans.

They walked along the remnants of the Roman guard wall from centuries ago, passing ancient buildings with mosaic-tiled floors. She wondered about those days of old, how the people had lived then, how they had felt about residing so far from their warm home by the Mediterranean.

Jack was a warm presence at her side, and together they drew in the quiet of nature, the freshness of the forest air. An immense sense of peace filled her soul.

When they reached the collapsed Roman gates by the pond, Catherine found a large rock to sit on, spreading out her green skirts around her legs. The Cathedral staff had been kind enough to provide her with some fresh clothing, and this dress, embroidered with Celtic symbols and dyed the color of cattail greens, suited her nicely. On her chest, as always, she wore the large circular spiral-design medallion of brass and green that seemed to glow with the reflected sunset.

Jack rested one leg on a nearby stump, gazing down at her with a look of fondness. He waited patiently for her to speak.

Catherine returned his gaze with tenderness. Jack was everything she could desire in a man; she would want no other here with her tonight. The settling dusk sent warm breezes across the meadow, and a robin warbled softly in the trees.

She sensed again the distant billowing of storm clouds and took in a deep breath.

"I am not even sure how to broach this," she stated truthfully. "I have given it a lot of thought over the past few days. Every way I try to phrase it, it seems to create a challenge that you have to accept for honor's sake. So I will just say it straight out, and ask you to think about it - truly give it serious thought - before you give me an answer."

Jack stilled, and she had a sense of the turmoil of emotions that he was caught in. He still harbored concerns about their differences in station. She was now the Lady of her land, although her holdings consisted of a destroyed, destitute keep with burnt remnants of fields. He was an orphan of a craftsman, and his foster father was now undoubtedly sailing his way toward Ireland.

She offered him a reassuring nod, then continued.

"Jack, I love you. I know I will worry about you daily when I am apart from you. I will imagine that something will happen to you and I will not know. In the same way, you will worry about me."

She smiled gently. "There is, in fact, a way to help at least alleviate some of this."

She put her hand to the spiral medallion at her neck. "You recognize this heirloom I wear?"

Jack nodded, his eyes moving to the necklace. "Yes, of course, everyone knows about the Bowyer medallions. They are the symbol of your family. Your mother was famous for her golden yellow medallion."

A flood of loss cascaded over Catherine at the memory. It was still hard to take in, that her mother, her entire family, had been slain in an instant. When she spoke again, her voice was subdued.

"When my mother came of age, she had many men who wished to court her. Her favorite - my father - was brought to a special ceremony. He was given a blue medallion as a sign of his right to woo her."

She smiled slightly; her parents had been deeply, madly in love with each other from the first time they met at a harvest celebration. Her mother had told her countless stories of how they had ridden together for hours in the ensuing months, shared heartfelt discussions beneath the stars, and pledged their love to each other.

She drew her eyes up to Jack's. "My father wore his sapphire blue medallion until the day he died, and she wore the golden yellow. When they traveled separately, the locals would note the medallions as they passed and a communication network would spring up. All my mother had to do is hand a note to any local merchant or farmer, and within no time at all it would have found its way to my father."

Jack's eyes were intent on her as she took her medallion's chain up over her head and held it in her hands, looking at it for a few moments. Then, making a decision, she gave the edges of the medallion a sharp twist. There was a slight cracking noise, and suddenly she held two overlapping discs in her hand, each a brass circle with colored glass set within it. Brass spirals adorned both pieces. One disc was a deep blue, the color of the ocean at night. The other was a golden yellow, as the embers of a glowing campfire.

Catherine finally found the strength to look up at Jack, to meet his gaze. "I am not holding you to any obligation," she hesitantly whispered. "I am not asking to be courted. I have not that right, considering the situation I am in. I own nothing ... I can offer ... nothing."

She took in a long, deep breath. "Even besides that, if we choose to openly wear these emblems, it will make both of us obvious targets. In order for the communication to work, we both have to bear our medallions in plain sight, so that villagers know when we pass through. The risks are great ... immensely great."

Her heart constricted. There was so much danger in what she was offering, and yet she craved it with all her heart, with every ounce of her being. She fought to keep her voice steady. "Still, to know that I would be alerted if you were in trouble - and to know that you would be called if I were under attack -"

Jack was kneeling at her side in a heartbeat. "Yes. Yes, a thousand times yes," he breathed softly. "I understand the risks. I accept them wholeheartedly."

He tenderly kissed her hand, then looked back up into her eyes. "I will not presume to hold you to any future obligation. That can be left for quieter times." His gaze became serious. "But please know this; I would be honored to have you as my wife if you had not one coin to your name or anything but the clothes on your back. I have no desire for wealth or goods. My desire is solely for you to share my life, to be by my side."

Catherine's eyes shone, and with gentle reverence she lay the blue medallion chain over his head, settling it down on his neck. She handed her own chain to him, and lowered her head. She felt him place the golden medallion over her head. His hands rested on her shoulders, and she looked up to meet his. When he spoke, his voice was low and full of strength.

"I swear that I will do all in my power to be worthy of this honor," he pledged in a hoarse voice.

"Oh, Jack," she breathed, and then they were in each other's arms, kissing, drawing strength for all which would come ahead. For a moment the world vanished and it was just her and him, united, immersed in love.

Finally she pulled back from him, drawing herself to her feet, holding down her hand. He took it and rose to stand beside her. A warm shiver ran down her spine, as she gazed up at his strength, his well-muscled form standing at her side, with her blue medallion shimmering on his chest. She could see the same pride and love shining in his eyes.

The walk back to the Cathedral seemed almost magical. Catherine found she could not keep from smiling. There were pairs of mallards paddling down the stream, and she spotted a nest of eggs tucked in at the water's edge. They passed a hexagonal pigeon house, full of cooing and fluffing birds.

When they passed under an aging stone bridge, Jack pulled her hard to him, turning her to press her against the cool stone and kiss her ... kiss her ... each kiss billowed in the depths of her soul. With an effort he broke off, smiling at her ruefully as he led her on toward the main building.

Peter met them at the entry gates, and his eyes went immediately to the medallions they were wearing. His face reflected both concern and contentment. "Congratulations," he offered heartily to Jack, clasping him on the arm. Jack drew him into a warm hug, patting him on the back.

Peter turned to Catherine, a smile spreading across his face. "I know you two will be truly happy together, and I hope your time together is long and peaceful." He tenderly held her for a moment, giving her a kiss on the cheek. "Although you have the worst timing," he added with a gentle laugh.

Catherine looped her arm in his as they walked into the hall for dinner. "The way our lives work, now is always the best time to take action. If we continued to wait until 'later', nothing would ever get done," she explained with a smile. She looked up at Jack with dancing eyes, and he brought her hand to his lips in silent agreement.

There were many toasts that evening, both to the memories of their fallen friends and to the future of Jack and Catherine. When the two retired back to her room, it was a long while before they fell into a contented sleep.

When Catherine sat to organize her gear the following afternoon, Jack did not try to stop her. Instead, he helped her go through her belongings, making sure she had key supplies and that she knew the route to take. She knew he struggled with the burden of responsibility to keep her safe. She could see in his eyes what it cost him to let her leave, and she loved him for that.

It seemed all too soon when her black steed was ready and waiting by the main courtyard. Jack stood with her, just holding her hands for a while. Then, suddenly, he pulled her into a long, passionate kiss, pouring all of his love and strength into the embrace.

After a while he pulled back to look down at her. "Come back to me soon," he instructed in a deep voice, his eyes smoky with passion and concern. "Every hour apart from you will be a trial."

Catherine touched his cheek gently with her hand, willing herself to memorize his face. "I promise."

He boosted her up into her saddle, and after one last glance down, she looked ahead, spurring the horse on the road northwards. The team of soldiers rode in escort. She reined in as they came to the crest of the hill, turning back for one last look. Jack stood by the gate, watching her, and she gave him a last wave farewell. Then, with a shake of the reins, she moved forward toward her goal.

Chapter 21

Jack felt as if he was pushing through dense fog. Around him the cathedral swirled with activity, but he could not see the attentive guards or hurrying pages. All of his thoughts were focused on Catherine, on her safety during her trip.

Father Berram's newly assigned personal guard stayed by the frail man's side, but there was no sign of danger as the elderly priest and his friend, Father Oswold, immersed themselves in long discussions in the study. Peter and John spent much of the day in sparring practice, John throwing himself into the activity with fervent focus.

Jack sighed as he watched the two. Both religious men seemed vastly unlikely to have plunged a dagger deep into Michael's chest. The watch would be kept, but it seemed more and more certain that only Walter's death had been part of the initial attack. There had been no other reports of any murders after that one fateful night.

He turned from the courtyard, walking into the main building with resignation. He knew he would not take five steps before being drawn into a heated discussion of what all of the recent events signified. Nobles from all corners of England were descending on the cathedral to gain news and make wild conjectures. The fury with King John over the schism with the Pope was rising to new heights. Many were certain that the wholesale slaughter of the Bowyers was only the first bloody step toward nation-wide chaos.

After a few days the cathedral was bursting at the seams and little progress had been made. Father Oswold finally called Jack and Peter into his study. Father Berram sat to one side, his elderly face still heavy with grief.

Father Oswold nodded to the two, waiting for them to be seated before he spoke. "This business with King John, the Pope, and the Bowyers is setting brother against brother," he warned the pair, his face tense. "The meeting that Lord Epworth held was a noble enough attempt, but after this wholesale slaughter people want stronger action taken. I have to say I agree."

Jack leant forward. "What do you suggest?"

Father Oswold glanced at Father Berram, then back at the pair of men. "A more official enclave should be held, in London, with all ranking officials present. That way their decision can hold weight. Also, if each man uses every resource at his disposal, perhaps we can finally get to the bottom of just what is going on here."

Peter nodded in understanding. "If this panic continues to grow, there may be more fighting as people see threats where there are none. We have to rein this in as quickly as we can."

Jack's heart pulled in two directions. From a logical sense, he agreed with the men. It was critical that the growing chaos be stemmed as quickly as possible. But he could not bear the thought of moving further away from Catherine, not now, not when the threat was still imminent.

"When would we need to depart?" he asked, his voice hoarse.

Father Oswold glanced at Father Berram. "It would take us several days to set the wheels in motion. Something of this magnitude will require messengers to be sent to all corners of England."

Jack nodded. As soon as he was able, he enlisted one of the messengers to run a message up to Catherine, laying out the plans.

It was a long four days before the messenger came riding in through the front gates of the curtain wall. Jack turned from his sparring practice, his heart rising as he took the scroll from the young man and pulled it open.

His brows creased in puzzlement. Catherine's response was short and cryptic.

Jack -

Your course seems to align with mine, for London is where I must head next as well. I promise to be there by the evening before Easter. Probably sooner, not later. Watch for me. I will be with you again soon.

Love,

Catherine

Jack re-read the message several times, wondering why she had not been more detailed in her response. Was she that concerned about someone intercepting the message? What had she learned that she feared others might overhear? Was she intending to be in London for the enclave, or was there another purpose which drew her there?

His shoulders tensed in frustration, and with effort he rolled them, keeping them limber. She had a good escort of soldiers, and the road to London was a well-traveled one. He would need to be patient until she once again was by his side.

Now that he knew she would be waiting for him in London, he was eager to get into motion. He worked with the staff to get all final preparations done, and by the next morning the wagons were stocked. Father Berram climbed into the wagon to take his usual spot, and John was at his side in an instant. A handful of local nobles joined their party, and Father Oswold insisted that ten of his own guard accompany the group for added protection. Jack did not mind the extra manpower. He and Peter, their gaze ever vigilant, brought up the rear of the group.

The road between St. Albans and London was a steady stream of merchants, pilgrims, soldiers, and other travelers. The group moved at a slow but steady pace, stopping at the numerous pilgrim's inns that were laid out in easy succession along the trail.

Jack found that his blue medallion was attracting a wealth of attention. He maintained a mental checklist of who made those looks, if they seemed friendly or hostile. Some seemed merely curious, while others nodded their head as if in salute. A few averted their eyes or slid into a shadow, and these were the men he committed to memory.

He fully prepared for trouble along each leg of the journey, coordinating with Peter so that as little time as possible involved only one of them being awake. They slept in inns with stout doors and a low number of rooms, taking all of the rooms for their party as a precaution. Jack and Peter slept in the room with their two charges, and rarely let either man out of their sight.

Jack even had the servers take a bite of each meal brought, and a sip of each ale. While all reported deaths until now had been violent - in some cases it seemed unnecessarily so - Jack did not wish to take any chances.

Despite the concerns, Jack made no effort to press hard to reach their destination. The priest and boy were in double grief over the deaths of their friends. Father Berram was finding it harder and harder to move about, blaming his old bones for his lack of energy. He took a while to get going each morning, and asked to stop when it was barely mid-afternoon. While the roads were in better care as they approached London, the slow pace dragged on further with each passing day.

Between the numerous stops and long, drawn out mornings, it was many days later when they pulled into the King's Arms Inn near the center of London. Jack had sent a messenger ahead and the entire Inn had been cleared for the party. It was within walking distance of Westminster Abbey, where the meetings were to take place.

Once they settled into their rooms at the inn, Father Berram sent word to the Abbey of their arrival. Trusted guards were sent over at once, and the inn became, in essence if not in fact, a fortified garrison. Jack appreciated the help, but even so he walked the perimeter several times that day, testing the windows, watching the people who were nearby.

Father Berram went up to bed shortly after dinner, and Peter nodded to Jack before climbing the stairs after him. Jack watched the pair ascend the ancient wooden stairs, then turned his gaze back to the inn's main room. Several round wooden tables were scattered beneath a post-and-beam ceiling, with a fire crackling in a large, stone fireplace to one side. The windows along the street side were all mullioned, and the burgundy curtains drawn tightly.

John had been sitting with the priest, and now came over to join Jack at his corner table. He brought his pewter mug with him, setting it down onto the worn table with a soft clink. He seemed to have aged ten years in the past few weeks. He took a sip of his ale, then looked up to meet Jack's eyes. "You miss her, do you not?" he commented quietly.

Jack blinked in surprise. Thoughts of Catherine had snuck into every corner of his life, and he had just been wondering how she was doing. He had not realized it was that obvious to others. "Yes," he admitted to his younger friend. "I do miss her greatly."

John nodded and took another sip. "I miss Walter and Michael. Not a moment goes by that I do not wonder why they died, or what I could have done differently to prevent it. Maybe if I were a lighter sleeper, or maybe if I had talked with them more so they trusted me with their secrets."

Jack said nothing, simply looking at John with compassion. They had been over this ground numerous times during their ride.

John took another pull and went on morosely. "We still cannot find any link between Michael and the Bowyers, and nobody else we have spoken with has talked about any non-Bowyer killed in these mysterious manners. The only deaths were on that one night."

He looked down into his ale. "It seems that Michael killed himself – but why? Was he riddled with guilt over Walter's death? Was he part of the cause?"

He sighed wearily. "It seems likely that Michael knew of the plans to wipe out the Bowyers. Every other Bowyer was slain on that one, same evening. Catherine was the only one who survived, and she barely did so. Maybe Michael felt guilty at the thought of having to face her?"

John took a sip, absently wiping the foam from his lip. His monologue continued unabated. "Does this all have to do with Prince John? Raymond's plans? Father Berram and that book?"

Jack let him talk, let him work through his mix of emotions. John wasn't looking for answers; there were none to find with what they knew. They had talked about each point for hours during their travels, gone over every small hint of meaning. Their only hope lay in meeting up with other people who had been involved with the Bowyers and try to find a common thread, or perhaps news of any repercussions.

When John finally wore down into silence, Jack reached over and put his own hand over John's. "We will find out who has done this," he promised quietly. "We will bring them to justice. I am sure in a few days, with other eyes and ears providing information, this will all make much more sense."

John finished down the rest of his ale, then stood. Jack went with him up to their room, nodding to Peter as they entered. He sat alongside Peter on the wooden bench as John climbed into the low bed.

Jack shook his head, looking between the two men. Michael's suicide had hit the pair hard. Jack wished he knew what turmoil had driven the lad to that decision.

Jack sighed and patted Peter on the shoulder before climbing into his own bed. He needed to get a few hours of sleep before his own watch came up.

* * *

Jack was in good spirits the next morning as the group ate breakfast by the low fire. The food was delicious - an assortment of spiced sausages, numerous varieties of cheese, and fresh bread. The weather outside was sunny and warm, although they kept the curtains pulled for security reasons. Every time the front door opened, he looked over with hope, waiting for Catherine's smiling face to appear there. Each time, it was a messenger from another arriving dignitary, letting them know which inn he was staying at and relaying information. Jack chided himself to be patient. She was not due for another day, yet, and there was still much to be done.

Once the morning meal was complete, Jack left the two in Peter's capable hands and walked over to Westminster Abbey. The building was stunningly designed, with arched windows, famous shrines, and numerous examples of fine metalwork within.

Jack looked past these details to the ones involving security. He knew that he was being overcautious - the Abbey had been guarded for years against numerous threats and their security men were some of the finest in the land. Still, he liked to be familiar with the layout for his own needs. He walked through the building throughout the day, learning where the exits were, where the dead end corners lay.

He focused primarily on the Chapter House, a round meeting room with a mosaic floor and high stained-glass windows surrounding it. The windows' sills lay just above his head, and with the colorful scenery depicted on them, there was no chance of any outsider being able to look in on the proceedings.

He had left word at the inn for them to send a messenger the moment Catherine arrived, but as the day drew on, none came for him. He had a brief meal with the soldiers at the Abbey, then renewed his investigations.

When the sunset streaked the sky with red and orange, he made his way through the cobblestone streets to the quiet inn. As always, he kept a sharp eye out for anyone lingering nearby who looked out of place or overly watchful. A 'no vacancy' sign hung beneath the main inn's symbol, swaying slightly in the gentle wind. All seemed clear, and he walked in with a light step, scanning the room for Catherine. She was not there, and Peter shook his head no when their eyes met.

"I am sorry, Jack. She has not yet arrived," apologized Peter as Jack came to join him at a table by the curtained windows. "We have had someone watching for her all day. It is still a day early, though. I am sure she will be here tomorrow, as promised."

A barmaid brought over a pair of mugs and a plate of cheese, which they picked at as they talked. Peter glanced occasionally over at the larger table where John and Priest Berram sat with some friends, talking in relaxed voices. "They are all eager for the meeting to begin," added Peter with a nod toward the group. "Perhaps once we have all the pieces in place, the whole picture will make more sense."

Jack looked over at the talking men, doubt and hope mingling in his mind. "You would have thought that if there were pieces to assemble, that we would have at least one," he pondered. "With all of the times we have gone over the deaths, nothing stands out. We were right there when both Walter and Michael were slain. Nothing in either case seems to be helpful.

Dinner was brought over - a roast duck with vegetables. The room grew louder as the men talked, ate, and relaxed. Peter kept a steady eye on his charges while Jack watched the room in general, his eyes straying frequently to the door. The evening wore on. Eventually John stood and helped Father Berram up the stairs to bed. Peter clapped Jack on the shoulder before following along behind the pair.

Jack watched them go, then sat contemplating the room as it fell into quiet, the dancing warmth of the fire throwing flickering shadows across the worn, wooden plank floor. He sat there for several long hours, lost in thought.

Chapter 22

Jack watched from a chair by the window, looking out over the cobblestone street, its edges still lost in pre-dawn shadows. Fresh dew gave the buildings and rooftops a soft glimmer.

He sensed Peter's stretch and spoke without turning. "We will leave as soon as the evening sun touches the horizon," he stated in a low but clear voice. "A few of the Westminster guards have been helped by Shadow over the years in their travels; we spoke of it yesterday during my tours. They can help us find out where she is."

Peter nodded in understanding. He sat up in his bed, putting his arms behind his head as he thought. "If she came down from Lord Xavier's, she would be on the northwest road," he commented. "We can work our way back to Xavier's, asking at each village. We should be able to trace where she has gone in a matter of days." He paused, then glanced down at the two slumbering forms in the beds furthest from the door.

Jack's eyes followed his. "This inn is a veritable fortress, and the Cathedral guards have assumed all responsibility for the care of its inhabitants. They let no one in or out who is not one of this conclave. At this point, we could do no better. I am sure they can postpone the meeting for a few days."

Jack went through the normal routines of the day - washing in the basin on the dresser, eating the fried eggs for breakfast, talking to the soldiers as they changed shift, walking patrols in the streets around the inn. The day crawled on, minute by minute. No word came of Catherine. Jack knew, somehow, that she would not appear today. Something had happened to her, and every second that crawled by meant that her situation was even more dire. His patience was sorely tested as the sun, ever so slowly, crept lower and lower in the sky.

Peter readied the horses and brought them over to stand in front of the inn as evening's shadows stretched across the alleyways. Three guards in black livery came with him, ready with their own steeds. Jack made the final arrangements with the guards who were handling the inn, and gave farewells to John and Father Berram.

John nodded to Jack. "Good luck," he offered, standing at the doorway of the inn. Father Berram nodded his prayers, his shaking hand resting on John's shoulder. Jack had his eyes focused down the length of the street, watching the sun. It passed through a layer of clouds, turning them a rich orange color, then ever so slowly, it rested against the far-off hills.

He mounted smoothly, and the other men followed suit. Jack looked down to John. "We will be back soon," he promised. Then he turned to ride north out of the city.

They galloped at a fast clip to clear the city limits, then slowed in order to keep a watch on the side of the road. Every few miles they stopped at an inn to ask about Catherine and to make it known they were looking for her. No one had seen or heard of her travels, and they pressed onward.

They rode until they had covered about ten miles; by then the shadows at the side of the road had become thick and impenetrable. Jack reluctantly reined in. If they continued, and she were lying hurt at the side of the road, they could easily pass her by. The group set up camp in a small clearing. Jack forced himself to get some rest, to be fresh for the morning's ride.

Morning arrived thick with swirling fog, and frustration billowed in Jack's soul. When they set in motion again, he held the group to a gentle trot, all eyes attentively scanning the road's side for any sign of horse or rider. They passed a priest walking in their direction, but he had no news to share of their quarry.

Jack pressed grimly onward, resolute to check every mile between here and Lord Xavier's. He was torn between haste in wanting to get to Catherine, and a need to go slowly in case her body lay just over the edge of a tumbled-down wall or behind a pile of boulders.

A thundering came from the foggy road ahead; Jack motioned to the others, and the group pulled to one side to let the rider pass. A tan horse came at a gallop through the mist, a young, brown-haired man astride. He slowed to a canter to pass the group, his eyes scanning them as he went. When he spotted the dark blue medallion on Jack's chest, he pulled hard at his reins, wheeling his horse into a skidding stop.

"Catherine is in trouble," he called out without preamble, catching his breath and wiping the dust from his eyes. "They are under siege in the town of Wilstead. I was sent to find you."

Jack's heart thundered in his chest. "Lead on!"

The boy took another deep breath, then urged his horse into a hard canter and streamed back the way he had come. Jack and the others followed in hot pursuit.

Jack calculated quickly in his mind as they rode. That trip would be at least fifty miles. They could get there just after nightfall - maybe - if none of their horses foundered.

In a few miles they rode through a tiny hamlet. Jack saw a small group of men lingering on the outskirts, and lowered his hand to the hilt of his sword. If bandits thought they were going to take them on, he was in no mood to stop for an idle chat.

To his surprise, the group fell in beside them without a word and rode along, apparently joining the party. At the next village, another four men silently joined in. The men were not soldiers, but appeared quite able and were well armed. Jack realized with grim pleasure that Catherine's support in this region was strong indeed. These men seemed ready to lay their lives on the line. He only hoped that it would not be necessary.

The miles passed beneath the horses, rolling by as meadow and forest, village and farmyard. An hour passed, then two. As the sun passed the midday mark, Jack reluctantly waved the men to a stop as they came into the next small village, pulling up around a large, well maintained tavern to give their worn out horses a short break. He begrudged every moment not spent moving along the road, but knew it would be folly to drive the beasts to exhaustion.

Peter was off his horse the moment they drew in, running through the tavern's main door to fetch help and food. A flurry of activity ensued as boys washed down the horses, servants prepared ale and roast duck and the men stretched, making their way inside. The tavern's main room quickly filled up, but it was a somber group that drank and ate amongst the wooden tables and beams. Only a few quiet conversations murmured between groups of friends.

Jack glanced around once he was sure all was settled, looking for the messenger who had begun them on their way. He saw the boy sitting at a table in a quiet corner with Peter and moved over to join them. Peter pushed a mug of ale in his direction as he sat on the sturdy chair, and Jack gratefully drank it down.

Peter nodded at the slender lad. "Jack, meet Nicholas," he introduced. The boy put out his hand, and Jack clasped it in thanks.

"We owe you a debt of gratitude for coming to find us," offered Jack quietly.

Nicholas shook his head at once. "There is no way I could even begin to repay Catherine for what she has done," he insisted with fervor. "If it was not for her, my dearest fiancée -"

He swallowed and looked down into his drink, his face going pale. After a long moment, he looked up again at Jack. "Catherine nearly died to save my Zoe. I promise you I will gladly risk my life in return."

Jack glanced at Peter, his eyes sharpening with interest. "What happened?"

Nicholas's eyes widened in surprise. "She did not tell you? But you are *her* intended! Surely she had to explain the injuries to you when -"

He cut off, nodding. "If she did not, it was out of loyalty to my Zoe. However, you deserve to know to what lengths she went to for us."

He took a long drink of his ale. "Catherine had been visiting the villages on and off for as long as I can remember. She wore a disguise at times, but we knew well enough who she was. In recent years, she made a point to talk with the parents of any teen girls, asking them to keep a special eye on the lasses. She asked for word to be sent to her if any girl went missing, no matter how innocent it seemed. She said she would much rather go on a wild goose hunt than risk a girl's safety."

Nicholas glanced with shame at Jack. "Zoe and I thought she was being overzealous, and laughed about it, the times we snuck off together."

He took another swallow of his ale. "Then, not long ago, Zoe went off to visit a friend for the afternoon and never came back. Her parents thought she was with me; I thought she was at home. It was very late that evening before we realized she was gone. The moment it was clear she really was missing, I did not hesitate. I sent word to all of the nearby villages, letting them know that Catherine was needed. We started a search for Zoe, to no avail. By dawn Catherine had arrived; she was exhausted from a recent long ride but she did not hesitate in joining the hunt."

Peter looked up at Jack. "That must have been just after she distracted Conrad's men from your trail."

Jack nodded in agreement. "It seems to fit." He turned to look at Nicholas. "What happened then?"

Nicholas' eyes grew unfocused as he thought back over the events. "It was a long, harrowing day. Catherine was able to pick up the trail where others had lost it, and we followed it through the forest, across several streams and rocky ravines. Zoe had met up with two others, it appeared, and she went with them willingly. I could not understand it."

Jack looked over at Peter, his eyes morose. "They were skilled at their craft, apparently," he murmured quietly.

Nicholas nodded. "It seems so. It was past dark before we heard voices up ahead. Catherine made us stop before we came within sight, and made us swear to wait there for her. We would have argued, but she convinced us that she would do better with stealth than having us all move in together. Then she was gone. It was a long half hour, but we waited, not moving, not making a sound." He took in a long, deep breath. "Then suddenly Zoe was there with us, bruised, her wrists red from ropes, wrapped in Catherine's cloak. She said that Catherine had told us all to flee back to the village, to get Zoe to safety."

Jack held Nicholas's eyes with his own. "What did you do?"

The boy's eyes flashed with pride. "Zoe absolutely refused to leave. We could hear the swordplay by now, and knew there was trouble. If there was any way we could help – even slightly – we would do it. We crept slowly to the edge of the clearing. Then, suddenly, everything went quiet. We moved in more quickly - and we saw …"

He glanced guiltily at Jack, his eyes moving down to the medallion at Jack's chest. "You undoubtedly saw the result of that beating, and the images will be forever seared into my mind. All three lay there without moving. We thought they were all dead, that she had truly given her life for Zoe's escape. But somehow, fantastically, we found she had breath in her, slight though it was. We rigged up a sling and between us we got her back to the village."

Nicholas looked between the two men. "To protect Zoe, Catherine worded the public story so that it was Shadow having a fight with known bandits. Zoe was merely caught in the crossfire. That way Zoe's injuries could be explained without further discussion."

Jack nodded to Nicholas. "Is Zoe … healed?" he asked with concern.

Nicholas took a drink of his ale. "It is due to Catherine that she is. I saw the two of them together, during the days she stayed with us, talking long into the night. Catherine showed Zoe something on her arm, and I know they spoke of being survivors, that they had the strength to face any obstacle. It meant a great deal to Zoe, that she had a sister, of sorts, in Catherine now."

He sighed deeply. "I know Zoe was hurt, and that nothing will erase that. Still, she seems … stronger now, in a way. She is more determined to do what she feels is right, and less concerned about what others might think."

He looked at Jack then, holding his gaze. "Catherine saved Zoe's life, and she saved her soul as well. If I can do anything – anything at all – to help Catherine, then I shall do it."

A stableboy ran into the crowded room, threading his way over to Jack's table. "The horses are ready, sir," he called out in a high voice.

Jack needed no further encouragement. He stood at once, and in a moment there was scraping and thumping as the men in the room saw his movement and joined in. Peter quickly paid the bill, and in a few minutes the troop was back on the road, riding strongly toward their destination.

The hours passed in steady riding. Afternoon darkened into evening, with golden colors spreading across the sky. Jack pushed the group even harder, thundering across the roads with fierce determination. They could not ride heavily at night without danger of a broken leg or worse. If they did not make it by full darkness ... but Jack promised himself that they would. The sun slipped down below the horizon, its last reddish haze fading from the sky.

Yet the sky was not dark. There was still a rosy, orange glow ahead of them, flickering on the horizon. Nicholas pulled up alongside Jack as they half cantered, half galloped down the forested road. "That is Wilstead," he called out, making sure he was heard over the hoofbeats and heavy breathing of the horses.

Jack's gaze was intense. "It is on fire."

Chapter 23

Jack's group now numbered thirty or so men, and they needed no exhortation to ride at the limits of their steeds' abilities. The flames were plain to see and grew brighter as they rode closer. It seemed only minutes before they pulled up on a hill overlooking the small village.

Every structure in view was fully involved in flames. Orange and red streamers danced from small homes, barns, a mill, and a granary. A scattering of horses fled wild-eyed from the heat and smoke. Jack could see dark shapes moving about in the village, but these appeared to be soldiers, not villagers. The figures made no attempt to put out the fire or seek shelter - instead, they methodically moved from structure to structure, searching.

A shout came from their left, and a group of archers came out of the woods toward them, cheering in relief. A lean man strode up to Jack's group.

"Nicholas! Thank the Lord. How did you make it here already? We only sent word an hour or two ago!" He shook his head in surprise. "We have already lost three of our group trying to stop the raiders who are burning the village. It is no use; we cannot pierce their armor with our bows, and they come up to attack us whenever we start our volley."

Jack took in a few deep breaths, his heart still pounding from the long ride, then dismounted from his weary steed. "We have just come from London. What is happening?"

The archer looked baffled at the reference to London, but pressed on without question. "A small party came flying through town early this afternoon; I imagine they were coming from Bedford. There was a force in pursuit - but a larger force was waiting for them here, in this town. I do not know if that larger group was here for other reasons or specifically to catch that party."

He glanced down at the flames, his voice becoming hoarse. "In any case, the fighting broke out immediately. It was like oil and water to see the two. I was cutting wood up here when it began. The townsfolk all raced into the stone church - you can just see it there, to the right side of the green. That is where they have been holed up ever since. The attackers put a torch to everything else and are trying to smoke them out."

The archer looked back to the newcomers. "We tried a few times to run interference for them, but when it was clear it was hopeless, we sent for help. We thought the soldiers would not get here until morning, though. I was amazed you had arrived so quickly."

Jack glanced at Peter. "I do not know for sure if Catherine is down there, but it seems likely." He turned to call out orders to the gathered men. "Half of you stay with me, and we will approach the church from this side. You others, circle with Peter around carefully to the north. Only come down when you see us move. If nothing else, we should have surprise and darkness on our side."

He turned back to speak down to the archers. "Please give us whatever support you can when we launch our assault. I know your arrows might not be ideal, but every bit will help."

The archer nodded his head. "Good luck. " He and his friends slipped back into the cover of the forest.

Jack, Nicholas, and their group picked their way quietly down through the trees, attempting to stay hidden for as long as possible. The forces working below seemed to pay little attention to the woods, and it was quite easy to draw relatively close to the church without being noticed. Jack saw that a group of fifteen or so well-armed soldiers were camped on the green in front of the church, watching the closed doors with careful attention. Another ten men roamed the village area with torches, making sure the homes were fully aflame and that there were no survivors hiding anywhere.

A large, burly man wearing a long, textured cape and fine sword at his hip was standing at the edge of the green, conferring with a bandit with a long mane of white-streaked hair. Jack recognized the latter at once.

Conrad.

Glancing through the other faces present, Jack felt that he could pick out other members of that same crew.

He looked back to the green. As he watched, the two men nodded to each other. The caped man stepped forward into the light of the many torches his men had placed around the church's entrance.

"Catherine!" he called out. "I want to talk. Come out to the stairs and I swear you will not be harmed. Let us find a resolution to this."

There was a long pause, then Jack's heart caught in his throat as the door slowly creaked open. Two figures stepped out through the doorway into the light. One was a middle-aged man with coarse brown hair falling to his shoulders. A deep scar traced its way down one cheek. Jack recognized him instantly. This was Lord Xavier, the man whom Catherine had gone to negotiate with.

Catherine came out right behind him, her face weary, but her eyes flashing fire. Jack saw with anger that her right shoulder was stained crimson with blood, and that there were blood stains on other parts of her clothing as well. Things had not gone easily for the pair. He was tempted to ride in immediately, but if a truce was forming, he wanted to give her the opportunity to end things peacefully.

* * *

Fury welled up in Catherine as she gazed across the dark green at her cousin. When she had first spotted him outside the church, she had the fleeting hope that he had come in a rescue effort. It had quickly become all too clear that he was the mastermind behind the current inferno.

And now he wished to treat?

Her mouth curled in disdain. "Dear Cousin Raymond," she snarled with cold hatred, "There is no oath you could swear that I could believe in. As I recall, you made a promise many years ago to defend the Bowyer people from all harm. Surely that was betrayed a hundred times over when you put every man, woman, and child to the sword."

She shook her head, still not fully believing what he had done. "What sort of power could you possibly hope to gain? If you wanted to rule in my stead, and my exile was not enough for you, why not just kill me and have it done with?" Her voice broke on the last question, but she tossed back her head in defiant challenge.

Raymond's ringing laughter rolled across the valley. "Oh, dear Catherine, do you still not understand what is going on? Of course I am going to kill you. Your noble sacrifice ..."

He chuckled to himself with mirth. "Oh my, you were always the one to try to do the honorable thing and save others."

Catherine held Raymond's gaze and tossed out her offer. "You wish my death? Then come forward and meet me in battle. Let us see once and for all who is the better fighter. Leave the rest of these innocents in peace."

Lord Xavier put his hand on Catherine's arm to restrain her, but she shook it off, taking a step forward.

To her chagrin, Raymond only laughed with glee. "Me, fight you? Oh my girl, that is not my style at all. I prefer a more supervisory role. It is my mercenaries who will cut you down. You will have the ignominious task of fighting - and falling to - the swords of hired hands."

His eyes swept the landscape. "As for your villager friends, why they will all die, of course. I was simply offering to make the deaths quick, if you would come out quietly. If you wish, we are quite happy to burn you out and do this the hard way."

Catherine shook her head in disbelief. "Why are you doing this?"

Raymond grin was a wolf's smirk of delight. "Oh yes, I could reveal for you my motives - why your friends had to die, why your mother was slain while I watched. I could even tell you my end game; what all of this means."

His smile became toothy. "However, I rather enjoy the thought of you dying in complete ignorance. Your last thought will be that you understand nothing at all. That sounds perfectly delightful to me."

Raymond turned to the man at his side. "Conrad, you might be amused to learn that this woman in front of you is no other than Shadow, the lone wolf who has thwarted you several times in the past."

Conrad's eyes flashed, going over Catherine's figure in a long, smooth look. "Well, look at that," he commented with a low whistle. "First I was robbed a commission by her feigned death, and then she shows up in disguise to cause yet more problems."

Raymond nodded in sympathy. "I do apologize about her assassination. The previous one had gone so smoothly that I had not expected any problems when we got down to her. Still, that is all behind us now."

Conrad's eyes sharpened, and he gave a knowing grin. "So you *were* the client on that one. I thought as much. Well then, what is the plan here?"

Raymond waved his hand. "She is all yours. I have been waiting for this for many years, and it will be sweet to watch as the last of the family is snuffed out. Kill her, please."

Conrad gave a gleaming smile in response. "My pleasure," he called out, then turned to face the pair standing on the church steps.

"Catherine, or Shadow, whatever name you wish to have on your stone, you have been a thorn in my side for far too long." He drew his sword in salute, and touched it to his forehead. He held the gesture with a grin.

Catherine had been watching this exchange with forced detachment, willing herself to remain calm and focused. It did not matter now what list of crimes Raymond was responsible for. All that mattered was surviving this fight and protecting the innocent people who huddled in the church. If Raymond was going to allow her to face Conrad one on one, she would count her blessings in having that opportunity. One step at a time.

Conrad patiently waited for her move. Catherine drew smoothly and returned the salute, her eyes dark. At that, Conrad swung his sword to his right, finishing the salute. Then he gave his sword a spin and then called out to his men, "Attack at will, but the girl is mine!" A hearty cry went up, and the band stormed toward the church's door.

To Catherine's surprise, an echoing yell surrounded them from all sides. A voice sounding eerily like Jack's rose above it.

"Defend the church!"

In an instant there was thundering of hoofbeats descending from both sides of the green. Most of the mercenaries wheeled, completely taken off guard by this double-fronted attack. Conrad, however, did not hesitate a moment in his drive. He had set his target and was driving toward Catherine. A wiry blond at his side zeroed in on Lord Xavier, and in a second the swords clanged as the pair of combatants locked in deadly combat.

Catherine fought with every ounce of her strength. There was no holding anything in reserve now. She was exhausted from a hard day of riding and from the fighting that had come and gone during the day. With the village in flames and the attack finally launched, it was time to either take down the mercenaries or die trying.

She had held out hope that her cousin could be reasoned with, but whatever his plan, it apparently involved the death of everyone here. She had to do her best to stay alive to protect them.

She feinted left, then drove hard right. The throbbing in her shoulder sent waves of pain throughout her body from where Raymond had caught her unawares earlier. It seemed like a lifetime ago.

She shook her head and blocked a twisting swing from Conrad, stumbling back a step. She had to focus.

Catherine desperately wanted to help defend Lord Xavier from this blond assailant, but Conrad was a skilled soldier and she had her hands more than full keeping his sword from her flesh. He was taking great care in his attacks, not underestimating her in any way. She glanced up at his eyes. They were dancing with delight - he was enjoying himself. He answered her look with an amused smile.

"If I had known before that you were Shadow, I would have spent much more time with you," he laughed with a grin, flashing the sword in a deadly combination that nearly took out her eye. "It will be a shame to see you dead. If I had my way, I might keep you as a pet for a while."

"I am not dead yet," gritted out Catherine, making a quick stab to his left, which he avoided easily. The fight moved back and forth across the stairs, caught up in feints and quick movements. Conrad was quite her equal, and she felt it in every exchange. She was running out of tricks, and her strength was quickly fading.

It was time to gamble. Feigning a stumble, she went down hard on one knee. The move almost took the wind out of her, and she hoped against hope that he would come in quickly against her.

He did, moving hard, driving his blade home for the sure kill. She rolled easily out of the way, and came up with her dagger straight into his stomach.

He cried out in surprise, his momentum carrying him sailing past her. The motion ripped her dagger out of her hand. He landed on the bottom stair, looking up into the sky in shock. Then the light faded from his eyes, and he was dead.

Barely hesitating, Catherine spun to run up alongside Xavier. His opponent was Marc, the second in command of the mercenary group. Marc had already been wounded several times in the exchange, and as she reached the top step, Xavier gave a final blow to his neck. Marc dropped like a stone, and lay still.

Xavier looked up at her approach and clapped her on her good shoulder in pleasure. "You are all right, thank God," he breathed gratefully.

The two turned to put their back to the door again, surveying the scene. The horsemen who had ridden in were circling through the village, engaging the mercenaries. Then, through the smoke and fire, Catherine spotted a spiral medallion with a deep blue center. A sweeping sense of relief gave her fresh strength.

Jack had come for her.

She watched as he fought with a mercenary, flinging himself down off his horse to topple the man over. He rolled twice and then came up with a sharp slash that opened the man up across his chest. The mercenary dropped back, dead. Jack surged to his feet, his eyes turning toward the church.

Looking up, his eyes met with hers. For a long, powerful moment, their connection spanned the green, the world around them quieted, and it was as if her breath suspended. Jack's face glistened with sweat and determination as the fires raged behind him and the smoke welled up toward the sky in thick billows. She knew from his eyes that there had never been any question of his coming to her rescue.

With a shout, he raced across the green toward her at a hard run.

She called out in anguish as a man stepped between Jack and her, causing him to pull up short. Exhausted as she was, she started forward at a sprint, only to be restrained by Lord Xavier's strong arm around her waist. The new combatant was her cousin Raymond, untouched by any wound, barely involved in the fighting. He was fresh, well fed, well rested, and he eyed the medallion at Jack's chest with unabashed interest.

"Well, well, now. What have we here?" crooned Raymond with bright curiosity. "I have not seen a blue medallion in, what, fifteen years. Not since dear Catherine's father passed away. Tragic, that. Is not that right, my sweet cousin?"

He looked over his shoulder at Catherine, who had fallen to her knees in exhaustion and frustration. Xavier still held her on the steps by one arm. “Ah yes, I see now that yours is golden. How silly of me not to have noticed it before. I am afraid I had other things on my mind. Your death, the destruction of the village ...”

* * *

Jack drew in a calm breath as the elegant noble turned from Catherine to stare at him with renewed interest. Catherine was safe. His men surrounded the green in a ring, and would ensure Raymond did not escape, whatever the results of this battle. She would have her justice.

He balanced his sword in his hand, eyeing his opponent. Raymond looked to be in excellent shape, and he moved across the green with the smooth agility of a cat. His sword was of high quality construction, and from Catherine’s tales he was a superb swordsman. Jack circled him warily.

Raymond pursed his lips as he ran his eyes down Jack’s form. “You are not any of the Bowyer; we seem to have accounted for all of them. Surely dear Catherine would not pledge herself to a random outsider. Yet, you seem familiar ...”

Jack’s voice was smooth and clear. “I am the foster son to Lord Epworth. My name is Jack; you know me as Southerner.” He continued to circle, firming the grip on his sword.

Raymond’s eyes lit up in surprise. “Ah, so Catherine saw through that little deception, did she? Yes, that was quite an amusing game to play with her. I saw no harm in humoring her mother’s petty plans for a while.” His eyes narrowed. “Still, surely you seem more familiar than that scruffy ...”

Suddenly Raymond’s mouth dropped open in shock. When he spoke again, his voice was slower, and had lost some of its cock-sure banter. “You are a Tanner. You are a Tanner, just like the villagers here,” he gasped softly, shaking his head in amazement. “I was positive Carl and Craig killed all who had left here, had ensured we had every one corralled within these borders.”

Fury washed over Jack. "You were responsible for my parents' deaths?" he called out in ringing challenge, his voice icy steel. "You are behind the other abominations wreaked by those two men?"

Raymond recovered his poise quickly, and laughed with mirth. "While they were excellent killers for hire, those two did have their little side hobbies, did they not? I admit they proved themselves to be incompetent kidnappers. I suppose your troublesome fiancée told you all about how they captured her, but became distracted with her … ah, charms … and she was able to escape her bonds and make it home again. I was amused when it spawned her intense interest in learning to sword-fight."

His eyes scanned up and down Jack's body. "As far as taking out the Tanners, why yes, I always did appreciate a bit of theatricality. I tell you quite freely that the man who killed your ma and pa is about to take you down as well. Although why I always have to clean up after that lecherous pair is beyond me." He grinned over at Jack. "Well, then, come on, lad. Avenge your family."

Jack nearly gave in to the surge of anger which filled every corner of his being. With supreme effort he remained still, maintained his guard. He knew Raymond was taunting him, drawing him in to make a mistake. The man could not succeed.

Jack's voice rang out with icy calm. "This will be for everyone you have harmed, in all of our families," he vowed. His men formed a loose ring around the green, and in a moment Peter moved up the stairs to stand over Catherine, taking the side opposite Lord Xavier. She was still on her knees, her eyes desperately focused on the scene. She held her hand to her chest, the dark brown ring pressed to her heart, and he could tangibly feel the wave of love and support she sent to him.

Jack took in a deep breath, then let it out, rolling his shoulders. He nodded at her, giving her a half smile. Then his eyes returned to Raymond. He brought his blade in a high guard, waiting.

Raymond suddenly flew into action, drawing his sword down and in, aiming to end the fight with a quick decapitation.

Jack's deflection was instant, sending the blade skimming over his head. Raymond twisted the blade instantly, sending it back toward Jack's waist. Jack slammed his own blade down on top of Raymond's, driving both points into the dirt. The two men leapt back, resetting their guards, preparing for the next strike.

Raymond moved again, and Jack knew exactly where the blow would land, exactly what the next turn would be. He realized suddenly why Raymond's style seemed so intimately familiar. It was the same as Catherine's; it held the same imprint of training that Jack had learned and studied over these past few weeks in sparring and training with Catherine.

He smiled, pressing his advantage. He allowed his left thigh to momentarily be unguarded, and sure enough, Raymond's sword arced high first, then twisted and drove down. Jack deflected the blow with ease, spinning his blade tip to rip open a gash in Raymond's calf.

Raymond's eyes widened with surprise, glancing down for a moment at the wound. When Jack deflected another round of attacks, and then the next as well, a sudden realization came to his face, and he let out a low oath.

Raymond spared a glance for Catherine, his voice guttural and harsh. "God's teeth, you harpy, will you never cease to cause trouble for me?" Then with a yell he turned and flung himself at Jack with the fury of a battering thunderstorm.

The battle was a whirlwind, and both men were soon riddled with wounds and cuts. The swords slammed into each other, a fist pounded into a shoulder, a whirling blade nearly took off an ear.

Then Jack spun sideways, throwing the full weight of his body behind his shoulder, driving into Raymond's torso. There was a scream of panic from the church; Raymond saw the opening and swung his sword high in triumph, drawing it down to cleave Jack at the shoulder.

Jack twisted, ducked, and barely avoided the whistling blade. At the same time, his own sword came up from below, driving hard up through Raymond's chest.

Raymond threw his arms out, teetering, his eyes wide with shock, and then keeled over backwards. His body slammed into the ground. He lay there motionless, his life's blood pouring out of him.

Jack's heart pounded in his chest as he looked down at the fallen figure. A stampeding of feet came at him fast, and he turned hard at the sound, his dagger in hand, his chest breathing in long draws.

Catherine skidded to a stop before him, her hair a wild tangle, her eyes on his.

In an instant he was dropping the dagger, drawing her into his arms, kissing her with a passion which nearly overwhelmed him.

He wrapped his hands into her long, thick hair, holding her body against his, soothing her shaking. A low murmuring came up from her, half lost against his chest.

"You are safe ... you are safe ..."

It was several long moments before she pulled back from him, gazing up in weary relief.

He ran his eyes over her injuries. "Are you seriously hurt?" A bandage had been tied around her upper arm, and there were various stains and scrapes on other parts of her arms and legs as well.

Catherine smiled fondly up at Jack. "I will heal," she vowed, her hands never leaving his. "We are together, and that is all that matters."

She turned to look down at Raymond. His eyes were dimming with every passing moment. She dropped to one knee at his side, bringing her face down to be near his pale visage.

"Raymond," she pleaded softly. "Do not let your legacy be one of madness and genocide. Help me to understand. Why did you wipe out my home town?"

Raymond laughed softly, and bloody foam bubbled up on his lips. "I am far from insane," he rasped hoarsely. "The council called me crazy; they scoffed at my plans. They said they would rather die than work alongside the slave shipments I had ordered from the Holy Lands. Well, look at who is laughing now!"

His face twisted in a paroxysm of coughing and choking. Then his breathing drew shallow. In another moment he was unmoving, dead.

Catherine knelt there for a long minute, seeming to search for a sign of familiarity, of family, in the glassy stare. Finally she reached forward to close his eyes, and stood wearily.

Lord Xavier stepped forward, looking between Catherine and Jack. "My dear, I realize this is difficult, but there may still be wolves' heads around. We need to get these people to safety."

Nodding in agreement, Jack turned from Catherine and retrieved his dagger and sword. The men in their group gathered in to hear the plans. There were over fifty men in the group now including the archers who had come down from the overlooking woods. Jack quickly scanned the surrounding area, but there were no bandits in sight. All had apparently either been killed or had fled.

Jack returned his gaze to meet Lord Xavier's. "Are the villagers still in the church?"

Xavier walked toward the stone building, and Jack and Catherine fell in step beside him. Xavier's voice was tired but steady. "The priest feels that they do have everyone who is alive in the building; a few people were killed by fire or by the bandits." They reached the heavy church doors, and Xavier pounded three times on them. "It is all right," he called in. "This is Xavier. The danger is over."

There was a muffled cheer from inside, then the sound of heavy furniture scraping on a wooden floor. In a few moments the doors swung open, and grateful villagers poured at them, giving thanks and praise. A graying priest stepped forward to shake Xavier's hand with a grateful smile. "I do not know how we can repay your efforts," he shakily thanked him. "We would have been lost."

Xavier placed his own hand over the frail one of the priest's. "I am still not sure that the force which laid siege to your town was not either bait to draw us in or a trap to which the others drove us," he pointed out. "It may be because of us that this tragedy occurred. We will determine that shortly." He turned slightly to indicate Jack. "Father Jeffrey, may I introduce ..."

He paused, surprised to see that Jack and Father Jeffrey had locked eyes and were looking on each other with wonder. It was the priest who spoke first. "You ... you are Jack, are you not? Son of Robin and Sarah?"

Jack nodded mutely staring at the priest in wonder.

"My boy, you are my nephew," continued the priest warmly. "Your parents left here because ... but that is a long story. I am so glad that you survived ..." A tear trickled down his cheek.

Jack stepped forward to give the man a gentle hug, holding him for a moment.

Jack looked down to his uncle's eyes. "You can tell me everything when we get to safety," he promised quietly. "Right now your peoples' welfare needs to be our top priority."

"In a moment," responded the priest, moving back toward the altar. "First, there is something that I would have given you long ago, if I had known you were alive."

He knelt behind the altar moving his hands against the stonework. In a moment he stood with a wrapped bundle. "We will wait until we get back to Kempston; that is the nearest point of safety. There will be plenty of time for explanations then."

Jack nodded in agreement. In a moment the villagers were all in motion, streaming onto the green. The soldiers had brought down the horses, and in short order they gathered up a few of the local horses who had fled from the fire. By double-loading many of the animals and retrieving a few carts they were able to get the entire group mobile and moving in the direction of the castle.

It was a tense trek for the next few hours, rolling slowly through dark forest. The soldiers kept a vigilant watch over the villagers, listening carefully for any noise besides the creaking of the wagon wheels and soft tread of the horse hooves. Catherine and Jack rode side by side at the front of the group, never far from each other, taking quiet comfort in each others' presence.

It was with great relief that they saw the castle ahead of them and made their way up to its gates. The guards on the wall bustled around like agitated bees on the walls as the large group approached, and the voice which shouted down at them was tense with concern.

"Who goes there?"

Father Jeffrey stepped forward, his brow creased with confusion. "It is Father Jeffrey, of the Tanners," he called out. "Surely you got the news that we were under attack?"

"Attack?" cried the guard in surprise. "We heard no such alert. We would have come out to help! Is there still trouble?" He waved down below, and the main doors were swung open with a drawn out creak.

"The danger is past for now," Father Jeffrey reassured. "We have all of the townsfolk here, and solely seek refuge for a day or two until we can figure out how things stand."

Soldiers trotted out to help guide in the wagons, and in only minutes Lord Sutton, wrapped in a thick bearskin cloak, strode down to greet his friends. He gave a hearty embrace to Lord Xavier, then a more tender one to Catherine. His handshake to Jack and Peter was firm and welcoming.

"There will be enough time for discussion tomorrow," he instructed in a hearty voice. "Right now you are safe. These walls have not been breached in decades." Around him the castle had sprung to life, with pages guiding all of the villagers and fighters to places to sleep.

Lord Sutton nodded in approval at the bustle in the courtyard, then turned back to the smaller group before him. "Come, please follow me to your sleeping quarters."

Jack supported Catherine as they wearily followed Lord Sutton up to a series of adjoining rooms on the top floor of his keep. Each had a freshly stoked fire blazing in its hearth, and a plate of food set on a table. Jack and Catherine gave their fond good nights to Peter and Lord Xavier, then Jack guided Catherine into her room, closing the door firmly behind him.

He turned to face Catherine, and she came into his arms instantly, drawing close against his chest. He wrapped his arms around her, gratitude swelling through his soul.

She was safe.

It was long minutes before he could release her, could help her over to the table. She fell at the roast chicken and steamed turnips as if she had not eaten in weeks, and he smiled in appreciation before making short work of his own meal.

Then her eyes were closing, and he half-carried her the short distance to the bed. She tumbled on it without removing her clothing, raising a hand to draw him down against her. He went willingly, laying an arm protectively across her. Deep calm filled him as her breath eased into the quiet rhythm of sleep.

At last – at long last – his world seemed absolutely right.

Chapter 24

Catherine wondered if she was in a dream. Afternoon sunbeams stretched across the large bed, pleasantly warming her through the green tapestry covers. Fragrant breezes danced through open windows, tickling the delicate curtains at the bed's corners into drifting motion. At her side, Jack was breathing easily in a deep sleep, his features serene. They were both fully clothed, the dust of the road incongruous with the freshness of their surroundings.

Catherine hated to disturb his sleep, but she could not help herself. She tenderly kissed Jack on his cheek. His eyes opened instantly, relaxing into a smile as they focused on her own. He brought up his arms to tenderly wrap them around her, to draw her down against him in a full embrace.

A few hours later, the sky tingeing to ebony and the breeze turning chill, they climbed out of bed and sat on its edge. Jack carefully tended to her wounds, replacing the field dressings with care. Then they drew on the fresh clothes which had been laid out for them. Jack had been provided black tunic and leggings with silver embroidery at the hems. Catherine wore a long, burgundy dress with a white chemise, and she draped her black cloak over her shoulders for extra warmth as Jack shuttered the windows.

Peter was waiting for them as they entered the main hall. "Catherine, how are you feeling?" he asked with tender care, giving her a gentle hug. "Are my salves helping?"

"Yes, as always," she agreed, returning his embrace. "I think the solid night's rest was the best medicine of all, though. It seems like an eternity since I have slept that well."

"I am sure that Jack had something to do with that," chuckled Peter, putting out his hand and shaking Jack's in welcome. "I am glad to see you both up and about."

Jack glanced around the torch-lit room. "What is the current status?" Catherine and Jack followed Peter as he led them toward the head table. The dining area was laid out with numerous wooden round table, but only a few people huddled around the main table at one end.

Peter nodded his head toward the main archway. "The villagers and soldiers are out in the courtyard, holding an enthusiastic celebration of survival," he explained with a smile. "They are amply stocked with ale and food, and last I heard there was dancing. Only a few of us have remained inside, to plan out the next step."

Lord Xavier and Lord Sutton nodded in greeting as the trio approached. Father Jeffrey came out from behind the table, his eyes misting, looking over Jack from head to toe. He then put out his arms, embracing Jack with hearty warmth.

"My nephew, I had not dreamed you were still alive," murmured Father Jeffrey after a long minute. "When I heard of your parents' deaths, I thought all hope was lost. It is a solace to me that you live on for them, to carry on their name." He motioned with his hand. "Here, come sit beside me while we talk."

The six found seats along the head table, with Peter and Catherine taking either end. Servants hurried in with meat pies and mead, and in between bites Catherine and Jack poured out the entire story from the beginning.

Lord Sutton nodded as the two recounted their tales, his sharp eyes calculating the details. When they were done, he spoke in a musing tone.

"At this point we have accounted for every member of the Bowyer clan, including Raymond. It seems clear that Raymond was involved in the assault. But why? His deathbed comment about slaves is cryptic at best. What could they use slaves for? The Bowyer lands were running quite efficiently. Why would this have turned into such a point of contention between Raymond and his council?"

Catherine nodded slowly, drawing her cloak close around her. "I agree with you completely, Lord Sutton. And even if he were fighting with the council, why rain death on everyone in town – and even those beyond its walls?"

She shook her head. "Also, what of the two mercenaries who left before the assault began? Why would they leave, if they were known to the attackers? Why not remain and cause further damage from within? It is hard even now for me to think about what happened - but it makes it worse for its senselessness. If at least there had been a reason, a motive, it might be reconciled. There seems to be none at all. The wide-flung deaths were not for power or glory."

A curly-haired young page cautiously approached the group, waiting for a moment to interrupt. Sutton spotted the young man and motioned for him to speak.

"I apologize, My Lord." The page gave a brief bow. "You asked me to let you know if any strangers came into our walls. A pair has indeed appeared and asked to speak with you." The lad gulped, then continued. "They say they are from the town of Bowyer."

The group instantly stilled, all eyes riveted on the nervous young page. It was a few moments before Lord Sutton spoke. "You are sure?"

The page nodded. "I know something of the current situation, my Lord. I made very sure - they say they are from Bowyer."

Jack looked with concern at Catherine, but she was already pulling her hood up over her head. "I will stay hidden and silent," she vowed both to Jack and to Lord Sutton. "Please admit them, and question them. I will watch as well, and see what they might reveal, not knowing I am here."

Jack hesitated a moment, then dropped his hand to the hilt of his sword and nodded grimly.

Lord Sutton's eyes roamed the party assembled at the table. "Make sure that none of you, by word or look, betray the trust of the woman who sits with us," he instructed solemnly. "This may be our only opportunity to find out the truth of this matter. If you feel you are not up to this task, please retire now, and no shame will attach to you. It is not an easy thing, to hear lies without a flicker of reaction."

His eyes went around the table, resting heavily on each person. In turn, each member nodded his assent, taking on the responsibility of controlling every reaction in order to pry the necessary information out of these visitors.

Satisfied, Lord Sutton turned back to the page. "Send them in."

When the brown-haired page vanished through the front archway, it seemed to Catherine that the world held its breath. She focused with absolute attention on that dark opening. Who would return through its mouth? Rough cut mercenaries whom she had never met? Council members whom she had laughed and played with, trusting them for years? Catherine stared at the stout wooden gateway of the hall as if it held the secret to life itself.

There was a shadow, and a movement, and two figures came striding purposefully toward the table.

Catherine gave a soft cry of disbelief.

"No ..."

Jack placed his hand over hers, comforting her as best he could with his presence. She barely felt his touch, focused solely on the figures approaching the table. Both were relatively short, with one figure appearing slender, the other a bit stout.

As the two approached, they put back the hoods on their long cloaks. Catherine's heart jagged with pain, as if a razor-sharp dagger had speared her through. It could not be ...

The two women knelt easily before the table, bowing their heads to Lord Sutton. The taller one spoke in a light, melodic voice, her golden hair shining in the afternoon light. "My lord, I bring you greetings from Bowyer. My name is Susan, and my companion is Marcie. We have been traveling many days on our journey, and we beg lodgings from you as well as assistance on our quest."

Lord Sutton looked neutrally down on the pair, his face not registering a flicker of recognition. "Ah yes, I have met your Lady several times in the past years. How was she when you left her?"

Susan stood, her face weary but genial. "She was well, My Lord. It was she that sent us on our journey. Once we rest, we will set out on it again shortly. We are looking to meet up with Catherine. Have you seen or heard of her?"

There was not a movement in Lord Sutton's eyes or face to betray Catherine's nearness to the party. His voice held casual interest. "What is your business with Catherine?"

Susan immediately became guarded, her eyes flickering to her companion before answering. "I am afraid that is privileged information, My Lord. We are only allowed to give this information to Catherine herself. If you have not seen her recently, then we will continue on our way once we take some rest."

Jack's voice broke smoothly into the silence. "Exactly when was it that you left Bowyer?"

Both women swiveled their attention to Jack, and their tension became visibly thicker. Marcie spoke up. "It was on the night of the last full moon," she replied testily. Her eyes narrowed. "I believe I know you, sir. You are the man who is known as Southerner."

Susan spoke quickly, directing her comments to Lord Sutton. "My Lord, if this man has spoken against us, I insist that we be heard. He is rumored to be a recluse and a miscreant. The Bowyers have been known to you for many years as trustworthy and valuable allies. Do not take his word against ours in this matter. It is critical that we reach Catherine and have a private conference with her."

Lord Sutton's eyes flashed at this, and his voice gained an edge which caused both women to recoil. "Be cautious, emissaries of Bowyer," he warned with a sharp tone. "You are in my territory now, and this man is trusted by me. You are not. If you have a case to make, it is best that you make it clearly."

Susan spoke more slowly this time, choosing her words with care. "We have been entrusted personally, by Lady Bowyer, to deliver a dispatch to her daughter," she stated formally. "You do not hold power over us. We will only provide our news to Catherine directly, in private.

Jack rose in a fluid motion, moving to stand in front of the two women. "Just when was it on that day that you left the company of the Lady?"

Susan's eyes flared at the repeated questioning. Both women's hands dropped to their hilts at his approach. In a flash Jack has his sword at the neck of the taller one, causing her to stand perfectly still.

Jack's voice was low, holding a core of steel. "I think you were about to drop your sword."

Without a flicker, both women moved their hands to their belts, releasing their swords to the ground with a clatter. Susan's jaw was tense as spoke to Lord Sutton. "I protest this mistreatment, My Lord. If you do not know where Catherine is, simply tell us and we will leave you in peace. This hostility is uncalled for."

Jack kept his sword at Susan's throat, and Catherine could see how tightly he held check on his anger. "When you get Catherine alone, then what? What sort of a *present* will you be offering to her?"

Susan's eyes flashed with barely controlled fury as she followed the path of Jack's questionings. "You go too far, sir," she snarled. "You know nothing of our bond with Catherine. We would give our lives for her, and we will find her to protect her."

Her eyes flicked to meet Sutton's, then returned to face Jack's again, meeting his gaze levelly as she regained her composure with effort. "You could not possibly understand. Catherine is as dear to us as our own families."

Lord Sutton's voice cut smoothly into the tension between the two. "Then would it upset you to hear that the town of Bowyer was put to the torch the evening you left, and that every man, woman, and child was slain?"

There was a long moment of silence as both women looked, with shocked faces, to Lord Bowyer. That they were surprised by this was plain to all present.

Marcie spoke out first. Her voice was low and hoarse. "You cannot be serious, my Lord. This is but a lie spread by Southerner. I cannot imagine for what twisted reason he would say such a thing."

Lord Sutton shook his head, keeping a close watch on the pair. "This information has been confirmed by many sources. It is true. The entire town has been eradicated."

Marcie sagged against Susan at this. Susan put her arm out automatically to her friend, her own face white with shock.

Lord Sutton did not relent. "If you have something for Catherine, it is time for you to lay it out before us. You admit to having left the compound the day of the attack. The burden is on you to prove to us you were not involved." He paused for a moment before adding, "We can, of course, take any item you carry by force. We have sworn to get to the bottom of this matter."

Susan only hesitated a moment before shaking off Jack's sword and reaching into her backpack. She withdrew a squarish box, slightly larger than a man's head.

"This is our mission," she stated, her voice breaking. "If what you say is true, then our need to find Catherine is even greater than we thought. She must be desperate ..." She looked away, the enormity of the situation hitting her fully.

Jack returned his sword to Susan's throat, and she did not resist the motion this time. Tears trickled down her face as she gently patted Marcie on the shoulder.

Shielded from view by Jack's body, Peter passed the wooden box into Catherine's cloaked hands. She quickly worked at the intricate lock to release the latch. The lid sprung open and she unrolled the scroll which laid on top, reading quickly.

When she finished, she stood and laid a hand on Jack's arm, drawing him back alongside her. "It is all right," she breathed softly. As he retreated to her side, she spoke up more loudly, relating the contents of the scroll.

"My daughter Catherine," she read, catching the attention of all present. "I write this in haste. We have only just discovered that Raymond has betrayed us. There is not enough time to mount a defense. The two spies in our midst have been discovered, and we can only send out two in their stead."

She paused, looking up at Marcie and Susan from her hooded depths. "We have chosen your two friends in the hopes that they, of all people, can discover your location and bring these items to you. Please accept that they know nothing of what is about to take place. If we had told them, they would have insisted on staying and defending their homes. We know that is a lost cause. It is far more important that they reach you, that they bring these items to you."

Catherine slid back her hood, and Marcie and Susan embraced each other in relief, crying out in joy amidst their sorrow. Catherine smiled at them fondly, then continued reading.

"You have spoken out for action when we counseled retreat. Now our reticence has brought us our doom. I regret so many things, and there is not time to put them right."

Catherine paused for a moment, her face flushed. She looked around at the group present, then continued. "I also accept now that I was wrong to keep you away from Jack. Word has reached me that you have become close to him. I wish you both joy and, if you end up together, know that I give you my blessing. Yours, Mother."

Catherine slowly withdrew the other items in the box. She realized with awe that her mother had sent the master set of the Bowyer scrolls. These documents held all training notes for each of the military and diplomatic works done by the Bowyers. She lingered over these for a few moments, fully realizing all they signified.

Then she looked up at her friends, and her resolve broke. She moved past Jack to embrace Susan, closing her eyes and giving herself over to her sweeping emotions.

After the trio had finished reuniting, a page brought a pair of chairs for the two newcomers, and they settled down at the near side of the table. Jack retook his seat by Catherine, and as he did, his pendant fell forward out of his tunic. The two women looked sharply at this, then over to Catherine, their eyes drawn to her golden necklace.

Catherine smiled at her friends. "Let me introduce you to my fiancé, Jack, of the Worcester Cathedral."

Susan's eyes widened with shock. "But surely Jack and Southerner are not the same person?"

Catherine laughed merrily at her friend's confusion. "There is much that you will have to re-learn," she consoled her with a smile. "There are many things we were told which were not exactly true."

Father Jeffrey spoke up. "Let me help as I can. Yesterday I retrieved an item from our family altar. It is time I made that known to you all." He reached beneath the table and brought up a carefully wrapped object. With reverence, he slowly removed its coverings.

The item was revealed to be an ornate register, surrounded by a finely tooled leather covering. "This is the church's records," he explained to the group. "The mercenaries and Lord Raymond were both insistent on finding it, but it was well hidden. It traces the Tanner family back many generations. The records show that the Tanners are direct descendants of the same line Sir Magnor is a member of. Sir Magnor is currently without an heir, which as you know has caused quite a strife-filled situation."

He tapped his hand on the register. "All of those lands, according to these records, would descend to my older brother.

With him dead, they would go to ..." his eyes moved across the room to meet with Jack's. "To you, Jack."

Jack looked at his uncle in surprise. "Why would Sir Magnor not have known of this?"

Father Jeffrey chuckled softly. "Ah, but he did know of it. My mother and Magnor were cousins. The battle goes back a previous generation, when two men fought for the love of a woman."

His aging eyes lost their focus. "My grandfather won the heart of the lady, but his younger brother swore to kill both of them out of spite. The lovers fled, abandoning their land in order to be together. They came here, and helped to found this village. They deliberately chose to live in quiet exile."

The priest held Jack's eyes. "The couple had one daughter, my mother, your grandmother. She made it clear to Magnor that she would not make any pretensions to his position, as long as he left her family alone. It seemed there would be a truce."

"So what happened to start the fighting?" asked Jack, unraveling the layers in his mind.

Lord Xavier spoke up. "I can answer this. Raymond happened. As a neighbor, his greed for land knew no bounds. He spurred other bordering lords into causing trouble, to weaken Magnor's forces. From his point of view, the situation was ideal."

He leant back in his chair, talking through the sequence of events. "Raymond used the strife to lure in Catherine's father, and then had him assassinated. He almost succeeded in killing Catherine there, many years later. In the meantime, to remove any other claimants, it appears that he had arranged for your parents to be killed, Jack."

Lord Xavier nodded wearily as he recounted the tale. "I suspected some of this, but I could not tell who was working with Raymond. I was unable to determine if other Bowyers were behind the assaults on Magnor, or if the Tanner family was somehow involved, seeking revenge."

Father Jeffrey looked fondly at his nephew. “I thought that all three of you had been lost, so many years ago. I am grateful to find that you, at least, slipped through their nets.”

Catherine shook her head, entwining her fingers with Jack’s. “Yet, this cannot be the whole answer. It is one thing for Raymond to have sought the death of those in line of our leadership, to expand his land base. That, at least, makes some sense.”

She looked over at Marcie and Susan, her eyes shadowed. “However, why would he have killed off the entire clan? Why, only now, move against the rest of your village, when he had killed Jack’s parents so many years ago?”

Lord Xavier nodded in agreement. “Until recently, it seems that Raymond felt he had things under control. He was working at a slow pace, so as to not raise suspicion. It would even appear that, with Catherine’s exile, he had succeeded. He would have had control of Bowyer on one side, and once Magnor died, moved into that area as well. He would have tripled his holdings with minute effort; certainly no true battles. That seemed very much his style.”

He looked around the table. “We still do not have all the pieces. Catherine has convinced me to come to London, to join the conclave. Maybe with all of us present we can sort out what is happening.”

Jack nodded. “Then we should leave first thing tomorrow morning. We have three days’ travel in front of us, if we pace ourselves more properly for the journey.”

Lord Xavier smiled. “Then let us get you properly ready!” He clapped his hands, and servants streamed in carrying roast goose, steamed turnips, and mugs of ale. Catherine took down a long drink, then leant against Jack. His arm came up around her shoulder as naturally as if they had been together for years. She looked over to Marcie and Susan, and ease settled into her center.

Somehow, they would figure it all out.

* * *

Catherine pulled the cinch on her horse's saddle, gathering up the reins to guide him out into the center of the courtyard. The early morning sun drifted in golden sparkles across the gathered group. Peter, Lord Xavier, young Nicholas, and Father Jeffrey were already mounted, and Marcie and Susan emerged from the stables right behind her. Lord Sutton had his head down with Jack, sharing some last minute thoughts.

Catherine stepped forward to embrace Lord Sutton as the others sat ready on their horses. "Thank you again for all your support," she offered warmly. "We will send word once we have any news for you."

"Thank you, I appreciate that immensely." Lord Sutton looked across at the spread of villagers moving about in the walled enclosure. "I will make sure these villagers are resettled securely, and that any wolves' heads who remain on our lands are tracked down and brought to justice."

Catherine mounted, and in a moment Jack had pulled alongside her. The group walked along the road to London, taking an easy pace to get them there within three days. The weather was turning toward summertime and the travel was quiet and restful. Catherine found herself relaxing on the road, falling into the easy rhythm with her friends all around. The time passed quickly with the telling of tales, either of Susan and Marcie sharing tales of Catherine's youth, or Father Jeffrey filling Jack in on tales of his parents' younger years.

It seemed only a short while before they were riding into London itself, down the familiar streets. When they turned onto the lane which held their inn, John was waiting out front, a large grin on his face. He ran down the street toward them, calling with loud joy. "Catherine! Jack! Peter! You are all right!" He ran up to grab onto Catherine's reins, holding her steed while she dismounted and swept him up in a warm embrace.

She looked forward to the inn with a smile. Father Berram stood by the door, leaning against the door frame for support, waving feebly at the group. She waved back, her spirit lightening.

They were all together again. Somehow they would find an answer to all of their problems.

Jack was at her side, looping his arm around her waist, and all concerns fled her mind. Whatever came tomorrow, they would face it together. She knew with certainty that she would never leave his side again.

Chapter 25

Tuesday morning dawned with shimmering light, and Catherine took it as a good omen. She stretched in the warm golden glow, turning to nestle against Jack. He drew a hand slowly along her waist, his eyes thickening with passion as she slid her hips against his.

His voice came out as a hoarse murmur. "We do have somewhere to be ..."

"Not for another hour or two yet," she responded with a chuckle, giving an additional movement of her hip.

He moaned, and then he was kissing her, and time stood still, tracked only by the progress of the sun across the polished wood floor.

A while later, there was a knock at the door, and Peter's cheerful voice came calling through the wood. "All right, you two, time for breakfast," he teased merrily. Catherine gave a final kiss to Jack before rolling out of bed. The two dressed quickly, joining the group down in the main room.

Breakfast was complete before they knew it and in short order they all walked together to Westminster Abbey. A full complement of guards accompanied them, seeing them safely from the inn's quiet courtyard, through the awakening streets of London and finally up to the massive wooden doors of the abbey.

The soldiers halted outside the doors, watching over the group as they relinquished their arms and entered the holy walls. Catherine and Jack both paused for a moment before handing over their weapons into the safekeeping of the brothers.

For the first time in many weeks, Catherine felt truly safe as she and Jack walked side by side through the halls of the Abbey. All of the threats were in the past now. Carl and Craig were dead. Conrad and Marc were slain. Raymond himself was now buried. It was just left to figure out why this had all happened.

Passing a row of low windows, she caught her own reflection. She wore a tan tunic, with her hair flowing loose down her back. She twined her fingers into Jack's, looking up at him with fondness. His leather armor was well used but neat, and she could see the cuts from the recent battle in the seams. On his chest, the blue medallion shone. His answering smile was calm and content.

Turning a corner, they found that Sir Magnor was standing in the hall before them. Magnor's eyes sharpened at their approach, and he walked up to stand before Jack. He spoke without preamble.

"My lands are mine. My parents made me swear it on each of their deathbeds. I will hold to my oath. None from your line shall ever have them."

Magnor paused a minute, then continued with a steely undertone. "As you know, I have no heir. Therefore, I have signed my rights away. All of my lands go over to the church on my death, to guarantee that you cannot lay claim to them. This cannot be revoked."

Jack met his gaze steadily. "I have no need of your lands," he replied without malice. "I already have all I need, right here by my side."

Sir Magnor considered this for a long while, his eyes considering Jack with sharp attention. Then he put his hand forward.

Jack took it, and the men clasped hands for a long moment. Satisfied, Magnor turned and escorted them through the short hallway into the circular chapter house.

The chapter house was lined with stone benches around its outer walls, and the members of the enclave filed in, sitting on the benches in two rows. Catherine found many familiar faces in the group around the walls, and nodded her greeting to several old friends. John had not been allowed to attend owing to his youth, but Father Berram stood to one side, waiting for her. His embrace seemed more feeble than usual, and as she moved to find a seat, he stayed close to her, gratefully accepting her assistance in negotiating the worn steps.

Jack waited for the two to get settled before sitting on Catherine's other side, his hand absently going to where his sword usually hung. Peter noticed the gesture and smiled slightly. He leant over to whisper, "I must have done that ten times myself."

Peter helped settle Susan and Marcie on his other side, then sat. Lord Xavier stopped to converse with an old friend before coming over to join the group as well.

Catherine carefully ran her gaze across each person in the room. Most she knew, but a few she did not. There were still too many questions left unanswered to assume all were friends. In all, there were perhaps thirty people in the room, preparing to share what they knew to get to the bottom of the situation.

Soon the bells rang eleven a.m. and the gentle murmur of conversation in the room settled down into quiet. All eyes turned expectantly to the main doors, waiting for the Abbot to join them and guide the discussions. Footsteps sounded and approached the entryway of the chapter house.

Lord Epworth stepped into view, his richly embroidered purple cloak billowing theatrically around him. He smiled with delight as the shock of recognition ran around the room.

"Greetings, my brethren," he intoned in a clear, smooth voice which echoed around the stone walls. "Word reached me of the tragic recent events. I felt it my duty to postpone my travel and come lend my aid. This situation was far too important to leave in the hands of other men."

Jack stood slowly, and Catherine found her gaze moving between the two men, realizing that Jack wore the symbol of his engagement to her on his chest. She realized that Lord Epworth would surely understand the significance at once. This was not the way she would have wanted him to learn that she had replaced his rejected courtship with a pledge to his foster son.

Jack's voice was low but steady. "Father, it is good to see you. If we might have a word outside -"

To Catherine's relief, Lord Epworth barely glanced at his foster son, and waved for him to sit down.

"There will be time enough for reunions later, Jack. For now, let us focus on the task at hand. First, are we all here?"

The group looked around slowly, and murmured assents came from all sides. The room was comfortably full, with people seated evenly around its outer edges, resting back on the low stone bench. The tiled floor in the center was open, with Lord Epworth standing in its center. The high sills of the stained glass windows began over their heads. None could look in through that thick, colored glass to spy on their proceedings. They were ready.

"Wonderful," agreed Lord Epworth with a smile. "Well then ... Father Berram?"

Catherine turned to see what the elderly man on her left would bring to this discussion. He had brought the small, bound codex in with him, refusing to allow anybody else to carry it. He struggled to his feet, and Catherine gently helped him stand. He leaned on her gratefully as she supported him down the steps and into the center of the room to stand with Lord Epworth.

Lord Epworth nodded. "Ah, here you are, my old friend," he greeted congenially. "I have heard from the Abbey priests what has gone on until today. It appears there are still some outstanding issues. I believe it is time for us to resolve those."

Father Berram fumbled awkwardly with his parcel, and in the process of turning it in his hands, he dropped it with a loud, soft thud onto the stone floor. Feeling sympathy for the elderly man with so many eyes watching him, Catherine stooped down to retrieve it for him.

The sharp bite of cold steel pressed against her throat. She froze instantly in shocked instinct. To her side, Lord Epworth had not moved - he simply watched with amusement. Slowly she was pressed back into a standing position by the sharp dagger of Father Berram, held by a rock steady arm.

She saw Jack and her friends frozen in mid-movement, a tense look of focused attention on Jack's face.

Jack face held a mixture of bafflement and fury. "Lord Epworth, what are you doing?"

Lord Epworth basked in the attention, and bent down theatrically to pick up the codex at his feet. He tossed it easily to Jack, who caught it in one hand. "Why, see for yourself," he offered with a smile.

Jack looked down to turn through the pages. He stopped suddenly, his brow creasing in confusion. He turned and held the codex up to the assembled group, turning the pages to face them.

Catherine blinked in bafflement. Every page that he turned was empty and unblemished by a single spot of ink.

Her voice was hoarse. "I do not understand ...?"

Lord Epworth's eyes twinkled. "Nor did Michael, although he did not have long to think about his findings. He was always too inquisitive for his own good." He turned to grin down at Catherine. "Still, I am surprised that you do not comprehend the significance. Perhaps that training your family gave you was not as thorough as it should have been."

He looked up at the crowd, pitching his voice to fill the room. "From those first fortuitous days that Carl and Craig brought Jack to me, I have been planning my future. Have you not been following the changes in fortune of King John? His base of support shrinks with each passing day. He has been excommunicated by the Pope, and is desperate for assistance. He is willing to levy huge taxes from our starving population to serve his own needs. In particular, he has offered to pay incredibly large bounties to those who bring him land with mineral wealth. He needs fuel and ore for his plans of conquest. All I needed was the land and the workers to mine it."

Jack held up the book. "So you invented a story to prod Lord Raymond into action? Making him think that his plans were not foolproof enough?"

Lord Epworth smiled in delight. "Exactly. We allowed Raymond to hear rumors that the diary contained proof of what he was up to – that it laid out the genealogies in clear detail."

He chuckled quietly. "As I knew he would, Raymond panicked. Once he failed to get his hands on the diary itself, he felt he had to quickly acquire both Lord Magnor's land and the Bowyers' before either could prepare for his actions. He felt that once the lands were in his name, he could move in his forces and easily hold off any subsequent claimants."

Lord Epworth shrugged and spread his arms. "I simply had to allow him to wipe out the existing leaders of each side, and then take him out myself. I would be the savior - the church moving in to protect the war-torn innocents. To assist in my own claims, I had Catherine practically guaranteed as my wife, which covered the Bowyer side, and you as my son, taking care of the Magnor angle. Everything was working out perfectly."

A small pout appeared on Lord Epworth's lips. "I admit I was a bit surprised when Raymond razed his own family's town. I knew the man was unstable, but that show of temper was rather much. He had several shipments of slaves coming in to handle the mining operations, and the Bowyers threatened to free them, to fight him in every way to keep their home from becoming a slave state. They said they would rather die, and Raymond granted them that option."

He shrugged. "I would have found a way to enslave the Bowyers along with the rest. Why waste the resources of able-bodied men and women? Still, what can you do. He chose his path, and it did not concern me much either way. I had the slaves coming in, and the land ripe for plundering."

He shook his head. "Then you, my darling foster son, became unexpectedly rebellious. The next thing I knew, you had caused my wife-to-be to run off. However, even with your interference, it still seemed that at least her death was guaranteed, as she was moving in Raymond's direction. Not quite as neat as if she had become my wife, but still an acceptable solution."

Jack stepped forward in anger, and Catherine gasped as Father Berram's strong grip pressed the dagger tightly against her neck. A warm trickle of blood traced a slow path down her throat. Jack froze instantly, his face a mask of fury.

"Let her go," he gritted through clenched teeth. "You cannot get away with this."

Lord Epworth cocked an eyebrow. "Ah, my dear foster son, but we already have," he commented lightly. "King John is very pleased with my offerings. Magnor's lands are mine; he signed them over to me himself, as the representative of the church. Raymond's lands will shortly be mine, as he died an enemy of the state. Who is left to rival my claim to the lands of the Bowyer? It is all quite legal and proper. I have the minerals to mine, and the slaves to mine it with. Any resistance has been wiped out for me. I am now one of the wealthiest men in the nation. The only question remaining is one for Catherine."

He turned slightly to face her furious gaze, and chuckled condescendingly at her. "What will it be, my dear? Will you voluntarily agree to wed me, and stay alive? If you choose death, there will be no more contenders for the Bowyer property, and it will fall to me anyway. You do realize that your mother made me guardian of you and your estate, planning forward to the fateful day of our joyous union. Since you have no other kin alive ..."

Lord Epworth smiled at the irony of the moment. "In fact," he continued with quiet glee, "Father Berram is a consecrated priest. He can marry us in the holy bonds of matrimony, right now. We will be done with it in only a few minutes time."

Jack spoke up hotly. "If you force her to marry under duress, that vow will be declared invalid. I will go to the Pope myself and -"

Lord Epworth waved his hand as if an annoying insect had come nearby. "Ah, Jack," he rebutted mildly. "Do you think King John or I am overly concerned about what the Pope says at the moment? We are already excommunicated. John's word is the alpha and the omega. All that concerns us is that she goes through the motions, and that the land is signed over to me. Once our forces get onto the property, I believe possession is nine-tenths of the law. If she does not choose to wed me, we simply slay her, and the land falls to me quite legally anyway."

He turned to look over at Catherine again. "So, what shall it be?"

Catherine looked down for a moment, then turned and steadily met Jack's gaze. Her voice did not waver. "I am promised to Jack," she solemnly vowed. "There will never be another man in my life." Resolve steeled her heart. She would rather die than to let herself become a pawn of Lord Epworth.

Quiet fatalism spread over her. The only reason Jack and Peter were frozen in place was that she was being held hostage. She could drive an elbow into Father Berram's ribs and take her chances. Whether she got free or not, Jack would see to it that these two did not harm any other person, ever again.

Jack's face froze, and she knew he read the desperation of her plans in her eyes. His grey eyes held hers, the swirling clouds in his gaze dark and unreadable.

His voice came to her in a distant call, soft and low. "Catherine, do you trust me?"

Catherine took in a deep breath. Her mood calmed as she allowed herself to be caught by his gaze. She held her head high, time slowing for her. She felt herself treasuring each moment she had spent with Jack. Even if it all ended now, it had been worth it. A smile spread slowly on her lips. "Infinitely," she promised, her eyes locked on his.

Jack looked around the room to the stunned members. "Everybody, please move back against the wall. Make no move against Lord Epworth or Father Berram."

As instructed, the various members stood and moved back to press their backs against the circular stone walls of the room. Lord Epworth smiled with pleasure as his plans moved forward so easily.

Jack and Peter stood side by side against the wall, in line with everybody else. Jack held Catherine's gaze, his face tense with concentration. When he spoke again, his voice was low but firm. "My love, for me ... kneel at Father Berram's feet as Lord Epworth has instructed."

Lord Epworth clapped his hands in glee. "Why, this is perfect! Her true love pushes her into my arms, and into my bed!"

A soft growl sounded in Jack's throat, and Lord Epworth's grin widened in response.

Lord Epworth then looked over to Catherine. She watched his gaze move from the dagger held tightly at her throat, down to the thin line of red which she could feel tracing a path between her breasts.

His voice became condescending, shaking his head at her as he might to a child. "Little one, listen to your beloved. He is speaking sense. It is about time you agreed to marry me, as your mother and council ordered you to. You were willful to disobey them."

He paused for a moment, then his grin grew wolfish. "Do keep in mind, though, that I am a jealous man. Once we are wed, you will not be allowed to see Jack again. Still, at least you will be alive, and he will remain alive as well. He can think of you, every day – of how you warm my bed for me ..."

Catherine did not deign to respond to Lord Epworth's taunts. She turned to focus on Jack's eyes, drawing a rein on her anger, willing herself to believe in him even as she was bewildered by his instructions. Surely Jack would not condemn her to a life as Lord Epworth's wife.

Jack did not say anything further; his eyes pleaded with her to trust … to trust ...

Catherine took a deep, steadying breath, the sharpness of the dagger cutting into her skin with the action. It was time to make a choice. Whatever else Jack had said, he had asked her to trust him. She would do that without question.

Sensing her movement, Father Berram slightly released the pressure at her throat, and she obediently lowered herself to her knees. Her cheeks flushed crimson with shame.

Father Berram moved around to stand between her and Lord Epworth. Lord Epworth gazed down at Catherine with a lecherous grin, sweeping his eyes along the length of her body. Catherine deliberately did not return that gaze. She kept her focus on Jack. If this was to be her last look at him, she would burn it into her memory.

There was a pause that seemed to last an eternity, and then suddenly Jack and Peter whirled into motion. Their hands went to the ledges of the windows high overhead. A split second later, two metal streaks blurred inches over her head. Lord Epworth and Berram gave strangled cries of shock, then both men toppled over backwards, a dagger sticking from each man's chest.

Even as they fell, Jack was hurtling toward her, sweeping her up in his arms, pulling her away from the two men. Peter slid in front of the pair, watching both falling bodies, alert for any counter attacks.

The room echoed in silence as the watchers stared open-mouthed. The two fallen men lay still in the center of the room, not moving. Leaving the ring of onlookers, Lord Xavier strode forward to check the bodies, stopping by first one, then the other. He glanced up at Peter. "Fetch the guards. They may yet live, and it will be a great pleasure to see them answer for their crimes." Peter was gone in a flash, his footsteps echoing down the hallway.

Catherine clung to Jack, shaking in his embrace. It was several long moments before she opened her eyes. She looked up into her lover's gaze, weariness threatening to overcome her.

"I love you, and there will never be any other in my life," she vowed, all else fading from view.

Jack tenderly kissed her on the forehead, her cheek, her neck where the thin line of red ached. "I will always be there for you," he whispered. "No matter what, I will come for you."

Catherine closed her eyes, and the world fell away.

Chapter 26

Catherine drank in the warmth of the inn's dining room, leaning forward to clink a toast to her friends around the table. Lord Xavier and Nicholas drew down the last of their ale in a long pull.

Lord Xavier shook his head. "Really, my dear, we must be off," he teased with a chuckle. "I have many things to tend to." His eyes moved to his side. "I am sure Nicholas here wants to get back to his darling Zoe."

Nicholas's reply was instant. "I will stay as long as Catherine needs me," he vowed, but Catherine saw the longing in his eyes and knew at once how he felt.

"You two get on your way," she encouraged with a soft smile. "You have done more than I could have ever asked for. It is thanks to your efforts that we were able to get through this."

She stood and moved around to hug each man fondly in turn. The group moved out the door, and in a short while they were waving as the two men moved out of sight.

A familiar bear of a man strode down the street toward them, and Catherine nodded in greeting as Sir Magnor came up before the inn. His face had lost its stubborn glare, and now held a hint of abashed shame.

"It seems I was taken for a fool," he admitted to the two in a quiet voice, "but there may be some good to come out of all of this yet. I have talked with the council at the Abbey, and they have agreed to use my land to set up a scholastic center. They will keep it safe from King John's prying hands, and ensure it does not fall victim to whoever moves in to take control of Raymond's lands."

He nodded to Jack. "I believe that young religious friend of yours, John, will be in charge of some of that operation. They find he has a good mix of religious knowledge and soldiering skills."

"Good for him," grinned Jack. "I am sure he will do very well."

Magnor's eyes moved wearily to hold Catherine's. "That only leaves your Bowyer lands to keep safe," he muttered. "I am afraid I do not have the manpower to help with that."

"Do not worry," replied Catherine, looping her arm through Jack's with easy grace. "We will cover that end, I believe."

Magnor looked between the two, then nodded, offering his forearm to Jack. Jack took it with a strong grip, and then Magnor was turning, walking back down the street toward his inn.

Catherine watched him go, then turned thoughtfully to head back into the main room. She had not spoken to Jack of any future plans, and she found her throat growing tight, wondering what he had hoped for, what he expected. She knew where her own dreams lay.

She sat at the large table in the room's center, and in a moment Jack and Peter flanked her, with Susan and Marcie filling out the remaining chairs. The innkeeper brought over bowls of chicken stew without waiting to be called, laying pints of ale next to each serving. A fire roared in the fireplace, and Catherine ate slowly, the gentle normalcy of the place infusing into her bones. The world would go on. It was time to start thinking about the future.

"I realize there is not much left to Bowyer," she mused, staring into her tankard. "Even so, I find myself wanting to return there. With King John's difficulties, there will be an even greater need than usual for diplomacy and negotiation skills to represent the poor and the weak. If we can set up even a building or two, we can offer that training to those who seek it.

Marcie smiled gently at her friend. "These students will need something to eat," she offered. "I could set up an inn, providing room and board for those who wished to come to learn."

Susan looked shyly at Peter, and Catherine realized that the two were sitting close together, almost touching on the bench. She wondered how she had missed this before, that the two had seemingly become a couple under her nose. "We could set up a market area for traders," added Susan cautiously, "If we could somehow offer safe passage, this would draw in commerce as well. The roads still cross through our town, and it is convenient for many reasons.

Peter spoke up. "It would be my pleasure to help undo some of the damage that has been wrought."

Catherine turned to Jack, and found herself lost in his grey eyes, so full of intelligence and strength. He reached into his tunic, drawing out the leather thong, revealing the small carven snowdrop. Marcie and Susan smiled in recognition, nudging each other with a smile.

"I have gotten my wish, after all," he murmured, leaning forward. He ran his hand tenderly down the side of her face. "You know where I will be," he vowed. "By your side, wherever you choose to go. Together I am sure we can rebuild your forces, train a guard to keep the lands safe, and draw people in to begin anew. After all, Father Jeffrey and the Tanners need somewhere safe to start over, and we could use a church."

Catherine's eyes dropped to the brown ring she had worn all these months.

He followed her gaze, taking her hand in his, lowering his mouth tenderly to press a kiss on it. His voice came out smoky with passion. "Only another eleven months and eight days until our engagement period is over," he added with a smile.

Catherine raised her glass to Jack in a toast, and the others joined in without a word. She smiled at him, then turned and gazed at each friend in turn. She thought about the trials they had passed through, and her heart filled with hope at the new future they could forge together.

Their scars had made them stronger; had branded them as survivors. As long as they stayed together, and worked as a team, she knew they would succeed.

"To honor," she offered, raising her glass high.

The words echoed all around her, and her gaze swept to join with Jack's. She became lost in the depths, and she knew that she had finally found everything she sought in life.

At last warm laughter from the next table over shook her out of her spell. She looked over and smiled. There was a woman about her age sitting with an older woman who might have been a beloved aunt. The two were laughing and joking together. The younger woman had a scabbard at her hip.

The older woman said, "I tell you, Morgan, I am just so glad I have you as my bodyguard. The men I've worked with in the past simply did not understand my rhythms or interests. You are a sheer delight."

Morgan grinned with pleasure. "Donna, I'm just glad someone appreciates my skill with the sword!" She shook her head, drawing the sword out of the scabbard and laying it on the table. "But I swear, what they say about the cobbler's child going barefoot is absolutely true! My father is so backlogged with work for others that I'll never get this sword back in good shape. And then where will we be if some bandit prince wants to run off with you?"

Donna grinned. "It all depends on how handsome he is."

The two burst into gales of laughter.

Catherine's heart was warmed. There were indeed other female sword fighters out there in the world, and they were finding their way. The more the women all supported each other, the more respect they would build.

She wished Morgan all the best of luck in her quest.

There was a hum at Catherine's hip.

She looked down to the sword she carried – the one given to her when she was a lost child of thirteen. At the time, she had barely understood what Joan had told her about the sword.

She'd been more fascinated by Joan's travels in the Holy Land and her exploits in saving innocents.

But one phrase did ring in her mind –

Do not become too fond of Andetnes. When you have at last found contentment, there will be another whose fate balances on the point of a pin. You will know when it is right. And the sword will have a new mistress.

Catherine nodded. She'd had Andetnes for thirteen years now. It had seen her through all her training. It had helped her win the tournament against Raymond. It had kept her safe countless times as Shadow.

She smiled and unwrapped the hilt, removing her emblem from within it. She could select another sword for her remaining years as reeve. This one had brought her the man she loved – and her best friends at her side. It had seen her through trials and tribulations.

It was time to let a fresh set of hands wield it.

She smiled and called over to the two women. "Morgan, Donna, my name is Catherine Bowyer. I would love for you to join us. I think we have much to talk about!"

* * *

The Sword of Glastonbury series continues with Book 11, *Seeking the Truth* -

http://www.amazon.com/Seeking-Truth-Medieval-Romance-Glastonbury-ebook/dp/B006GIYE5W/

If you enjoyed *Badge of Honor*, please leave feedback on Amazon, Goodreads, and any other systems you use. Together we can help make a difference!

https://www.amazon.com/review/create-review?ie=UTF8&asin=B007WMKZUY#

Be sure to sign up for my free newsletter! You'll get alerts of free books, discounts, and new releases. I run my own newsletter server – nobody else will ever see your email address. I promise!

http://www.lisashea.com/lisabase/subscribe.html

As a special treat, as a warm thank-you for reading this book and supporting the cause of battered women, here's a sneak peek at the first chapter of *Seeking the Truth.*

Seeking the Truth - Chapter 1

England, 1212

Happiness depends upon ourselves.
-- Aristotle

Morgan wriggled her way through the bar's noisy throng, a feisty salmon struggling against the almost overpowering current, heading always upstream, driven by her instincts. She paused a moment to take a long draw from the tankard of ale in her hand, balancing the other two mugs close against her waist, her hand strung through their handles. A boisterous farmer bumped into her as she weaved past a heavy oaken table, and she laughed as she hip-checked him back into place. The rowdy crowd was certainly enjoying the harvest celebration. The sun had barely slipped past the horizon and already half of the pub seemed well on its way toward drunken abandon.

She plunked herself down on a worn stool, sliding the tankards out across the small round table with practiced ease to her two friends. The men called out their thanks, grabbing at their ales and each downing half the mug in a smooth motion.

Christian grinned up to her. "You are a saint, Morgan," announced the red-head, a twinkle in his eye.

"Sure, and you get the next round," she joked merrily, pushing her long, jet black hair back from her face with one hand. The men were still wearing their guard uniforms, having come right from watch duty to join in the festivities. Morgan knew Lady Donna's keep was well enough protected – there were plenty of guards still left on the walls. Her friends deserved some time off. It was harvest, after all. A season to relax, to have some fun.

She rolled her head, loosening the ache from her shoulders and neck, taking another long draw on her ale as the chaos of the place washed over her with comfortable familiarity. The pub was normally ample for its patrons, but tonight it was overflowing with the crowd, both with the farmers celebrating their crops and the soldiers in from London. It made for a tightly-packed night.

"And just why are those outsiders here?" she asked Christian, looking over at the soldiers. She'd grown up in Shamley Green, knew every man, woman, and child here. The trio of well-built men stood out like hawks in a flock of sparrows.

"Something about a funeral for a friend of theirs," responded Christian, barely sparing a glance for the newcomers, his eyes warm on her face. "Felix said they should be in town for another few days, perhaps. They are staying down at the inn."

"Was there bandit action in the area?" Morgan pressed, her interest sparking. Maybe she could talk with Lady Donna, get some time off from her bodyguard duties.

Christian was shaking his head, sending his red curls dancing. "Nothing so exciting," he calmed his friend, his eyes twinkling. "Rumor has it that the man got on the wrong side of a loan shark and was put out of his misery."

Morgan sighed. It was always the same; nothing exciting ever happened around here. She put the strangers out of her mind, rolling her shoulders again; that stubborn ache in her neck just would not ease. She turned to her right, to the man who leant back in watchful relaxation. She swatted playfully across the top of his brush-cut blond hair, riffling the gently greying tips. "So, Oliver, what about putting that medical training of yours to some good use?" she teased him with a smile.

He arched an eyebrow, then slid a hand behind her back, unerringly kneading at the knot immediately above her shoulder blade. She sighed softly in pleasure.

God's teeth, but he was a good man to have handy at the end of a long, wearying day.

Then, suddenly, he stopped. She looked up with a toss of her head, protest on her lips.

Oliver was staring over at the bar, his eyes sharp. Morgan glanced over and saw that Felix, the portly barkeep, was waving one hand toward their table with a wry grin. His red nose practically shone in the dusk as he nodded his head to the right. Morgan followed the look and spotted one of the elderly farmers tottering to his feet, a look of outrage on his face.

Morgan could barely hear his curse over the din of the room. "How dare you say your turnips are better than mine!"

Morgan felt Christian begin to rise beside her and patted him playfully on the arm. "You two hold tight; I will be right back," she promised, draining her ale. "Sometimes a woman's touch is what is called for."

"You certainly have that touch," agreed Christian with a smile, his eyes sweeping her curvaceous form with appreciation. Morgan leant over the table for a moment, dipping the front of her scarlet dress lower than necessary as she swept up the empty tankards, winking at Christian as his grin grew wider. Then she was turning, dropping the mugs off for refills as she swept past the bar on the way to the corner table.

"Come now, Jonas," she called out to the balding farmer as she came up alongside him, "I think it is time for you to head on home." Offering a friendly smile, she tucked her arm in against his. Jonas seemed caught between his pride in his produce and the well-built woman who was insinuating herself against his side. The latter won out, and he turned, his face glowing.

Morgan chuckled. "Let us get you home to your wife," she suggested, walking him to the door. She dropped her voice down a notch. "Besides, I am sure everyone here knows that your turnips are the best in the county. Let that braggart make a fool of himself if he wishes."

Jonas' face shone with pride, and he nodded blearily in agreement. Morgan released him as they got out into the dark street, watching fondly as he ambled his way down the dirt road toward his small cottage. The noise rang out behind her, but the houses were peacefully quiet as they spread out in three directions, lights from candles and fires glowing softly in several windows.

Morgan glanced toward the end of the street, toward the two-story building which housed her parents. The forge would be quiet now, but she knew it would not be silent in the home. Her father and mother were undoubtedly at it again, raging over some perceived slight, some invented ill. No, she would not be heading home until well near dawn. Thank all that was holy that she was due back at the keep tomorrow afternoon and her short visit was nearly at an end.

Pushing her family out of her mind with well-practiced effort, she turned and dove head-first in the roiling chaos of the mob. She saw the fresh tankards waiting for her on the scuffed bar top and began weaving her way through to retrieve them.

She was jostled hard to the left by the tumultuous crowd, staggered, and a spray of liquid misted her arm. She looked down at her stained dress with a wry smile, wiping herself down as she turned.

It was the soldiers from London, their dark green uniforms crisp and neat, an island of order in the stormy sea of muddy turmoil. The man she had hit was shaking drops off his hand, a small metal cup on the table now only three-fourths full. She sized him up in a long glance. He seemed perhaps thirty, his body long and rangy, well-muscled beneath his tunic. His chestnut hair was cut relatively short, brushed back from his face, emphasizing his strong cheekbones, his grey eyes flecked with gold.

One of his companions looked over. "Hey, lass, fetch us another round of ale," he called out, his speech slightly slurred. Morgan turned her gaze with mild annoyance. This soldier was more muscular, about the same age as the first man, his birch-brown hair cut close to his head. He stared with hazy interest at her buxom form spilling out of the close-fitting dress she wore, then slid his look back up to her face. “Be quick about it and there might be a nice bonus in it for you,” he added suggestively. He glanced over at the well-built man she had hit. His voice became slightly more formal “Did you want a refill on your mead, Sean?” he asked the man.

“No thanks, Roger” replied Sean, wiping the back of his hand on his leg, not looking up. “Take it if you want.” He gave his leg a final swipe. “I wonder how the locals can tolerate the brew - it is foul enough to drop a horse,” he added with a shake of the head.

Morgan’s eyes flashed in outrage. It was bad enough for strangers to take up space in an already crowded pub, but for them to badmouth the homemade liquor Felix took such pride in pricked her to the core. She swept up the cup and without hesitation tossed the entire drink back down her throat, the raw liquid slithering into the depths of her being with the familiar warm sensation. Her world stopped for a moment as the mead sent its curling tendrils into every corner of her body.

Oh, but that felt good.

She slammed the cup back down onto the table with a firm ring. All three soldiers were now staring up at her, their mouths open in shock.

Morgan was not done. “Felix!” she called out, her voice ringing in command. The bar’s patrons turned instantly at the shout, and the place hushed to a murmur, all eyes focused on her with bright interest.

“I think this soldier here would like some milk,” she announced to her audience with a deliberate smirk. “It seems he cannot handle the harder stuff.”

There was a rolling cascade of mirth from the crowd in response. Sean looked up at her in amusement, a ready smile playing on his lips. “I promise I can drink anything you choose to put before me,” he answered in challenge.

A voice rang out behind her. "Two pounds on Morgan!" Christian had come up alongside her, his face split in a wide smile.

Oliver tossed coins on the table. "Make that three," he added evenly.

The room became a hubbub of bets and offers, and the center of the area was cleared out to make room for the spectators. Morgan sat to one side of the soldier's table, settling her red skirts around her with practiced ease, getting her feet set up sturdily beneath her. Sean took the chair opposite her, swinging his sword out of the way as he sat.

Roger patted Sean on the shoulder. "You pace yourself," he advised his friend with a teasing wink. "These village girls can be feisty."

"I suppose you have some advice, Peter?" asked Sean, looking up at the other man. "You are nearly forty now; you are our senior man here."

"Never make assumptions," responded Peter thoughtfully, his eyes sparkling with amusement as he looked over the scene. "Still, I think you have this one easily." He leant forward. "Four pounds on Sean."

Sean turned back toward the table. He gave a long look down Morgan's healthy build, her lush curves. His eyes brightened with anticipation as he sized up his opponent.

"I would hate to cause any real harm to such a lovely creature," he commented with an appreciative smile.

Morgan watched as his eyes moved from her body toward the pair of men standing just behind her. She could almost read his thoughts in the narrowing of his eyes. Swords on their hips, protective stances, well-toned builds. Not simple farmers, these two.

He muttered quietly to Roger, his voice low, but not low enough. "The wench certainly knows how to choose her admirers."

Morgan leant forward slightly, drawing his attention with the subtle movement. “Are you sure you are ready for me? You can always back out now,” she teased gently.

Sean's eyes flickered toward hers for a moment, then returned to consider the two men who stood over her. He addressed Oliver, his gaze steady. “You know how to get her home, I imagine, once she can no longer walk?” Morgan sensed a hint of probing in there, of Sean's desire to know just how well she was acquainted with her two friends. She grinned. She had hooked this one almost too easily.

Oliver looked down fondly at Morgan, running a hand absently through his blond hair. “Oh, we will take good care of Morgan,” he agreed with a tender nod. “We are quite familiar with Morgan's haunts and habits.” His mouth quirked. “Now as for you … you are staying at the inn, I hear?”

“Do not worry about me,” replied Sean absently, leaning back in his chair, sizing up the two men as if they were a part of the challenge before him.

Felix trundled over with a large wooden tray, five shot glasses apiece lined up down each side of it. He placed the tray theatrically on the table between the two contestants. Sean looked at the offering almost dismissively before giving an indulgent smile to Morgan. “Well then, I will go first,” he offered chivalrously. He took one of the glasses, downing it with a quick movement of his wrist. A cheer went up from his supporters. He then turned the glass over in the air and placed it firmly, upside down, at the center of the tray.

Morgan sat back for a moment, closing her eyes, fighting the urge to smile. Her friends would win good money tonight, but there was no reason to rush. She enjoyed the showmanship of the process.

She pouted her lips prettily, adding hesitation to her movements, acting as if she had suddenly realized just what a mess she had gotten herself into. She reached forward tentatively, taking the full glass in her hand, staring thoughtfully at it for a long moment. Then, slowly, carefully, she poured the liquid down her throat.

She closed her eyes as she did. As much as she could fake the tenuous hand movements, the trembling of the lips, she doubted she could hide the shine in her eyes as she drank the luscious ambrosia and felt it course down her throat, warming her. She made sure to give a little shudder before opening her eyes again. With a shaking hand the glass was turned over in the air and placed down on the table.

Felix raised his hands in the air. "One!" he announced with delight, and the crowd roared with pleasure.

Sean went glass by glass down the line, matching her at each step, and she watched with interest as his eyes began to betray his growing enjoyment of the liquid, the appreciation showing in his lips as he sensed the hidden layers of flavors. She knew he was watching her with equal interest, and she focused on the hesitation on her movements, giving the sense that she might give up at each stage, but somehow she managed to draw out the inner strength to keep going. His eyes flickered with surprise when, even after the fifth shot, she was able to put her glass securely down on the table.

Felix spun to the crowd. "Round Two!" Cheers and applause rang out on all sides. Sean scanned the crowd which clearly expected the contest to continue for quite a while, and after a moment he chuckled in appreciation. He picked up one of the smaller coins on the table, flipped it in his fingers a time or two, and then tossed it past her shoulder. Morgan had been gazing down at the table with a listless attitude, but out of habit she plucked the coin out of the air easily, and her eyes snapped with laughter when she realized she'd been found out.

She flipped the coin back to him with an amused grin. "All right, then," she acknowledged in delight, her voice clear and rich. "Let us do this the straightforward way. I find it so much more fun when I face my challenges head-on."

"You think you are a challenge for me?" asked Sean, his eyes brightening with interest, lingering on her lips for a long moment.

Morgan ran her tongue slowly along her bottom lip, and she watched with delight as his face flushed red with heat, as his breath drew in a ragged inhale. Her smile widened further as she basked in the reaction she had caused.

"I think I will be the one on top tonight," she agreed throatily, her eyes sparkling.

"We will see about that," murmured Sean, his voice going hoarse as she shifted slightly in her seat, as her curves moved and realigned.

There was a shadow across the table, and Felix was between them, setting down the wooden tray with a fresh set of five shots each. Sean looked at the line of mead, shaking his head, his eyes reflecting his admiration.

"I imagine a working hazard of being a waitress is building up a tolerance to alcohol," he murmured to Roger, his voice rough. "Still, it will be a cold day in Hell when one of them can keep up with me."

Roger's mouth quirked up into a smile. "You have indeed honed drinking to an art form," he agreed readily.

Sean's eyes moved back to meet Morgan's, to drift down her length appreciatively, taking in her ripe curves, her healthy strength. He gave a long sigh of relaxation. "Even if she does not last long, it will certainly be a pleasant distraction for us," he mused to his friend.

Morgan held in a snort. Not last long indeed. The amused sparkle in her eyes did not dim as they went through glass five … glass six … Sean seemed almost enthralled by her deep brown eyes, by the ruby red of her lips as her tongue danced out to wet them. She leant forward to take glass seven, making sure the swell of her breast was tantalizingly near. He shook himself, renewing his focus on the contest at hand.

"Round Three!" roared out the room gleefully. Sean gave a toast to his temptress with his next glass, his eyes shining, apparently honestly impressed. She chuckled again. Perhaps he did not know many women who could have lasted this long. Her smile grew wider. On the other hand perhaps none of his drinking companions back home had a form as she did. She gave a glance down the length of her body. She had dressed well for tonight's festivities. The red dress curled deliciously along her shoulders, drawing close at her waist. Her dark hair cascaded down her torso in thick curls.

She brought her gaze back up to meet Sean's and she grinned as she saw him wavering slightly, as he blinked again to keep his eyes in focus. It had begun.

She leant forward for glass number thirteen and her hair fell down across her face in a wave. Christian moved forward with comfortable ease to brush it back for her, and let his hand rest on her shoulder for a moment in a casual gesture of familiarity. Laughter bubbled up within her as Sean's eyes flared with jealousy, as he bit back his emotions with visible effort. Already she had him hooked well. She held his gaze through glass fourteen … fifteen …

"Round Four!"

Morgan could see in his movements that the liquor had taken a hold of him. He narrowed his eyes as if the room was beginning to shimmer. His body weaved slightly; he seemed to be riding on a ship at sea. There appeared to be two sets of each glass before him now, and he concentrated hard to determine which one to pick up. The crowd was continuing to chant the number, giving a roar of approval as each glass was brought to the lips, downed, and placed upside down on the table.

"Seventeen!"

Sean reached out carefully for his eighteenth glass. By his slow hand movements she would have almost guessed that this one was heavier than the previous. He watched with focus as he brought it toward his lips. His tipped it up with a quick motion.

The liquid rolled down his throat, and she saw it in his eyes, the connection they shared, that the mead was bringing him a smooth oblivion, an erasing of the past, the focus on now. She felt guilty, as if she had glimpsed into his soul, into a private haven.

He looked at the empty glass in his hands for a long while, appearing to marvel at its texture. There was a small air bubble in its base, a spherical drop of perfection, and he was entranced by it.

Then he gave himself a small shake, as if remembering that there was something he had to do. He had to put it down on the table. He reached forward with it, his attention a pinpoint focus, watching as the glass approached the table, its edges wavering … wobbling …

The edge of the glass came in contact with the table, and it seemed he found he could not bring it upright. His eyes strove to focus, but his hand slipped. The glass tumbled on its side, rolling in a long circle.

"Ohhhh!" groaned the crowd, half of the voices tinged with panic, the other half in greedy delight. There were hushing noises from all sides as countless pairs of eyes turned to look at Morgan.

Morgan watched the glass make its lazy circle, bringing her eyes slowly back up to the man sitting before her.

God's teeth, he was handsome.

His thick, lustrous hair lured her to run her fingers through it. His physique was solid but lean, like a racehorse built for speed. Desire built up within her as a tangible force, and his eyes held an answering kindle as he read her look. To think he had almost made eighteen shots … she shook her head. There was work still to be done. Enough time for play later.

She reached her hand out, proud that it remained fairly steady. She had never had to drink eighteen before, never been pushed to this limit. She would not let down her friends, not destroy her reputation. She focused on the glass, on lifting it carefully, on bringing it to her lips. The release of the alcohol, its potent power, thrilled through her as it always did. She kept her eyes open this time, letting Sean see the pleasure it brought her, her comfortable familiarity with its effect. She saw the answering knowledge in his eyes, that he drew the same solace from its deep pools of darkness. She took down every last drop, then with a firm hand she reached out with it.

She placed the glass solidly, upside down, at the center of the table.

The place erupted into cheers, yells, curses, and congratulations. Morgan found herself hoisted up onto Christian and Oliver's shoulders, paraded around the room as a conquering hero. Money changed hands with laughing good nature as Felix cleared away the glasses and began his last call for the night. Morgan glanced out the window and realized to her surprise that a soft pre-dawn light was beginning to spread across the town. It was later than she had thought!

Her soldiers deposited her down by the table again, and Sean slowly stood. He held out a hand in friendly defeat.

"That was well played, Morgan," he commended with a smile. "I have not seen it done better. You have my congratulations."

Morgan put her fingers in his palm, watching as he lowered his head to her hand, brushed his lips sensually over the skin of her knuckles. An answering tremor ran through her, and she gave a soft chuckle. Two could play that game. Her thumb was on the underside of his hand – she ran it slowly, seductively along his skin, her lips pursed with promise. A flush of heat rose into his face, and his grip tightened on her fingers.

Christian pulled her back against him. "All right, Morgan," he joked, his red curls bouncing around an even more rosy face.

Oliver chimed in with a low voice. "Time to get you home, Morgan, or your parents will tan my hide."

Morgan smiled. "Even worse, my father will not deliver your new sword for another month in punishment," she teased, allowing her fingers to slip free from Sean's grip, allowing herself to be drawn along by her friends. Together they made their way out into the lightening world, weaving their way along the village's one main road. Here and there they saw other of the bar's patrons making their way home.

They got to the sturdy oak door of her house in only a few minutes, and Morgan gave each man a warm hug in farewell. "I will see you at the keep tomorrow," she promised with a wink. She glanced up at the gentle tracery of light drifting across the sky. "Oops, I suppose I mean today," she amended. "Keep the fires warm for me!"

Christian nodded. "We will," he vowed with heat.

She gave a wave, then turned to move along the lavender-lined side alley of her house toward the back fence.

Gazing in a low window, she could barely make out her mother, a mug of ale near to her hand, sprawled on the bench in the main room of the forge. Her father was sitting on the sturdy side chair, his head down against his chest, snoring in steady rhythm. Morgan had no interest in waking the pair and being drawn into whatever fight had consumed them this evening.

She grabbed the ladder from its nook, laid it up against the side of the house, and scrambled nimbly up to her bedroom window. Once inside, she gave the ladder a kick, sending it back into its corner with a soft thud. She waited a long moment, but there was no answering sound from below.

Chuckling with pleasure, she made her way over to her bed, flinging herself onto it with satisfaction. She had won. She had taken down and bested a Londoner. Now there was an achievement to be proud of!

Her mind went back to that last glass of mead, the moment when she had allowed Sean a glimpse into her soul, when she had felt a connection with him that went beyond words, beyond any man she had ever met before. Her heart kindled …

She pushed the warmth away, rolling herself under her blankets, pulling them up over her head with a firm tug. Tomorrow he would be gone, and she would return to her carefree life. No man alive had yet put the yoke on her, and with God as her witness, no man ever would.

http://www.amazon.com/Seeking-Truth-Medieval-Romance-Glastonbury-ebook/dp/B006GIYE5W/

Medieval Dialogue

I've been fascinated by medieval languages since I was quite young. I grew up studying Spanish, English, and Latin, and loved the sound of reading Beowulf and the Canterbury Tales in their original languages. I adore the richness of medieval languages. How did medieval English people speak?

There are three aspects to this. The first is the difference between written records and spoken language. The second is the rich, multi-cultural aspect of medieval life. And the third is how to convey this to a modern-language audience.

Let's take the first. Sometimes modern people equate the way medieval folk would talk, hanging around a rustic tavern, with the way Chaucer wrote his famous *Canterbury Tales*. Something along the lines of this (note this is a modern translation, not the original Middle English version):

"Of weeping and wailing, care and other sorrow
I know enough, at eventide and morrow,"
The merchant said, "and so do many more
Of married folk, I think, who this deplore,
For well I know that it is so with me.
I have a wife, the worst one that can be;
For though the foul Fiend to her wedded were,
She'd overmatch him, this I dare to swear."

Sure, it seems elegant and rich. But did worn-down farmers sitting around a fireplace with mugs of ale really talk like this?

Do we think the London street-dwellers in the 1600s skulked down the dark alleys emoting like Shakespeare –

Two households, both alike in dignity
In fair Verona, where we lay our scene
From ancient grudge break to new mutiny
Where civil blood makes civil hands unclean.

And, in the 1920s in Vermont, did farmers really wander down their snowy lanes murmuring to their farming friends, a la Robert Frost:

Whose woods these are I think I know.
His house is in the village though;
He will not see me stopping here
To watch his woods fill up with snow.

As someone who lives in New England, I can pretty resolutely say “no” to that last one. And, given my research, I’m equally content saying “no” to the previous two. There is a big difference between poetry written with deliberate effort and the way “normal people” talked, flirted, cajoled, and laughed day in and day out. People simply did not talk in iambic pentameter. I’m a poet and even I don’t talk in iambic pentameter :).

Modern people sometimes think of the medieval period in terms of the plays we see. We imagine actors on a stage, speaking in formal, stilted language, carefully moving from scene to scene. But medieval life wasn’t like that. It was a rich cacophony of people struggling hard to survive amongst plagues and crusades, with strong pagan influences and the church trying to instill order. People fought off robbers and drove away wolves. They laughed and loved in multi-generational homes. It was a time of great flux.

England - A Melting Pot

England wasn’t an isolated, walled-off island. It was continually experiencing influxes of new words and sounds. The Romans came and went. The Vikings came and went. The French invaded. Nearly all of the English men headed off to the

Crusades, leaving behind women to gain strength and position. The men returned with even more languages. Pilgrims went to Jerusalem. Merchants arrived from all over. This was a true melting pot.

So, in part because of this, Middle English was a rich, fascinating language. People in this time period had a wealth of contractions, nicknames, abbreviations, and combinations of words they used. Often people could speak multiple languages - their old English, the incoming Norman language, Latin from church, and random other words from tinkers, merchants, and pilgrims they encountered. Medieval people had all sorts of words for drinking, for fighting, for prostitutes, you name it. They had slang and shortcuts just like any other language does. After all, these are the people who turned "forecastle" (on a ship) to "foc's'le" and who pronounce the word "Worcester" as "Woostah."

But, here's the trick. With the medieval language being so rich, varied, intricate, and full of fascinating words, how can we bring that to life for a modern audience?

Centuries of Change

Let's start with a basic issue - most modern readers simply cannot understand authentic medieval dialogue. They don't have the grounding in Middle English, French, and Latin that would be required. Even the fairly straightforward, basic Chaucer works look like this:

And Saluces this noble contree highte.

Modern readers generally wouldn't know that "highte" meant "was called" as in "And Saluces this noble country was called."

This happens over and over again. Words change meaning. In the Middle Ages, if you *abandoned* your wife it means you subjugated her. You got her under your thumb. It didn't mean you left her - quite the opposite. Awful meant *awe-ful* - as in stunning and wonderful. It had a positive connotation. Fantastic wasn't great - it was a fantasy; something that didn't exist. Nervous didn't mean worried or agitated - it meant strong and full of energy. Nice meant silly, and so on.

If a book was written with proper medieval words and meanings, first, even if the words are reasonably close to what we use now, modern readers would have to struggle with the spelling -

By that the Mauncipie hadde his tale al ended,
The sonne fro the south lyne was descended
So lowe, that he nas nat to my sighte
Degrees nyne and twenty as in highte.

But, again, that is just the tip of the issue with medieval language. The word "bracelet" didn't exist until the 1400s. Necklace wasn't a word until 1590. The word "hug" wasn't around until the mid-1500s. We also didn't have the words tragedy, crisis, area, explain, fact, illicit, rogue, or even disagree! Shakespeare invented the words "baseless" and "dwindle" in the 1600s. Staircase is from 1620. A story written solely with words that existed in the year 1200 - and that still retain their modern meaning so modern readers could understand them - would be fairly basic.

(Speaking of which, the word "basic" didn't exist until the mid 1800s.)

Conversely, some words we might think of as thoroughly modern, like "puke", were also used in Shakespeare's time. "Booze" traces back to the 1500s. And these are just the proofs we have. While "shiner" for a black eye can be traced definitively to the 1700s, it could easily have been used for centuries before then and we just don't happen to have a letter or newspaper article which mentions it.

It's fair to say that people in medieval days did get black eyes and had a wealth of interesting terms for that situation. After all, it could be a rough life back then. Was one of the terms used "shiner"? Maybe, maybe not. Out of the ten fun phrases they used, probably nine of them would make zero sense to a modern reading audience. So authors strive to find phrases that provide meaning to a modern audience without being too *133t* and techno-speak. It doesn't make sense to completely avoid the word "bracelet" simply because it technically didn't exist in the 1200s. Surely people in the 1200s had several words for "bracelet" and we are simply using the word modern readers understand. Similarly, people in medieval times hugged! They just called that action something else.

Medieval people loved playing with words. They called their kids "dillydowns" and "mitings". (little mites). They called sweethearts "my sweeting" and "my honey. They loved snapping out insults, from "dunce" to "idiot" to "pig filth" and "maggot pie." And, again, these are just the ones that happened to get recorded.

Medieval people loved contractions. There's a phrase "ne woot," meaning *knows not*. They'd simply say "noot". They did this with all sorts of words.

So writing in modern English should have this same sort of loose, fun sense to the writing. It's important to remember that even the kings, in this era, were rough fighters. They were out with soldiers, crossing multiple countries, and experiencing a range of languages. They weren't necessarily concerned about speaking in iambic pentameter. They were more concerned about breaking down their enemy's walls to plunder what lay within and then drinking themselves under the table to celebrate.

So, certainly, treasure the poetry and prose of the time. As a poet, I appreciate that immensely. But also keep in mind that people did not talk in poetry. They did not speak in fantasy-speak of *Lord of the Rings* or *Game of Thrones*. They talked and laughed, flirted and cursed, gossiped and cajoled in a rich, multi-lingual, contraction-filled, sobriquet-laden dialogue which mirrors how we talk in modern times.

About Medieval Life

When many of us think of medieval times, we bring to mind a drab reality-documentary image. We imagine people scrounging around in the mud, eating dirt. The people were under five feet tall and barely survived to age thirty. These poor, unfortunate souls had rotted teeth and never bathed.

Then you have the opposite, Hollywood Technicolor extreme. In the romantic version of medieval times, men were always strong and chivalrous. Women were dainty and sat around staring out the window all day, waiting for their knight to come riding in. Everybody wore purple robes or green tights.

The truth, of course, lies somewhere in the middle.

Living in Medieval Times

The years in the early medieval ages held a warm, pleasant climate. Crops grew exceedingly well, and there was plenty of food. As a result, their average height was on par with modern times. It's amazing how much nutrition influences our health!

The abundance of food also had an effect on the longevity of people. Chaucer (born 1340) lived to be 60. Petrarch (born 1304) died a day shy of 70. Eleanor of Aquitaine (born 1122) was 82 when she died. People could and did lead long lives. The average age of someone who survived childhood was 65.

What about their living conditions? The Romans adored baths and set up many in Britain. When they left, the natives could not keep them going, and it is true they then bathed less. However, by the Middle Ages, with the crusades and interaction with the Muslims, there was a renewed interest both in hygiene and medicine. Returning soldiers and those who took pilgrimages brought back with them an interest in regular bathing and cleanliness. This spread across the culture.

While people during other periods of English history ate poorly, often due to war conditions or climatic changes, the middle ages were a time of relative bounty. Villagers would grow fresh fruit and vegetables behind their homes, and had an array of herbs for seasoning. The local baker would bake bread for the village - most homes did not hold an oven, only an open fire. Villagers had easy access to fish, chicken, geese, and eggs. Pork was enjoyed at special meals like Easter.

Upper classes of course had a much wider range of foods - all game animals (rabbits, deer, and so on) belonged to them. The wealthy ate peacocks, veal, lamb, and even bear. Meals for all classes could be flavorful and well enjoyed.

Medieval Relationships

Some movies present a skewed version of life in the Middle Ages. They make it seem that women were meek, mild, and obediently did whatever their father or husband commanded.

This was *far* from the truth!

Medieval times were times of immense change. Men were off at the Crusades, leaving the women to run things. Christianity was trying to get a foothold, but many areas of Britain were still primarily pagan, with all the Goddess worship and female empowerment which had been tradition for centuries. The vast majority of brewers were female. Most innkeepers were female. Women's knowledge about herbs, health, and food was respected. Healthy women were treasured as the key to a child-rich partnership.

Medieval life was heavily focused on fertility. Farm animals had to be fertile in order to create meat to feed the family. Women had to be fertile to create helpers for the farm and household. Celebration after celebration in medieval times focused on fertility. These people weren't shy about the topic. They watched their horses, cows, and dogs continually engage in these activities. Their festivals focused on the topic with bawdy delight. Their songs lusted about it.

The church tried, again and again, to squelch this behavior so that all aspects of relationships could be regulated by the church. However, half of all medieval couples were together outside of a church marriage and, for those sanctified by the church, a large proportion were "sealing the deal" for a couple already pregnant.

This was the way the medieval people looked at it: they needed to know their partner could create children. This was a key consideration for a relationship.

The Medieval period was far from an era of Victorian prudity. Quite the opposite. People of this era celebrated fertility, felt it was wholly natural, and even felt it was unhealthy for a man or woman to go for too long without sex. The celibacy would block critical flows of the body.

It was considered natural that a male noble might take on mistresses and that unmarried couples might seek out partners. It was the same as someone needing food if they were hungry. It was a bodily function which had to be tended to for the health of the person.

So where does marriage fit in with this mindset?

Medieval Marriage

In medieval times, marriage was primarily about inheritance. It was almost separate from sexuality. Sexuality was an important part of bodily health, like eating well and getting enough exercise. Marriage, on the other hand, was about ensuring one's lands and chattel were cared for from generation to generation. Sex, within a marriage, was focused on creating family-line children to then tend to that wealth.

For this reason, wealthy families would put immense energy into arranging optimal marriages for their children. This was about the transfer of land far more than a love match. Parents wanted to ensure their land went to a family worthy of ownership - one with the resources to defend it from attack. It was not only their own family members they were concerned with. Each block of land had on it both free men and serfs. These people all depended on the nobles – with their skill, connections, and soldiers – to keep them safe from bandits and harm.

That being said, both the woman and man would be consulted about the match. Their input was a critical aspect of the decision. Choices were often made with intricate selection processes. Keep in mind that the woman and her suitors would have been raised from birth to think of this process as natural. They would participate in that choice-making with an eye as to how it would secure the stability of their future family.

Yes, villagers sometimes married for love. Even a few nobles would run off and follow their hearts. Even so, they would have first seriously considered the potentially catastrophic risks which could result from their actions.

Here is a modern example. Imagine you took over the family business which employed a hundred loyal workers. Those workers depend on your careful guidance of the company to ensure the income for their families. You might dream about running off to Bermuda and drinking martinis. But would you just sell your company to any random investor who came along? Would you risk all of those peoples' lives, people who had served you loyally for decades, to satisfy a whim of pleasure? It is more likely that you would research your options, map out a plan, and made a choice with suited both you and your responsibilities.

Medieval Women

In pagan days women held many rights and responsibilities. During the crusades, especially, with many men off at war, women ran the taverns, made the ale, and ran the government. In later years, as men returned home and Christianity rose in power, women were relegated to a more subservient role.

Still, women in medieval times were not meek and mild. That stereotype came in with the Victorian era, many centuries later. Back in medieval days, women had to be hearty and hard working. There were fields to tend, homes to maintain, and children to raise!

Women strove to be as healthy as they could because they faced a serious threat - a fifth of all women died during or just after childbirth. The church said that childbirth was the "pain of

Eve" and instructed women to bear it without medicine or follow-up care. Of course, midwives did their best to skirt these rules, but childbirth still took an immense toll.

Childhood was rough in the Middle Ages – only forty percent of children survived the gauntlet of illnesses to adulthood. A woman who reached her marriageable years was a sturdy woman indeed.

You can see why fertility was so important to medieval people!

To summarize, in medieval days a woman could live a long, happy life, even into her eighties – as long as she was of the sturdy stock that made it through the challenges of childhood. She would be expected to be fertile and to have multiple children, which again weeded out the weaker ones. This was very much a time of 'survival of the fittest.' Medieval life quickly separated out the weak and frail. Those women who ran that gauntlet and survived were respected for that strength and for their wisdom in many areas of life.

So medieval women were strong - very strong. They had to be. They were respected. Still, would they fight?

Women and Weapons

Queen Boudicia, from Norwalk, was born around AD60. She personally – and successfully - led her troops against the Roman Empire. She had been flogged - and her daughters raped - spurring her to revenge. She was extremely intelligent and quite strategic. Her daughters rode in her chariot at her side.

Eleanor of Aquitaine, born in 1122, was brilliant and married first to a King of France and then to a King of England. She went on the Second Crusades as the leader of her troops - reportedly riding bare-breasted as an Amazon. At times she marched with her troops far ahead of her husband. When she divorced the King of France, she immediately married Henry II, who she passionately adored. He was eleven years her junior. When things went sour, Eleanor separated from him and actively led revolts against him.

Many historical accounts talk of women taking up arms to defend their villages and towns. Women would not passively let their children be slain or their homes burned. They were able and strong bodied from their daily work. They were well skilled with farm implements and knives, and used them with great talent against invaders.

Many of these defenses were successful, and the victories were celebrated as brave and proper, rather than dismissed as an unusual act for a woman. A mother was expected to defend her brood and to keep her home safe, just as a wolf mother protects her cubs.

Numerous women took their martial skills to a higher level. In 1301 a group of Italian women joined up to fight the crusade against the Turks. In 1348 at a tournament there were at least thirty women who participated, dressed as men.

This is not as unusual as you might think. In medieval times, all adults carried a knife at their belt for daily use in eating, chores, and defense. All knew how to use it. Being strong and safe was a necessary part of daily life.

Here is an interesting comparison. In modern times most women know how to drive, but few choose to invest themselves in the time and training to become race car drivers. In medieval times, most women knew how to defend themselves with a weapon. They had to. Few, though, actively sought the training to be swordswomen. Still, these women did exist, and did thrive as valued members of their communities.

So women in medieval times were far from shrinking violets. They were not mud-encrusted wretches huddling in straw huts. They were not pale damsels locked away in towers. They were strong, sturdy, and well versed in the use of knives. Many ran taverns, and most handled the brewing of ale. Those who made it through childhood and childbirth could expect to enjoy long, rich lives.

I hope you enjoy my tales of authentic, inspiring heroines!

Glossary

Ale - A style of beer which is made from barley and does not use hops. Ale was the common drink in medieval days. In the 1300s, 92% of brewers were female, and the women were known as "alewives". It was common for a tavern to be run by a widow and her children.

Blade - The metal slicing part of the sword.

Chemise - In medieval days, most people had only a few outfits. They would not want to wash their heavy main dress every time they wore it, just as in modern times we don't wash our jackets after each wearing. In order to keep the sweaty skin away from the dress, women wore a light, white under-dress which could then be washed more regularly. This was often slept in as well.

Drinking - In general, medieval sanitation was not great. People who drank milk had to drink it "raw" - pasteurization was not well known before the 1700s. Water was often unsafe to drink. For these reasons, all ages of medieval folk drank liquid with alcohol in it. The alcohol served as a natural sanitizer. This was even true as recently as colonial American times.

God's Teeth / God's Blood – Common oaths in the middle ages.

Grip - The part of the sword one holds, usually wrapped in leather or another substance to keep it firmly in the wielder's hand.

Guard - The crossed top of the sword's hilt which keeps the enemy's sword from sliding down and chopping off the wielder's fingers.

Hilt - The entire handle part of the sword; everything that is not blade.

Mead - A fermented beverage made from honey. Mead has been enjoyed for thousands of years and is mentioned in Beowulf.

Pommel - The bottom end of the sword, where the hilt ends.

Tip - The very end of the sword

Wolf's Head – a term for a bandit. The Latin legal term *caput gerat lupinum* meant they could be hunted and killed as legally as any dangerous wolf or wild animal that threatened the area.

Parts of a Sword

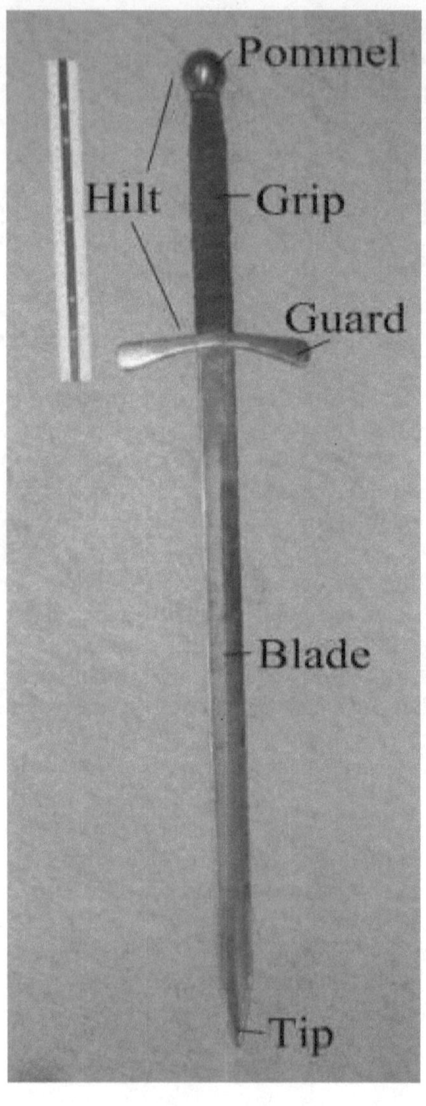

Medieval Clothing

Medieval people - despite modern stereotypes - did have noses and did like to stay clean. Public baths were popular, and people liked to swim as well. However, they did not have the luxury of bathing daily. Also, in medieval times people were often cold. Castles were damp and drafty. Fireplaces were not kept blazingly hot all night long. There is a reason that people wore many heavy layers including cloaks. That way they could add or remove layers as necessary to keep warm.

The basic under-layer was a chemise. This thin nightgown would be worn at night as well as during the day. Because it was against the body it kept the actual clothes clean from sweat. That way you could wash the chemise regularly and not have to wash your actual dress every day. Think of it like when you wear a turtleneck and a wool sweater. At the end of the day you would wash the turtleneck, but you would not wash the wool sweater after every wearing. If you wear a t-shirt under a jacket, you would toss the t-shirt into the washing machine but just hang the jacket on a hook again. The same is true for medieval outfits. The inner layer would be washed, while the other layer would be reused multiple days before it had to be washed.

The chemise was generally not meant to be seen, especially in colder months. It was underwear. There would always be an over-dress with a floor-length hem on top of that. Perhaps a glimpse of the chemise would show at the neckline or at the end-of-sleeve area. In hotter months the chemise might be more visible as the outer dress had short sleeves or no sleeves.

Men would typically wear a tunic over leggings. Men working in summer heat would sometimes wear simple linen "shorts" without anything else. Their chest and lower legs would be bare. This is a stark difference from how covered up women would be.

Both sexes would wear boots or shoes. There was no "left" or "right" - both halves would be made in the same oval shape.

Cloaks would be worn when going out into poor weather, to help keep you warm. These cloaks could be quite heavy if they were full circle cloaks, and incredibly warm.

Monks would wear similar clothing to non-religious men, but the monk's hair would be cut short and have a "tonsure" - or bald spot - shaved out of its center. The tonsure was a sign of their humility. This illuminated image is from a 12th century manuscript at the library at Cambridge University.

Women's Clothing

A number of readers had specific questions about women's medieval clothing so I created this page with those specific details. To illustrate it, I have included a drawing done by Andreas Muller, a famous German artist known for his work restoring ancient paintings. This drawing was published back in 1861, so it's now out of copyright. As you might expect the drawing shows German people, not English, but the fashions are from the 1200s and are quite similar in style.

So, the basics. Women wore at least two layers of long dress. The bottom layer, or "chemise," was often plain white but could be fancier with nobles. This was what was against the skin, got sweaty, and would be washed. The chemise was often slept in, again especially if the person was poor.

The outer layer, what we would call the "dress," was the prettier layer. This would have the nicer stitching and designs. It could have embroidery or different fabrics stitched together to create designs. The outer dress could have long sleeves, short sleeves, or no sleeves, depending on how hot the weather was. In general, though, a woman's arms and legs were covered by the inner chemise and perhaps also by the outer dress as well. Women in medieval times did not tend to show skin from those parts of the body.

You might see images on the web with medieval women wearing long "trumpet" sleeves which made housework impractical. These were sometimes worn by French nobles who were showing off that they did not have to do menial labor. They were not a normal fashion in England or most other areas.

By the same token, women who had to work hard would wear shorter dresses - ending above the ankle rather than dragging on the floor. That was so their dresses did not catch or drag while they went about their work. Noblewomen who had a quiet day planned or a formal event would wear longer, floor-dragging dresses. These subtle differences helped to show off their status.

If it got even colder women would wear cloaks. These range from light, like the woman in the middle is wearing here, to heavy and full-circle, which could be amazingly warm. I have one of those.

Here is an illuminated image done between 1285 and 1292 which shows the famous poet Marie de France. Marie primarily wrote between 1160 to 1190 and was well known by nobility in France and England. Again, you can see how her outer long dress goes to the floor and the inner dress is visible at the arms. This copyright-free image comes via the National Library of France.

Women had an immense array of colorful dyes to choose from, some more expensive, some less expensive. So clothing could be quite bright and cheery. Just as in modern times, practicality had an aspect here. If someone was going to work in the pig pen all day long they'd probably wear something brown and old. If they were going to church they'd wear their best outfit they had.

In modern times we can sometimes think of dresses as "fancy" items we wear to "dress up" that are hard to move in. In medieval times, a dress was normal and natural! These were the outfits they wore every single day. Women made their dresses so they could do all their normal activities in them. To them a dress was like our modern t-shirt and sweatpants. So they're no question about "could they do chores in a dress" or "could they ride a horse in a dress." Of course they could - that's what the clothing was made for. Medieval women didn't generally hide out in tower rooms. Noblewomen would do archery and horseback riding for fun. Working women would scythe hay, ride to the market, and do a myriad of other chores in their dresses. It was what one wore. So those outfits absolutely were made to easily let them do those tasks. Dresses were loose to allow all of that. Women didn't ride side-saddle in medieval days - they simply put their legs on either side for stability. And their clothing was made for that. To ride, a woman could either tuck the skirt beneath her, like when one sits on a chair, or let it flow behind her. Either way works!

In terms of underclothes, most medieval women did not wear a bra. Their simple, straight dresses were meant to keep the body hidden rather than emphasized. A large breasted woman might wear a "binder" to keep the breasts from jiggling around while they tried to work. Current thought is that women didn't wear "underwear" (underpants) either. With their long multi-layer dresses it would be a challenge for underwear-wearing women to go to the bathroom. Instead, they would just move to a section of the field, fluff out their dresses, and go. Then they could get back to work. The same in the outhouses.

Even during the time of their periods, many researchers feel that the philosophy of the time was that binding or constricting a woman's flow would damage her fertility. So she simply bled into her underdress and that was washed. This free-flow practice continued long after medieval times. It was mentioned in doctors' journals in the 1800s. Even as recent as the 1900s there were cotton mills in the United States that had straw-strewn floors to absorb female workers' blood, so again this was not a short-term trend. And given that tampons can cause toxic shock syndrome, maybe those medieval women knew what they were doing :).

Let me know if you have any other questions about medieval women's clothing! I have a library of books here to help with research.

Dedication

To my mom, dad, siblings, and family members who encouraged me to indulge myself in medieval fantasies. I spent many long car rides creating epic tales of sword-wielding heroines and the strong men who stood by their sides. Jenn, Uncle Blake, and Dad were awesome proofers.

To Peter and Elizabeth May, who patiently toured me around England, Scotland, and France on three separate occasions. Elizabeth offered valuable tips on creating authentic scenes. Visiting the Berkhamsted motte and bailey was priceless.

To Jody, Leslie, Liz, Sarah, and Jenny, my friends who enjoy my eclectic ways and provide great suggestions. Becky was my first ever web-fan and her enthusiasm kept me going!

To the editors at BellaOnline, who inspire me daily to reach for my dreams and to aim for the stars. Lisa, Cheryll, Jeanne, Lizzie, Moe, Terrie, Ian, and Jilly provided insightful feedback to help my polishing efforts.

To the Massachusetts Mensa Writing Group for their feedback and enthusiastic support. Lynn, Tom, Ruth, Carmen, Al, and Dean all offered detailed, helpful advice!

To the Geek Girls, with their unflagging support for my expanding list of projects and enterprises. Debi's design talents are amazing. I simply adore the covers she created for me.

To the Academy of Knightly Arts for several years of in-depth training and combat experience with medieval swords and knives. I loved sparring with Nikki and Jo-Ann!

To B&R Stables who renewed my love of horseback riding and quiet forest trails.

To my son, James, whose insights into psychology help ground my characters in authentic behavior.

To Bob See, my partner in love for over 19 years and counting. He enthusiastically supports all of my new projects.

About the Author

Lisa Shea is a fervent fan of honor, loyalty, and chivalry. She brings to life worlds where men and women stand shoulder to shoulder, steady in their desire to make the world a better place for all. While her medieval heroines often wield a sword, they equally value the skilled use of their intelligence, wisdom, courage, and compassion.

Lisa has studied the Middle Ages since she was quite young. She has trained in medieval swordfighting for several years. She studied medieval dance and music with the SCA. She has been to England numerous times and loves exploring old castles and churches.

Please visit Lisa at LisaShea.com to learn more about her background and interests. Feedback is always appreciated!

You can also contact Lisa at her many social networking accounts:

Facebook - http://www.facebook.com/LisaSheaAuthor
Twitter - https://twitter.com/lisashea
Google+ https://plus.google.com/+LisaSheaAuthor/
GoodReads – https://www.goodreads.com/lisashea
Wattpad - https://www.wattpad.com/user/lisasheaauthor
Instagram - https://www.instagram.com/lisasheama/
Pinterest - https://www.pinterest.com/lisashealowcarb/

23 Free Ebooks

Do you enjoy free ebooks? I have 23 free ebooks that you can download and enjoy on your PC, tablet, smartphone, or other device!

If you have trouble locating any of these for free, just let me know and I'll lend a hand.

KNOWING YOURSELF
A MEDIEVAL ROMANCE
LISA SHEA
ASPEN ALLEGATIONS
LISA SHEA

ONE SCOTTISH LASS
Regency Time Travel Romance Novella - Book 1
LISA SHEA
THE LUCKY CAT
Black Cat Vol. 1
A Salem Massachusetts
Mini Mystery
LISA SHEA

Destiny Interrupted
1
ETERNAL TIME SHADOWS
LISA SHEA
AQUARIAN AWAKENINGS
The Collective Saga book 1
LISA SHEA
RIVER JORDAN
A JERUSALEM SHORT STORY
book 1
LISA SHEA
The Dove and the Wolf series
INTO THE WASTELAND
a dystopian journey
LISA SHEA

ACROSS
the RIVER
LISA SHEA

RUMBLE
STRIP
Book 1
LISA SHEA

the
PREENING
PEACOCK
a Rosalinda Alameda Mystery
1
LISA SHEA
A Cozy Zoo Short Story

SNIFFING OUT
a CRIME
An Art Detective
Dog Lover's
Short Story
LISA SHEA

DINER DEEDS
DONE DIRT CHEAP
an Aspie girl in Massachusetts
BOOTH
SERVICE
Diner
Short Story
Mysteries 1
LISA SHEA
The Proposal
A Romantic Short Story
Book 1 - NYC
LISA SHEA

STEPPING
OUTSIDE
ONESELF
book
1
Astral Out Of

CHARTREUSE
A Sci-Fi
Short Story
LISA SHEA

YOGA for
Stress Relief
and Forgiveness
Lisa Shea

Ten Minute
YOGA
for Stress Relief,
Focus,
and Renewal
Lisa Shea

YOGA
in Bed for All Ages
Start your day or
Prepare for sleep with
Calm relaxation
and serenity
Lisa Shea

YOGA
for Traveling by
Plane Train Bus & Car
Enjoy your Trip
Relaxed, Serene &
Energized!
Lisa Shea

JOURNALING
BASICS

JOURNAL WRITING
FOR BEGINNERS
LISA SHEA

Five Minute
MEDITATION
LISA SHEA
MEMORY
Brain Training
Book 1: Amusement Parks
LISA SHEA

CHAKRAS
In Yoga, Meditation,
and Stress Relief
Lisa Shea

Romantic
LOVE
Poems
poetry
collection of
adoration
and
praise
LisaShea
RomanceClass
Green Living
SAVING WATER
Water your Garden while
Conserving our Water Supply
Lisa Shea

COCKTAILS
Low Carb Recipes Series
Delicious recipes
perfect for unwinding,
relaxing, and enjoying!
LISA SHEA

Namaste Aloha Servus

Many languages have a single word that can be used both as a greeting and a farewell. I imagine it's because, in thoughtful relationships, the person is never really gone. They stay within your thoughts until the next time you are able to be together again. While there was technically a beginning, once that connection is made it is always there. There is a continuation of memory and care.

Over the years, countless people have helped me with my writing. My dedication earlier does not even come close to touching them all. Every time a new reader picks up a book and becomes part of the story process, their comments enrich our entire community. Often it's a random thought or idea from one reader which then causes improving changes in the storylines for future ones.

I then am able to pass along those ideas and suggestions to all the authors I help. That allows them to blossom and grow in their own projects.

If you have feedback on this or any of my stories, please share it! I'd love to hear from you.

Thank you so much to all my readers. Thank you to my fellow authors who encourage me. Thank you to the wonderful creative spirits who provide inspiration for me.

Perhaps most of all, I want to send my warmest of wishes to the battered and emotionally burdened women who struggle each day to face the world. All of the proceeds from this series support shelters. This mission is extremely important to me. It is tragic we still live in a world where those shelters are necessary. Until our society rises to a level where they're no longer needed, I will strive to do my part to support them.

We all share this big blue marble we call home. It's the only place we have to live. And we're only on it for the blink of an eye before we're gone again.

We should treasure each day.

We should care for those around us who have walked a rough road.

And we should be grateful for all we have.

Thank you for being a part of my journey.

Namaste.

www.ingramcontent.com/pod-product-compliance
Lightning Source LLC
LaVergne TN
LVHW050925080826
845145LV00001B/211

9780979837708